IN HER DEFENSE

CHUCK DRISKELL

Copyright © 2015 by Chuck Driskell
Published by Autobahn Books
Cover art by Nat Shane

First Edition: January 2015

autobahn
BOOKS

"Courage is like a muscle. We strengthen it with use."
– Ruth Gordon

Chapter One

SPRINGTIME in the Greek Isles—blooming flowers, shining sun, light winds—the perfect time to kill someone. The sniper was confident he could shoot his target and get away before anyone realized what had happened. His target was a woman. She was currently living on a yacht, moored approximately one kilometer from where the sniper stood, eyeing her through binoculars.

The sniper had sailed alone from Naxos City, approximately ninety minutes away, in this small rental craft that seemed dingy alongside the surfeit of fancy yachts and sailboats in these waters. He'd mitigated the disparity of his craft by doing nothing to stand out. Just an average man on an average boat taking an average cruise. Once he'd reached the mooring area off Santorini, he'd motored slowly while leaving no wake, carefully searching for a spot away from the other boats. From that point on, it had simply been a waiting game.

Elena Volkov, dubbed the Ukrainian oil princess, occasionally showed herself, typically carrying a large hardcover book or fussing over her dogs. She seemed modest enough, wearing a cover-up over her unexceptional white bikini. Behind her back, the male crew leered at her, even making ribald gestures to one another when she wasn't watching.

It was a shame to kill her, but the windfall would certainly smooth over any sorrows the sniper had.

He'd been in place since mid-morning and it was now well past lunch. He feared the yacht might move on, forcing him to follow at a distance. Rather than do that, he might be better off reacquiring her at a later date. While he fashioned himself as a professional sniper, he'd never done such a thing as this before. Oh, sure, he'd killed people with his sniper rifle, but he'd done so while serving as a soldier in the Serbian Army's Special Brigade. After his discharge a year before, he'd begun doing small jobs for an underworld boss in Athens, slowly building his reputation before this opportunity landed in his lap.

Now he was caught up in the intoxicating dream of becoming one of the world's faceless assassins. It was a fraternity occupied by many but dominated by few. And those elite few commanded fees that could be only described as obscene.

Some of the whispered recent transactions...

A million euro had been earned through the killing of an abstaining board member at a multinational chemical corporation. The assassination had been done via syringe, using naturally occurring bodily chemicals to induce a heart attack—which was indeed the cause of death. The authorities weren't even suspicious. Whoever had pulled off the killing was a master of both disguise and body chemistry. The rumor suggested the assassin was actually a wayward physician who'd lost her license due to her aggressive practices.

Three million pounds sterling were supposedly paid to an Irish assassin who disposed of a stubborn landowner in Wales just last year. The inflexible old landowner had suffered a gruesome death from an unfortunate tractor accident. The authorities were suspicious in this case, but could never prove anything other than the deceased's own negligence. Supposedly the men behind the contract were the landowner's two rebellious sons, eager for their inheritance. One had since died of a heroin overdose. The other son, now genuinely wealthy and living a life of booze, drugs and debauchery, was still on the clock.

And the most recent high-profile assassination involved the ultra-conservative mayor of a large Chinese city. Apparently, the mayor had been blocking civic progress, preventing a significant amount of development from occurring. Those developments would have filled the coffers of certain contract-holding Chinese construction firms. The assassin, rumored to be Argentinian, earned more than 15 million yuan—roughly equivalent to 2.5 million dollars—for a grisly knife beheading that was to also serve as a message to other non-visionary Chinese politicians. In his first months in office, the deputy mayor—now mayor, after the murder—earned a reputation as big-business and construction-friendly.

If you had the creativity, the vision and, of course, the skill for a clean assassination, you could get filthy rich. The pay was transcendent and the work infrequent. This was the life the shooter wanted.

Currently, his target was nowhere to be seen. He ate a piece of cold chicken and an apple from his small cooler, watching as the crew busied themselves on the deck of the yacht. Several clouds passed over as rain threatened from the east. The sky darkened but no rain fell. In the early afternoon, a pleasant breeze blew and swept the sky to cobalt brilliance.

The beaming sun brought her back to the deck—Elena Volkov, the Ukrainian oil princess.

Her bathing suit contrasted nicely against her sun-burnished skin. Though she wasn't tall, she had the body of a tall lady. Long, lean legs topped by an attractive torso and medium-size breasts. It was a shame she had to die—she'd be great for a roll in the hay. The princess positioned the chaise lounge in the sun before spreading her towel and lying on her stomach.

Her two little rat-looking dogs plopped down in the shade underneath the lounge and were asleep almost immediately.

The shooter checked his surroundings. No one seemed to take any notice of him. In fact, the closest person was the princess. Her crew had gone belowdecks. The only other boat nearby was moored and quiet, its inhabitants having taken their launch ashore over an hour ago.

"It's just me and you, sexy," the shooter whispered, peering through his scope and brooding over the difficulty of this shot. While rather calm, the sea still rolled, generating a gentle up and down movement of the shooter's small craft. Though much larger, the yacht rolled, too, albeit to a lesser degree. These movements exacerbated the shot, providing two axes of motion to deal with. And that didn't even take into account the wind that had grown more brisk as the day had worn on.

All in all, a difficult shot.

Now the princess was moving. *Damn it!* Perched on her belly, with her toned ass tantalizing anyone who might be looking, she just couldn't seem to get settled. First, she adjusted the towel. Then, she sipped her drink. Next, she shooed away an insect. Between the motion, the wind, and her fidgeting, the shooter dared not pull the trigger. He lowered the rifle below the gunwale and waited.

A short time later, as if the heavens intervened, she rolled to her back and placed the large hardcover book on the deck. Her motions ceased and soon thereafter it seemed the princess was asleep. At that moment, in the heat of the day, the breeze slowly lessened, thereby calming the sea.

The conditions couldn't get much better.

It was time for this lady to die. It was high time for the shooter to earn his first consequential payday.

He scanned the nearby waters. There were other moored boats, but none displaying any activity. He was all alone.

Once again, the shooter settled the stolen Zastava M07 rifle onto the foam rubber pad he'd taped on the rail of the starboard side of his small rental craft. He nestled the rifle into the indentation he'd made on the rubber, giving himself a stable platform.

Here we go.

Elena Volkov was now in the crosshairs. She was motionless, her exposed skin slowly absorbing the sun's energy. Little did she know that 250 meters away, a rifle loaded with 7.62 millimeter 175-grain long-range ammunition was trained on her.

The sniper tried to get in sync with the gentle swell, estimating the combined rise and fall of both crafts as no more than ten centimeters. The crosshairs remained in the kill zone at both ends of the movement spectrum. With essentially no wind, his shot should still rip into her ribcage, either high or low. And a single shot should do the trick.

The shooter struggled to swallow. He felt perspiration running down his face.

Relax. You've done this a hundred times. Breathe easy and fall back on your training.

He began to apply pressure to the trigger. Slowly. Steadily. Wait for it. Wait for it.

Crack!

Just as his finger had pulled backward with the release of the trigger, a slightly larger swell had elevated his boat. It had come without warning. The shooter sighted Elena Volkov, realizing he'd not even hit her. Just above and behind her he could see the small black mark in the white composite finish of the boat's cabin.

Sranje!

The shooter hurriedly rotated the bolt, seating another round. By this time, several of the crew appeared on the yacht's deck. Elena Volkov sat up. Her dogs circled her. No one seemed to know what had happened, but there were too many people milling around her to keep shooting.

In the closest boat, this one a large sport fisherman, several people had appeared and now pointed toward the shooter. They'd obviously heard the report. He lowered the Zastava to the deck and made the decision to abort. Although it appeared quite average, this rental boat was highly-powered. Despite this being a no-wake area, the shooter roared away. He wasn't followed.

Cursing himself, he stayed out until nightfall, replaying the shot in his mind again and again. One simple swell had lifted his boat only a few extra centimeters. But that scant amount over such a distance, even with the minute corrections he'd made as he pulled the trigger, was enough to cause his bullet to travel on a trajectory that was too high.

And the Ukrainian oil princess lived on.

Once dusk had fallen, the shooter leaned over the stern and ripped the fake registration from the rental. He crumpled the temporary letters and tossed them into the Adriatic. Then, vowing to try again soon, he motored back to Naxos.

He was arrested seconds after tossing his line to the dockworker at the Port of Naxos.

His arrest had nothing to do with the shot he'd taken earlier. The authorities apprehended him for his sloppy heist of a large quantity of silver several weeks before in Poland.

While he fancied himself as a tier-one assassin and criminal, the shooter was a much better woodworker than a criminal or sniper. He simply wasn't adept. The cooperating Greek authorities charged him with illegal possession of the Zastava sniper rifle, but couldn't connect it to a crime. They simply added it to a laundry list of other charges. The Serbian was soon extradited. After sentencing, he would be remanded for a period of 41 months without the possibility of parole. In prison, he'd soon become a trustee for his furniture-building skills. Not quite the opulence he'd dreamed of, but it beat getting raped in a disease-infested community cell.

This had been the second failed attempt on Elena Volkov's life. Rather than report the bullet the crew had found lodged in the composite of the yacht, she simply sailed away, seeking shelter to the west.

Unfortunately for the Ukrainian oil princess, the attempts on her life would continue.

***

Nine days after the failed sniper attempt on Elena Volkov's life, Gage Hartline heard the proposition. Actually, it didn't come in the form of a proposition. It came as a dismissal, once Gage had finally coaxed it from Colonel Hunter. Hunter was Gage's mentor, friend, father figure and landlord. He'd once been Gage's commander, too, having recruited him from the U.S. Army's Special Forces. Together, they'd been a part of a small team that never existed. Now, however, they were both retired, residents of the state of North Carolina.

Gage had been back from Lima, Peru for several months. He felt good, his mind was fresh, and he was itching for purpose. His most recent "regular" employer, a retired credit card magnate, had sensed Gage's reluctance to return to the north of Canada. Rather than force Gage to do something he didn't want, the magnate proposed that he hire someone else for the day-to-day work.

"And rather than you pay me back by coming here to do something you don't want to do, I'll bank what you owe me. That fair enough?"

"I'll come back. I owe you," Gage had said.

"Nah. I may never need you and, if not, your debt will simply be forgiven. But, if I do need you, then I expect you to cooperate. How's that?"

Gage had been pardoned. "You just yell and I'll come running." That had been two months ago—two very long months with nothing to do.

Now, the oppressive heat of the North Carolina summer had finally settled in after a cool and damp spring. Once the rains had stopped, Gage had taken on several large projects around Hunter's house and completed them faster than he thought he would. Since then, the only thing that needed doing was mowing the lawn and watering the grass and garden. He'd spent the morning using the large turf sprinklers to irrigate the grass. The sun was out and hot. Once the lawn dried, Gage would cut all five acres on the colonel's Massey Ferguson tractor.

It was lunchtime. Gage enjoyed a heaping pimento cheese sandwich while reading a classified incident report that had been entrusted to him by one of his friends from Delta. The report involved the elimination of several ISIS members in Syria and quite a bit of the report involved details that would never make the evening news. Supposedly, a few of the less forgiving boys from Delta had allowed a few of the ISIS members to suffer a bit more than necessary.

Pity.

Just as Gage was finishing his lunch, he heard Hunter rapping on the screen door of his converted shipping container. "Around back," Gage yelled, placing the report off to the side of his empty paper plate.

One of his spring projects had been the construction of a small patio behind the converted container. He'd soft-set pavers in a herringbone pattern and surrounded the patio with bushes and flowering plants. Hunter had warned Gage that the plants would likely die. He said bushes and trees had to be planted in the fall in the south; otherwise their roots wouldn't be mature enough to get them through the summer heat. Gage had vowed to water the plants twice a day and thus far, while somewhat wilted, they were all surviving.

Hunter ambled around to the back of the shipping container. "Bushes dead yet?" he asked, just as Gage's dog, Sheriff, slathered kisses on the colonel's hand.

"Thriving and well-watered."

"Give it time. We haven't sniffed the dog days yet…have we, Sheriff? You miss a couple of days and you're gonna have brown plants everywhere."

"Sometimes I think you want stuff like that to happen just so you can be correct."

"Yeah, I know. One day I woke up and realized I'm a grumpy old man. It'll happen to you, too, someday."

"If I live that long."

"If you live that long," Hunter agreed. He sat, encouraging Sheriff to rest his paws on his lap.

"Well?" Gage asked.

"Well, what?"

"You know, 'well what.' What about the job?"

"What job?"

"Didn't you talk to your guy in D.C. about a job in Europe?"

"Konrad."

"Yeah, Konrad."

"I did and it's no good," Hunter replied dismissively, rubbing the dog's neck.

"The job?"

"Yes," Hunter clarified. "The job is no good. It's a non-starter."

"Why?"

Hunter shook his head. "More work's coming. Got two gigs to talk to a friend about next week."

"Tell me about the one in Europe."

"It's not you. It entails things you don't want to deal with. It's built for failure. Trust me, okay?"

"I do trust you. Tell me about the job," Gage said monotone.

"Damn, son. You don't let up, do you? Thought you were gonna cut the grass."

"When the grass dries, I'll mow it. Till then, I'm all ears."

"Why don't we chat after dinner? Alice is making country-fried steak tonight."

"Seriously?" Gage closed his eyes and leaned his head back to the heavens. "Mmm, fried steak." He opened his eyes. "But I won't be able to focus after that calorie-bomb, so will you please just tell me now?"

"I don't have all the details."

"Don't need all the details, just the high points."

"Put simply, there's a Ukrainian woman who thinks her family is trying to kill her. She wants professional protection."

"Okay, is it a team job?"

"Solo."

"Why solo?"

"Exactly. That's part of the problem."

"Do you know why she wants just one man?"

"From what Konrad said, she doesn't want to hire a professional security firm. She's got some sort of crowd phobia…doesn't want a lot of people traipsing around in her life. She wants someone discreet."

"Why? Discreet is fine when you're not in danger."

"Again, exactly. I told them she needs to get over it. If she wants true protection, one bodyguard ain't gonna cut it."

"Where is she?"

"Sicily. My guy says she's exposed—doesn't know what she's doing."

"How long's the job?"

"Doesn't matter."

"How long?"

"A few weeks."

Gage was silent for a moment. He moved a few remaining breadcrumbs around with his finger. "You know, if someone really wants to kill her…"

"That's the thing—that's why it's a no-go, especially with one man trying to do all the work."

"Okay, I get you don't have any appetite for the job," Gage said witheringly. "*Why* is someone trying to kill her?"

"It's got something to do with a business deal that's going down. There's a deadline, too. Once the deadline passes—I think it's the end of June, but I can't recall because I wasn't listening too intently by that point—but once that passes, the threat should dissipate." Hunter laced his fingers over his trim stomach. "What else do you want to know?"

"How much does it pay?"

"Fifty grand, plus expenses."

"For two weeks?"

"That's what I was told."

"In Sicily?"

"Yes."

"You said she thinks someone is trying to kill her."

"There've been two verified attempts on her life," Hunter answered. "On the first, someone tried to run her over. The second was a sniper shot that went awry. Since then, she's tried to go dark and leave no trail."

"Same person each time?"

"Don't know."

"So, if there's a deadline, I'm guessing she wants someone there ASAP."

"Good guess."

"How many people has the job been offered to?"

"No idea."

Gage folded his paper plate and sipped the last of his tea. He removed his lemon slice from the remaining ice and ate the pulp, making a face due to the sourness. "Call Konrad right now, please. Let him know I'll leave tomorrow."

"You kidding me?"

"No, sir."

Hunter rubbed his short gray hair in obvious frustration. Then he nodded and shook his head all at the same time, wearing a matching expression. "I'll go call him."

"C'mon...don't be angry with me."

"I'm not, Gage. It's just..."

"What?"

"It's not what you do."

"You're thinking about what happened to Monika."

"Yeah, I am. If something happens to this lady, I'm not so sure you can go through that again."

Gage nodded. "But if I don't take the job, and something happens..."

"I know you're not changing your mind at this point. I'll go call."

"You pissed?"

Hunter deflated but appeared relaxed. "No, son. Not at all."

"Thank you. And could you give Konrad some simple pieces of advice so the Ukrainian lady doesn't get dead between now and then?"

"Already did. He said she's real stubborn but he'll pass it on." Hunter stepped into the grass, rubbing his shoe through the tall blades of Fescue. "Almost dry."

"I'm on it."

"Dinner's at six and by then I should have all the details. You'll pay for your flight and she'll reimburse you."

"What's her name again?"

"Elena Volkov," Hunter said, spelling it. "They call her the Ukrainian oil princess."

"Princess?" Gage asked. "You didn't tell me that part."

"It's a moniker due to her fortune. Konrad says she's good people."

"Guess I'll find out."

As Hunter walked to the house, Gage walked into the grass and felt the remaining moisture with his hand. By the time he gassed up the tractor and checked the oil, the lawn would be ready for a haircut.

Later that afternoon, after his bag was packed—while he was craving Alice Hunter's country-style steak—Gage read about Elena Volkov on the Internet.

***

Once he'd heard the basics from the colonel, there had been no question in Gage Hartline's mind about taking this job. Despite Elena Volkov's obvious eccentricities, Gage believed that he could adjust her lifestyle enough to safeguard her for the time being. In Gage's current, admittedly uninformed line of thinking, he would meet this lady and get the lay of the land from her. Then he'd bring in a few people he knew, people who currently worked in Europe, people with the right connections. He'd work through them to place Mrs. Volkov somewhere anonymously, with the type of protection she needed. Piece of cake—fifty grand in the bank, plus expenses.

As Gage had learned earlier, traveling to Sicily by air wasn't too difficult. He would travel with US Air out of Charlotte. His first leg to Frankfurt wouldn't depart until tomorrow in the early afternoon. There, after a brief layover, he'd take a two-and-a-half hour flight down to Fontanarossa Airport in Cantania, located on Sicily's eastern shore. According to Google Maps, Mrs. Volkov's home was a brief taxi ride away.

After an early dinner with the Hunters, Gage had decided to head to Charlotte to spend the night. He had a close friend who lived in the Upstate of South Carolina, about two hours southwest of Charlotte. Like Gage, his friend was an ex-Green Beret and current "operator"—meaning, he did the same sort of work Gage did. It had been a while since they'd gotten together so they'd agreed to a late night chat at a dive bar outside of Charlotte.

"The bar may not look like much," Gage's buddy, Ron, told him over the phone, "but the beer's ice cold and they've got the best wings south of Buffalo."

"I don't drink," Gage had reminded Ron. "And I already ate."

"Once you smell the wings, you'll eat again."

Gage had taken the back way to Charlotte, a two-lane route he used to run with regularity back before he'd become Gage Hartline. He'd pushed west, past the backside of Fort Bragg. He'd driven his old pickup through Aberdeen and up to the town of Carthage. From there, he headed due west over to Biscoe and Troy, then over the so-called mountains of the Uwharrie National Forest. After that came the bustling little city of Albemarle followed by a straight shot toward eastern Charlotte. According to Ron, Gage would find the bar on the edge of the sprawling metro area, just off Route 27.

Gage couldn't have missed it if he'd tried.

Just after the skyline of the Queen City came into view, Gage slowed when he approached the brightly-lit old roadhouse. An enormous hand-painted sign by the road advertised the Hog's Breath Saloon. Below the name, true to Ron's word, was a tagline advertising "Ko-Beer, Hot-Babes & Flamin-Wingz."

Something for everyone.

The dusty parking lot was crammed full. At least two thirds of the vehicles were motorcycles, most of them Harleys. Gage had to actually drive back onto Route 27 and park on the shoulder a short distance down the road. As he walked through the parking lot, two shadowy figures from the other end of the lot began to curse him for no reason. Gage turned his head but kept walking. The two men yelled and mocked him with obscene gestures. They were both quite portly, leaning on their monstrous, chopped-out motorcycles and cursing Gage for, among other things, his femininity and his affinity to provide oral favors to men. Gage made the wise decision to ignore the drunken idiots, turning his head to the door and chuckling at the insults that continued to fly.

He stepped inside, greeted by the tangy smells of sweat and hot fried wings and that other indistinct scent known to dive bars the world over. AC/DC blared over the sound system, as Brian Johnson encouraged patrons to have a drink on him in his ever distinct, screeching voice. Gage took a seat at the bar.

While he awaited one of the bartenders' attention, he texted Ron to see if he'd already arrived. With the teeming crowd, Gage could have easily missed him. Ron texted back in seconds, replying that he'd been hung up in traffic due to a wreck on I-85.

Prob be there in 30. Get 50 nuke wings or more. Hungry.

Nuclear wings? Gage would probably need a beach towel to deal with all the sweat. And he didn't even want to think about the by-product aftermath tomorrow morning. But he felt his mouth watering. He glanced at his watch—nearly six hours since he'd eaten dinner. Oh well…it wouldn't be the first time he'd eaten a fourth meal in a day.

Finally, the oldest bartender, a short fellow with a gray beard and a leather vest, leaned over the sticky bar and asked Gage what he would have.

"Pitcher of ice water and fifty nuclear wings."

"That it?"

"My buddy's on his way. He'll be drinking all the beer." Gage eyed the older bartender as he nodded and sent a ticket back to the kitchen. His ear was trickling bright blood and there was a fresh cut over his eye. The bartender's lip was swollen, too.

While Gage waited for his water, he noticed the other male bartender also had fresh injuries. Most prominent were an eye with red blood on the sclera and a swollen nose that appeared to be broken. The second bartender, who was probably about thirty, was pretty large and well-muscled. Upon closer inspection, Gage could see the tissue stuffed in the man's nostrils.

When the older bartender returned with the pitcher of water, Gage asked what happened.

The bartender shook his head dismissively. "You wanna run a tab with your credit card or pay as you go?"

Gage slid a ten and twenty over. When the older bartender brought change, Gage told him to keep it before leaning over and gently grabbing the man's leather vest. "Tell me what happened. Why are you and your buddy bleeding?"

With leaden eyes, the bartender glanced left and right. "You a cop?"

"No. But I can see the wounds on you and your coworker, there. None of the women servers seem worse for the wear, though."

The bartender gently removed Gage's hand from his vest. "Was a fight earlier. When we broke it up, coupla' the fighters turned on us. Happens all the time."

"Who got in a fight?"

"Excuse me, friend, but I've got customers," the bartender said, walking away.

"It wouldn't be the two guys out in the parking lot, would it?" Gage yelled.

The bartender came back. "What two guys?"

"Two fat assholes at the end of the parking lot, running their filthy mouths, leaning on their choppers and harassing people as they walk in."

Closing his eyes upon hearing the news, the bartender nodded. "That'd be them. The Colton brothers. Kenny Earl and Harlan Lee. They start trouble in here damn near every week. Then, if they don't have anywhere better to go, they hang around outside and take on all comers."

"Why do you let them in?"

"Who's gonna stop 'em?"

"A couple skilled bouncers should do it."

"Bah, those two are like cockroaches. You can't kill 'em and they always come back."

"Did you call the cops?"

"The cops?" the bartender snorted. "We don't call the cops here, son. First time we did that we'd go outta business."

"Well, maybe the owner of the bar should call the cops."

"I *am* the owner." Shook his head. "No cops."

"Why not?"

"Look, friend, I run a legitimate business here, but my customers are the type'a people who don't want cops hanging around. Understand?"

"Who'd the brothers fight?"

"Coupla other bikers. Knocked one of 'em unconscious over by the dance floor and kept beatin' on him. That's the kinda people these guys are, whuppin' on an unconscious man." Shook his head. "That's when we jumped in. At least we got 'em outside. They'll get bored and leave soon. Believe me, I've seen this movie before."

Gage turned his head to the door. "Brothers, huh?"

"Nasty as they come." The owner hitched his thumb toward the kitchen. "Your wings'll be out in about fifteen."

Gage glanced at his phone again. If Ron had estimated his arrival correctly, he was still 22 minutes out.

The Colton brothers. Kenny Earl and Harlan Lee…certified pieces of shit.

Gage was keenly aware that he had a significant task in front of him. A woman whose life was in danger was counting on him.

Not a good time to get in a brawl.

But just look at that bartender's face. And the other one, too.

Gage took a long sip of water. Closed his eyes.

No, Gage. Bad idea. Bad…freaking…idea.

Turning on the barstool, he glanced around the bar. A few couples danced to the beating rhythm of an old Whitesnake song. Leather and jeans everywhere. Most everyone here looked like they'd arrived via one of the heavily-chromed motorcycles out front. But bikers nowadays aren't what they once were. This was a peaceful group, drinking beer, listening to 80s-era rock and roll and having a good time.

Then Gage saw what had to be one of the Colton brothers' victims. He was sitting at a table, his head tilted back to the ceiling while his lady held a bag of ice on his forehead. The lady was crying a bit, mascara streaming down her face.

The victim seemed to be reassuring his lady and their friends that he was okay. There was a large knot on the man's head and his ear was swollen. The group was probably stuck here due to the two assholes lingering outside.

Those pricks.

And the owner refused to call the cops. Without police intervention, Gage knew those two dickheads out in the parking lot would continue to come back and do the same thing, again and again and again.

Gage smelled a fresh batch of wings come out of the fryer. The smell made him realize just how hungry he was—despite all he'd eaten earlier. And when he was hungry, he was easily irritated. There were peanuts on the bar but Gage didn't want peanuts. He needed something with substance.

And Gage wouldn't eat the wings till Ron arrived. That'd be plain rude.

So, Gage needed a way to pass the time. A way to pass the time till he could eat. He eyed the front door again.

Damn, boy, you're just inventing an excuse…

Stop. Think. Are you crazy, Gage? It'd be a shame to live through all you've lived through and die in a dusty parking lot at the hands of two pudgy Neanderthals who live to brawl. They could have knives. Hell, they might even be packing.

But…it *would* pass the time.

If you go out there, you'd better hope they're bullies and not bad-asses. Big difference…

Gage wrote Ron a text but didn't send it. He called the owner over and handed him his phone.

"Hey pal," Gage yelled over the music. "You know how to work an iPhone?"

"I know I look old, but I ain't that old."

"Do me a favor? I wrote a text and it's ready to send. If I'm not back here in five minutes, will you press send for me?" Gage spoke his four-digit password to the owner.

The owner seemed confused. "What're you talkin' about?"

"Five minutes, okay? If I'm not back in this seat…please…send that text. All you gotta do is unlock the phone and touch the green button to send the text."

Gage took a great sip of water, slapped both of his own cheeks very hard, and headed for the door.

The owner wiped his wet hands on a dishtowel. He tapped in the four digits and held the phone at a distance so he could read the short text. Head snapping up, he saw the screen door at the front slam shut.

"Oh, shit!"

As it turned out, the owner might have to call the cops, after all.

Or maybe the coroner.

***

The Colton brothers had moved to the big city of Charlotte as teenagers. They'd never really had a place to call home before coming here. Home had been wherever their mother's latest fling was. From the time they were ages 5 and 6, the brothers had learned the value of strength in numbers. At first they'd terrorized playgrounds together. Then it was them working together as bathroom toughs in junior high. Then, of course, came juvie. Once adulthood arrived, they began a string of dominant stints in bars, local jails, Carolina beaches and apartment complexes. Most recently, they'd taken to harassing or beating drug store managers in order to create a pseudoephedrine supply line for the Colton family's burgeoning crystal meth business.

The Colton brothers were a formidable duo.

Now 32 and 33, the brothers had grown roots—and big bellies—in Charlotte, and found their true calling in the meth business. The product they sold was as substandard as existed on the streets of the Queen City. But there are always buyers for illegal drugs, and the customers for such low-grade stuff are usually those with nowhere else to turn. Weakened by years of drug abuse, the Coltons' customers were perfect for them. And if someone dared complain, they got the ever-loving shit kicked out of them. Although there was a constant churn of clientele, new customers always materialized. Running meth was a poor man's trust fund—it paid off each month. Certainly enough to fund a steady stream of motorcycles, leather, Carolina barbecue, cocaine and the occasional skinny hooker.

Tonight, just as the Coltons were kicking around the idea of roaring off to terrorize another bar, they saw a stranger walking in their direction from the Hog's Breath. Kenny Earl, the elder brother, hocked up a loogie and spat it on the ground, sullenly watching and awaiting the stranger to adjust course.

Probably just some dumb drunk headed to his bike. But…

The stranger kept on coming.

"Th'hell is this here?" a smiling Kenny Earl asked his younger brother, Harlan Lee, who'd been busy dabbing the abrasions of his knuckles with the Confederate flag that flew from the back of his motorcycle.

Harlan Lee, blessed with better vision, looked up. "That's the asshole that done walked through the parking lot a few minutes ago."

"You want some of this, faggot?" Kenny Earl yelled, stepping off his chopped Fat Boy.

The stranger walked on. He was well built, probably a bit over six feet tall and maybe 210 pounds. He wore boots, utility pants and a gray t-shirt. As the stranger finally stopped in the bluish light ten feet away, Kenny Earl could see that he was probably in his mid-forties.

"So, tell us, *dad*, you lookin' to score some Oxycodone from the E.R. tonight?"

"No," the stranger replied. "I just got here a few minutes ago and I heard you two roughed up a few of the patrons."

The brothers looked at each other and burst into laughter. "Patrons?" Harlan Lee asked. "Now we know you're a faggot."

The stranger laughed, too. That caused the Colton brothers' laughter to cease.

"Why you laughin'?" Kenny Earl snarled.

"You know…I was laughing *with* you."

"Laughing with us?" Harlan Lee snarled.

"Sure. Why not?" The stranger gestured to both of them. "Hell, I like you guys. Like your style. Like your swagger."

"Like us?" Kenny Earl asked.

"Yeah. I was kinda hoping we could become, you know, *really* close friends."

Talking time was over. They might not have been all that bright, but the Colton brothers were perceptive enough to know when they were being mocked. And no one—no damned soul on mother-freaking-earth—made fun of the Coltons without earning an emergency room visit—at minimum. No more talking: it was now…

Go time.

And since the Colton brothers possessed more than a quarter century of side-by-side fighting experience, they didn't even need to verbalize their intent. Each could read the other with ease, as they both did when they began to slowly approach the stranger from angles that would put him at a distinct disadvantage.

Though the Colton brothers certainly weren't informed enough to understand the principles of their tried-and-true system, they attacked their enemies much in the way lions take down dangerous prey, such as a water buffalo. The front lion acts as a distraction to the water buffalo, while the rear lion stealthily pounces and drags the buffalo to the ground.

A primitive, yet effective, technique.

The Colton brothers certainly had the primitive part down pat.

Kenny Earl took up a fighting stance, hands poised like a boxer. Unlike a boxer, he wiggled his fingers and waved his hands as he slowly circled. He sneered and made noises, using all his diversionary skills to occupy the stranger who would soon require the services of a licensed medical professional.

Meanwhile, Harlan Lee, who was slightly less fat and quite a bit stronger, edged away and out of the peripheral vision of the stranger. As he'd done hundreds of times before, he would then put his hands on his hips, as if he decided to avoid the fight altogether. Just a polite little brother letting his big brother fight the stranger one-on-one. When the stranger—their "quarry"—eventually glanced Harlan Lee's way, he would realize the younger brother was a non-combatant. The stranger would then focus solely on the older brother.

Big mistake.

Because that's when Harlan Lee would attack, coming quietly at first before sprinting the last few feet. In a 2-on-1 fight such as this one, the technique had never failed the brothers.

"Me and you, faggot," Kenny Earl growled, bobbing and weaving and continuing with his extravagant hand movements.

The stranger had adjusted his stance to a more athletic posture, placing his left foot forward and bending his knees. While lightly bouncing, he brought both hands up to a fighter's position, indicating he was right-handed.

"Get him, Kenny Earl!" Harlan Lee yelled from a distance.

Right on time, the stranger glanced back to see Harlan Lee standing at a distance, hands on his hips.

"Come on, faggot," Kenny Earl taunted. "It's a fair fight…just you and me. And I'm gonna whup your ass, bitch."

The stranger settled in, seeming to buy the brothers' ruse.

Both brothers grinned as their little game began.

***

Although Gage felt pretty sure he knew the brothers' plan, it didn't mean he had the antidote. The crazy hand movements by the sweaty, bearded fool in front of him were an obvious diversion. That, combined with the slightly shorter brother ducking back out of Gage's vision, told Gage all he needed to know.

The first attack would come from Gage's rear. Then the brothers would be on him with all their combined girth, aiming to pound him into the dusty gravel of the Hog's Breath parking lot.

Gage had no illusions about this fight. If he screwed up, he'd need more than an ice pack on his forehead. He'd grabbed the tiger by the tail and now he had to perform.

Minutes earlier, as he'd approached, Gage had noted both men's engineer boots—big, clunky boots with lugged soles. Provided a loud motorcycle didn't roar in at the wrong moment, Gage knew he should be able to hear the shorter one when he made his approach.

Playing dumb, Gage continued to slowly circle with the taunting brother.

"Make a move, pussy!" he yelled, cackling afterward. "Scared, ain't ya?"

Gage made no sound, nor did he betray any emotion. He kept his eyes on the taller one's eyes, watching for any reaction that might tip Gage to the other one initiating his opening move.

Attempting to irritate the one in front of him, Gage grinned.

***

"Th'hell you smilin' at, faggot?" Kenny Earl roared.

"Just knock his ass out," Harlan Lee said, making his tone sound as if he was growing bored. He quietly set his feet.

"That's just what I'm about to do," Kenny Earl replied, feinting at the stranger, making him react.

The Colton brothers knew this was the key moment, especially now that Harlan Lee was directly behind the stranger. He should be unconscious in mere seconds. Then the brothers could really go to work.

***

The owner of the Hog's Breath Saloon operated by a number of rigid personal policies. The first was, of course, no cops. The second, and nearly as important, was his prohibition of firearms in the bar. In fact, the only firearm in the bar, a shotgun, belonged to him. But he refused to brandish it inside the four walls.

Now, however, since blood was about to be spilt in the parking lot, he'd gone into his office and retrieved the shotgun, a Rossi 12-gauge riot gun with a pistol grip. Followed by the other bartender and a group of regulars who'd seen the owner retrieve the gun, he stepped out into the parking lot just in time to see all the action.

The stranger who'd given him his phone seemed ready to engage the older Colton brother, Kenny Earl. The two were slowly circling, hands up.

And, true to form, Harlan Lee Colton was behind the stranger, crouched to pounce.

The owner shook his head, wondering if someday those two assholes would get theirs.

He would soon be witness to the answer of his question.

Just as the owner was opening his mouth to yell a warning to the stranger, Harlan Lee Colton lurched into action. For a 32-year-old man who was 85 pounds overweight, the younger Colton still moved cat-quick. And just as he lowered his shoulder for a form tackle to the stranger's lumbar plexus, the stranger spun to his left, ducking out of the way.

Harlan Lee grabbed nothing but air. His girth plowed forward, making him sprawl on the rough gravel, his face absorbing much of the energy required to slow his 265 pounds. He was back to his feet quickly, the parking lot lighting revealing a wide-open chin fissure that would leave a nasty scar.

The stranger now faced both brothers, bouncing on his toes and urging them on with his fists.

Now it was Kenny Earl's turn to attack. Almost like a cartoon, when the person's feet begin running but the person stands still, he let out a warrior yell as he lurched into motion, his right fist pulled back for a knockout punch.

This was not how the Coltons typically brawled, and it showed. The stranger moved at the last second, using his left foot to trip the onrushing Kenny Earl who suffered the same fate as his brother, bulldozing into the gravel in a hail of rocks and dust. He lay there a moment, like a beached whale unsure of what to do next.

It went on like this for a few minutes. The stranger didn't throw a punch. The two brothers couldn't get into sync. Before long, their cholesterol-clogged, diseased hearts failed them as neither had wind to generate an attack better than the previous one. After four attempts each, the brothers were scraped, dirty and spent.

Harlan Lee, the younger one, was on his back doing all he could just to breathe. Kenny Earl, however, had managed to come to his knees, wheezing as he cursed the stranger for his cowardice.

The stranger finally demonstrated some aggression when he pulled his right fist back and stepped in front of the older Colton.

"Do it, ya faggot!" Kenny Earl managed, trying to maintain some sense of machismo.

For a moment, the stranger tensed before he relaxed.

"He's scared!" Harlan Lee shouted, still in his supine position.

"You proud of yourself?" Kenny Earl yelled, knowing there was an audience. "We was already wore out after whuppin' ass inside. You didn't do shit other than run from us."

"He ain't gone do a damn thing!" Harlan Lee added, managing to lift his abraded head.

Gage tensed his arm again.

"Do it!" someone urged from the crowd. Several others chimed in.

"Yeah, do it, faggot!" Harlan Lee dared.

"C'mon, you pussy, do it!" Kenny Earl agreed, still on his knees but puffing out his chest.

Gage did it.

He unloaded a straight right, catching Kenny Earl on the front of his chin. The heavier Colton fell backward, both of his lower legs trapped under his significant girth. The effect was comical, as the unconscious brother bounced like a spring as his knee tendons had to be close to their tensile strength. After a fraction of a second, both feet sprung forward. Because of the kicking motion, gravel shot from Kenny Earl's heavy boots, striking Harlan Lee and making him yelp.

The stranger was still at the ready, but there appeared to be no more threats. After a moment, Kenny Earl came to and rolled to his side. He moaned something unintelligible, laced with curse words. Harlan Lee, his chin wound leaking like a sieve, finally sat up cross-legged and helpless, trying to stop the bleeding by clasping both hands under his chin.

Everyone watched as the stranger rifled the saddlebags on both Colton motorcycles, pitching several items that looked like handguns into the thick kudzu at the edge of the parking lot. Then the stranger lightly slapped Kenny Earl until he sat up. The group watched as the stranger knelt between the two felled brothers, speaking a brief sermon as he pointed fingers at both of the wounded men. Then, to everyone's surprise, the Coltons stood—quite unsteadily—before mounting their motorcycles and puttering slowly into the night.

Wiping sweat from his brow, the stranger headed back to the Hog's Breath. At that moment, a ghost-silver Mustang Super Snake roared into the parking lot, skidding to a stop with a spray of gravel. The driver stepped out, his face intense. He spoke a few words to the stranger, listened for a moment and laughed. Once the driver had parked, he and the stranger walked to the front door.

"My wings ready?" the stranger asked the owner.

"On the bar and on the house, along with anything else y'all want to eat or drink." He stared at the spot where the scuffle had occurred. "How the hell did you do that?"

"I didn't really do anything."

"You took down the Colton brothers and, until the end, you didn't throw a punch."

The stranger shrugged. "Those two are brawlers. I'm not. But I made an educated guess that I might be in slightly better cardio shape than them, so I brought them to my world rather than meet them in theirs."

"You punched them at the *end*?" the stranger's friend asked.

"Just the one," the stranger answered. "Hell, he asked me to do it…twice." The crowd laughed.

"What'd you say to them before they left?" the owner asked.

The stranger chuckled. "You won't see them again."

"No, they'll be back," the owner muttered, looking worried.

"I don't think they will." The stranger clapped his larger, tattooed friend on the back. "This is my buddy, Ron. He's a Green Beret and does, er…*security work* for the right price. If you've got a few bucks, you can hire him to make damned sure the Coltons don't come back."

"Why wouldn't you want the job?" the owner asked, ejecting the shells from the shotgun.

"Because I'm heading to a different job tomorrow. It's out of town," the stranger replied. "And can you double that order of nuclear wings? I'm starving."

The group went inside. The Coltons never returned.

And no one will ever know if the owner hired the stranger's friend, Ron, the Green Beret.

Chapter Two

CANTANIA, SICILY, ITALY

Elena Volkov wasn't at home. After the Air Berlin flight from Frankfurt to Fontanarossa Airport here in Cantania, Gage had first made sure he wasn't under any surveillance. When he was positive he was all alone, he'd taken a taxi to the address Mrs. Volkov had provided. Now, having rung the bell for the third time, he stood out in front of the home, baking in the high western sun as he listened for footfalls in the house. There were none.

But we'd agreed upon the time. He checked his watch, making sure that he'd set it forward six hours. *Of course I did. What if someone's gotten to her already?*

The home itself was basic and seemed quite old. Built on the side of a steep hill, it adjoined the other homes bordering the narrow street that wended around to the left as it climbed. Most of the homes had flower boxes or planters. Mrs. Volkov's home had none. Just as Gage turned to walk back down the hill, a young man on a motorized scooter roared around the bend and stopped. He couldn't have been more than twenty. The young man nervously cleared his throat, then, in passable English, asked, "Are you Gage?"

"Excuse me?" Gage asked.

"Your name...Gage. Is that how you pronounce it?"

Shutting his eyes, Gage tilted his face to the heavens. Here less than an hour and already exposed by a kid on a motor scooter. When he reopened his eyes, the young man asked to see Gage's tattoo.

"Are you kidding me?" Gage asked, flabbergasted.

"Please, signor, your tattoo."

"Who told you to approach me?" Gage asked, glancing into an alleyway that might provide him an escape path.

"Do not worry, signor. It's for Signora Volkov."

Gage's arrival was supposed to be private. This method of verification seemed a poorly executed scheme to verify Gage's identity. He lifted the sleeve of his utility shirt. "There's my tattoo. And don't use my name anymore."

"Yes, signor." After studying the tattoo of Themis for a moment, the young man nodded his satisfaction. "Get on. I will drive you."

"Me ride on the back of that?" Gage shook his head. "Sorry, pal, but I'm not doing that."

"But that's what I was paid to do."

"This isn't her home?" Gage asked, motioning.

"I don't know. But right now Signora Volkov is in Belpasso."

"No *names*."

"Yes, signor. *She's* in Belpasso."

"Belpasso? How far away are we talking?"

"Several kilometers."

Gage cinched his pack on his back and fastened the chest strap. "Tell you what. You ride ahead a little bit and I'll follow, how about that? Just stop every now and then till I catch up."

"I'm afraid Signora won't like that."

"Blame me. But I'm not 'riding bitch' on the back of a scooter." Gage motioned down the narrow street. "Let's go."

The walk wound up taking nearly two hours and it was certainly more than "a few kilometers." While the actual distance might have only been five or six miles as the crow flies, the actual distance he'd walked had to have been twice that by curvy road. Added to the distance, Gage estimated that he'd probably gained 2,000 feet in elevation on the steep journey. The weather, while not as humid as summertime in North Carolina, was blisteringly hot.

Such a delight after 13 hours of flying. And to think—he'd been hoping for a nap.

When they finally reached the town of Belpasso, the kid waited for Gage, excitedly telling him that Signora's house was just ahead. After a few turns, they climbed another steep hill that took them into a residential area with modest homes surrounded by cacti and rock gardens. Once the street leveled out, to Gage's left a broad field sported brilliant yellow flowers surrounding a rock formation. It was obviously arid here, and due to the altitude, Gage was occasionally able to catch glimpses of the Mediterranean.

Soaked from head to toe in his own perspiration, he stepped into the shade at the carport of Elena Volkov's supposed home. The house itself was modest, the outside constructed of tile, exposed timber and stucco. It was situated on a surrounding lot consisting of red dirt, rock and scrub brush. The young man had gotten off the scooter and nervously motioned Gage to hurry to the front door. Gage removed a t-shirt from his pack and mopped the sweat from his face and arms before walking to the young man.

"Your odometer broken?"

"Mi scusi?"

"Never mind." Gage rang the bell, watching through the side glass as two small dogs raced to the door, yapping away as they viciously bared their tiny teeth.

Mrs. Volkov herded the killer dogs into another room before she opened the door, her mirthless face looking Gage up and down. "Your flight landed three hours ago," she said in lightly accented English. "What took you so long?"

"Nice to meet you, too," Gage said. He motioned to the young man who'd stepped back and dipped his head. "Is he your employee or just someone you hired to pick me up?"

"Why?"

"It's important."

"He's Paulo, the landlord's son. He lives down the street."

"Pay him."

"I paid him half earlier, but he obviously didn't do his job since you're so late."

"He *did* do his job. Pay him."

Mrs. Volkov reached into the back pocket of her white jeans and produced a folded bill. She handed it to Paulo, shooing him away at the same time. Then she turned to Gage, eyeing him irritably.

"What now?"

Gage stepped back and viewed the house. "Who knows you're here?"

"No one."

"Not true. The kid called you 'Signora Volkov.'"

"Paulo's not really a kid, and he's not a threat. Like I said, he lives down the street. His mother rented me this house."

"They both know your real name?"

"Yes. I tried paying in cash but she had to see my passport to fill out the papers."

"So, at a minimum, two people know who you are?"

"They're good people," Mrs. Volkov replied, exasperated.

"But you're not anonymous. And who knows who the landlord filed those papers with."

"Mister Hartline, you do realize I have a well-known face? It's difficult for me to go anywhere and remain anonymous. Believe me, I despise living in the public eye."

Gage eyed her closely. Her face was indeed well-known, although before he'd been told about her Gage had never heard her name. But one Google search revealed hundreds of pictures of Elena Volkov, the Ukrainian oil princess, in various wardrobes and doing a variety of activities. Elena in Kiev buying groceries. Elena in London walking her dogs. Elena at the symphony. And of course, before his passing, hundreds of photos of Elena with her husband. In the Ukraine, she was royalty—the classic pauper to a princess—and her fame had quickly burgeoned onto the splashy society magazine pages of Europe.

Her age was listed as 38 years old. If Gage hadn't known, he would have guessed a very well-maintained age of 32. She had a narrow face and blonde-brown hair that was pulled back into a ponytail. She wore no makeup that Gage could see and her green eyes and high cheekbones suggested Nordic heritage. She was rather lean and had long legs, although she was probably an inch or two shorter than average.

All in all, Gage found her quite beautiful. For whatever reason, he had the feeling she didn't see herself that way. But it was just his feeling...

She tapped her plain fingernails on the front door. "So..."

"Do you have a car here?" Gage asked.

"Yes."

"Yours, or a rental?"

"It's mine."

"I was told you haven't been here very long."

"I haven't."

"Yet you've bought a car?"

"Yes."

"Registered in your *name*?"

"I just got it." She crossed her arms. "Why all the questions?"

He rubbed his eyes. He was tired and now frustrated. "Got cash?"

"Excuse me?"

"Do you have loose currency like you just paid the kid? Your English seems excellent—don't you understand me?"

"Yes, I understand English quite well," she snapped. "But I don't care for your brusqueness and irritability."

"Good words. Your English is obviously better than mine. But when I was briefed, my friend sent a set of instructions that you were to follow until I arrived."

She waved her hand as if shooing a fly. "So many people have advice. I didn't read the instructions."

"Missus Volkov, I was told you're convinced someone is trying to kill you. And I was paid to come here so we can prevent anything bad from happening to you. This is not what I typically do, okay? But I'm doing my best, here. So, please, will you at least work with me for now?"

She pursed her lips and nodded. "Do me two favors?"

"What are they?"

"First, be nice."

He nod-shrugged.

"I mean it...truly polite and courteous."

Gage reset himself and forced a respectful smile. "Yes, ma'am."

"Second, call me Elena. I loved being married but I don't like being called 'missus' or any other title."

"So, I'm guessing you don't like being called the Ukrainian oil princess?"

There was a moment of silence. Hands on her hips, she stared at Gage with leaden eyes. "If you say that again, I'll no longer be the potential murder victim. Rather, I'll be arrested for murder."

Gage showed his hands in a mock surrender. "Understood. From now on it's Elena." He glanced left and right. "Now, Elena, where's your car?"

"Around back."

"Please bring it around."

"Now?"

"Yes. Right now."

"Do I need anything?"

"All your loose cash."

"What about my dogs?"

"Leave them. They won't be alone for long."

"I can't have someone else take my dogs."

"They'll be with you. Please, trust me."

Elena eyed him for a moment before walking away. Seconds, later, she was back with the two killer dogs on leashes. "Take them to the lot across the street so they can do their business."

"Yes, ma'am." While there, Gage remained alert for anything out of the ordinary. He slowly scanned the residential street, eyeing each home and car. Nothing seemed out of place.

The dogs finished and he walked them back to the house, placing them inside. Elena parked on the street and gave him a key.

"Can the dogs be alone for a few hours?" Gage asked.

"If they used the lot, then they're fine for about four or five hours."

"Hopefully we'll only use half that time." He locked the deadbolt and again surveyed the area. After a brief discussion, they were off, heading west in Elena's new Lancia Flavia Cabriolet.

Per her wishes, Gage drove.

***

Gage was famished. They parked the small convertible in the charming Sicilian town of Adrano, walking all the way across the square to a café and sitting under a Cinzano umbrella at the corner of the patio. Gage chose the spot because it was bordered by two walls and several large planters, both teeming with foliage. At his direction, he had Elena face him with her back to the street and the other patrons. He then ordered enough food for three men and set about gorging himself as soon as bread was placed on the table. Elena sipped mineral water and frowned at his wolfing.

"Did you not eat on the flight?"

"Ever fly coach? The food wasn't very good...and I'm not even picky. The chicken tasted the way old tires smell." He dipped the bread in olive oil and held it in front of his mouth. "Then, when I arrived here, I marched uphill for maybe ten miles...rather unexpectedly." Popped the bread in his mouth. "Sorry...but I can't help but be hungry. Need calories."

"What happened to your face?" she asked.

After all the travel, Gage had forgotten about the cut over his eye, courtesy of the Colton brothers. He wasn't sure when it had happened— maybe he caught a fingernail when one of their off-target punches had whizzed by. He shrugged. "I had a little disagreement before I left."

She shook her head as if she had no desire to understand what he was inferring. "Would you like to know exactly why I hired you?"

Gage swallowed a mouthful of bread with the aid of his ice water. "Yes, but first I'd like to explain something to you."

"And that is?"

"If someone is truly trying to kill you, I don't think they're trying very hard."

"Why do you say that?"

"Unless they're not very bright, you should be dead by now."

"Explain," she demanded, leaning back in her chair and crossing her arms.

"You have no security here, correct?"

"None, other than my dogs."

"That's what I thought. So, for starters, the landlord and her son know your name. That's bad. Then, you tried to be discriminating by sending me to some false address and have the kid verify me by way of identifying my tattoo."

"Was that wrong?"

"Not necessarily wrong, per se, but you made a few mistakes in the process. Did you give the kid a picture of me?"

"No. I don't have a picture of you."

"But you knew about the tattoo."

"My friend, who is a friend of your friend, the colonel, learned about the tattoo."

"That's all fine, but what if I was a hit man impersonating Gage Hartline? All I'd have had to do is show up with a fake tattoo of Themis and the kid would have led me right to you." Gage pointed across the square. "That car's in your name, right?"

"Yes."

"Someone with Italy's licensing and registration, or highway department, or tax department could be bribed to reveal where you are." Gage motioned east. "And another thing about the landlord and her kid—if they learn you're famous, they might tell their friends, thinking such information is harmless. Word spreads, especially about famous people...you get the picture."

"Mister Hartline...the people who I believe want me dead do *not* know I'm here. They wouldn't know to *start* in Sicily or even Italy, for that matter."

"That helps," he replied as the waitress began placing platters of food before him. "But if they have any sort of brains, they'll find you if you're leaving electronic signatures."

"What are those?"

"Credit cards. Tax information. Driver's licenses. *Car registration.*" Gage slid the steaming mussels in front of him. "Essentially, anything that enters your name into a computerized database can be homed in on. Meaning, you can be tracked, found and..."

"Killed."

"Yes," Gage replied soberly. "Among other things."

Elena removed a fresh pack of Treasurer Silver cigarettes and carefully removed the cellophane and foil.

"Bad for you," Gage said, already five mussels in.

"If you can prevent my killer from succeeding, I shall stop smoking," she replied, smiling warmly for the first time.

"An additional motivation to save you...I like it." Gestured with his fork. "You sure you won't eat? This marinara the mussels came in is spicy and tasty." He dragged a piece of bread through the sauce until it was sopping and popped it into his mouth. "Amazing," he said with a full mouth, recalling when he ate the same meal in Spain with a Spanish crime lord.

They chatted idly while Gage devoured most of the food. In addition to mussels, he had prawns, two planks of sautéed fish and vegetables. Each time someone sat near them, Elena eyed them nervously.

"You're okay," Gage said. "I'm watching."

"It's not that I'm scared. I just...I don't do well around crowds."

"This isn't a crowd."

"Normally a place like this wouldn't be bad. But I'm already nervous, so that sets me off worse. I was getting help before Dmitry died."

"Is it some sort of social anxiety disorder?"

"No," she replied, tapping the unlit cigarette on the table. "I love meeting new people and even socializing in familiar settings. Mine is a fear of crowds and crowded places—strangers, primarily. And it comes and goes unpredictably."

"That doesn't sound like much fun."

"Tell me about your flight over the Atlantic. About the boarding."

"Excuse me?"

"Describe the boarding, how many people there were in the gate area...that type of thing."

"Well, it was a US Air flight. The aircraft was an Airbus 330. Pretty sure it seats about three hundred people, maybe more. I was in the last zone to board so, as you might imagine, it was a zoo, especially with all those assholes crowding around the gate before their zone was called. The jetway was packed and by the time I was onboard there was only a little space in the overheads. People were clogging up the aisle and—"

Gage halted himself, as it was clear his description was having an effect on Elena. She was breathing heavily and had grown splotchy around her neck and upper chest.

"You okay?"

Elena closed her eyes for a moment and nodded. "See? Even a description can set me off."

"And you say it doesn't always happen?"

She shook her head. "I've attended concerts, flown on flights like the one you took…it doesn't always hit me the same way."

"What do you do if it does?"

"If it's a flight, I sit down and shut my eyes and put on white noise headphones. Then I think about someplace serene. If I feel an attack coming on at a show or some event that doesn't require me staying, I leave."

"Then we'll do our best to keep you away from crowds." Not wanting to dwell on her condition, Gage leaned back and took great breaths. "I'm officially stuffed."

She slid the cigarettes in his direction.

"No, thanks."

"Will it bother you if I smoke?"

"Go for it."

Elena used an ornamental lighter to ignite the cigarette she'd been holding.

"Interesting lighter," Gage remarked.

"It was Dmitry's." She signaled the waitress and ordered two double espressos. When the waitress had gone back inside, Gage asked why Elena believed someone was out to kill her. He'd heard the high points from Colonel Hunter, but the details had been sketchy. Gage wanted the full story.

"You know my background, yes?" she asked.

"Just the little bit that I've read. Go ahead and tell me everything."

"I'm from Shostka, in the northeast, near the Russian border of Ukraine. My family was neither rich nor poor. We were just normal. I'm the youngest of four girls," she said, her eyes on her cigarette. "When I was nineteen, I moved to Kiev and managed to get a job in data entry at UkeOil. I'd only been there for about three months when Dmitry appeared at my little shared desk. I'd seen him before but I didn't think he'd seen me." Now Elena stared at the ornamental lighter, smiling wistfully at the memory. "He took a sheet of empty paper from my printer and, in his beautiful handwriting, he wrote the address of a restaurant and the request for a date that night. He folded it and handed it to me and told me to open it after work. Of course, I met him there that evening. He was such a gentleman." She blinked away the thoughts. "We married two years later."

"One of the wealthiest men in Ukraine chose you without ever having talked to you before? No wonder you're famous."

"It amazes me to this day but, remember, we dated for two years." She leaned forward, her eyes intense. "Dmitry was a fine man. And at that time, while he was doing well, he wasn't one of the wealthiest men in Ukraine. It wasn't until later that his small oil company grew so rapidly." Elena looked away for just a moment. "While this isn't altogether proper to say, over the balance of those two years of courtship, he only kissed me. Nothing more. As I said, he was a gentleman. And I also know he wasn't seeing other women in any way during that time."

"Okay," Gage replied. "But why are you telling me this?"

"Two reasons. First, I want you to know that Dmitry was good. Despite the *rest* of his *family*…" she let that hang for a moment, "…he was an ethical and decent man. And second, I want you to know that, while he first approached me because I guess something about me attracted him, our love was genuine and it grew every day we were together. I've been in mourning since his death although, admittedly, all the energy around the attempted killings has seemed to quell my grief."

"Can I ask you a personal question about him?"

"You can ask."

"In business, was he ruthless? I ask this because I thought most oligarchs from the former USSR were ex-KGB types who essentially took the oil fields by force."

"No, he was not. UkeOil's initial fields were hard to get to, and until the price of oil went up dramatically, the company withered. But in the early 2000s, when the price of a barrel made it worth going into those mountainous oil fields, the company grew rapidly. And to answer your other question, Dmitry wasn't ever KGB. He was a smart businessman. He was upright." She leaned back and set her jaw.

"Thank you for telling me about him," Gage said, believing her—or at least believing that she thought she was telling the truth.

A mirthless smile formed on her mouth. "You believe me, but you wonder if I know the truth about Dmitry."

Gage nodded. "Correct."

"It's the truth. Feel free to research it when we're done."

"Thanks, Elena. And I'm sorry for your loss. Dmitry sounds like someone I'd have liked."

She nodded.

Mildly embarrassed, Gage changed the subject. "Your English is excellent."

"I read constantly. All the books are written in English." She finished her cigarette and gunned the espresso. "Now, Mister Hartline, what would you like to know about why I hired you?"

"Gage."

"Gage, it is."

"I'd like to know about the attempts on your life. And, I want to know who was behind them."

"I'm almost certain I know who. And, as far as the attempts, they've happened twice."

"Tell me what happened each time."

There was a long moment of silence as she looked away. Gage watched as a range of emotions flitted over her face. Finally, nostrils flaring as she pulled in a bolstering breath, she turned to him.

"The first happened almost two months ago, in Prague. It was spring but felt like winter." She narrowed her eyes as her features grew momentarily harsh at the memory. "I'd rented a small apartment before the holidays and had been there all winter and into the spring. I'd just gone grocery shopping in the morning, when I knew the market would be least busy. My apartment was on a narrow alleyway and when I was almost home, an idling sports car roared right at me. There was nowhere to go because the alley was so narrow."

"Who was driving?"

"I have no idea. Didn't see."

"What happened?"

"At first I couldn't believe it. I just stood there frozen, holding my bags and gaping as the car sped at me. It was like watching a movie."

Realizing he was clawing the table, Gage reminded himself she was okay. He forced himself to sit back and try to act dispassionately. "But you somehow avoided it?"

"Barely. I guess it was instinct, but since the car was so low and coming so fast, I dropped my groceries and leaped just as it reached me. I'm pretty sure I hit the windshield and was spun over the top as the car sped away. I can't recall clearly."

"Were you hurt?"

"Yes, but not as badly as I could have been. The most painful injury was a cracked bone in my pelvis, called the iliac wing," she said, touching her side around the area of the beltline. "It's just recently stopped hurting. I also had a concussion, a sprained left wrist, and plenty of cuts and bruises."

"But you're okay."

"I am."

"What happened afterward?"

"I was in the hospital for two days."

"Did anyone see what happened?"

"No. I was able to stagger to the closest street and a kind older man called the paramedics."

"Why were you in Prague to begin with?"

She shrugged. "It's a beautiful city, the Paris of the east. I'd never been there with Dmitry and was hoping to spend Christmas in a place that wouldn't make me sad. I liked it, so I decided to stay."

"Did you know anyone there?"

"Just a few painters I met."

"Painters?"

"Painting is my hobby. I paint people."

"Even though people scare you?"

"*Crowds* scare me…sometimes."

"Understood. About Prague—did your painter friends know your true identity?"

"Yes."

"Did you use credit cards or other electronic methods like I referred to?"

"Yes. I didn't know I was in danger."

"Exactly how long had you been in Prague?" Gage asked.

"About four or five months."

"How long did you stay after the accident?"

"As soon as the hospital let me go, I paid for a ticket to Greece."

"Airline?"

"Yes."

"What about the crowds on a plane?"

She shrugged. "Like I said, sometimes I have no choice. I managed to get on a very early flight that was half-empty and I boarded at the last moment, after everyone had taken their seats. It helps."

"Did the second attempt occur in Greece?"

"It did. Based on advice from one of my attorneys, I rented a small yacht to convalesce. He thought that'd be my safest option. It was an extravagance that I regret to this day."

"You flew into Athens?"

"I did. Then I rented the yacht in Pireas."

"All of this in your name?"

She nodded and frowned at the same time. "Credit card."

"Go on."

"I never even knew the second attempt on my life happened." She fingered another cigarette. "The yacht was anchored off Santorini. I had a small crew with me, along with my dogs, and spent my days reading and relaxing while I healed. It had been many weeks and I grew very bored. I thought I was safe and was even thinking about painting again. For all I knew, the first attempt was just some maniac."

"What happened?"

"I truly don't know. I'd spent the afternoon sunning on the chaise and must've dozed off. Before I knew it, several of the crew awakened me, asking me if I'd fallen."

"Why'd they think that?"

"They'd been belowdecks and heard a loud thumping noise." She toyed with the cigarette, twirling it. "I told them that I'd fallen asleep. The dogs were sleeping, too. I thought nothing more of it and went to my cabin to continue my nap. Later, they showed me."

"Showed you what?"

"A hole in the boat." She displayed her little finger. "It was made by a bullet about the size of my finger. The captain estimated the angle and pronounced that the bullet had missed me by only a centimeter or two."

"Were there other boats nearby while you were sleeping on the chaise?"

"Yes, dozens. We were moored."

"How far from shore?"

"Maybe a kilometer?"

"Did the shot come from the shore?"

"The captain said it couldn't have, given the direction the yacht was facing. He said it came from another boat."

Gage rubbed his chin in thought. "Boat-to-boat makes for a tough shot. Rolling seas, wind, multiple axes of motion. I wonder why the sniper stopped at one bullet?"

"The crew appeared as soon as they heard the sound."

"I guess the sniper wasn't confident in his escape," Gage mused. "Or else he'd have kept shooting."

"You seem disappointed he didn't."

"It's not that. If it's the same person as the one in Prague, I'm just trying to get a feel for how he...or *she*...thinks."

"Regardless, at that point, I knew someone was after me. I knew I had to alter the way I was living. That's why, when I left the yacht, I told no one where I was going or what I was doing."

"But, as I've said, you've left quite a trail."

"And that's why I've contacted you. I know enough to know that I don't know anything about this type of thing."

"Did you contact the police either time?"

"They questioned me in Prague. I was supposed to call them when I was released from the hospital but I didn't. And I didn't report the shooting in Greece."

"Why?"

"You'll excuse me for not explaining myself."

Gage allowed a moment to pass before he asked, "Who do you think wants you dead, Elena?"

Her eyes welling with tears, she turned away. "I need a bit of time. I haven't talked about all of this in one sitting. It's a strain."

"That's fine. We can discuss it later, but I need to tell you something." He leaned forward. "You cannot go back to that house in Belpasso. We'll take the cash you brought today and get you some temporary lodgings. Over the coming days, we'll work at setting you up anonymously." Gage gestured around him. "Once we get you in a secure place, it'll free me up to bring in people who can go to work finding the person, or people, responsible for the two attempts."

As soon as he mentioned other people she straightened. "What?"

"I need to bring in help."

"I don't want help brought in. That's why I hired *you*, one man. One very discreet and ethical man." She abruptly stood as her voice became strained. "Those were my conditions. Were you not told this? Have I wasted all this time finding you and waiting for you?"

"Please calm down," Gage replied softly, fighting not to glance at the faces around the café. "Please sit back down and relax. Don't call attention to us."

"Did you hear me?"

"I heard every word you said. Now, please…"

She obeyed, lighting the cigarette with a trembling hand.

"Listen carefully," Gage said. "Are you at least okay with me setting you up in an anonymous place?"

"What about my dogs? They need—"

"I'll get your dogs," he interrupted, patting the back of her hand. "I have a dog back home and a dog that lives in Poland. I love dogs."

Elena made a face. "A dog in Poland?"

"Long story."

"Well, I don't want anyone else knowing about me. About my personal affairs. About my situation." She poked the table and drew her next words out. "No one."

"Elena, I will do this exactly the way you want me to do it. Okay?"

She seemed to relax. "I'll tell you who I believe wants me dead—just not right now."

"When can we discuss it?"

"Soon. I just…I just want my mind to be blank for a little while."

"You can rest once I get you a room. Then I'll go get your dogs and pack a suitcase."

"I'm sorry about my hysterics. I don't usually act that way."

"Don't be. And believe me; I've had people try to kill me before." He winked. "It'll make anyone a little bit crazy."

Elena Volkov smiled from the corner of her mouth. "I was a little bit crazy before all this."

"Aren't we all?" Gage signaled for the check.

Chapter Three

IT WAS well into the evening by the time Gage had completed his initial list of tasks. Earlier, after they'd left the café, he found a small, family-owned hotel there in Adrano. Gage parked far away and booked the rooms using his false passport. The manager was fine with well-behaved dogs, provided Gage was willing to pay a steep surcharge of 25 euro per night, per dog. What choice did he have? So, the lodging situation was settled for the moment.

Gage brought Elena in through the hotel's back door. No one saw her. Once she was situated in one of the two rooms, he drove back to Cantania and packed three suitcases with Elena's things, guessing at items like bras and underwear. She'd asked him to retrieve her travel cosmetics case under her sink. Gage was impressed when he found the case to be as small as a shoebox. Dogs in tow, he departed the house by the back door, leaving a number of lights on.

He drove back to Adrano with the top up and the passenger window down, allowing the two small dogs to hang their heads out the open window. While the two pets jockeyed for the forwardmost position, Gage negotiated the curvy Sicilian roads deep in thought.

Not being able to enlist any type of help had thrown his plans for a loop. He hadn't expected Elena to slam that door so hard. Personal protection was definitely not his specialty. He was out of his depth.

And Gage also hadn't expected her grief to be so severe. In actuality, he'd not even thought about that too much. He figured she was the youngish wife of a now-dead billionaire. Maybe it was societal conditioning but, for whatever reason, he hadn't thought she'd be the demure and grief-stricken widow. He shook his head at his cynicism before petting the dogs, trying to wrap his brain around what lay ahead.

As he patted both dogs, he wondered if Elena would ever be able to openly discuss who she thought was after her. Her grief, the shock over the attempts on her life, and her obvious reclusive nature proved to be a powerful combination that led to her silence.

She said she'd tell you. Trust her.

Regardless, this job was going to be tricky. Somehow, Gage knew he needed to uncover whatever it was that motivated Elena Volkov. What did her core being center around? What made her tick?

For now, Gage needed to deliver the dogs and luggage. He also needed to get rid of this car. That was on tomorrow's list of things to do. For now, he'd keep it far away from Elena in case there was someone tracking the car's movements.

Earlier, after they were safely in Elena's hotel room, he asked her how much cash she'd brought with her.

"Two hundred thousand euro," she'd replied. "Perhaps a little more. I haven't counted it in a while."

Gage was certain he didn't hide his astonishment very well. After struggling to swallow, he said, "Then I think you'll be just fine for a little while."

She'd shrugged in an embarrassed fashion that he couldn't help but find amusing.

Who would want to kill this lady, this likable widow? She seemed refined, honest and understated. She certainly didn't seem the type to create enemies. But Gage reminded himself of her net worth—and whatever business transaction Colonel Hunter had said was currently pending. Such an immense monetary dynamic brings incalculable pressure to otherwise normal situations.

He couldn't help but guess at who might want her dead. She'd mentioned Dmitry's family with obvious derision. As he parked across town, he uttered the age-old phrase aloud, "Follow the money."

Gage then took a circuitous route around Adrano, lugging the suitcases and dogs. He used back streets and alleyways; places he knew wouldn't be covered by security cameras or the like.

Having entered the hotel by the back door, Gage hurried upstairs with the dogs and luggage. He was excited about an idea and asked Elena if he could come inside.

She sat cross-legged on the bed, laughing as she accepted the adulation of her dogs.

Gage let the moment pass before asking, "You rented that house from an individual, correct?"

"Yes."

"Not a company?"

"No. She owns several houses on that street. I told you this."

"Just confirming. And, after the shooting, you took your rental yacht from Greece to Cantania?"

"I did come from Greece, but we sailed to Naples."

"Good. Now, tell me you *didn't* rent a car in Naples."

"No, I stayed there for two days before taking the train to Sicily."

He frowned. "You can take a train to Sicily?"

"Yes. It's quite a unique process, which is why I wanted to do it. They actually load the cars of the train onto a ferry upon reaching the Villa San Giovanni Port in Reggio."

Gage leaned forward. "This is important. Did you buy that ticket with your identification?"

"No. I paid cash."

"You're sure."

"Yes."

He exhaled with relief. "Okay, next question: I know you put your car in your name. Were there any problems buying it because you're here on a passport?"

"No. I have an international driver's license. I purchased the car from a dealer and they handled everything to do with the registration, for a fee, of course."

"Did you need a visa?"

"I have a visa."

"You do?"

"Yes."

"When did you get it?"

"The day before I got the car."

"Damn it!"

"What?"

"Elena, what date was that?"

She thumbed her iPhone. Catching his look, she said, "It's been in airplane mode since we left my house. Don't worry."

"I'll get you a phone soon," he replied. "The visa?"

She swiped through the calendar pages. "Okay, I got the visa four days ago. I went and picked out the car three days ago and picked it up two days ago, with tags and registration."

"So, there's a visa in your name as well as a car registration?"

"Yes."

"And the police in Prague didn't have some sort of warning registered with the Ukrainian embassy or consulate demanding you call them?"

"None that I was told of."

"Before you got the visa and car, did you leave any sort of electronic trail here? Any credit cards, mobile phones, hotel stays…anything like that?"

"No. And I knew not to use my mobile phone. The only time I've used it has been with Wi-Fi."

"Don't use Wi-Fi, either."

"You already told me that."

Gage looked out the window at the blackness of the Italian evening. "So…my guess is they think you're in Naples, or somewhere near there, since that's where the yacht let you off. But they're going to find out about the visa and the car if they haven't already." He turned back to Elena. "Did you use the address of the Belpasso rental house for the visa and car?"

"Yes. I had to."

"Shit," he hissed. "And you haven't seen anyone lurking around in the past few days?"

"No."

"Are you sure?"

"Of course. I've seen no one. You're scaring me."

"You're fine now. Don't read my intensity as a reason to worry. I'm concerned about catching whoever is after you, but they don't know you're here in this hotel." Gage stood and paced the room for a moment. He pulled the window open and sat on the ledge as the thick and humid evening breeze pushed in around him. He turned to Elena.

"How long had you been in Prague before the car attack?"

"Almost five months."

"And how long after you rented the yacht did someone take a shot at you?"

"Weeks."

"They're growing more impatient."

"There's a reason for that."

"The business deadline."

"Yes." She fingered an unlit cigarette and shook her head. "But I don't want to talk about that now."

"Colonel Hunter told me the end of June?"

She turned away. "Later."

"Well, whoever's after you will find out about the visa and the car, and that's when they'll come to the rental house in Belpasso."

"And they won't find me there."

Gage lifted both index fingers for emphasis. "That's why it's critical you don't give any clues about where you are now. None."

She frowned. "Please, now that you've told me, it won't happen again. I'm a fast learner."

"Elena, we don't have to go too deep into this, but I need to know more about this business deal. Knowing will help me protect you." He squeezed her shoulder. "Please."

Both sides of her mouth trembled as she took a steadying breath. "This is the part I have a hard time talking about, so I'll just tell you quickly." She walked to the bathroom and came back with a wad of tissue. "I own fifty-one percent of UkeOil, Dmitry's company."

"Go on."

"And we were presented with a lucrative offer to sell the company." She explained who wanted to buy the company—a global American oil and gas company called Suntex Energy. "And the offer expires by a certain date."

"But killing you won't help the sale go through."

"Yes, it will."

"Who will it benefit?"

She dabbed her eyes. "Dmitry's family. They're after me to agree to sell."

"Tell me about them."

She shook her head. "Not tonight...I just can't."

"Will you please tell me the date?"

She took Gage's spot on the wide windowsill, lighting her cigarette and inhaling deeply. "The offer to buy UkeOil expires June thirtieth."

"It's a good offer?"

"It's an incredible offer. My advisors tell me the American company is offering four times what the company is worth."

"Why?"

"The oil business is strange. Speculation runs rampant and, as you know, oil is a finite resource. Something about UkeOil's makeup, geography, oil fields...something, has set those Americans aflame. But I really don't care about any of that. I'm satisfied to let the managers run Dmitry's company."

"So, if you don't care, why not just sell it?"

"Dmitry didn't want to. Unlike those ex-KGB oligarchs you mentioned, he actually built the company with his own hands. He wanted it to remain in the Volkov family."

Gage didn't want to press her but he felt it important to ask the next question. "And you feel strongly about upholding his wishes even though he's gone."

Elena's green eyes smoldered. "As long as I breathe, I will honor him."

That answered that. Gage changed tack. "If someone wants you dead to make the sale go through, why not change your will so that, if you die, it absolutely prevents the sale of the company? In fact, you should put out a public statement that, not only does it block any sale of the company, but it's also bad for business because you'll tie your ownership up with lawyers, et cetera."

Elena blew smoke out the window. "Good idea but it won't work."

"Why?"

"My stock ownership has a clause. Since it's private stock, in the event of my death, the company pays my estate the fair market value at the time of death and the stock is absorbed back into the company."

Gage was surprised that her husband had built a company on such a draconian ownership policy. "Does that clause stand even in the event of foul play?"

"There are no exclusions," she replied in a low voice. "It's a simple clause and only applies to owners who received their stock via transfer. My stock was received via transfer after Dmitry passed. I didn't buy it through investment." Elena pulled in a long breath through her nose. "Any manner of death is enough to satisfy the conditions in the charter. All the other shareholders need is my death certificate. This legal act has already played out. I have no recourse. The charter might as well been written a thousand years ago."

Gage shook his head. Big business never ceased to amaze him. It wasn't all that different from his own world of mercenaries—only with better clothes and fine hotels. "Elena, are you okay staying in this room for a few days?"

She looked around the room and shrugged. "Yes."

"The manager said you can order food through the front desk."

"Fine."

"When you take the dogs outside, you need to wear sunglasses and conceal your hair. Put on crazy makeup, too. Anything to conceal who you are."

"Okay."

"And come up a new identity, just in case you're asked. Make sure it's quite different from the truth."

She nodded. "Fine. I'll do as you tell me. Where'll you be?"

"I'll be at your house in Belpasso."

"You think they'll come there?"

"Maybe. It's the best place for me to start."

"You're going tonight?"

"I'm going right now."

"You think they'll come this soon?"

"That deadline is approaching."

Elena's face clouded with worry. "What'll you do if someone does come?"

Gage paused for a moment. "It depends on a number of factors."

"So, you have no idea?"

"Correct."

***

In Cantania, the newly-hired killer, an American, paid cash for his room and carried his small bag to the elevator. Upstairs in his room, he quickly ate the wrapped sandwich he bought at the ferry port, chasing it with a large bottle of water. After setting his alarm for 3:30 A.M., the American lay flat on the bed and eyed his pictures of Elena Volkov—his target. Hired nearly a week before, he'd followed her trail south from Naples, finally learning her address this morning through a series of steep bribes to low-level government employees. Just before he'd checked into this hotel for a bit of sleep, he'd cruised by Elena's rental house, not seeing her car but noticing numerous lights inside.

Killing Elena Volkov wouldn't bother the American. In fact, this would be the job that set his star. Thus far, following his discharge from the military, he'd recorded several unsolved killings in the U.S. along with two assassinations in South America. Each of the killings had kept him afloat for a few more months. They'd been okay for starters, but they paled in comparison to this contract.

The American knew, once he pulled this kill off, he'd be one of the world's preeminent silent killers and could demand exorbitant fees in order to ply his trade.

He breathed deeply as he stared at the photos of the Ukrainian oil princess. Damn if she wasn't smoking hot. Those long legs and perky tits...

He reached over to his backpack, digging into one of the inner pockets and producing a condom. He slid the condom into his pocket and shut his eyes, envisioning. Tonight...perhaps...but only if the opportunity presented itself...

Who knew, she might even enjoy it?

Satisfied with his planning, and the handsome advance he'd been paid, the American fell quickly asleep.

***

Having driven to the end of Elena's street and turned around, Gage parked on a small rise, diagonally across the street from Elena's rental home. He pulled the seat lever and leaned the driver's seat all the way back. It was nearly midnight and streaky gray clouds occasionally scudded by the quarter moon.

Using Elena's keys, Gage went into the house by the back door and turned off all the lights other than a small lamp in the entry hall. He grabbed a knife from the kitchen and made his way back to the Lancia. With the seat back, he was invisible to passersby.

With only a kitchen knife, there wasn't a whole lot Gage could do even if someone did come. In the unlikely event that tonight was the night, Gage made the educated guess that her killer would arrive between 2 and 4 A.M.—the time when the majority of humans were least active. And here, in a Mediterranean country where people typically stayed up later, it might actually be best to approach a house like this between 3 and 5 A.M., although the sun would begin its ascent quite early at this time of year.

Regardless, Gage was betting that, if someone did come, it would be in the wee hours of the morning. Feeling his own alertness fading, Gage knew he desperately needed sleep. After making his hypothesis about when the enemy might come, he set the alarm on his phone for a three-hour snooze and was asleep in seconds.

The three hours might have been three minutes.

Later, as Gage's Timex showed a local time of 4:18 A.M., he remained reclined in the driver's seat, fighting the sleep that had felt so good earlier. The sun would show itself soon, after which time he vowed to get some serious sleep. He'd just pinched his arm for further wakefulness when he heard an engine and saw the halo of lights turning onto Elena's street down below. Few cars had passed since he'd parked and this was the first one since the alarm had awakened him.

The lights shone upward as the car ascended the steep portion of the street that passed over the tree-filled ravine. Gage peered through the small gap at the top of the steering wheel. Because of the headlights, he couldn't see who was driving or how many people were in the car. He ducked down. As soon as the car passed, it accelerated slightly and motored down the street and out of sight. Gage had marked the car as a new, mid-size Fiat. It was silver.

Moments later, headlights appeared to Gage's rear before they went dark. Gage stayed low, watching through the door mirror as the darkened car kept coming before parking on the side of the street 300 meters away. He was almost certain it was the Fiat. The driver had turned around and approached with stealth.

"You have got to be shitting me," Gage whispered to himself, incredulous. There was no way this was Elena's pursuer—not on night number one.

After making sure the Lancia's doors were locked, Gage watched as a man exited and boldly walked down the center of the street, the cherry from a cigarette swinging in his hand. Gage lay below the window-line, the knife pressed to his side.

If he sees me, how do I play this? Certainly he's armed.

The keys were in the ignition. Gage's best bet might be to crank the car and use it as his weapon.

As Gage's mind had raced over what he might do, the man finally reached the Lancia. His feet stopped for a moment before Gage heard him walk behind the car.

Must be checking the license plate.

Gage didn't dare breathe. He'd have been in trouble if it weren't so dry here. Because of the arid conditions, the windows showed no condensation from Gage's breath.

Thankfully, the man continued on without ever so much as glancing inside the car, which made sense. Why would the man suspect someone to be in Elena's car when her house was right there? But it demonstrated the man's lack of thoroughness. She might have left one critical item on the front seat that could have clued her pursuer in on something important.

Still, it was best not to underestimate this man.

Gage peered over the dashboard again. The man was eyeing Elena's house as he slowly approached it from the street. A tall and slender person, he walked with an athlete's elegance. He seemed completely nonchalant about prowling around the outside of a house at the hour of the wolf. After circling the house he came back to the street and lit another cigarette. He stared at the house for half of the cancer stick, as if considering every potential consequence of his next move.

And smoking the whole time.

Real disciplined, this one.

Then Gage watched as the man walked around to the back of the house but didn't reappear.

He'd picked a lock. Gage would bet anything.

Okay...now what?

The Gage 101 Playbook said to take the man down as soon as he exited the house. Or, perhaps when the man was most vulnerable, such as when he was entering his car. But Gage was lacking a proper weapon and this guy might be a trained killer.

Might...

Regardless, Gage was capable but he wasn't stupid. There was no point in being reckless, especially since Elena was safe and sound in another town.

Ten minutes after disappearing around the back, the man reappeared and walked swiftly back to his car. There was no more elegance or nonchalance. He was in a hurry. The man cranked the Fiat and roared by Gage, obviously unconcerned with his headlights or noise.

Gage started the Lancia and sped down the hill, doing his best to catch up without alerting the driver. Unfortunately for Gage, at this early hour there weren't many cars on the streets for him to blend in with. Because of that, he left his lights off as he raced up through the gears, accelerating to better than 100 kilometers per hour on the curvy, two-lane road that headed to the east.

The man was speeding but wasn't driving excessively fast. Gage followed him through the small towns of Nicolosi, Trecastagni and Viagrande before seeing the signs for Autostrada-18. There was no way Gage could follow the man onto the highway without turning on his lights. They'd already driven about ten kilometers, over which time Gage was thankful to have not encountered the *Polizia Stradale*. There'd been several times where Gage had found himself in complete darkness and had barely been able to discern the gray strip that represented the road.

If the police did stop him, Gage could only imagine having to explain why he was driving a car not registered to him, speeding, driving with no lights—all mere hours after having arrived in Sicily. Assuming Gage's false identification held up, the *poliziotto* would probably have "George Howell" explain all that to the judge. Of course, "George" would do all this after he spent a night—or two—as a guest of the local jail.

Thankfully, Elena's pursuer didn't turn onto the highway. He continued on to the east as the road dropped precipitously when the Mediterranean came into sight, marked by a faint strip of orange on the eastern horizon. Twice Gage passed cars going the other way. One flashed its lights and honked, probably trying to signal Gage to turn on his lights. Unfortunately, the signaling occurred in a switchback, allowing the man Gage was pursuing to see all the commotion.

By the time Gage had reached the sharp curve of the switchback, he could tell his mark had made him and therefore sped up. The first thing Gage did, despite the increasing light of day, was to turn on his headlights. No sense in hiding now. Downshifting, he accelerated down the steep grade, nearly losing sight of the Fiat, which had rapidly braked and skidded to the right at the bottom of the hill. Resisting the urge to brake, Gage whipped the Lancia to the left side of the street so he could sweep wide into the right turn and maintain most of his speed. As he did, he slid onto a four-lane road that was bounded by numerous homes and businesses—a coastal highway.

There was a bit more traffic here, but not so much that Gage couldn't see his target. Now, in a role reversal, Gage's mark had turned off his headlights and was racing south with a 500-meter head start.

Time to see what this Lancia could do.

Gage redlined the car in each gear until he found himself nearly maxed at 200 kilometers per hour—about 125 miles per hour. There weren't many curves on this southbound road and Gage was pleased to see he was slowly reeling in the Fiat. Judging by the coast and topography, if Gage didn't know he was in Italy, he might think he was driving on the PCH between Malibu and Santa Barbara—with far less traffic. When Gage had closed within 200 meters, he watched as a delivery truck pulled out in front of the Fiat. The driver of the truck was probably unable to see the speeding car due to the Fiat's lights being off, especially with the low light of the early morning.

White smoke boiled from the Fiat's tires, allowing Gage to end up only a few meters off his mark's bumper. Gage noticed a yellow sign flash by, announcing the town of Aci Trezza. The road narrowed and snaked several times through the town. Gage breached the peace by nudging the Fiat's rear bumper several times, wondering if he was going to cause an unwanted airbag deployment in the Lancia. After a kilometer of hard turns, they shot out of the south end of Aci Trezza. Unlike before, when there had been homes on the left, now the Mediterranean was beside the road, bordered only by a guardrail and a steep drop of rocky cliff.

With the full realization he was about to head past the point of no return, Gage revved the Lancia and moved to the left of the Fiat's rear quarter panel. As they accelerated to twice the legal speed limit, Gage utilized the pit maneuver, turning smoothly to the right and watching as the Fiat spun to the left. The driver didn't brake and overcorrected as the spin began, causing the small car to shudder before it caught a lip in the pavement and cartwheeled to its side.

Gage slowed as the small Fiat did two-and-a-half rolls, leaving a trail of spangled safety glass cubes. For a moment, it seemed as if the Fiat would flip over the guardrail but, instead, it wound up askew and upside down, its rear end elevated on the aluminum safety rail. Steam hissed from the front of the car as a thick dark liquid dribbled onto the asphalt.

Sliding to a stop next to the crashed car, Gage jumped out and ran to the shattered driver's window. The driver of the Fiat, despite his contorted position, was frantically searching for something amidst the smashed safety glass and deflated airbags. Kneeling, Gage threw two underhand rights, hitting the man in his cheek and ear before dragging him from the window of the car. When the man was free of the Fiat, Gage saw what he'd been looking for, as a small suppressed pistol tumbled from the seat down to the headliner. While holding the dazed man with his left hand, Gage grabbed the pistol, pounding it into the side of the man's already abraded head.

By this time, several drivers had pulled over to rubberneck, gaping in astonishment as Gage tucked the pistol in his waist band and dragged the half-conscious man to the Lancia.

"Ospedale?" Gage yelled. *"Ospedale?"*

One man, a uniformed driver of what looked like a trash truck, pointed south.

"Grazie!" Gage yelled, stuffing his dazed captive into the passenger side of the Lancia.

Gage hurried around to the other side, squealing the tires as he headed south. As soon as he accelerated to fourth gear, he produced the pistol and unscrewed the short suppressor. By this time, the man had regained his senses and begun to groan.

Holding the pistol in front of the man's face, Gage fired, shattering the passenger window glass of the Lancia. The roar from the pistol—it felt like a Sig, but Gage didn't have time to confirm—made the man wince and yell at the same time.

As they approached the tunnel, Gage asked the man if he spoke English. The man replied with a fearful nod.

"One wrong move and the next bullet goes into your head!" Gage yelled, wheeling the car onto the first right turn after the tunnel. By this time, the sun wasn't fully up, but the ambient light had increased significantly. The road was dirt and gravel.

"Put your hands on the dash," Gage commanded. The man didn't comply and his eyes seemed a bit glassy.

"There!" Gage yelled, gesturing. The dazed man leaned forward and placed his palms on the dashboard.

Slowing as he continued up the dusty hill, Gage pointed the car slightly left when he crested the rise, able to see a medium-sized railway yard in the distance. As Gage drove in that direction, he noticed the man eyeing the gun.

"Don't think about it, asshole." And for good measure, Gage twisted the pistol and fired it into the floorboard, nicking the sole of the man's leather shoe in the process. This caused another yell from the man as he squeezed his eyes shut.

When Gage reached the edge of the quiet rail yard, he looked around and estimated he was no less than a kilometer from the closest residence. The seaside road couldn't be seen from here, either, giving Gage the confidence that the police wouldn't know to look here for the crash victim— if they looked at all. When the victim of the rollover accident didn't show at the emergency room, Gage guessed a call would go out with the Lancia's description and that'd be the end of it.

Unless one of the drivers had seen this pistol. Well, too late now.

Gage shut off the car. He yanked the parking brake and covered the man through the windshield as he made his way around to the passenger side. There, Gage quickly thumbed the magazine release, finding the mag nearly full. He'd been correct; the pistol was a Sig P220.

"Get out and keep your hands in front of you," Gage commanded. He continued to aim the pistol at the man, watching as he slowly obeyed.

The man couldn't have been more than thirty. He had dark hair and a swarthy complexion. Two streams of blood had run down both sides of his face. The injuries appeared to be superficial. By this time, the man seemed to have recovered his senses. He stared at Gage with no emotion as Gage patted him down, finding an iPhone, a knife and a large syringe in a toothbrush case. Inside the syringe was a clear liquid. Gage had the man sit down and lean against the rear tire of the Lancia with his hands clasped in front of him.

Pistol aiming between the man's eyes, Gage knelt in front of him. "We're going to have a little talk. If you lie to me, I'm pumping this syringe's liquid, whatever the hell it is, into your neck. *Capisce?*"

The man nodded.

"Good. Let's start with who the hell you are."

No response.

Gage pounded the pistol into the side of the man's head. "You want more?"

The wincing man shook his head.

"Then, make it easy on yourself and talk."

Imagine Gage's surprise when he heard the man begin speaking American English with a decided northeastern accent.

Chapter Four

WHILE the aspiring American killer began telling Gage the little bit he knew, a crestfallen Russian man prepared to go to sleep 1,034 miles to the northeast. His name was Georgy Zaytsev. Behind Georgy was the Black Sea, already bathed in rich morning sunlight. To both sides of him sprawled the mansions of Kyivs'kyi Beach, one of Odessa's most popular strands and, in Georgy's mind, the finest place on earth to live in hiding. He'd just finished a long night with two underfunded young tourists and had sent them on their way with the vial of cocaine he'd dangled like a carrot throughout their entire sordid affair. Now, having called his contact in Switzerland for about the hundredth time, Georgy hurled the phone in disgust, watching it fall impotently against the long drapes that would soon block out the sunlight of what promised to be a beautiful summer day.

Georgy dipped his chin to his bare chest, taking measured breaths. He needed to maintain his composure if he were to see this through.

A man of average size, Georgy stood out mainly because of his tan. His 40-something-year-old skin was as dark as saddle leather, and shiny from the expensive oils and treatment that were constantly lavished on the sun-burnished cutaneous tissue. He was physically fit, but not overly so—a fact marked by his muscular chest perched above his well-fed gut. He preferred heavy gold jewelry and spent no less than 351 days a year basking in warm weather.

Two weeks per year, and never more, Georgy the Russian would enjoy a snow skiing vacation, usually in late March when the snowy slopes were sun-splashed and not very cold. As soon as the vacation was over, he'd be whisked somewhere extremely warm to reheat his bones.

With a shiny bald head, a prominent nose and a salt-and-pepper moustache, Georgy could easily pass for the head of a global Fortune 500 company – if he wore a suit. But typically he only wore a bathing suit, sandals and a silken robe. Georgy hardly ever bothered with a shirt.

He'd rented this exclusive villa through a corporation run by his Swiss banker. And despite the fact that he always rented this same villa, few knew Georgy was in Odessa, and there was a reason for that.

Trudging across the open bedroom, he lifted his recently hurled mobile phone and made sure it still functioned. He redialed a number he called often and waited for the woman to answer. She did on the fourth ring, breathless.

"You sound like you were running a marathon."

"I wasn't," she huffed.

"Are you here in Odessa?"

"Yeah."

"Where?"

"Not far from you," she gasped.

"Are you okay? What the hell did you do to lose your breath?"

"I *was* getting my brains fucked out till you interrupted," his wife griped. "What the hell do you want, anyway?"

Georgy closed his eyes and shook his head in disgust. Dirty *shalava!* His wife's name was Nastya, and, even after all these years, her bluntness still managed to shock him.

"Well?" she spat.

"No word from the American. He missed two times that he was supposed to check in."

"Meaning, you failed...*again*."

"Your man chose the American."

"But you, dipshit, put it in motion and made the plan. I'll call you later."

Before the line went dead, Georgy heard Nastya requesting something particularly vile and vulgar, even for her. He hurled the phone again, this time shattering it for good.

The Russian cuckold lay down in his silken sheets, wondering who was servicing his wife this time. Georgy knew she'd slept with dozens of men, including nearly all of her domestics. She'd also participated in an on-again/off-again affair with a Spanish rock singer. About a year ago, the singer's wife had found out about his paramour and threatened to separate him from his manhood with a *navaja* knife. Since then, as far as Georgy knew, the Spanish affair had ended.

If I know for sure about 20 or 30 of the guys she's banged—imagine how many I don't know about...

He rolled to his side, shaking away the thoughts. Nothing would ever change her, or him, for that matter.

But what to do about Elena? Elena the oil princess... Elena the bitch...

Surely there had to be a way to kill her. She was a glorified typist, for heaven's sake. How could she outsmart professional assassins three times now?

You don't yet know that the American failed, Georgy reminded himself. *He's just late with his phone calls. Maybe he was just in a hurry to get away.*

Georgy closed his eyes, his consciousness quickly claimed by sleep and the two Ambien he'd chased with cold vodka a half-hour before.

Before he slept—as he did every morning when he finally went to sleep—he vowed to make sure Elena Volkov wouldn't live to see June 30th.

That *sooka's* luck would eventually run out.

***

The sun was rising quickly. In order to gain some trust, Gage had gone into his prisoner's shirt pocket and retrieved a cigarette for him. While the American smoked, he swore he'd not been behind the previous attempts on Elena's life. He'd been chosen specifically for this attempt due to his Italian heritage and fluency.

They chatted for several minutes, with Gage learning that the man had been in the U.S. Army and now fashioned himself as some sort of debonair assassin. Though he attempted to come off as urbane, it became readily apparent that he'd kill anyone for the right price. Some assassins live by a code of honor, only eliminating people who they believed to be scourges. This one, however, willingly admitted to some of his past kills regardless of the reason. His two U.S. kills amounted to spousal murders in a gun-for-hire arrangement.

Gage learned all this by telling the killer that they were both professionals, simply hired to do work that regular people were unwilling to do.

"Who are you?" the killer asked.

"I'm just like you. I was paid to assassinate Elena Volkov."

The killer had narrowed his eyes. "Why two of us?"

"I guess that's how badly someone wants her dead. I chased you just because I thought you were some sort of personal protection."

"Really?"

"Yeah. I thought maybe she was in the car with you."

After telling Gage some of his background, the killer asked the key question. "Where is Elena Volkov?"

"I don't know," Gage answered, playing along.

While the killer might have been crafty and brazen, he obviously wasn't very bright. "Were you hired by the Swiss man, too?"

"No. But the woman who hired me *was* Swiss," Gage smoothly lied. "You think they work together?"

"That makes sense." The killer had briefly looked away. "How much were you paid?"

"I got twenty-thousand euro up front. I'm to get ten times that amount if I make the kill and get away clean. You?"

"I get more than twice that," the killer said with a smile.

"I never do seem to get paid as much as others," Gage mused, allowing the Sig to dip a fraction. "Say, do you have a phone number for the Swiss man?"

"He called from a different number each time."

"Do you have them?"

"They're in my phone."

"Show me," Gage replied, handing the phone to his fellow American.

The killer punched in his four-digit iPhone code that Gage memorized. The man turned the phone so Gage could see the call history. The phone numbers from Switzerland all started with the country code of 41. The numbers might come in handy later.

"Did the Swiss man have a name?" Gage asked.

"Not that he told me."

"Ever worked with him before?"

"No."

"How did he find you?"

"Through a man I know in New York."

"What language did he speak to you?"

"English and some Italian. He wanted to make sure I was fluent."

"How was he with those languages?"

"Excellent. And I think he speaks Russian, too."

"Why do you say that?"

"He used several Russian words and he spoke them just like a Russian. I know because there was a Russian neighborhood one street over from where I grew up." The man placed his phone beside him. "Are you going to keep holding my pistol on me or should we work together? We can be there in fifteen minutes."

"She's not at home."

"She might be by now."

"Just a few more questions. Who knows, maybe we can call our Swiss handlers and demand more money...together," Gage replied casually.

"That's an idea."

"The woman who hired me seemed older. Any idea how old your Swiss guy was?"

"Middle-age maybe? Forty or fifty?"

"Good. What else?"

"There wasn't much. He called me four or five times—first to see if I wanted the job, then to give details."

Gage nodded. "They sent me to Naples, first."

"Me, too."

"When did they tell you about Sicily?"

"Yesterday," the American said. "I found out on my own."

"How?"

"Paid off some locals."

Gage nodded. "Did the Swiss man care how you killed her?"

"He asked that I do my best not to make it look like a blatant murder. That's why I brought that syringe."

"Wouldn't they see the needle mark?"

The American's grin was wicked. "The doctor I bought that stuff from said it's pretty much untraceable. I was going to poke it into the skin inside her snatch."

Gage struggled with himself upon hearing that. "How'd you get paid?"

"The Swiss man set up a bank account for me. That's where the deposit went and that's where the rest'll go after the kill is confirmed."

"I'm assuming it's an untraceable Swiss account?"

"Yes."

"That makes sense. Anything else?"

"No."

Gage lowered the pistol a bit more. "Don't move, okay? I need to know a few more things."

The killer narrowed his eyes. "You're being very careful."

"Yeah, I am. It's kept me breathing this long and if we're going to work together, I'd like to be sure." Gage sucked on his teeth as he pondered his tack. "You mentioned what you were going to do with that needle. Were you…you know…tempted by what you might do with her before?"

"What do you mean?"

"The oil princess is pretty damned hot from the pictures I've seen."

A wily expression came over the American as he inclined his head toward the needle. "That syringe is loaded with something called SUX. It causes paralysis in small doses, deadly in large. I was going to give her just a taste and then get mine before giving her the rest. I was gonna bang her with a rubber, of course."

There was a long moment of silence, the only sound being the distant noises of the ocean road. Gage eyed the man harshly.

"What?" the killer finally asked. "What's your problem?"

"SUX stands for succinylcholine."

"I guess."

"Do you know what an awful death that would bring?"

"The fuck do I care?"

Trembling, Gage's knuckles turned white on the grips of the pistol. As he shuddered in his rage, the two men shared a look that predated history books, psychology and recorded war. It was the glare of mortal enemies, when both belligerents realize the talking is over and there's but one thing left to do.

At the very second Gage was going to throw a punch with the pistol, the American killer surprised Gage with a fast kick upward, knocking the Sig from Gage's grip. Gage was still in a dominant position and didn't want to lose it. Rather than scramble for the firearm, he thrust forward with both of his arms, trapping the killer's head against the Lancia just above the wheel-well.

The only sounds were growls, grunts and sibilant breaths as the two men labored against one another. Despite the American killer's lithe build, he was young and extremely strong. Two times he unsuccessfully attempted to sweep Gage and come to his feet. As in many grappling bouts, the person who tires first loses. This bout was no different. The American killer had to expend too much energy trying to get out from under Gage. Had Gage not begun with the dominant position, he wasn't sure he'd have bested the younger man.

When his opponent's struggling legs finally gave out, Gage slammed the man's head against the Lancia, dazing him. Reaching back and palming the pistol, Gage swung it in a looping arc into the side of the killer's head, close to where he'd struck him before. The man went down in a heap as Gage walloped him two more times.

As the killer lay silent but breathing, Gage unloaded the syringe into the downed man's jugular vein without a second's hesitation.

"Sweet dreams, you psychopathic prick."

The killer lived about two more minutes and his death was particularly horrid, just as Gage had predicted. As the man's life noisily expired, Gage leaned against the car, catching his wind. This was not going at all to plan.

Finally, suddenly aware of his great hunger and thirst, Gage struggled to cram his fellow American into the small trunk of the Lancia. After collapsing in the driver's seat and guzzling from his bottle of water, Gage pondered his best course of action. He knew he'd be taking an immense risk by driving the car. The Lancia was probably already associated with the wrecked Fiat. Some enterprising *polizia* was going to pull prints from that Fiat and, eventually, a police database was going to spit back the fact that the Fiat had been driven by a world-class piece of shit.

And that's when the police would turn their attention to the driver of the Lancia convertible that witnesses had told them about—the one with the dented front right fender. Gage imagined that somewhere nearby there was a traffic camera that would provide the Lancia's license plate. That would lead the police to Elena Volkov and the address in Belpasso. But it was there their dead ends would begin.

She was no longer in Belpasso, but she wasn't very far away, either.

The best-case scenario, in Gage's mind, gave him 48 hours to escape. Hopefully the police didn't even cock an eyebrow at the wrecked Fiat. Provided no one told them the two cars had been dueling prior to the wreck, it might just be another crash on the curvy road. If the traffic cop was lazy, he'd have the Fiat towed and wouldn't check with the emergency room at the hospital. In that event, who knew how long it might take the police to become suspicious?

But if the police had already pulled the prints, and Gage had to assume they had, he felt they'd be knocking on the door of Elena's rental home by late afternoon. After that, the search would be on.

Therefore, Gage had no intention of being on this rock by sundown.

He drove over the dusty red hills to the large rail yard, assuming it was associated with the numerous shipping facilities to the north. For now, perhaps because it was still very early, there seemed to be no activity in the rail yard. Once at the rail yard's edge, Gage stopped and studied the bevy of utility implements. It took him only a few minutes to find something he thought might work.

The 55-gallon drum had only been half-full of a gritty substance that looked like cat litter. In the Army, they'd called it "dry sweep", a product utilized to soak up oil and fuel spills. Gage dumped out a pile of the dry sweep and replaced it with the American killer. Gage then used his hands to scoop the dry sweep back in, partially covering the killer's crumpled body before re-sealing the top and rolling the barrel to the rear area of dozens of barrels.

It might be months before the dead American was found.

Now, the car. He lowered the top and rolled down the windows.

Sticking exclusively to back roads, Gage made his way south, into the city of Cantania. Once there, he relaxed a bit when he saw several Lancias just like the one he was driving. He cruised around a bit until he found what appeared to be a depressed area. Gage located a small grocery store and parked in an alleyway next door. He stood on the sidewalk and waited for the owner to unlock the door. As the store's first customer of the day, he purchased glass cleaner and paper towels. Back at the car, Gage put the top down and set about spraying and cleaning all surfaces that he or Elena might have touched, including the outer door handles and the key fob.

When he was finished, Gage gripped the key fob with his t-shirt, placing it on the driver's seat in plain sight—in a rather bad area of town.

A nice, shiny Lancia—with a few fresh dents and bullet holes in the passenger window and floorboard—was now available to the first person who came along. Gage was hoping the mafia would grab it. He banked that it would be taken to a chop shop where one of two things would happen. Either it would be cut up and sold for parts or, since it was so new, the VIN number and associated serial numbers might be changed, after which the mafia would use their influence to re-register the car in the governmental database.

Then the car could be legally sold and the mafia would be about 25,000 euro richer.

Despite his fatigue and hunger, Gage felt markedly better. Elena's piece-of-shit pursuer had been dispatched.

And now it was time to get the hell off this island.

***

The taxi ride inland to Adrano was quite expensive. During the journey, Gage rolled down the rear windows. He then leaned his head back, allowing the warm air to rush over his face as he thought through all his options. Foremost in his mind was getting Elena away from Sicily without leaving a trail. After that, it was as simple as hiding her somewhere until the June 30th deadline passed. At that point, they could reassess her situation to determine if the danger had passed.

What am I missing? Something niggled at Gage's mind, but due to his exhaustion he couldn't put a finger on it.

After instructing the cabbie to park around back, Gage tipped the man with his remaining cash and hurried into the hotel, taking the stairs by twos and threes. He'd barely reached the landing when he saw Elena's door whip open, startling the hell out of him. But her angered mien gave him quick relief. Gage knew a pissed-off woman when he saw one.

"Where have you been?" she snapped as both dogs burst from the room to sniff Gage's feet and legs.

"Please, go back inside," Gage said, following her back into her room.

"I've been going crazy waiting for you. I hate being confined in hotel rooms."

"You hate crowds, too."

"Don't be cute."

Gage went straight to his pack, producing two protein bars and ripping one open. With his mouth full he said, "You need to get packed."

"We're leaving already?"

"Yes."

"When?"

"As soon as possible."

"Where are we going?"

"I'm working on that." Gage hoisted the largest suitcase to her bed. Most of the items were still inside. "They know you're here."

"Who does?"

"Whoever's out to get you," he replied, stuffing the last of the first bar in his mouth.

"How do you know that?"

Gage held up a finger until he was done chewing. "We all get lucky sometimes, Elena. I can't believe it happened on the first night you were away from your house. If you'd have hired me a day later…"

"What happened?"

He looked at his watch. "I'll tell you later. For now, I need to know if you're willing to spend a bundle of that cash."

"Are you sure you're okay?" she asked, narrowing her eyes at him.

"I'm fine," he answered, going to work on the second protein bar. "The money?"

"I don't mind using it, provided it goes to good use. What'll we be buying?"

"Travel and then safety." Gage produced his mobile phone and powered it on as he kept eating. "Keep packing, please." He moved by the window, running a few ideas through his mind. They could charter an airplane. They could also continue further inland and pay cash for a cabin. He stared at the rooftops of the sun-drenched Sicilian town as the phone connections clicked several times before Gage heard the ringing.

"Calling me already?" Hunter asked.

"Morning, colonel. Didn't wake you, did I?"

"Prostate woke me at three and my guilty conscience took over from there. How's Italy?" He said it like "It-Lee."

"Not so good. Had a little problem last night."

"Already? You okay?"

"I'm fine. It was amateur night, thankfully. Listen, assuming she's compromised, would you stay on this rock or head elsewhere?"

"Haul ass."

"Thought so. Would a private plane leave too many loose ends?"

"Yep. You need mass transit that doesn't require an I.D."

"Roger that. Then I need a few favors. Big ones. You up for it?"

"Name it."

"Check the *account* for instructions, will you?"

"Involved?"

"Yes, sir. Pretty involved."

"How soon are we talking about?"

"I need you to check the email within the hour. You'll have all day today to get what I need, then you'll need to world overnight the stuff for tomorrow."

"Sheeyat!" Hunter griped. "World overnight means I'll have to hand-carry whatever you're wanting to the airport in Charlotte by probably...I dunno...eighteen hundred, at the latest. And it'll cost a damned fortune."

"I know. My friend here's good for it."

Hunter blew out a loud breath that made the phone squelch. "Anything else?"

"That's all for now. I do appreciate it."

"Is what you're asking for doable?"

"Part of it is doable today. Maybe all of it."

"I'll do what I can. Email me soon so I can plan my day."

"Thank you, sir." Gage hung up the phone.

"Who was that?" Elena asked.

"My friend who knows your friend. Keep packing," Gage said, twisting open a bottle of water. "And don't leave the room. I'll be right back. We're leaving soon."

"I'm completely confused."

Gage was about to open the door but stopped. "I'm sorry for acting so abrupt. Like I said, something happened last night at your house in Belpasso. It's okay, for now, but we really need to get moving." He gave her a tight smile. "If we go soon, we'll be fine."

Elena nodded although her expression changed to one of worry.

"May I have some cash?"

She handed him a bundled packet and he hurried out the door and down the stairs to the front desk. The clerk was no more than twenty and extremely short. Her hair was dark, highlighted in streaks of purple. When she gave Gage a bright smile, the hoop piercings in her bottom lip canted outward before she asked him something in Italian.

"*Mio italiano ist non è buono. Lei parla inglese?*" Gage asked, realizing he accidentally threw a German verb into his stilted phrase.

"English is no prob," the young lady said, her English nearly devoid of accent.

"Does the hotel have a guest computer?"

"Yeah, but it's old. It's around the corner by the lift," she said, pointing.

"Is it connected to the Internet?"

"Dude, it's old but not that old. What'd be the point of having a computer that wouldn't surf?"

"Good point. And would you happen to know if there's a taxi service near here that'll accept a long fare?"

"How long?"

"I don't know, yet. Maybe an hour away?"

"Not that far. You could probably call Cantania and find a car service that would do it."

"Damn. I don't have time."

"I could drive you."

"Would you? What about the hotel?"

She shrugged. "This is my parents' hotel. We don't have any upcoming reservations. And anyway, my parents are here," she said, gesturing to the attached building. "We live in the cottage right over there."

"I'll pay you for the ride. Pay you well."

"Good," the girl said with a grin. "That was going to be my next question. How much?"

"Couple hundred euro?"

"I knew you were cool. Just let me know when you're ready."

"You got it. Go ahead and check me and my friend out of 303 and 304." As she went to work on the receipts, Gage found the hotel computer and accessed the Internet.

Provided this computer wasn't compromised—and he couldn't think of any logical reason why it would be—what Gage was about to do was a method first devised by terrorists for secure international communication. The NSA had since figured it out, but for purposes such as Gage's, when no sophisticated entity was after him, it was an excellent way to send secure messages with little hassle and no special equipment.

He logged into the Yahoo email account he shared with Colonel Hunter and composed a new email:

```
Morning Sir,

Apologies for asking you to do this.
The situation here is much hotter than
I thought.  She was already blown so I
have to assume the worst.  Please send
me my only I.D. packet from the safe
(along with the debit and credit cards
and the fake keys.)  I brought my
second I.D. packet but I'm afraid it
could be traced since it's been used
before—that's why I want the clean
third I.D.  And can you call Charlie M.
to see if he can pull off an I.D. set
for my friend in time for the shipment?
He'd have to drive up and bring it to
you at CLT.  Money is no object at all.
If he can't do it in time, go ahead and
have him make her one and I can give
you a future shipping address later.

Make her residency somewhere in Central
or Eastern Europe but not where she's
from.  There are tons of photos of her
online.  Tell Charlie to Google her and
do his Photoshop magic with something
he can find.

(Oh yeah, make sure you call Ron and
ask about what happened at the biker
joint in Charlotte.  Good times.  I
```

never threw a punch. Well, that's not
completely true. Just call Ron.)

Send everything overnight to a Genoa
hotel, your choice. Something near the
port. And would you mind making me a
reservation for two adjoining rooms?
Please let them know a package is
coming, too. Secure packaging please
with our normal procedure.

Finally, if possible, can you get me a
source for implements in Genoa or
nearby? A phone number will suffice.

I'll check this computer in an hour for
the response.
Thank you. Thank you. Thank you.

(And don't spoil the dog!)

Rather than send the email, Gage saved the email draft. This
prevented the email from being sent out over dozens of networks between
Sicily and North Carolina. Instead, the email was saved directly into Yahoo's
servers. Minutes from now, Colonel Hunter would log into the same account
and read the draft email and simply respond via the same message.

Nice and secure, unless Yahoo was reading draft emails.

After finding Elena packed and ready with her dogs beside her, Gage
pulled his scant items together and asked her to wait before he hurried back
down the stairs. Although only 10 minutes had passed, Hunter had already
responded. Charlie Mink, former sub driver, former engineer, and current
master forger, said he'd meet Hunter in Charlotte with her I.D. So, Hunter
agreed to drive Gage's I.D. packet to Charlotte and ship both items to Genoa
on the last flight tonight, meaning Gage would have the items sometime
tomorrow.

...I was supposed to spend the day
with Alice so now she's coming to
Charlotte with me. That means
lots of shopping. That means this
trip'll cost me $500, easy, and
that's not counting gas and food.

```
That means you owe me...big time.

Your hotel is the Genova Marina
Hotel and it's under the name of
the Garrett Healey I.D. that
should be waiting with the hotel
concierge.  Delivery is guaranteed
to Genoa by 2 P.M. local,
tomorrow.


I guess you know the locals call
it Genova, but we call it Genoa.
I spent some time there way back,
so in the envelope I'm including
the name and address of an old
friend who lives there.  He almost
certainly has access to the
implements you need.


For the record, I told you not to
take this damn job.
Check back in with me soon...

(And damn right I'm spoiling the
dog!)
```

The colonel comes through again.

Fifteen minutes later, Gage, Elena and the two dogs departed with the daughter of the hotelier. Her tiny red car was older than she was and didn't seem to have been cleaned since it left the factory in the early 90s. Although the group idly chatted, Gage, who was crammed into the backseat with one of the dogs and two suitcases, could hardly hear over the throbbing industrial music from some obscure band called Pailhead. Even though the car was old and on the verge of ruin, the stereo and speakers were new and powerful.

Ah, the priorities of youth.

After a torturous hour-long drive, the young woman dropped her passengers at the small railway station in the inland city of Dittàino. The city was on the main railway line to Palermo. And in Palermo, Gage planned to purchase ferry tickets to Genoa.

Chapter Five

IT WAS early evening in Odessa and the scent of intrigue charged the air. Earlier in the day, Georgy Zaytsev, frustrated by the numerous failures of the previous hired killers, did something he knew he should have done a long time ago. He called his most trusted banker and confidant, a Zürich-based Russian, and told him he finally wanted to discuss hiring "the Assassin."

"The Assassin" was the first person the banker had advised Georgy to hire, long ago when Suntex Energy had first made the offer for UkeOil. A professional killer of unknown name and origin, the Assassin supposedly commanded ridiculous fees that Georgy feared would be escalated due to the fortune associated with the Volkov name. When Georgy's banker inquired about the price, he was told the fee would probably fall in the $20 million range.

Before now—unfathomable.

Today, however, with the American killer having gone completely dark—meaning, he failed—Georgy was beginning to panic. There was a finite amount of time between now and the deal date—only 9 days, counting today. If the deadline passed without a shareholder vote agreeing to the sale of UkeOil, billions of dollars would be lost. Many, many billions. And despite the hundreds of millions associated with Georgy's statement of net worth—due to a number of unfortunate legalities—his money, and subsequently his lifestyle, could evaporate with a few deft strokes of a pen.

If the Assassin was as good as advertised, his fee would be well worth it.

Amazing how time can greatly alter one's perspective.

Georgy had done exactly as he'd been told and wired a "discussion payment" to the numbered account that had been provided. Because it was done on such short notice, the bank charged an extra 2.5% of the full amount to expedite the wire.

Fleeced at every turn by pen-wielding crooks.

Now Georgy sat alone in the quiet bedroom of the sprawling Odessan vacation home. His phone lay dormant on the table, next to the half-empty vodka bottle he'd taken from the freezer. Six agonizing minutes had ticked by after Georgy received word that the wire had been successfully placed.

According to his banker, the Assassin was supposed to call immediately.

When the phone finally did ring, 22 minutes after the wire went through, Georgy yelled out in alarm. He'd set the ringer at maximum volume and it startled him and his already-frayed nerves. The caller ID displayed all zeroes. Georgy lifted the phone, his manicured fingernail hovering over the screen.

Don't pick it up till the third ring…

When he touched the green on-screen button, Georgy could hardly get his greeting out due to his scratchy throat. Once he'd croaked his hello, he drank deeply of his ice-cold vodka and put the phone on speaker, carefully replacing it on the bedside table.

"Tell me who you would like killed," the voice said. It was obviously modulated by some sort of computerized device, but didn't sound robot-like at all. Instead, there was a faint digital choppiness to the otherwise normal elocution. It sounded as if the computerized voice spoke with a central Russian dialect, similar to what one might hear in Moscow.

"Tell me," the voice commanded.

"Ah…yes…I would like Elena Volkov…" Georgy tripped on his words.

"Killed?"

"Yes."

"When?"

Georgy was uncomfortable at the abrupt way the conversation had so quickly begun. "Shouldn't we discuss other things first?"

"What other things?"

"I don't know. This just seems…you know, quick. I'd like to get my brain around this before telling you everything."

"You're not ready so this call is over."

"Wait!" Georgy urged. "It's just…well, you're moving rapidly."

"I have neither the time nor the patience to mince words. When would you like Elena Volkov killed?"

"Are you concerned our call might be recorded by the government, or even some group like the NSA? I'm on a cell phone."

"No, I'm not concerned and the call isn't being recorded. Tell me when you'd like Elena Volkov killed or I'm hanging up and keeping the discussion payment."

There seemed to be a slight delay between their verbal exchanges. Georgy assumed the Assassin had to wait for the computer to translate his words in the event the man wasn't Russian. Georgy's banker had said he'd heard whispers that the Assassin was French or Belgian. Through Georgy's other inquiries, he'd heard the Assassin was Nordic or perhaps even Moroccan.

"When?" the voice persisted.

"She must be killed before the end of June. In fact, she needs to be killed no later than the twenty-ninth of June. That's when we have a shareholder...well, never mind." Georgy took another sip of the vodka. "Let's make the deadline June twenty-eighth, okay? Because we need time to get a death certificate."

"Getting the documentation can be done quickly with the proper cooperation from the authorities. Money buys that cooperation. Make sure your attorneys are ready."

"I will."

"Have you already attempted to kill her?"

Georgy stared with wide eyes at the phone. "Why does that matter?"

Slight delay. "It matters."

"Yes. I...*we* have."

"How many times?"

Georgy squeezed his eyes shut. "Three times. In Prague, Greece and Sicily. The first two failed."

"And the third?"

"We think it failed."

"Those previous attempts will have significant impact on my fee."

"And what is your fee?"

"Before I calculate my fee, why did you not initially list Sicily with the failures?"

"I haven't heard from the man we hired and he should have checked in by now."

There was a long pause followed by a faint clicking sound. "Regardless, you should hire me immediately. There is very little time between now and the twenty-eighth of June. Each hour is critical."

"How much to hire you?"

"Ten million U.S."

Georgy slumped in relief. That was still high but not the $20 million he'd been told by his banker back when they'd first received Suntex's offer. Massaging the bridge of his nose, Georgy said, "That's an incredible sum of money. Though the first two attempts definitely failed, I only paid a slight percentage of what you're asking. However, due to the quick timeframe and your reputation, I'll agree to this exorbitant amount."

"That's my *retainer*."

Georgy's jaw muscles momentarily malfunctioned.

"And, of course, the retainer is non-refundable no matter what happens. I will spend a great deal of the upfront money finding Elena Volkov who is now *spooked* due to three botched attempts on her life."

"She's not spooked enough that it will make your job more difficult. Elena hates people...she has some sort of social angst. She'd never agree to outside help. So, all you need to do is find her. Meaning, your upfront amount is too high."

Silence.

Georgy continued. "She even rented a small yacht and I later found out that she could hardly mutter words to her crew. She's alone somewhere…that's why your fee shouldn't be higher due to the previous attempts."

"The retainer stands at ten million, U.S."

"Then, what's your full fee? And, also, we still don't know the third attempt, by the American, even occurred. She could already be dead and you'll get to keep my money."

"Assume the attempt occurred and your American is now dead."

"Why do you say that?"

"That's the last free tip you'll receive. My full fee is an additional forty million U.S. dollars. If you want me, I'll have the full retainer fee in my account by tomorrow fifteen hundred hours, Greenwich Mean Time. If it's not there, I keep today's discussion fee and life goes on. If the retainer is there, I will attempt to find Elena Volkov and, when I do, I will kill her. At that point, you will pay me the remaining forty-million dollars, U.S. Failure to pay me within twenty-four hours of a verified kill will result in the death of you and everyone you hold dear." There was a slight pause. "Your deaths will not be pleasant."

Georgy stood beside the bed, both hands involuntarily kneading his scalp upward. "Are you mad, man? Fifty million and change? That's more than double what I'd been told!"

"I will not justify my fee with another word. If you continue on your current course, this conversation is over and you can hire another lazy American ex-soldier who lied about his past. Or maybe you can pay another poorly-trained Serbian sniper who couldn't hit a wounded fat man from two hundred meters on a calm day. Or, perhaps you could find another Slovakian thug who can barely operate a straight-drive automobile. You can hire any of those, and more…but you won't have me."

Georgy gaped at the phone. How did the Assassin know about each of the hired would-be killers?

"I know many things," the voice said, as if divining Georgy's thoughts. "So, do we have a deal?"

Hands massaging his face and pulling it downward into an over-tanned, ghastly mask, Georgy slumped onto the side of the bed and mumbled his assent.

"Wire the retainer by the deadline and I will go to work."

"How will you reach me for questions?" Georgy asked, grasping the vodka around the neck.

"Keep your phone charged and beside you at all times, day or night. Once the payment is in my account, I'll go to work. I'll call you only if need be. I will also call you when she is dead. And that will be one very brief call. After that, you will have one day to pay me, or else. Do you understand?"

"Yeah."

"Are you certain? The stakes here are quite high and I will be completely inflexible from here on."

"I understand."

"Do we have a deal?"

"Yes."

"Are you absolutely certain?"

A pause. "I am."

"Then, on good faith, I shall begin at first light tomorrow, even before the wire has been received. I'll do this due to the tight timeframe. So, this is your last chance to say no. Because once I begin, I shall assume your payment is coming. If it doesn't come, you'll be dealt with as discussed."

Georgy blew out a long breath. "We have a deal. The money will be wired tomorrow before the deadline."

"Fine. Good day."

There were two clicks before the line went dead.

Fifty million U.S. dollars, not to mention the two hundred grand and change Georgy had just spent to have a somewhat disturbing ten-minute phone call. Because he was so illiquid, the retainer would essentially clean out Georgy's accounts, leaving him with only a few million for living expenses. He'd have to get the remaining amount from Nastya.

But, given the riches that awaited them, that shouldn't be a problem.

And then that simple, money-grubbing bitch, the Ukrainian oil princess, will finally have her date with the maggots.

Georgy swigged deeply from the sweaty bottle of vodka. When he'd had enough to soak his liver, he placed an urgent call to Switzerland.

***

The Assassin removed his headset and closed his laptop. He was currently living in Lagos, Portugal, located several time zones west of the Russian. Lagos was on the sun-splashed rocky shores of Portugal's south-facing Algarve coast. While the morning had been cloudy and cool, the afternoon sun had ultimately won out and now bathed the shirtless professional killer in warm sunlight. He reclined in his chair, a wisp of a smile appearing on his bearded face as he massaged his bicep with his hand. There'd been a time several years before when the Assassin had packed on muscle, thinking it would do him good. But he'd found the extra weight cumbersome. Now he was lean, focusing on healthy eating, cardiovascular exercise and weight training for repetitions rather than maximum kilos.

The smoking helped keep the weight off, too. The Assassin knew it would probably end his life twenty years before genetics eventually would. But he had no desire to grow old. To be hunched over in pain, lining up pills morning and night simply to keep on living in that horrid state. To be relegated to a nursing home for military veterans, having his ass wiped by some underpaid nursing assistant who wished he'd just die…

No…

The Assassin would rather eat, drink, smoke and end things a bit early. And if a doctor pronounced his death sentence, the Assassin would enjoy a final meal, smoke one last cigarette and find some clever way to quickly end things. But for now, he was quite alive.

Invigorated, actually.

What had been a restful and enjoyable two-year holiday would come to an end tomorrow. There had been several proposals floated the Assassin's way during the two-year period, but none he'd been keen on. This one, however, intrigued him. He certainly knew the Volkov name and had discreetly learned the staggering numbers that were at stake with the buyout offer from the American company, Suntex Energy. This was the big payday the Assassin had always dreamed of.

The Assassin viewed himself as a critical cog in the machine of big business, no different than a lawyer or investment banker or some other white-collar type, making what amounted to a sizeable fee off of such a large transaction. Numerous professionals—many who amounted to nothing more than hangers-on—would be made virtually untouchable by the amount of money that was to be doled out in the sale of UkeOil; so why shouldn't the Assassin profit, too?

Besides, after his last job, he'd started his two-year holiday with nearly eight million dollars to his name. In the last month, he'd finally lost the most important of his two net worth commas, watching the remains of the handsome fee dwindle down to six-figures. Given his lifestyle, the Assassin needed work—and soon. The payday for this Volkov job, invested properly, could finance the rest of his life. Sure, after the Ukrainian oil princess was dispatched, he might someday kill again, but the Assassin was currently neutral on the prospect. He neither enjoyed killing, nor abhorred it. To him, killing was a means to an end.

Like having sex with a person you're not particularly attracted to. Nothing to look forward to, but you can sometimes find yourself surprised by the gratification you receive, the Assassin thought with a chuckle.

From what he'd gleaned, there was too much at stake for that Russian glutton, Georgy Zaytsev, not to have hired the Assassin. And there was no doubt the Assassin was the best on the planet, especially now that the South

African sniper was dead after that business a few years back in Mallorca. Word of the Assassin's prowess had definitely gotten around. He was the very best and the very best is almost always very expensive.

When I kill the oil princess, if I decide to keep working, what might my next fee bring?

The very notion made him giddy. In celebration of his newfound wealth, tonight the Assassin would dine at his favorite waterside restaurant in Alvor and hope to find some premium female companionship. He'd quickly seduce her with his magniloquent style. She'd have long, smooth legs. Eyes like cerulean pools. A woman to laugh with and taste and enjoy and pleasure all night long. Then, tomorrow, he would depart at first light with only a small bag of clothes, his computer, his phone and several bundles of cash.

For now, the Assassin planned to cool off with a chilly dip in his rental villa's pool. Afterward, he'd enjoy a blisteringly hot shower and dress in his finest linen suit.

Tonight's meal might be the last good one he'd have until July.

***

The 21-hour ferry journey from Palermo to Genoa sailed at 11 P.M. The northwesterly route would follow the western shore of Italy, up the shin and knee of "the boot." Earlier, at boarding, Gage had managed to secure the very last suite for Elena. He purchased a regular seat for himself and had to pay an extra fee for the dogs' voyage. Elena had waited in the hotelier's car as Gage had walked back and forth from the ticketing area, giving her the details.

Gage had wanted to board the dogs himself, just in case someone might be watching. Anyone who knew Elena knew about the two dogs. Breaking them up during boarding might help Elena avoid detection. As he leaned down to the car window, she objected to not having the dogs in her suite.

"Their policy is rigid, Elena. You can visit them once we're underway."

After several more rebuttals, she relented.

The ferry itself was quite large and reminded Gage of the ferries in Puget Sound. Once he and Elena were on the same page about the accommodations, he boarded and took the dogs to the kennel. Ten minutes later, after all the passengers were aboard, Elena boarded wearing a large hat and a scarf. She made her way to the suite without incident. Gage arrived minutes later.

The suite was better than he'd expected, the largest of its kind on the ferry. It was roughly equivalent to a standard hotel room, outfitted with a queen size bed, a private bath and even a narrow balcony on the ferry's port side.

"It'll be after eleven by the time we get underway," Gage said, pulling the curtains shut. "Since we're headed northwest, the sun will come up on the other side so, in the morning, maybe you can enjoy the relative darkness and sleep in."

"I believe it's you who needs the sleep."

Without responding, he placed the smallest suitcase in the bathroom and the others beside the bed. "Okay, I think you're all set. I'm going to be outside the suite and right down the hall in the aft cabin. The porter switched my seat with someone else's. It faces the hallway, so I'll be able to see your door."

"Why? Do you think they know we're on the ferry?"

"No."

"Then why watch the door?"

"Why not watch the door? Why risk it?"

"Are you implying that the person who is after me *may* know I'm here?"

"Not at all. We weren't followed and we didn't use your identification to buy the ferry tickets."

"I thought your friend said to use a method of transport that didn't require identification?" she asked.

"I have a second identification."

"But you asked your friend to send you a second identification."

"I asked him to send me my third one. Because, in the event someone might track my second I.D. to Genoa, then we will truly disappear."

"That makes me nervous."

"Elena, if we're going to do this…for this to work…you have to trust me. There's always a random chance that something could go wrong. But this ferry journey is our best move and I'm confident no one knows we're here." He walked to the door. "Once we get to the mainland, we will have clean identification and your cash. We will disappear and that deadline will pass without further incident. Okay?"

Elena glanced nervously about the small room. "Okay, but I miss my dogs."

"They're fine."

"You have no way of knowing that."

"I saw the girl who runs the kennels. She got down on the floor and rolled around and French-kissed both of them. I'd say they're in great hands."

"French-kissed?"

"Tongue-to-tongue."

She laughed while making a face. "That makes me feel a little bit better. Sort of."

"Once we get underway, I can go check on them."

"No, don't do that." She slid the drapes back open, the blackness of the Mediterranean sucking the light from the room. "It's so quiet in here, and with all the activity I'm not sleepy."

"Maybe you can read," Gage offered, opening the door. "I'll be right down the hall. Keep the door locked and don't open it for anyone but me."

She said nothing. Gage stepped out and pulled the door shut. He walked forty feet to the cavernous, aft-most seating area. It looked like an auditorium or a movie theater but with no rise in the floor. The ferry seemed to be about two-thirds full and the room buzzed with conversation. Many of the passengers weren't yet in their seats. A few children sprinted around the room, chasing each other and using up the last vestiges of the day's energy.

Gage purchased a large bottle of water and sat. Thankfully, the seats did recline and had a few inches of space between the armrests. As he reclined just a bit, Gage again verified that he could see Elena's door. He could.

Tonight was going to be brutally long. Though he hated admitting it, Gage was exhausted. There was a small café on the starboard side that was open 24 hours. He'd need the caffeine.

Gage added up the sleep he'd had since he'd left Fayetteville. In Charlotte, after the tussle with the redneck Colton brothers and dozens of nuclear wings, Gage had managed only about four hours at an airport hotel. The next night, he'd had two or three fitful hours on the airplane. Then, last night, after the long hike from Cantania to Belpasso, he'd had a few uncomfortable hours in the seat of the Lancia before having the run-in with the hired American killer.

Not nearly enough. No wonder Gage felt like he'd been run over by a truck.

Of course, once he calculated how tired he was, his mind took over and tried its best to pull a blanket of sleep over him. Ten minutes passed, feeling more like ten hours. Gage could feel the rumble of the side-thrusters as the ferry pushed away from its moorings. The vibrations made him even sleepier.

As soon as movement occurred, many of the passengers found their seats and the room began to quiet a bit. Gage eyed the café. The crowd had dwindled. There was a gaggle of teens drinking beer and wine. Next to them were three pathetic-looking 40-somethings. They were boozing it up, ogling women and, for whatever reason, laughing hysterically about a glass of milk they'd just ordered. *Weirdos.* Other than those two groups, there was a line of four people. The ferry was Italian so Gage made an educated guess that he could purchase good coffee in the café. He was thinking a double espresso with just a drop of milk.

That should do the trick for at least the next three hours.

Just as he'd been about to stand, he watched as the porter left the café with a bottle of red wine and a Burgundy glass. He made his way up the hallway and stopped at Elena's door, rapping twice.

Gage stood.

Elena greeted the porter warmly, tipping him. Then she leaned into the hallway and waved at Gage before disappearing back into the suite.

Puzzled, Gage walked to Elena's suite and knocked. She opened the door and told him to come in. Elena crossed the suite, sitting in the only chair while facing him. She lifted a glass of red wine and tucked her bare feet up under her legs.

"I told you I'm not sleepy."

"I can see that," Gage replied.

"Come and sit."

"I'd better get back to my seat."

"Nonsense. We're going to drink this bottle and, maybe if I relax enough…I'll tell you who I think is trying to kill me."

Gage stepped into the suite and closed the door. Despite his need of sleep, he was curious about what she might say.

***

Though Elena wouldn't admit it to him, she was glad he'd joined her. For whatever reason, tonight she didn't want to be alone. She offered to call for another wine glass. Gage declined, telling her he'd stick with water.

He was puzzling, this man. Never making eye contact for too long. Always seeming as if he was in a hurry to hear something, or go somewhere, or do something. He didn't like to sit still. He didn't seem to ever take a moment to enjoy little things, either, like the open air of a convertible or a fine meal. He was probably the type who ate to live but didn't live to eat, just as he'd done at the Adrano café, when he'd ordered food simply on the basis of having the most calories and protein. Sure, he said it tasted good but that wasn't why he'd ordered it. She suspected such a pattern existed in many areas of his life. Something about him reminded Elena of a lone wolf, padding all around the earth with distracted nomadic energy. Like any wolf, she could imagine him turning vicious when cornered. But otherwise, he moved about on his own, eyes always darting for a potential threat as he performed whatever his current job happened to be. There was a nervousness about him she couldn't quite pinpoint.

No…not nervousness. Perhaps it was angst. He never seemed quite settled. Unsettled with himself. Unsettled with his lot on this earth. Never happy enough. Elena Volkov understood such an existence, even from long before the attempts on her life occurred. In fact, the only time of her adult life that she'd felt whole had been during her time with Dmitry. But those years had been so fleeting they didn't even seem real now.

She closed her eyes for a long time, pulling in a deep breath through her nose, envisioning how she might try to capture Gage on canvas. It wouldn't be easy…

"Look, if you'd rather sleep, we can do this tomorrow."

Elena opened her eyes. He was sitting on the edge of the bed and looking at her expectantly.

"You must be exhausted," she said, the thought just occurring to her. His eyes were bloodshot. "I was rude to keep you awake."

"No, you weren't. This beats sitting out there."

"You're sure you don't want any wine?"

"I don't drink."

"You don't mind if I do?"

"If it'll loosen you up to tell me who's after you, I don't mind."

Elena took a large sip of the bold liquid. She hadn't even looked at the bottle but the spiciness of the wine made her guess it might be a *primitivo*.

"You never drink?" she asked.

"Not anymore."

"Why not."

He shook his head and shrugged.

She sipped again, swallowing thickly afterward. "Okay, Gage Hartline, are you listening?"

"All ears."

"I own fifty-one percent of UkeOil. The company is private and is valued at more than a billion dollars, U.S. My husband left me his share. And in a move that neither I, my lawyers, nor anyone else can understand, he somehow failed to change the original company charter which states that, in the event of shareholder death, all shares are absorbed back into the company. The beneficiaries of the deceased shareholder's estate would be paid fair market value for their share."

Gage was no businessman but he narrowed his eyes. "You told me a little bit of this. But since there's an offer on the table of such immense proportion, wouldn't the offer amount change the fair market value of the company?"

"Oh, no," she said with a sour smile. "The charter clearly defines a single archaic method for valuing the company. As of the last quarter, my portion would only be worth slightly more than two-hundred million."

"That's crazy."

"And not all that uncommon, so I'm told. Without the offer, and with a *valid* valuation, my shares are probably worth around seven hundred fifty million dollars. But, if I die, naturally or unnaturally, the remaining shareholders can sell the company after my shares are absorbed and my estate is paid by using the formula."

"Why wouldn't Dmitry have altered this so you wouldn't be faced with such pressure?"

Elena poured more of the wine and looked at the label. Suavitas, a Negroamaro wine from the "heel" of Italy. She liked it.

"I honestly don't know why," she replied, wondering how many times she'd said those exact words. "Like most of us, I don't think he had any intention of dying early. I don't think he ever focused on the charter. Dmitry didn't surround himself with attorneys and advisors, either. He ran the company extremely lean, which is probably why it grew so rapidly. For whatever reason, the charter slipped under his radar."

"Does the company have a board of directors?"

"Yes, and they're excellent. But they own only four percent of the company and have no authority to change the charter. That can only be done by shareholder vote."

"But, wait...you own the majority. Why can't you change the charter?"

She smiled a smile devoid of humor. "Because, Gage, a two-thirds majority shareholder vote is required for such a change. The board would vote with me, but the remaining shareholders, who comprise approximately forty-five percent, would not."

Gage straightened. "Would the owners of that forty-five percent happen to be who you think is trying to kill you?"

Elena guzzled the wine, feeling unladylike as a rivulet escaped the corner of her mouth and nearly ran onto her shirt. Gage hurried to the small bathroom and returned with a hand towel. After she dabbed her chin and neck, Elena poured more wine and had another sip before sucking in several whistling breaths.

"I'm drinking quickly to build up my courage." She glanced at the bed. "I may need to go to bed after I say this."

"We're on your timetable, Elena."

She placed the wine on the small, bolted-down table and cleared her throat. "The owners of the forty-five percent are Dmitry's sister and her husband."

"I read about them."

"I'm almost certain it's them."

"Trying to kill you?"

"Yes."

"Anyone else you could think of?"

"No. Since the second attempt, I've had a strong premonition that it's my in-laws. Very strong."

He shrugged. "Then I'm inclined to go with your premonition. Whenever I go against my gut instinct, it usually turns out to be a big mistake."

Elena stood and slid the door open. "Can we talk on the balcony so I can smoke?"

Gage followed her out. It was much cooler now that they were away from Sicily. The ferry was churning to the northwest, the water roiling and splashing twenty feet below as the V-hull ship skimmed along at 20 knots.

Elena managed to get a cigarette lit in the wind before looking up at the starlit night sky. The wine was hitting her bloodstream and, for just a brief moment, she felt quite relieved at having told this man what she believed. And she'd be lying if she said she didn't enjoy his enigmatic presence. There was a tiny bit of him that reminded her of Dmitry.

And speaking of Dmitry, how could that fine man have such an utterly despicable sibling, supposedly sired by the same father? While Elena had never met Dmitry's mother, Katarina, she'd heard whispers about her wandering eye. Dmitry's father had slaved in the coalmines, gone for days at a time.

There would have been plenty of opportunity.

His other two siblings died years before, rather mysteriously. The three of them favored one another, but not Dmitry.

"Mind telling me about your in-laws?" Gage asked, shaking Elena from her reverie.

She dragged deeply on the long cigarette. "Before I do that, can I tell you something?"

"Sure."

"I want you to know that I live on a set income. Since Dmitry's death, the only time I've exceeded that income and gone into my savings accounts was when I rented that ridiculous yacht." She crossed her arms in front of her, drawing close to herself against the cool ocean breeze. "Actually, that's not true. After that, I pulled out the cash that we're now carrying. But you get the point…before going to Greece, I lived on what roughly amounts to a hundred-thousand dollars per year, U.S. And my income from painting exceeds what I spend."

"In all that I read about you, I never found anything about your paintings." He arched his eyebrows. "You make more than a hundred grand a year painting pictures of people?"

She smiled, feeling the artist's combination of pride and embarrassment. "They sell through a variety of galleries under a pseudonym. I don't want them to sell because of who I am. I want them to sell because they capture the buyer's eye."

Though he seemed to want to say more, he clasped his hands in his lap. "Why are you telling me this?"

"I have anxiety, Gage. Anxiety over many things. And being rich, while it has its conveniences, carries an incredible burden. Dmitry wanted me to have everything I wanted. And I did...and I do. But other than food, clothing and shelter...and my babies down in the kennel...I don't need any more. Even the car you drove, the Lancia...I paid cash for it from money that I earned."

"Again, why are you telling me this, about what you live on?"

"Because I don't want you thinking I'm some spoiled brat. Everyone thinks I married Dmitry for the money and they're all wrong. I loved him!" she said, hating herself for her sudden outburst of tears.

"Hey...take it easy," he said, holding his hand for the wine.

She handed it to him, taking a final pull of the cigarette before crushing it in the small, built-in aluminum ashtray. Elena walked back into the suite and plopped onto the edge of the bed.

"Dmitry never wanted the company sold. Ever. He started it from a tiny field in the Dnieper-Donets basin and built it to what it was at the time of his death. He wanted it to stay in the Volkov family. He was fanatical about few things, but that was one of them."

"I see," Gage said, sliding the door shut and locking it.

"And his sister and her idiot husband want to sell it so they can have their billions and not be bothered with it anymore."

"All that may be true, but I doubt Dmitry would want you to die for it. Why don't you just give them what they want? Maybe cut a deal? Maybe just allow them to sell their portion?"

"I would rather die," Elena replied, aware afterward that she'd said the words through clenched teeth. She combed her hair backward with both hands, closing her eyes as she said, "Do you know what it's like to be hated from the bottom of your family's collective heart?"

"No, I don't."

"It's awful. To have everyone think you're just some money-grubbing bitch."

"But you're obviously not, otherwise you'd sell."

"They don't think that way...rationally. In fact, they don't believe I ever loved Dmitry."

"I can tell you did." He rubbed his hands together. "What about your own family?"

Elena leaned forward, staring at the floor. "It's sad to say, but they just want money, too. I've read about lottery winners, Gage. Everyone the winner has ever known comes out, hands extended. It's awful—a curse."

"I like having a little money," he admitted. "But only enough to get by. I have an old pickup truck and a dog, and I do like to throw a steak on the grill every now and then. That's about all I need to make me happy."

"You know what?" Elena asked, pointing a finger at him. "That's pretty much the first thing you've told me about yourself."

Though his mouth didn't smile, the rest of his face did.

"You left something out," she said.

"I did?"

"You need excitement. If you don't have it, you'd rather be dead. That's your currency."

He seemed amused. "What makes you say that?"

"I know it. If I were to paint you, that would be my biggest struggle...capturing that, along with your..."

"My what?"

"Your energy. It's hard to define."

She slid backward on the bed and rested against the pillows. "I'll tell you about his sister and two dead brothers tomorrow. I just can't do it tonight."

"You sure you're okay?"

"I'm fine."

"Can I get you anything?"

"No, thank you."

"Okay. I'm going to wash up in the community bathroom. I'll come check on you before you go to sleep. Lock the door behind me. Can you give me ten minutes before you crash?"

"It's silly to have you sleeping in a chair out there. Why don't you just stay in here?" she asked, surprised at the words as they escaped her mouth.

"I can't do that."

"You need sleep," she said.

"I'll be fine," he said, breaking eye contact.

"I insist. Go get your bag."

"Elena, this isn't a good idea."

She cocked her head. "Don't think for a second that I'm making a pass at you. You need rest, and so do I. Now, go. I'll fix everything."

"Elena."

"Do you know any Ukrainian women, other than me?"

"Uh...not that I can remember."

"Well, we don't do well with the word 'no'...or 'nee' or 'nyet.' Understand?"

Gage nodded. "Tak. Be right back."

While he was getting his things, she removed the extra blanket and pillow from the closet. Using the cushions from the small sofa as well as the chair, she fashioned a pallet for him on the floor by the door.

When he returned, she gestured to the makeshift bed. "Your feet will hang off but I bet it beats that chair out there."

"Horizontal always does. I appreciate it," he said.

"You can use the bathroom first," Elena said, retrieving some items from her bag.

Once they'd both brushed their teeth and washed up for bed, the American man checked the locks and settled onto his pallet, lacing his hands behind his head.

"Comfortable?" she asked, her hand on the bedside light.

"It's perfect."

Elena turned off the light and nestled herself under the covers, feeling safe due to his presence. Then, something occurred to her.

"Gage?"

"Yes?"

"The American who came to Belpasso to kill me."

Silence.

"Did you kill him, Gage?"

"Go to sleep."

"Will you tell me?"

"Not tonight, okay?"

"I want you to tell me," Elena commanded.

"I will...later." He fluffed his pillow. "By the way, I should warn you, I've been told I snore pretty badly, especially when I'm sleepy."

"Well...I snore when I drink wine," she countered. "Let's see who wins."

It was a tie.

Chapter Six

IT WAS just past 7 A.M. when the Cessna Citation Excel lifted off from Faro Airport in the south of Portugal. The aircraft was registered to a private Portuguese charter firm and had filed for a normal flight plan to Cantania, Sicily, Italy. The Citation was piloted by two of the charter firm's younger pilots, ferrying only one passenger who carried very little luggage. At the request of the passenger, there was no flight attendant. Because of the light load, and the captain's exuberance, the Citation roared into the sky in a steep climb, quickly reaching a cruise altitude of 35,000 feet.

The passenger could have passed for any businessman jetting around the Mediterranean by private charter. He was slightly taller than average, with deeply tanned skin and a well-manicured beard. His slicked-back hair was sun-streaked brown, flecked with gray over the ears and around the temple. His beard had notes of gray on both sides of his mouth and his teeth were brilliantly white and squared-off straight. If asked, the pilots would have estimated their passenger was in his early forties.

He was, of course, the Assassin. And his two-year vacation was officially over.

After stretching out in his leather seat, the Assassin slept from the moment the aircraft had lifted off until its downwind approach into Sicily, at which time the first officer gently woke him to ask him to put on his seatbelt. By the time they'd landed at the Cantania-Fontanarossa Airport, the Assassin had swilled three small bottles of mineral water. Unlike this morning, when he'd left his villa before sunup, he now felt quite refreshed. The lady he'd met last night had kept him up until well past midnight and the three-hour nap he'd just enjoyed seemed to have set him straight.

The Assassin found Cantania stifling hot and stagnant, especially compared to breezy Lagos. He made his way to the small rental car desk in the executive terminal and made reservations for a mid-size sedan from Sixt. After a handsome tip, the Sixt representative personally drove the Assassin by golf cart to the lot near the main terminal. There he allowed the Assassin to choose a silver Audi A3TDI Sportback. After dialing in Elena Volkov's alleged Belpasso address, the Assassin nestled himself in the sport seat and ran up through the gears as he exited the medium-sized airport. Using his tethered phone and encryption program, he called Georgy Zaytsev.

"Yes?" Georgy answered breathlessly.

"Is it there?"

"I certainly hope so. I sent the full amount."

"Do I need to check?" the Assassin asked, sitting at a traffic light and studying his fingernails.

"No, sir. Honest...I made arrangements when we hung up the phone."

"Very well, then."

"Have you begun? Will you provide updates? Do you feel good about your chances?"

"I'm a professional. There are many tasks ahead. After this, there will be no updates. When the job is done, I will call you. You'll only hear from me if I need something."

"Okay, well, please know that we—"

The Assassin hung up the phone. He had no desire to listen to the obsequious Russian's ramblings.

While the GPS continued to recalculate the route to Belpasso, the Assassin ignored the silent directions and instead drove to the area just west of the Acquicella train station on Cantania's east side. There, the Assassin parked on the street and entered a small, nondescript business advertising copies, fliers and printing. He'd been here before. The Assassin was inside for less than ten minutes and exited with an old nylon gym bag. The bag swung heavily, concealing his newly purchased Beretta 92 FS Inox and four boxes of ammunition. The Beretta seemed nearly new and was clean as a whistle.

Had his situation been normal, the Assassin could have purchased the pistol for 500 euro from a reputable dealer. But in Italy, at the very least, a person must obtain a purchase authorization, known locally as a *nulla osta all'acquisto*. Of course, the Assassin had no intention of making such an authorized purchase – therefore the Beretta, with ammunition, cost him five times what he would have paid otherwise.

A bargain for such convenience.

With the pistol concealed under the seat of his German sport wagon, the Assassin drove to the Acquicella train station. He parked nearby, using the screwdriver on his knife to remove his front and rear plates. It took him fifteen minutes to find a grouping of cars in the long-term parking lot that weren't covered by security cameras—even though he had his doubts that anyone was closely watching them. Without incident, the Assassin casually removed the plates from a late-model Citroen and attached them to his car. He then followed the directions of the built-in GPS to Belpasso. Once he reached the town, he'd check in with his bank in Singapore. If the Russian's money were there, he'd consider the hunt for Elena Volkov officially on.

Despite the huge stakes and the caution Mrs. Volkov should be demonstrating, something told the Assassin that it wouldn't take him very long to catch up to his quarry. He was correct.

***

There were now eight hours remaining on the ferry journey. Last night, despite the pallet's lumpiness, Gage had slept hard and, unless Elena was lying to be polite, he hadn't snored all that much. Nor did he hear her snore.

Now that he was well rested, he realized just how tired he had been.

After waking around 7 A.M., Gage ordered breakfast for Elena and showered while she ate outside on the balcony. The morning was overcast but warm and muggy. Gage then took his outer seat in the main cabin, eating there while Elena showered and changed. Most of the passengers were still sleeping. Elena emerged a half-hour later looking quite radiant, carrying a worn paperback and a towel.

"Where are you going?" he asked.

"I'm going down to check on my dogs, then I'm going up top to sit outside and hope the sun shows itself."

"I'd really rather you not do that," he said, glancing around. "Someone might recognize you."

She slid on massive, Jackie Onassis sunglasses. "I'm going."

"Hang on. Talk to me for a second."

Her chest rose and fell and her neck grew visibly splotchy. "I'd like to get away from all these people," she breathed. Although Gage couldn't see her eyes, he could tell she was eyeing all the people in the large, theater-like space.

"Too many?"

"Yes."

"Let's go," Gage said. He stayed with her as she hurried out the portside doors, leaning over the rail and breathing in great breaths.

"You okay?" he asked.

"I was fine for a moment, back there. The panic attacks come and go. When it hits me like it just did—out of the blue—it's as if I can't even breathe."

"Just take it easy for a minute."

She straightened. "I'm okay, really. Let's go find my dogs."

Gage guided her there by following the way-finding signs. He purposefully avoided the forward main cabin, which looked nearly as big as the aft cabin. Using a circuitous route, they made their way belowdecks and were allowed to visit the dogs in a small play area.

The dogs were brought in by the handler Gage had met yesterday. While Elena heaped love on her dogs, the handler provided a brief report in Italian, obviously satisfying Elena that her pups were in the care of a true dog lover. After a series of protracted goodbyes, Elena then took the stairs up to the sun deck as Gage followed dutifully along. The heavy overcast began to show traces of blue off to the west. Elena situated her chair as Gage followed her lead. The wind swirled in this area and the smell of the breakfast griddle occasionally wafted by, making Gage hungry despite his having already eaten. She took out her paperback.

"Where'd you get the book?" he asked, noting that the book appeared to be in English.

"Always keep a book with me. And I have many more books on my tablet."

"Something to eat or drink?"

"I'd enjoy a Coke Light."

"No food?"

"No, thank you."

Gage walked to the bar and returned with Europe's version of a Diet Coke along with a large bottle of water and a banana for himself. Elena thanked him and reclined with her book. Gage adjusted his lounge chair upright and readied himself for a long bout of silence.

She read for fifteen minutes. During that time, Gage watched as a few other couples sat down well out of earshot. At the aft rail, a group of teenagers smoked cigarettes and cackled about something that must have been hilarious. Gage listened to them speak, puzzled for a moment. He finally pegged the language as Luxembourgish, a cousin to the German language he knew so well. Despite it being a Germanic language, he was able to understand little of what they were saying. He scanned the sun deck, wishing this cruise would hurry the hell up and terminate in Genoa.

"Well, are you ready to hear?" Elena suddenly asked, laying the book on her stomach.

"Hear about your terrible in-laws?"

"Yes—*them*. I'm ready to get it over with. I can't concentrate."

"Sure," Gage said, turning his chair to face her.

"My husband, Dmitry, was the oldest of the four siblings. If he was alive today, he'd be fifty-two. The next in age was his brother, Vladimir."

"Was?"

"Yes. He died before I met Dmitry. From what I know, he was a mean and spiteful man who'd married five or six times...I can't ever remember. He lived in Moscow."

"How'd he die?"

"Self-inflicted gunshot wound."

"But you don't believe that?"

"No one does. There was no evidence to the contrary."

"And did he own part of UkeOil?"

"Nope. He was killed before Dmitry gifted a portion to his family."

"Okay, so we'll set him to the back burner," Gage said, sitting at the end of his chaise. "Who's next?"

"I'll skip to the youngest, Anton, because he's also dead. He was the least obnoxious of the bunch. He was also the most dangerous."

"In what way?"

"I could never really put my finger on it...just his demeanor. I only knew him for a short time. Other than Dmitry, he was the most successful of the lot—but incredibly different. He owned a large automobile dealership in Kiev. There were rumors not long before he died that he had his business partner killed."

Gage frowned. "Tell me about that."

"His partner was very conservative. Never wanted to pay dividends. Always wanted to reinvest all profits." She took a final drag and crushed out the cigarette in a glass ashtray. "One morning, his business partner's wife found her husband slumped on the steering wheel of his car. His head had been nearly severed by piano wire."

"Ouch. Did Anton do it?"

"It had to be him."

"Was he married?"

"Yes, and thankfully with no children. His wife was a complete slut, not that he would have noticed, given all the eighteen-year-olds he screwed."

"How'd he die?"

"He was at the dealership late one night, messing around with his secretary. Well...allegedly messing around with her—the security video showed her leaving late. She denied it but employees had seen her under his desk on more than one occasion."

"Seriously?"

"Oh, yes. She was married and far too old for his tastes...but she was willing and available. You know the story. Anyway, Anton never left that night. The sales manager found him dead the next morning, gunshot to the head. His time of death was several hours after the secretary left. It wasn't self-inflicted, either. The police never solved the crime and classified it as a robbery-homicide."

"What was stolen?"

"Cash from his safe. That was all."

As the ferry churned on, Gage let a silence fall between them. He thought he knew what was coming but he wanted to process all he'd heard. Finally, he said, "And then there's..."

"And then there's Nastya."

"*Nastya?* Are you kidding me?"

"What?" Elena asked, nonplussed.

"The name."

Elena seemed bored by Gage's amusement. "I get the joke, but Nastya is a very common name in Ukraine."

"Still…"

Elena eyed him. "I think she killed her brothers."

"Alone?"

"No, but I think her and her idiot husband *had* them killed."

"Why?"

"Because that was just before poor little helpless Nastya came and begged her big brother to bring her into his oil company. While I loved Dmitry with all my heart, he always had a blind spot when it came to his sister, that conniving…"

"Bitch?"

Elena's smile contained little humor.

"Blood can do that to people," Gage said.

"Yes, well, she really laid the blood on him thick, crying about their dead parents, crying about her dead brothers. Her pitch revolved around UkeOil being a family company. She wanted to help, wanted to be a board member, wanted to do anything she could to sink her hooks into his fortune."

Gage stood and retrieved a regular chair from a nearby table. He placed it next to Elena and sat. "So he gave her damn near half of his company?"

"Yes," Elena replied, blinking rapidly. "Gave it to her the same way an older brother pays his younger sister's rent."

"That makes no sense."

"And everyone told him that. His attorneys. His employees. His board members. He refused to believe she had bad intentions, and he wouldn't listen to talk that she and her husband might have been behind their brothers' deaths."

"What about you? Did you try to talk him out of it?"

"No," Elena replied firmly, shaking her head to the stops.

"Why?"

"Because I'd just married into the family. They were already calling me a gold-digger; the last thing I could afford to do was try to bar Queen Nastya from becoming a shareholder."

"Was he already giving her money?"

"Oh, hell yes," Elena replied. "Millions and millions and millions. All this did was redefine how he was supporting her and Georgy the idiot."

"And his two brothers who died?"

"All a part of her plan," Elena replied, lighting a fresh cigarette. "She created all this grief as the fulcrum, and in doing so she also carved out all that ownership percentage for her and Georgy."

"If accurate, that's pretty damned diabolical. Tell me about her."

"Nastya Zaytsev is one of the nastiest people I've ever met. She hates everyone, including her rotten husband."

"I thought they were in cahoots?"

"She still hates him. But they've been married for fifteen years, even though they despise one another. They're more like business partners."

"Why'd they get married in the first place?"

Elena turned to Gage with leaden eyes. "I don't know, nor have I ever cared to ask them."

"What else about her?"

"Like her dead brothers, she's a rampant cheater and does nothing to hide it. She prefers younger men, typically in their twenties. She likes the tattooed, muscular bad boys. With her money, she turns them into her lap dogs before she discards them."

"Is she bright?"

"Not really. She's just a miserable person and I could see her ordering me killed just as she rudely demands tall glasses of chilled vodka."

"So, you don't think there's any chance she'll try to come after you, herself?"

"No. She'll use Dmitry's money to have me killed."

"Tell me about her husband."

"Georgy...he's a patsy," Elena replied, exhaling her smoke into the breeze. "Not much else to say. He lives in Kiev and so does Nastya, most of the time. Georgy screws any tart he can and is basically at Nastya's mercy for money."

"Does he work?"

"*Neither* of them work, Gage, other than spending money and having sex with as many people as they can. They work hard at those things. Other than Dmitry, Anton was the only one who ever demonstrated any sort of drive, although most of what he did was illegal."

"You told me this already, but I just want to confirm...Nastya and her husband together own forty-five percent of UkeOil?"

"Nastya owns it. The board and a few others own four percent. I own fifty-one."

"Were they upset when Dmitry's will was read, when you were bequeathed the controlling share?"

Elena didn't answer. Instead, she laughed loudly and sharply.

"You mentioned Dmitry's siblings possibly being sired by another father?"

"Yes. There was a nine-year gap between Dmitry and Vladimir. Then, Vladimir, Nastya and Anton were all born within just over three years of each other. This bolsters my theory about his mother having an affair."

"Wow. She didn't waste time on the last three, did she?"

Elena dragged on the cigarette. "Want to see them?" She removed an iPad mini from her bag. "Don't worry…this one hasn't been connected to the 'net since I was in Prague."

She handed the iPad to Gage, telling him to scroll to the right. He viewed snapshots of various magazine articles about the family members. Vladimir, the eldest of the three, had not been a handsome man but he certainly dressed the part and had the deep tan of someone who enjoyed the beach or the golf course. It seemed he'd perfected his important pose for the cameras, always slightly frowning with slit eyes. The last picture must have been from a Russian gossip site. It showed him on a beach with a topless beauty of half his age. He was making a vulgar gesture at the camera as a brown cigarette dangled from his mouth.

"Classy photo," Gage mumbled.

"Google any of them and you'll find dozens like that one."

Next was Anton. He looked like a younger, thinner version of Vladimir, minus the tailored clothes. In each photo, Anton's eyelids hung heavily over his bulging eyes. And in most of the photos he held a clear drink of some sort.

"Is he drinking vodka?" Gage asked.

"Anton?" she asked, still not looking.

"Yes."

"He drank it all day, every day, when he wasn't having red wine. I suspect they were all alcoholics, but he was the worst."

"Show me Nastya."

Elena swiped several photos to the right and handed the iPad back to Gage.

Nastya looked like a cosmetically-improved version of Vladimir. Her lackluster looks were heavily camouflaged by premier makeup, perfect veneers and amazing blonde hair. She was overly tan and her massive breasts seemed to be the focal point of all her photos. In the seven images on Elena's iPad, Nastya was with a different man each time. As Elena had said, Nastya's suitors all had one thing in common: they were much younger and, to a man, they were overly-muscular and tattooed.

"What about her being married?"

"She doesn't care what people think," Elena replied.

Elena had two pictures of Georgy. He had a shaved head and in both photos he wore massive, jeweled sunglasses. Leathery from the sun, with expensive robes, swim trunks and flip-flops—Georgy looked like a bad caricature of a cheesy porn producer.

"Looks like a workaholic," Gage remarked.

"Yeah," Elena laughed as the sun overtook the ferry, instantly raising the temperature to a few notches beyond comfortable.

"Do you have pictures of Dmitry?"

"I do. Scroll all the way to the left."

Gage found the photos, oodles of them. After viewing Dmitry, Gage flipped back and forth to compare him with his siblings. Their mouths were similar but that was all. The other three all had bulging brown eyes while Dmitry's were small and blue. His nose was prominent and Roman while theirs was closer to the face and somewhat hawkish. The trio also had distinct downward lines on both sides of their mouths while Dmitry's face was more rounded.

Had no one told Gage otherwise, he'd have never even guessed Dmitry was related to his younger siblings. Gage turned to Elena.

"If Nastya's paternal heritage could be disproven, with DNA testing, would it nullify her ownership since Dmitry thought he was gifting the stock to his full-blooded sister?"

"No. That was the first thing the attorneys checked. Her ownership is secure no matter what his intentions were."

They talked for a few minutes more before growing silent. Elena opened her book and read for a moment, then she turned to Gage. "One more thing…will anyone know we're in Genoa?"

"Not unless someone has recognized you. As far as anyone knows, you're still in Sicily."

Appearing on the verge of tears, Elena said, "I'll never be safe, will I?"

"Yes, you will."

"How?"

"I'll take care of you."

A half-hour of silence passed. More people came to the sun deck but not enough to make Elena feel uncomfortable. Gage did his best to enjoy the solitude. It wasn't often he found himself lounging in the sunshine with nothing to do.

"What if I don't want to run and hide?" Elena suddenly asked without preamble.

"What do you mean?" Gage asked, shading his eyes so he could see her.

"There are 8 days before the deal expires. We've been assured by Suntex that there will be no extensions or additional offers if we don't sign." Elena tapped on her teeth with her fingernail. "There might be other offers someday, but I seriously doubt we'll ever get another offer like this one. In fact, our chairman is predicting a worldwide glut of oil. He said the price of a barrel will soon plummet and may not recover for a decade."

"What are you saying?"

"I'm saying, if I run and hide, I may regret it."

"Why?"

"It's just the way I feel. This pisses me off," she said, using a new edge to her voice that Gage hadn't yet heard. "Here I am, running away in fear, shedding tears on some ferry because people are trying to kill me over money."

"I get it, Elena. And I don't blame you, but this isn't permanent."

"Would you run and hide?"

"That depends on a bunch of factors."

She crossed her arms. "I hate when people answer questions like that."

"Okay, then…no, I wouldn't hide. I might run, but I'd have a plan to strike back."

"Exactly," she said, sitting up. "Instead of defense, you'd play offense."

He hesitated. "I guess."

"That's what I want to do."

Gage leaned forward. "Let me make sure I'm understanding you correctly. You want to go after them?"

"I want to go after whoever is after me."

"Who, the hit-men? The most recent one is already out of commission – I took care of that yesterday."

"So, you did kill him?" she asked.

"Let's discuss it later," he replied, glancing around.

"Well…believe me, they'll hire someone else. But I'd rather go after Nastya and Georgy."

"What exactly do you mean, 'go after them?'"

"Maybe get a confession. Use it to have them prosecuted."

Gage shook his head. "Wouldn't be easy. They won't just readily confess."

"Exactly. It'll be a huge challenge to prove what they've done and get them to admit it." Elena wore a satisfied smirk. "But it'll be worth it when we wave to them as they're taken to jail."

"I'll admit, this is fun to think about. Imagine it, getting revenge in the way you're describing." He sat back and clasped his hands. "But, in the end, despite my affinity for tasty revenge, I recommend we play it safe and hide you till the date passes."

"What if I refuse? What if I don't want to play it safe? Would you still protect me?"

"Elena…"

"Will you go along with me if I want to go after them?"

"We'd have to discuss it further."

"Admit it…it would make us unpredictable."

"True. But it also might lead us to the teeth of the tiger."

She shrugged. "Promise you'll think about it?"

"I promise."

Elena extended her hand. "Shake on it."

Gage chuckled and extended his hand, and she gave it a firm pump. Elena placed the book on the table and reclined her chaise fully flat, stretching out in the powerful sun.

She looked happy.

"Do you know where Nastya and Georgy are?"

"Somewhere warm."

"That narrows it down to about half of earth. But you don't know where?"

"They travel all year."

"Okay." After a moment, Gage said, "Elena?"

"Yes?"

"When I was scrolling through those pictures, I saw a painting of Dmitry."

She said nothing.

"Did you do that?"

"Yeah."

"I'm impressed. It looked like a presidential portrait."

She didn't reply.

"Can I see other paintings you've done?"

"Not right now."

Gage didn't press her. But he wasn't overstating the quality of the portrait.

Chapter Seven

IT WAS early evening in Sicily when the Assassin first saw the young man. He had ridden his scooter past Elena Volkov's house earlier, slowing and eyeing the home. He returned at sunset, probably having gone to the grocery store due to the bags netted on his backseat. The young man parked on the street, walking to the house and ringing the bell at the front door. He rang it again. When no one answered, he took a quick look through one of the front windows before motoring away. Knowing the street had no outlet in that direction, the Assassin did not follow.

Ten minutes later the young man was back, carrying a key ring. After ringing the bell again, he unlocked the front door and cautiously went inside, yelling his greeting. He was only in the house for about a minute. After that, the young man hurried from the house and sped away in the same direction he had before. This time, the Assassin followed at a distance.

The young man parked in the short stone driveway of a large house at the end of the residential road. The house was quite nice—the largest on the street. He walked to the back of the house and was eagerly greeted by two fenced-in Rottweiler dogs. The Assassin made the correct assumption that the young man lived there, but he seemed far too young to be the owner.

Landlord's kid, maybe? Or perhaps just a trusted worker. The young man's clothes, while extremely casual, advertised a premium designer in large block letters. The Assassin eyed the scooter. It was a late model Vespa GTS—not a cheap scooter by any stretch.

He's the landlord's kid and this is the landlord's house. Mommy and Daddy probably own every home on the street.

The Assassin decided not to approach the house. Too many bad things could happen if he tipped his hand this early. Instead, he drove back to Elena's home and idled slowly past. After her house, there were seven more homes before the quiet Belpasso street dropped steeply down to the intersection of the main road that led back to Cantania. On both sides of the steep drop was a dry creek populated by scrub brush and plenty of jagged rocks. He stepped out of the Audi, eyeing the ravine on the right side of the road.

Perfect.

The Assassin drove back to Elena's house and once again parked on the street. He rolled down his windows and smoked one of his handmade cigarettes. During his two years in Portugal, he typically journeyed to Lisbon for a few days each month. The Assassin normally had a fine time in Lisbon, staying in wonderful hotels, bedding vacationers and eating like a king. He also enjoyed Lisbon's fine shopping. The handmade cigarettes he carried were made to order for him by a kind little lady in Lisbon's tony Príncipe Real district.

Opening his airtight sterling silver case, the Assassin counted 26 more of the premium cigarettes, held in place by a gold clasp. When they were gone, he'd have to switch to a packaged brand.

The very thought made him ill.

It was the little things like these handmade cigarettes—they cost more than two euro *each*—that fueled the Assassin's desire to live the finer life. Although he only smoked five or six cigarettes per day, he enjoyed each one immensely. The youngest child of five, the Assassin hadn't spoken with a single member of his family since departing the military. That had been fourteen years ago. The Assassin then spent many years in Dublin and Bermuda, traveling to contract jobs and building his mysterious reputation through an increasingly impressive list of high-profile kills.

But they hadn't all gone perfectly. The closest the Assassin had ever come to being caught had been in Jamaica, of all places, about a decade before. He'd been hired to eliminate an English businessman for some reason or another—the Assassin didn't worry himself over such things unless there was a reason to—and in the commotion that followed the kill, the Assassin had been briefly detained by Jamaica's constabulary force. Fortunately, due to the Assassin's quick thinking and ability to mimic a London West-End accent, the police released him within minutes after numerous witnesses reported that the shot had come from one of the homes perched high above on the Oracabessan hillside.

Had the Assassin not presciently planted those remotely-fired squibs, he'd probably be rotting away in a Jamaican prison at this very moment. Or, more likely, dead…

Dragging deeply on the handmade cigarette, he closed his eyes for a moment, allowing the warm breeze to caress his skin as he sat there in the rental Audi, idly wondering what his insipid siblings were up to at this very moment.

Struggling to make ends meet—that he knew. He also knew they weren't happy. They couldn't be, could they? Bitter cold weather. Spousal jealousy. Vicious teen children. Expectant bosses. Bills to pay. Appearances to keep up. Why did anyone join the rat race in the first place?

To the Assassin, happiness could only be gained from self. And when it wasn't self-indulgence, it was self-pride. The Assassin did everything solely for the Assassin. However, his credo didn't prevent him from sometimes showing mercy. He didn't enjoy killing. The Assassin thought about the young man with the Vespa—he hoped there was some way to prevent from harming him.

I'm no savage.

The Assassin took another deep drag of the cigarette, neatly rolled with a rich blend of Virginian and Brazilian tobaccos. He reminded himself that there were now only 25 remaining.

I need to get this job done so I can properly refill my case.

In Lisbon? Probably not.

Though he truly loved Portugal, the Assassin felt it was time to move on. Two years, while enjoyable, had been enough. It was time to go elsewhere. His criteria, as he'd come to refine them with age, were quite simple. The locale must be industrially developed, meaning fine medical care, good transportation, low crime, etc. His destination mustn't be overly crowded. It couldn't have wild weather swings and generally needed to be warm but not overly hot. After growing up in the bitter cold next to that dreadful Blue Highway, the Assassin had sworn to never live in frigid temperatures again. Of course, the final requirement for his new home was ready access to the basic necessities in life: fine wine, wonderful food and beautiful, willing women.

While he'd definitely give it more thought as he reeled in Elena Volkov, his most recent frontrunners were Cape Town, Costa Rica's Central Valley and Kauai, Hawaii. But those were just off-the-top-of-his-head possibilities. Each had its drawbacks. There were almost certainly better destinations he'd come up with in due time.

The Assassin sucked greedily on the nub of the cigarette before flicking it from the Audi's open window. As the handmade cigarette smoldered on the asphalt, the Assassin kept his eyes on his mirrors, looking for the lone headlamp of a late-model Vespa scooter.

***

The ferry had reached port an hour behind schedule due to headwinds and rough seas at the tail end of the voyage. By the time Gage, Elena and the two dogs had reached solid ground, it was nearly 10 P.M. as the summer twilight lingered on. It wouldn't be fully dark tonight until around 10:30. They walked through the terminal area and immediately saw the hotel on the eastern edge of the port. Since accompanying dogs were common in Europe, especially in the ritzier areas, Gage didn't expect a problem from the hotelier about Elena's two pets. He whispered his new identity to himself and practiced what he would say to the desk clerk.

"What are you saying?" Elena asked as her dogs sniffed the base of a light pole.

"Just practicing my lines."

"What lines?"

"Just play along, okay? And keep those sunglasses on when we get inside."

"But it's almost dark."

"Doesn't matter," he said. "Just act arrogant. Keep your nose up."

They entered the hotel, finding it comfortable but modest. Not seeing a concierge stand, Gage stepped to the front desk and was warmly greeted by the middle-aged clerk. Gage introduced himself, saying that he and his wife had reservations and were also awaiting an international package.

The clerk nodded and stepped behind the blind, returning with a large rigid envelope fluttering with numerous carbon receipts. "May I see your identification, please?"

Gage smiled and shrugged as if he were embarrassed. "That's what's in the package, sir. Unfortunately, my wife and I suffered a burglary at our last hotel. My friend in the States sent us our extra passports."

"*Extra* passports?" the clerk asked, surprised.

"Yes."

"I didn't know a person could legally have more than one."

"We do," Gage replied with a shrug. Worried that this line of questioning might result in a small problem, Gage used a basic method to put the clerk on the defensive. "And I certainly hope this hotel is more secure than our last one. I don't want our things stolen *again*."

"I can assure you, sir, our hotel is most certainly secure," the clerk replied in his excellent English. With a warm smile, he handed the package to Gage and asked to see the identification that was inside.

Gage ripped open the envelope and displayed his fake passport. Ten minutes later they were checked in and in Elena's room.

"Now what?" she asked, sitting on one of the beds with her dogs.

"Now, we have a chat."

"About what I said this morning on the ferry?"

"Yes."

"I've thought about it all day," she said. "And I've come to the conclusion that I definitely don't want to run."

"We don't have to run. Now that we're in continental Europe, it'll be much easier to find a quiet place for you to safely hole up."

"I don't want to hole up, either."

"But if we go on the offensive, then we lose the edge we currently have. Right now, we have the tremendous advantage of being nimble and agile...and anonymous. Nobody knows where we are."

She listened impassively. "And we can't be nimble and agile and anonymous on the offensive?"

Frustrated, Gage opened his arms. "How? How do you suggest we proceed? If we somehow find Nastya and Georgy, they're not going to just roll over and admit what they've done."

"We have to trap them."

"How?"

"I don't know yet."

"And we don't even know where they are."

Elena motioned to his pack. "You told me you have the phone of the American killer, correct?"

"Yeah."

"We start there. You said the American was hired on the phone by a Swiss man who spoke Russian. We use the numbers in the phone to go find that Swiss man."

"The man called from a bunch of numbers. I'm sure they were payphones or public phones or, worse, numbers generated by a proxy device."

She raised a rigid finger between them. "Stop. Do not be Mister Negative. Don't give me ten reasons why we can't do something."

Unable to help being somewhat amused, Gage took a step backward. "I like that…Mister Negative. I'll have to tell Colonel Hunter—it'll become my new name."

"Gage, at least try to find the Swiss man with me. This'll be a trial. Then we go from there. If it doesn't work, I will 'hole up' as you say. If we find him, then we plot our next step."

Gage blew out a trumpeter's breath. "Find the Swiss man?"

"Yes."

"In return for me agreeing to this, you have to agree to something."

"What is it?"

"Do you even remember our first deal?"

She shook her head.

"You have to stop smoking when we're past the deadline."

She cursed in Ukrainian but nodded. "I do remember. I'd better start cutting back."

"And the second deal starts right now."

"And that is?"

"You have to change your appearance."

Her right hand floated to her long blonde hair, tugging on it. Gage nodded. "Makeup, too. New glasses. Different clothes. That kind of thing."

She nodded her assent. "It's no big deal."

"Tomorrow, we head to Switzerland…as a trial."

A broad smile formed on her face. "This'll be fun."

"Remember that when it's not fun."

She nodded, understanding his warning. Her expression changed. "I've agreed to everything. So, tell me about the American killer."

"I'll tell you later."

"Why not now?"

"Later, okay?"

"But you will tell me?"

"I will," Gage answered. After getting her settled, he departed to meet Colonel Hunter's contact and promised to bring back some food.

***

It was after 11 P.M. in Belpasso when the Assassin saw the single headlight in the rearview mirror. He stepped from the Audi, dropping the half-smoked handmade cigarette to the street and twisting his loafer on it. The Assassin stepped into the street and politely held up his hands to stop the oncoming rider.

As the light drew closer, the Assassin confirmed that it was indeed the young man from earlier. The young man stopped his Vespa several paces away, speaking rapid Italian to the Assassin.

"I can't speak Italian. Do you speak Spanish or English?" the Assassin asked in Spanish.

"Español," the young man warily replied.

The Assassin gestured to Elena's house. "Do you happen to know the woman who lives there?"

"Why?"

"I saw you earlier. I'd just pulled up when you left."

"What about her?"

"I'm very worried about her." Making himself seem non-threatening, the Assassin clasped his hands behind his back, shaking his head. "I'm afraid something bad may have happened to her."

The young man turned and took a long look at the house. "What makes you say that?"

"She was supposed to be here when I arrived." The Assassin eyed the young man. "You see, she hired me to travel here and protect her. But when I got here, she was gone."

The kid was wide-eyed. "*You* were hired?"

He knows something. "Yes, me. Why do you seem surprised?"

"Do you have the tattoo?"

The tattoo? What tattoo?

Without any reaction to the question, the Assassin gestured to the steep hill. "Before we get into all that, I found something of hers."

"What?"

"It might lead us to what happened to her."

"How do you know something happened to her?"

"Do you want to see or don't you?" the Assassin asked, making his voice panicky. "I'm really worried."

"I am, too."

"Then come on. It's right down here. You can leave your scooter." The Assassin began walking down the hill, toward the main road.

"What is it?" the young man asked with trepidation.

"It's blood," the Assassin replied. "Blood and a chunk of blonde hair." He kept walking. Behind him, he heard the metallic scrape of the scooter's kick stand.

With his knife concealed in the palm of his hand, the Assassin couldn't help but smile at his clever ruse as he pushed aside a branch and descended down to the rocky creek bed off the right side of the road.

***

Following the directions Colonel Hunter had left in the envelope, Gage walked northwest from the hotel. On the way, he passed a large petrol station reminiscent of the all-night variety seen in the U.S. Gage went inside and spent 300 euros on a bag of prepaid phones, earning a cocked eyebrow from the clerk. With that done, he left the petrol station and was soon walking through what seemed to be the old area of Genoa. In short order, Gage found the pub Hunter had recommended. It was on the bottom of an old, slightly askew four-story building.

The interior of the pub was old—perhaps hundreds of years old—its dark, roughhewn,wood scarred with countless names and phrases. One wall was covered with odes to lovers with dates scrawled beneath initials. Confirming his estimate, Gage saw dates ranging back almost 200 years. The only patrons in the bar were a couple sitting at a dark corner table in the far end of the establishment. The barman stared up at an ancient television, showing a grainy Formula One race. He spoke Italian to Gage before switching to English, proudly telling Gage that he'd spent a whole summer in New Jersey when he was a teenager.

"You serve food this late?"

"Till midnight. Best in *Genova*."

Gage read the menu and ordered the day's special of risotto and bread. The elderly barman wrote out the order before clipping it to a pulley on a thin strand of aircraft cable. He shuttled the order out of sight through a square notch in the wall and said, "Twenty minutes."

"Thank you. And before you go back to your race…" Gage beckoned him close and spoke in a low voice. "I'm also looking for Giuseppe."

"Who are you?"

"A customer."

"Do you know Giuseppe?" the old man asked in a warning tone. He had a bottom tooth that stuck out, protruding over his upper lip like Sarge and his dog, Otto, from the Beetle Bailey cartoon strip.

"My friend recommended I come see him."

"What friend?"

"Hunter."

"Hunter?"

"Yes."

The barman walked to the door that led to the rear and pulled a stained piece of string. A distant bell could be heard ringing above. Seconds later, the old telephone rang and the barman spoke a few words before hanging up. He walked back to Gage.

"Up," he said, gesturing with his thumb.

"You want me to go up?"

Nodding, the snaggletoothed barman pointed to the door, then pointed up.

"What about my food?"

"It'll be here when you come down."

Gage nodded, walking to the door, seeing the oil and grime on the right from decades of being shoved by dirty hands. He pushed through with his forearm, finding a small stockroom loaded with liquor boxes. In the center of the stockroom was a wrought iron spiral staircase. Gage took a look up and, feeling naked as a baby without any sort of a weapon, began his climb.

Hunter's recommendation carried all the weight Gage would ever require. But Gage wouldn't be himself if he didn't consider what might be awaiting him upstairs. This Giuseppe fellow obviously knew Gage was there to buy weapons. Therefore, Giuseppe could also postulate that Gage was currently unarmed and had a wad of cash.

Meaning, Gage was an easy mark…

Trust the colonel. Always trust the colonel.

Up Gage went. Clang. Clang. Clang. The spiral staircase swayed slightly as he ascended. It must have been at least three stories, bordered by boxes of liquor, beer and wine the entire way. The boxes gave the stairwell the clean, papery smell of a liquor store. Halfway to the top, there'd been a landing that led into another storeroom. Gage glanced in and kept climbing.

At the top, Gage's fears were allayed. The first thing he saw was a pair of large, highly polished pointy dress shoes. Gage's eyes moved upward, seeing a portly man in a double-breasted blue blazer with gold buttons. The man had a full head of dark, wavy hair and, once Gage was on the top landing, the man vigorously pumped Gage's hand and welcomed him.

"Are you Giuseppe?" Gage asked.

"The one and only," he said, speaking English. "I stayed late because I heard you might be coming." Giuseppe's round face was rubescent and jovial. He had an oversize pug nose and his brown eyes twinkled as he spoke. Gage guessed him to be about sixty, but it was hard to tell. Giuseppe was well-fed and his puffiness filled out whatever wrinkles he might have.

The stairs had led to an attic that seemed to be Giuseppe's office. There was a window on the far end, darkened by closed shutters. In front of the window was a battered old desk littered with papers. And all over the office were pictures of Giuseppe with women and children. There must have been a hundred photos. One wall swayed and undulated with children's artwork and finger painting, much of it emblazoned with the word "*Nonno.*" Contrasting sharply with the familial items were a shotgun, a pistol and AK-47, all located within an arm's reach of his desk.

Well…a man's gotta be prepared.

Feeling better about Giuseppe, despite the weapons, Gage said, "My friend told me you sell some items I might need. He said to come see you."

"This would be the honorable Lieutenant Hunter, I presume?" Gisuseppe asked, eyes closed, his voice taking on a formal air.

"He retired as a colonel."

"He will always be a lieutenant to me."

"You know him?"

"Know him? Ha! Hell, I only sheltered him for a full week, many years ago. Fed him my wife's food. Gave him my guest bed. And hid him from men who wanted his balls."

Gage realized his jaw had gone slack.

"Do you not believe me?"

"I didn't say that. I'm just…well, surprised."

"So was Lieutenant Hunter."

"I'll have to ask him about that."

"He won't tell you. And it had nothing to do with his job. It involved a woman, my cousin, and her four extremely pissed-off brothers."

"Hunter?" Gage asked, never imagining his father figure with anyone other than Alice.

"Oh, yes. Keep in mind, this was well before the lieutenant was married. I met him when I was skiing in Kitzbühl. He was a lieutenant then, based in Germany. I'd recently exited the *Esercito Italiano*, our army. We became friends. The next summer he vacationed here on leave and that's when he met my cousin. Unfortunately for him, he picked the wrong place to…*share passion*…with her. They were caught in a rather amorous act," Giuseppe said, eyes twinkling. "In the end, the brothers—also my cousins—accepted his apology, facilitated by me, of course."

"What changed their minds?"

"Lieutenant Hunter's apology was genuine—my cousin was very beautiful and he was caught up in the heat of the moment. He also promised to help her brothers with the acquisition of some contraband military hardware that, in those days, was hard to come by."

Gage chuckled. "I can't wait to ask him."

"When he denies it, just remember what I told you," Giuseppe said with a wink. "Every word is true and, for a while there, it seemed our friend might lose his family jewels. Thankfully, cooler heads prevailed."

The brief moment of silence and the fading of Giuseppe's smile indicated that the pleasantries were over.

Gage clasped his hands behind his back, a formality left over from his military days. "I need to buy some items from you. I'm not sure what you have so, before I start specifying weapons, is there any way I could view your inventory?"

"Come with me." Giuseppe began to descend. Gage's eyes shot up to the spiral stairs' mounting plate that was loosely bolted to the old timber ceiling, holding the ancient structure in place. The plate moved with each step. Giuseppe's considerable girth made the worn bolts groan under the tension.

"Come!" Giuseppe called out. "Someday it will break free, but it won't be today."

Swallowing, Gage started down, wondering how Giuseppe could know such a thing. Fortunately, they made it, their combined weight causing six inches of movement in all directions. Giuseppe stopped at the landing of the middle stockroom. Gage watched as the colonel's friend moved two boxes and released a hidden lever. The door pulled open, bringing boxes with it. Gage was instantly reminded of Tomas, the young man in Lima who'd outfitted Gage and Hunter with his illicit gang weapons for Gage's war against Sonny Calabrese.

Giuseppe hit the lights, displaying a square arms room that rivaled anything Gage had ever seen, including the armory on Fort Bragg's western edge at the Delta compound. He let out a low whistle. Most of the weapons were small arms from around the world. There were racks of M-4s. There were German pistols. There were dozens of submachine guns.

There was far more than Gage would ever need.

Fifteen minutes and twelve thousand euro later, he zipped up the black suitcase that Giuseppe had so benevolently thrown in as part of the major purchase. Gage rolled the suitcase to the door and turned, eyeing his new friend.

"Do you know the Marina Hotel, the one on the eastern dock of the port?"

"Of course."

"Giuseppe…I'm on the hunt right now, but I'm also on the run. Does that make sense?"

With a broad grin, Giuseppe's knowing chuckle emanated from deep in his belly. "More than you might think. Many years ago, my friend, I found myself in such situations quite regularly."

"The thing is, someone might come here looking for me."

"You were never here, my friend."

"It's not your discretion I'm concerned with. I'm afraid the person who is after me and my friend will learn about the ferry we arrived on, and the hotel where we slept."

"I understand."

"If he, or she, learns that, they will have our scent."

"So, you'd prefer they find nothing but dead ends in *Genova*?"

"Correct. Would you know a reputable person, or group, I could hire to watch the Marina Hotel and also the Palermo Ferry?"

"Watch them to find out if you're being followed?"

"Yes. And given all the foot traffic in that area, it'll be a tall task."

"Tall task?"

"It won't be easy," Gage clarified. "Even if someone is onto me and my friend, I think it'd be tough to spot from just a stakeout." He shook his head. "You know, now that I've talked it out, forget it. Too tough."

Giuseppe's affable face grew wily. "You underestimate me, my new friend."

"I do?"

"What if I could provide you with feedback from the hotelier as well as virtually anyone working at the port? And, in addition, provide two men for 24-hour surveillance."

"That would help," Gage said, not quite ready to commit.

"How long would you need this service?"

Gage sucked on his teeth as he thought about it. "About a week."

After a quick mental calculation, Giuseppe named his price. While Gage felt the man had not done him any personal favors on the price of the weaponry, he found this fee to be extremely reasonable. A week's surveillance plus payoffs to key people at a hotel and port should have cost double.

"You're puzzled at this low fee because the weapons you purchased were expensive."

"Correct."

"I paid nearly what I sold you those items for. Weapons in Italy are very expensive." Giuseppe smiled. "But the surveillance can be done in a much more cost-effective way. Make sense?"

"Yes."

"Then, do we have a deal?"

Elena had given Gage carte blanche when it came to her protection. Gage agreed to the financial terms of the arrangement and spent fifteen more minutes hashing out the plan. He opened one of the new burner phones and provided Giuseppe with the number.

"Call me if anything happens." The two men shook hands.

Now, with a full complement of weaponry and a plan to watch his back, Gage felt considerably better as he headed back to the hotel, their dinner and phones in one hand and a suitcase of weapons rolling behind in the other.

And he couldn't wait to ask Colonel—*Lieutenant*—Hunter about his one-time Genoan flame.

***

While the young man picked his way down the concrete portion of the run-off, the Assassin waited down below the street in the dry creek bed. To distract himself from the unpleasant task in front of him, he scrubbed his foot across the dry sand at the base, idly wondering when it had last rained. Probably not in weeks.

"Tough to see down here at night," the kid grunted as a limb smacked him in the face.

"Yes, watch your step. And brace yourself for what I'm about to show you." Blade open, the Assassin slid the knife into his back pants pocket.

"I haven't been down here since I was a little kid." When he reached the bottom, the young man peered at the black maw of the culvert. "How'd you even know to look down here?"

"From a few clues I found in her house."

"What clues?"

"That's what I'm about to show you. Come over here to the pipe and have a look."

The young man stayed where he was. "Are *you* the man with the tattoo?"

"That's me."

"But the man from a few days ago had the tattoo."

"Damn it!" the Assassin snapped. "Are you kidding me? There was another man? I told her it was going to be a full week before I got here."

"There was a man who came here a few days ago and I thought maybe they went away together." The young man glanced up the hill as if he might run. "Signora seemed happy that the man with the tattoo was who she was expecting."

"That sonofabitch must have impersonated me! I've been worrying about that all day, and I warned her to be careful." The Assassin opened his hands plaintively. "Don't you get it? He faked it. They can't have left together. Just come over here and I'll show you the blood."

"What's your name?"

"Excuse me?"

"Your name?"

"Look kid, I'm not going to play games with you. A woman's life may be at stake."

The young man produced a mobile phone, swiping at the screen a few times before blinding the Assassin with the built-in flashlight. "Either you tell me your name and show me that tattoo or I'm out of here."

"This is ridiculous," the Assassin breathed, correctly guessing that the tattoo in question was on the upper body. He began unbuttoning his light cotton shirt. "While I take my shirt off, sweep your light behind you and you'll see a small puddle of the blood I was talking about."

Reflexively, the young man turned with the light, scanning the rocks behind him.

The Assassin pounced like a cat.

The phone was the first casualty. It fell forward and smashed screen-first on a rock. The light flickered a few times before going dark, leaving the two men to struggle in scant moonlight. Given the Assassin's size and strength, and the element of surprise, the young man was no match.

Retrieving his knife from his back pocket, the Assassin pressed his blade tight up against the young man's neck. Then the Assassin used his left hand to pull the young man's considerable hair backward. The Assassin was on the young man's back, his weight pinning him fast against the rocky ground. The young man began moaning something in Italian before the Assassin repositioned the knife.

"You make another sound and I'm going slice your neck wide open," the Assassin whispered into his opponent's ear, sticking with Spanish. "Do not fucking try me."

"My hand," the young man rasped. "It's twisted under me."

The Assassin lifted himself slightly, allowing the young man to pull his hand out from under his chest. In the limited moonlight, the Assassin could tell it was badly broken. The young man quietly whimpered in relief before the Assassin thrust all his weight back down, cinching the blade back up against the young man's throat and wrenching his head back.

"Listen to me," the Assassin growled. "Answer me and you walk. Lie to me and I will bleed you out like a spring lamb, got it?"

The young man nodded eagerly.

"Does Elena Volkov live in that house up there?"

"Yes."

"Is she there now?"

"No. She's been gone for two days."

"Are you certain?"

"Yes. I checked on her."

"Why?"

"She was my friend."

"Were you involved with her?"

"No," the young man whispered, sounding as if he were on the verge of sobbing. "I just liked her, that's all."

"Who was the man with the tattoo?"

"I don't know. Some man she hired to protect her."

"From what?"

"She didn't tell me. She just said she had some personal things going on."

"What was the man's name?"

"Gage…it was Gage."

"Last name?"

"I swear I have no idea," the kid replied, shuddering.

"What'd he look like?"

"Maybe two meters tall and a hundred kilos. Short, light brown hair."

"Eyes?"

"I don't know."

"Handsome? Ugly? Scars? Tan? Pale? Beard?"

"Rugged looking. Kind of tan. He had a cut over his eye."

"The tattoo?"

"On his arm. It was that woman that you see in courthouses…with scales and a sword."

"Where was he from?"

The young man began to sob. "Are you going to let me go?" he asked, almost unintelligibly.

"Yes, if you keep telling me the truth," the Assassin answered, releasing some pressure. "Calm down. You're doing fine. Where was he from?"

"He was American."

"You're sure?"

"I'm sure," the young man replied, sniffling. "We get enough Americans here that I know the accent."

"What'd he say to you?"

"Not much. I took him to Signora's home and left him there. Soon after, she was gone."

"Why do you have a key to her house?"

"The house belongs to my mother. She rented it to Signora Volkov."

"How did you know her?"

"She hired me to do little jobs. I do that for most of my mother's tenants."

"So this American, Gage, shows up and then she leaves with him?"

"I guess she left with him. But I don't know that for sure. I just know she was gone."

"Did she tell your mother?"

"No, but she left an envelope of money. She wrote 'canone d'affitto' on the envelope and it was enough for two months."

"Note?"

"No note."

"What else can you tell me?"

The young man thought for a moment. "She had two dogs."

"What kind?"

"Little dogs. White with brown patches. She called them her babies."

"Did she have any other visitors?"

"Never that I saw."

"Did Gage have a car?"

"No."

"How did he get there?"

"He walked…followed me. He wouldn't ride on my scooter."

"Did she have the Lancia?"

"The cabrio, yes."

"Color?" the Assassin asked, already knowing the answer.

"It was white."

The Assassin could tell the young man was telling the truth. He eased off nearly all the knife's pressure and lowered the kid's head. "Is there anything else? Think very carefully."

"That is all I know, honest."

"You don't know where she might have gone? You don't know the Gage man's last name?"

"No, I swear."

The Assassin squeezed his eyes shut. He really didn't want to do this. Truly, he didn't. But he couldn't leave a trail, especially this early in the pursuit. This kid already knew too much.

If this hadn't gone so far, perhaps he could leave the boy to live his life. But the Assassin couldn't take that risk.

"Can I please leave?" the young man pleaded.

Kneeling to his victim's side, the Assassin patted him between his shoulder blades. "You did good, kid. I'm sorry I had to do that and I'm sorry I scared you." The young man began to push himself up.

"And I hate doing this, too," the Assassin whispered, shoving the back of the young man's neck straight down, smashing his face onto the gravel-size rocks of the creek bed.

The brutal beating lasted about a minute and exhausted the Assassin. He rolled to his back and caught his wind for several minutes.

When he'd recovered, the Assassin lugged his still-breathing victim halfway up the hill. He grunted as he hoisted the young man to chest level, throwing him off of a boulder so that he crumpled lifelessly on the creek bed. The Assassin walked back down, feeling the faint pulse from the carotid artery. It was weak. The young man would be dead soon—massive head and neck trauma. The Assassin used his penlight and surveyed the damage from a fifteen-foot fall onto jagged rocks. Blood leaked out onto the sand. The Assassin reached into his pocket and donned his surgical gloves. He moved the busted phone next to the kid's body.

Next, the Assassin made his way up to the scooter. The key was still in it. He turned the key to unlock the handlebars. Then, gripping the handlebars inside the grips, he walked the scooter down to the road's shoulder over the creek bed. After checking that no one was coming nor was he being watched, he shoved the scooter over the edge and watched it roll down the hill before banging into a large boulder and cartwheeling to the bottom.

The battered scooter was just a bit farther from the kid's body than the Assassin wanted, and his shoe prints would be down there…

Making his way back down, the Assassin slid the scooter closer and turned the key to the run position. That made the still intact headlamp come on. At least the taillight was busted and no longer burning. Using a rock, he smashed the headlamp in an effort to conceal this "accident" as long as possible. He then flattened the troughs that were dug by the scooter's weight as it was dragged. Finally, the Assassin used a broken branch to smooth away the footprints and disturbed ground. Then he eyed the scene. If someone were suspicious, they might bring in forensics. The Assassin swept his light over the area…

Would the overworked and underpaid police look at this as anything other than an accident? The kid was speeding down his own street— plausible. He lost control of his scooter on the steep hill—maybe a frightened genet ran in front of him—causing him to careen down into the jagged ravine. Shit happens. People die. And the first responders would likely trample the scene before anyone considered foul play.

The Assassin eyed the young man one more time. There was no more rise and fall to his chest. Poor kid, hadn't even begun his life. The Assassin cursed and shook his head before reminding himself of his goal.

Speaking his native language, the Assassin spoke a whispered apology to the young man's spirit. Then he pocketed the light and walked back to the Audi. As the Assassin walked, he spoke to himself, repeating the description over and over.

"Gage. American. Two meters tall. A hundred kilos. Tan. Light brown hair. Rugged. Gage…"

Back in the car, the Assassin drove several kilometers away and parked. There, he opened his iPad, searching his encrypted database for the correct individual's contact information. When he found it, he used his IP masking protocol to send a text in French. The text seemed innocuous but was a code for something much more important...

This is J. Hope you've been well. I will call you in five.

The Assassin fought the urge to smoke one of his handmade cigarettes. Instead, he drank water and allowed the cool evening air to calm him after the unpleasantness that had just occurred. When precisely five minutes had passed, he used his electronics gear to call his contact, but the Assassin didn't bother with the voice-modulating translation program.

"Good evening, friend," the Assassin said in English, his voice warm. "It's been some time."

His contact, a Frenchman named Gerard, was a ranking official with Interpol, based in Lyon, France. Gerard sounded peeved, probably because he hadn't made easy money in over two years. "I thought you might've been dead."

"Oh, no. I'm quite well," the Assassin answered. "I've been taking some much-deserved time off but now I'm back on the job. Might you help me with a few items?"

There was a pregnant pause. "It's different now. After that well-publicized leak, they're busting balls on anything that's not assigned a case number."

"You're an intelligent man. I'm certain you can find a case number that's open to use as the umbrella for the negligible items I request."

"I'll need more than before because I'm going to have to grease some palms."

The Assassin chuckled quietly. They all do this, eventually. Blame the organization to hide their own greed. "Fine, Gerard, but I won't pay unless the fees are reasonable. I have other contacts, you know."

"Don't be rash," Gerard countered. "Let me first hear your request."

Score! A direct hit! The threat of going elsewhere always gets them in line. The Assassin gave the description of the Lancia cabrio and its license plate number.

"Sicily?" Gerard confirmed.

"Yes, start around Cantania but check everywhere."

"We have several cases open in Italy. I should be able to handle this one without difficulty."

Shocker. "How much?"

"Um...thirteen."

"Thirteen it is. Same destination?"

"Yes. Exact same as last time. Euros. I'll go ahead and have my night officer begin the trace," Gerard said. "And when I get you the information, you will move the money?"

"Of course, I will. It's good to hear your voice again, Gerard. And it'll likely not be the last time you help me in the coming days."

"Call me in the morning?"

"Done."

Satisfied that the wheels were in motion, the Assassin drove farther inland and parked at a rest area. After eating horrid packaged food from the automat, he reclined the driver's seat and closed his eyes. Despite his regret over the killing of the handsome young man, the Assassin was asleep in minutes.

Chapter Eight

ON THE following day, after purchasing the items Elena requested, Gage had awaited her exit from the bathroom for a full hour. During the wait, he'd heard the faucet running, the shower, periods of silence and occasional sharp Ukrainian phrases that he correctly assumed were curses. Finally, Elena had shown herself. Her long blonde hair was now severely short and jet-black. Further changing her appearance were her eyebrows: once full and blonde, they were now extremely thin and plucked in such a way to give each one a slight peak on top. The effect of her work was breathtaking.

"You don't even look like the same person," Gage had remarked.

"That doesn't sound like a compliment."

"It's not an insult, either."

Elena's dogs both stared at her, their heads cocked as they obviously noted the transformation.

"I look like a vampire. Maybe I should buy some black leather and a whip."

Gage caught himself before he told her she looked beautiful. Instead, he said, "You look every bit as nice as you did before."

"Nice."

"Yes, nice."

"Girls don't want to look *nice*."

"You know what I mean."

She'd remained sullen and not said too much after that. Things had been that way for the balance of what should have been a five-hour drive north to Zürich. They were traveling in a rental car that Gage had secured with his new identification and credit cards.

Now, due to heavy road construction on Autostrada A7 around Milan, they were an hour behind schedule. It was past noon when they cruised through the picturesque Reuss Valley, just south of the Swiss town of Altdorf. The shimmering Swiss Alps towered all around them as the sparkling waters of Lake Lucerne emerged ahead. The beautiful scenery of the past hour had seemed to perk Elena up, so it was when Gage opted to take the slower but more scenic route on the lake's eastern shore that he began to question her about who might have been giving orders from Switzerland.

After going through one of her bags, Elena produced a large pad of paper and a pencil. She'd turned herself so Gage couldn't see the pad.

"What are you writing?"

"Just drive," she'd said.

After fifteen minutes, Gage asked again.

"It's killing you, isn't it?"

"You're obviously trying to keep me from seeing it."

She closed the pad and put it away. "I was sketching."

"I thought you haven't painted since your husband's passing."

"Sketching isn't painting."

"Were you sketching the mountains?"

"Maybe."

"Okay." He changed the subject. "Do you have any idea of a person your in-laws might have been close to in Switzerland?"

"No," she'd replied firmly. "No idea."

"Could the 'supposedly Swiss' man who called the American killer actually have been Russian?"

She shrugged. "I don't know. Why do you ask?"

"Because the American hired killer told me the Swiss contact spoke native-sounding Russian. Do Nastya and Georgy speak Russian?"

"Of course. Almost all Ukrainians speak Russian. Many speak it better than they speak Ukrainian."

"Could it have been Georgy who called?"

"No way. He wouldn't be in Switzerland this time of year."

"Why?"

"He likes beaches. He's almost always at a beach."

"Zürich has a beach on the lake."

"No. Georgy likes a party beach, with lots of young women."

As they slowed to a crawl due to heavy traffic, Gage twisted his hands on the wheel, recalling the American's testimony. "The hired killer said he thought the Swiss man was mid-forties. He said the man spoke English and Italian and said he sounded as if he were fluent in Russian, based on the way he spoke several words."

"If he spoke Italian, then it's definitely not Georgy. And if you're going to ask a bunch of tedious questions, then can I please have a cigarette?" Elena asked. "You haven't let me smoke the entire time."

Gage rolled down the windows. Elena's dogs had been snoozing but the sound of the electric windows woke them. Gage disabled the window buttons and watched as each dog took its place with its head hanging out.

"There. Now, about the Swiss man?"

"I can't think of anyone they would know there," she said, using the car lighter to ignite her long cigarette. "But, it's not like I would know, either. Do you have the phone?"

"It's in the top pocket of my bag."

Elena reached back and retrieved it, handing it to Gage.

"Per your suggestion, we can try to find out where the numbers are assigned. Maybe one will lead us to this mysterious man in Switzerland."

"What then?"

"Then, we will go and have a little chat with him."

"And this will be enough proof?" she asked.

"I don't know, yet. But it's the best place to start. You said, yourself, that Nastya and Georgy aren't going to willingly confess."

"True." Elena eased her seat back. The summer sun was high above, covering the right side of her body as she leaned back and stretched in the confined space. Gage was still driving very slowly due to the bumper-to-bumper traffic.

"Gage?"

"Yes?"

"What happened to the hired killer who came to my house? I've waited long enough."

"I interrogated him."

"And?"

"I got the answers that are leading us here, to Switzerland."

"Come on, Gage, you promised. What happened after you interrogated him?"

When there was a slight break in the heavy traffic, Gage moved to the left lane and accelerated. "You really don't need to know this, Elena."

"So, you get to ask all the difficult questions and I just get to sit here and smoke and be a good little girl?"

"No. I just don't want to disturb you with facts you don't need to hear."

"I want to know, dammit." She took a last drag of the cigarette before dropping it in a nearly empty water bottle. "Tell me all of it."

Gage glanced at her, his employer. She was eyeing him fiercely. He told her the entire story. He told her how his fellow American had cased the rental home. Gage relayed the tale of the car chase and subsequent wreck, and he told her about the interrogation on the dusty hill near the rail yard.

"Did you kill him?"

No answer.

"Well, did you?"

"You realize this is not cool."

"Not cool? He came to kill *me*. I think I have a right to know."

"Yes, Elena, I killed him."

"Why?"

"Now you're going to question me?"

"I'm not being judgmental." Elena briefly squeezed Gage's hand. "Did you do it because you didn't want the person who hired him to know?"

"That's part of it, but I hadn't planned to kill him."

"What's the real reason?"

"He tried to kill me. I had him under control and he kicked me. A struggle ensued, and...and he died."

"How did he die?"

Gage shook his head.

"I want to know," she snapped.

"He died by lethal injection."

She turned her entire body to face him. "A drug?"

"Yes."

"Where did you get this drug?"

As they passed a sign announcing their transition into the Canton of Schwyz, Gage downshifted and passed several cars. "He had the drug with him."

"Why did he have a drug?"

"Because that's how he was going to kill you, okay?"

The only sound for several kilometers was the road under the radial tires. Finally she said, "You're not telling me everything."

"He's dead, Elena."

"Why was he going to use a drug?"

"It's a clean way to kill someone, I guess."

"You're a shitty liar. Why?"

"He was going to rape you, all right? The sadistic sonofabitch was going to give you enough of the drug to paralyze you, and during that time he was going to rape you, sick twisted bastard he was. Then, afterward, he was going to kill you. There...satisfied?"

She took the news without emotion. "So, even though you're a professional, the fact that he might rape me changed him in your eyes?"

"You're damn right, it did. And, to your first comment about me being a professional, I don't have an ounce of sympathy for *any* contract killer." He eyed her, feeling his own nostrils flare. "In fact, I recently accepted a job to kill someone on contract. The man I was supposed to kill was a cold-blooded twisted murderer. So, for me to kill someone, I have to believe that I'm helping my fellow man. But some guy who blithely takes any job...no sympathy."

Eyes back on the road, Gage shook his head at his own credo. "I know that sounds warped..."

"No, it doesn't. Go on."

He licked his lips. "Anyway, when I found out that the American killer would kill anyone on contract, regardless of who they were, I'd already made up my mind that he had to go."

"But when you learned he planned to rape me..."

"That made the kill easy." Gage wanted to say more but decided he'd said enough.

"And where is the American killer now?"

Gage turned and eyed her. "He's stuffed in a barrel of dry-sweep at a Sicilian rail yard."

"Dry-sweep?"

"Kitty litter."

"That tiny gravel that cats pee in?"

"Yes."

She was amused. "And my car?"

"Hopefully, it's safely in the hands of the mafia." He told her how he sanitized the car and left it ready to be stolen.

They drove on in silence for quite some time. Gage felt wrong for telling Elena what had happened. As they passed a road sign announcing Zürich as 59 kilometers away, Elena's left hand touched Gage's right forearm. He looked over at her.

"Thank you, Gage."

"No need to thank me."

"Glad you don't have to lie anymore?"

"I wasn't lying. I just wasn't telling you everything."

Elena laughed. "Your lying is as bad as my new hairstyle."

"I think it looks very good."

"You said *nice*, earlier."

"Fishing for compliments, are we?"

"What's that mean?"

"Forget it," he said, chuckling with her.

Elena lifted the American killer's phone. "How will we find out about the numbers on this phone?"

"We might be able to Google them."

"Is that reliable?"

"I don't know. I think it works when the number belongs to a business. But if it's a cellphone, I think it just tells you which network the phone belongs to."

"Who could find out the fastest?"

"Law enforcement and the telecom companies."

"I doubt we want to ask the police."

"Agreed."

"So…we reach out to someone at a telecom company."

As they rejoined A4, Gage turned to her. "Do you know someone?"

"No. But I have an idea."

"What's that?"

"We go to a telecom company in Zürich, and I'll introduce myself to someone."

"Someone?"

"A man."

"How do you aim to do that?"

She tapped her lips. "I'll do some research on the computer, then I'll pick up the phone and call."

"I thought you were scared of people."

"Large crowds," she corrected.

"As long as whoever you call doesn't know who you are, I guess there's no harm in trying."

Elena settled back into her seat. There was a smile on her face.

"I've been thinking about what we're going to do," Gage said.

"Yes?"

"Your dogs."

"What about them?"

"I think we need to board them."

"I can't do that again."

"Elena, they could get killed, and they could also give us away."

She turned and viewed the two dogs, both smiling into the wind as their wet tongues curled and flapped. With a resigned countenance, she turned and slumped. "If we board them, it has to be somewhere nice."

"Zürich is a wealthy city. Surely we can find the Ritz-Carlton of boarding facilities."

Elena didn't respond. In the distance, the manmade spires of the Swiss lakeside city were visible.

***

It took the Assassin a half-hour to drive to the town of Adrano. He parked several hundred meters from the hotel, eyeing it for a moment before reviewing his hand-written notes. His Interpol contact, Gerard, informed him that Elena Volkov's Lancia had been driven to the town and parked. The traffic camera—a new one that stored a week's worth of video—showed a man and a woman exit the car. They returned about ninety minutes later and she sat in the car while the man walked away. A short while later, he came back for her and they carried the luggage on foot, headed north. There was only one small hotel in that direction, on the northern end of town. Later, the man returned to the Lancia and drove away from town, headed back to the east. Gerard said a white Lancia convertible was reported as having potentially been involved in a mysterious accident in the seaside town of Aci Trezza. The accident occurred the following morning, around sunrise.

Therefore, the Assassin hypothesized that this Gage fellow brought Elena to this town for her own safety. They parked while he secured a hotel room. He was careful not to park the car at the hotel, but the video told the true tale. Then, he went back to her Belpasso home to await the hired killer Georgy Zaytsev had spoken of. Contact occurred early the following morning and a chase ensued, terminating at the seaside town of Aci Trezza. According to Gerard from Interpol, several witnesses reported the driver of the Lancia "helping" the victim from the other car before speeding off to the south, allegedly headed to the hospital.

None of the nearby hospitals had any record of anyone fitting descriptions of either man seeking treatment.

Two days before, when the Assassin had said the American killer was likely dead, he'd been making an educated guess in order to appear all-knowing to Georgy. Now, the Assassin was sure of the American's demise. This Gage man had wrecked the American killer's car and spirited him away for interrogation followed by certain death.

While the Assassin had no use for the man named Gage, he respected him. Thus far, Gage did good, clean work. And he had a tattoo. He was approximately two meters tall with short brown hair. He had a cut over his eye. Rugged and quite capable.

Capable thus far. But the Assassin knew, at some point, this capable operator, Gage, would step on his cock. And when he did, the Assassin would be there.

For now, the Adrano hotel seemed to be the best place to start. Feeling the need of a shower and a nap, he sucked on a breath mint as he crossed the hot parking lot, truly considering renting a room for a bit. It all depended how things played out. A changeable sign on the door indicated the small hotel's office was open and someone was currently in. The Assassin entered the four-story establishment and glanced around. To the left was a small lobby. Straight ahead, a young woman sat behind the front desk, staring at her mobile device while her head bounced with the rhythm of whatever music she was listening to. She was probably in her early twenties, her hair streaked with purple dye. The Assassin had to wave to get her attention.

The young woman fake-smiled, removing her ear buds. *"Ci dispiace, la mia musica era troppo forte."*

"Nessun problema," he replied in a heavy accent, matching her smile—minus the lip rings. The Assassin switched to a perfect, Midwestern American accent, asking, "My Italian is poor. Do you happen to speak English?"

"Sure. Need a room?"

"I might," he replied, looking around. "I'm actually looking for my buddy, Gage. He's here with his girlfriend. They in their room at the moment?"

The young woman's brown eyes flickered with recognition. She quickly looked down at the old-fashioned hotel register and shook her head. "There's no one staying in this hotel by that name."

"Are you certain?" the Assassin asked, making his tone polite. "He's American and she's Ukrainian. Perhaps they didn't register by name when they checked in? Gage is funny like that."

She continued to look down at the register as she shook her head. "I'm positive. We have two parties at the moment, both are Italian families. That's all."

The Assassin placed his hand on the counter and looked out the window as if he might spot his friends. "That's odd because this is where Gage told me he'd be." He turned to the young lady. "Could you look at the last few day's registrations and see if they *were* here?"

The young woman flipped backward in the book. "No. They weren't here."

"Are you the proprietor?" he asked.

"My parents are the owners."

"Where are they?"

"They're around somewhere," she replied, one hand involuntarily tugging on her left lip ring.

The Assassin eyed her carefully, reading her nervous gestures. *She's lying. Lying about Gage and Elena. Lying about her parents.*

"Well, if Gage and Elena aren't here, then I guess it's pointless for me to get a room." The Assassin placed both hands flat on the counter. "Thank you for your help."

"You got it," she said, replacing her ear buds.

He remained, staring at her as he gently tapped his fingers on the counter.

She looked up at him, her irritation showing as she yanked the ear buds out again. "Anything else?"

"Yes." A long pause. "Did he actually use the name 'Gage' or was he using a pseudonym?"

That threw her. Flustered, she quickly recovered. "I told you, I *don't* know who you're talking about."

"Sure, you do." The Assassin let that sink in for a moment. "And Elena, did she try to disguise her identity? Maybe a change in appearance? Was she still blonde? She cut her hair? Is it dark now? Most amateurs go completely to the opposite."

Cheeks splotching, the young woman raised her voice. "They aren't here. They weren't here. And I don't know them." Her finger, led by a jet-black fingernail, pointed at the door. "Now, if you don't want a room, I'd like you to leave the property right now."

"Why are you protecting them?" the Assassin asked, keeping his voice soft and non-threatening. "Did they pay you?"

"What?"

"Why—are—you—protecting—them?"

She slid her chair backward, eyeing him as her left hand lifted the main telephone and tapped a few numbers into the keypad. "I don't take shit off anyone in my family's hotel. You can explain all of this to the—"

The Assassin reached over the counter, snapping the phone cord from the jack. He smiled.

The young woman snatched her mobile phone from the counter, standing up and moving out of range as she frantically swiped at the screen.

Controlling her was no more difficult than a parent handling a toddler. The Assassin deftly stepped around the desk, knocking the phone from her hand. The phone's case broke into two pieces. The Assassin kicked the phone, sending it smashing into the tile baseboard, finishing the job.

She screamed. He let it happen, making sure he seemed unconcerned. When she was out of breath, he asked, "Are you done?"

He didn't understand the Italian she shrieked at him, but he didn't let it bother him, either. The Assassin allowed her to yell herself out. He crossed his arms and arched his brows, making himself seem amused.

Afterward, she slumped, panting, eyes darting.

"So, where are those Italian families?" the Assassin calmly asked, gesturing all around. "And where's your mama and papa?"

Her next scream could have shattered glass. She shrank down into the corner, sobbing.

The Assassin grasped her right wrist, twisting it and making her stand.

"Now, don't resist and I won't add pressure." He walked her to the front door, turning the lock and changing the hanging sign to indicate that someone would be back in an hour. He led her back to the front desk and eyed the register.

"That's what I thought," he chuckled, pointing to today's page. "No one is here." The Assassin grabbed the key to room 201 and told her to lead the way.

More shrieks.

"We're just going to talk," he crooned into her ear. "But if you keep this up, this petulant behavior, I'll be forced to make things bad for you. Which will it be?"

When her blubbering subsided, she managed to say, "Please don't hurt me."

"Then calmly lead the way to room two-zero-one and let's have a little chat."

Sobbing, the young lady did as she was told. Up they went.

***

Gage had mentioned finding the Ritz-Carlton of kennels for Elena's dogs. In actuality, they'd found something even better. Just south of Zürich, a veterinarian had built a dog hotel that was essentially a five-star resort. The facility boasted a 1-to-1 ratio of employees to dogs. It had a swimming pool, doggie massage and a duo of chefs who prepared food per dietary guidelines for each dog. While Elena paid for two weeks in advance, Gage stood in the background and said nothing. When she'd stopped crying and they were back in the city, Gage asked if she was okay.

"I am," she breathed. "In fact, that was the right decision."

Unable to help himself, Gage said, "Didn't you say something about living frugally?"

She turned her head and stared at him. "Are you trying to—what is it you say?—ruffle my feathers?"

"Sorry," he said with a chuckle.

"My dogs are like my children."

"I won't say another word about it," he replied soberly. From that point on, they were all business.

It was early afternoon when Elena exited the outmoded Internet café, carrying with her a stack of printed papers. The sun was still high overhead, heating Zürich to the highest recorded temperature of the year. Scattered between the office buildings, outdoor cafés overflowed, most of the glistening patrons drinking iced drinks and fanning themselves with menus. The entire scene seemed very un-Swiss. Every businessman in sight had removed his coat and rolled up his sleeves. A few had even unbuttoned their dress shirts. Women who'd made the mistake of choosing long skirts for this day had bunched them up over their knees in an effort to cool off.

Hot weather has a way of making people forget about appearances—even the refined Swiss.

Two blocks away, the stout and gleaming headquarters of Klarheit Telekom AG stood proudly over the business district in Zürich's *Mitte*. While dominated by banks, Zürich is also home to a number of international business powerhouses including Zürich Insurance and ABB Group. Despite being an expensive locale to base a business, the favorable tax implications often tip the scale in Switzerland's favor. Klarheit wasn't a worldwide brand—at least, not yet. But its growth had been explosive and the telecom company currently boasted more than 2,000 employees.

Elena had the names of ten of those Klarheit employees in her hand.

She sat down in the air-conditioned rental car, placing the papers on her lap after she repositioned two of the dashboard vents, aiming them at her face. "It's freaking hot."

"Freaking?"

"I try not to curse, if possible."

"But 'freaking?'"

"Most television I watch is American. I read books in English. I should not have a good vocabulary?" she asked, letting her Ukrainian accent drip.

"Well, you're right, it is freaking hot," Gage replied, eyeing the scantily clad people gathered around a shaved ice cart on the left side of the street. "I'm just waiting for someone to break the glass ceiling and take off all their clothes. Hopefully it won't be some hairy man."

Elena ignored him, stacking the papers in order of importance.

"You sure you know what you're going to say?" Gage asked.

"Of course." She used the brand new, prepaid mobile phone that was charging via the car's 12-volt outlet. She dialed the Klarheit main line and asked for the first name from her stack. The papers were actually printouts of Klarheit executives' LinkedIn pages.

"They're putting me through," she said hopefully. "Argh…voicemail." Elena tossed the first sheet aside.

Gage picked up the paper. "Gunther Fernwalder, Director, Technical Services." He turned to her. "How did you decide who to print off?"

"All of these had nice faces," she replied, dialing again and striking out. She repeated this process four times, getting voice mail each time.

"Is the same operator answering?" Gage asked.

"No. Men and women. Must be a switchboard…"

She switched the phone to her other ear. "*Guten Tag. Konrad Schröder, bitte.*" She paused, waiting…waiting. She suddenly straightened. "*Hallo, Herr Schröder, sprechen Sie Englisch?*" Elena nodded. "Wonderful…Mister Schröder, I hate to be direct but I'm afraid, given my situation, I must. You will please believe me when I insist that I won't get you in trouble, and I truly am a nice person." She listened for a moment. "No, no, I'm not selling anything and, I promise, I'm coming to my point. Are you at the main Klarheit headquarters on Talstrasse? You are? Good. I'd like to speak with you, if I may, in person." She smiled. "It's a personal matter, and I will compensate you for simply listening. No, this isn't a scam. I have cash with me."

Gage shrugged. Elena nodded.

"The cash is for assistance. I'm in no way associated with law enforcement nor am I trying to make you do anything illegal. I simply need a favor."

It took nearly five minutes of her soothing before Herr Schröder agreed to meet with her beside the fountain in the plaza at the front of the Klarheit building.

"I have short dark hair," Elena said, winking at Gage. "I'll sit on the marble wall in front of the fountain. Five minutes?" She smiled and nodded. "No, I'm not Swiss. How did you know?" Another round of chatting and reassurances. "Fine, I'll see you then." She hung up, her expression triumphant.

"Are you nuts?" Gage asked.

"Why?"

"How do you go from a timid hunted woman to a flirtatious phone charmer so quickly?"

Elena's mirth faded. "Gage...I want to end this threat against me. And if I have to bribe a telecom executive to do it, I will. I'm probably capable of far more than you think."

"Whoa, now...don't be offended. I wasn't trying to underestimate you and I'm sorry if it seems that way. I'm simply learning that there are more layers to you than I realized."

Elena nodded as if satisfied with his apology.

"But what if Herr Schröder asks *why* you want those numbers?"

"I'll come up with something. Stay here. I'll walk," Elena said, removing a banded stack of bills from the briefcase. She stuck the money in her purse.

"But what about that crowd out there?" Gage asked, pointing to the busy sidewalk. "Doesn't that bother you?"

"It's not so bad in wide open spaces, unless people are crammed up next to each other." She opened the door. "I'll be back."

***

The Assassin situated the young woman on the bed in the hotel suite. He put her in the center with her back to the headboard, instructing her to spread her arms wide and grasp the tops of the simple headboard. She was wearing a black t-shirt and a mesh vest. Around her neck, numerous silver necklaces displayed gothic-style pendants. The Assassin noted that one of the pendants was an SS death head—she probably didn't even know who the hell the SS were. She wore a black leather mini-skirt, no hose of any type and chunky black lace-up shoes. It was almost as if she were wearing the very uniform of post-teen rebellion.

"Don't move your hands or I will shoot you," the Assassin said, sitting in the room's only chair at the end of the bed. "Tell me the truth—when will your parents be back?"

"I don't know."

"Do they live here?"

"Our house is attached to the side of the hotel."

"Where did they go?"

"They went to Cantania. Are you going to rape me?"

"I'm not a rapist. How long ago did they leave?"

She shook her head, her purple hair swinging over her face. "You didn't answer my question."

"No, dear. I am *not* going to rape you. But if you lie to me, I'm going to kill you," he snapped before softening his voice. "And I'd really rather not do that. Are you with me?"

She nodded.

"So…when did they leave for Cantania?"

"A few hours ago."

"When do you expect them back?"

She let out a deflating breath. "Probably not till evening."

"Very good," the Assassin said. "Now, I know you know more about Gage and Elena."

She nodded.

"Good. Tell me."

"You have to make a deal with me." She pulled in a wet breath through her nose. "You have to leave here, right now. You have to let me lock all the doors. And then, when I know I'm safe, you can call the hotel phone and I'll tell you everything."

"No deal," the Assassin replied, his derision mixed with amusement. "You're in no position to bargain."

"But you'll kill me," she cried.

"I won't kill you if you start talking right now. If you keep on stalling…" He walked beside her and lifted one of the pillows, holding it against the barrel of the Beretta pistol while aiming it at her head. "Then you get the bullet. Now, make it easy on yourself and talk." He leaned forward. "And I must tell you, any further delays will count as your being uncooperative."

"They were here. They stayed here," she replied frantically.

"Go on."

"They were here one night, then I drove them to Dittaino the next day."

"*You* drove them?"

"Yes. He asked about a taxi but I said it was too far."

"Why Dittaino?"

"So they could catch a train."

"A train? Where were they going?"

"I heard them talking about a ferry. Most people from here go to Dittaino to catch the train to Palermo. There are lots of ferries there."

"Aren't there ferries in Cantania?"

"Yes, but you wouldn't take the train to Cantania."

"Good point. But you don't know which ferry they took?"

"I swear I don't know. That's the honest truth. You don't want me to lie."

"No." He squinted his eyes, searching his mind. "Palermo is on the northwest side?"

"Yeah."

"When was this?"

"Two days ago."

"That you drove them?"

"Yes…so, they actually arrived here three days ago."

"What name did they stay under?"

"It's downstairs, but it wasn't that name…Gage…you keep calling him."

The Assassin lowered the gun and pillow. "You're doing fine, dear." Cocked his head. "But I have the distinct feeling there's a bit more."

Her eyes widened.

"I'm right, aren't I?"

Her lips, covered in Byzantium lipstick, pursed as she nodded.

"Tell me."

"He gave me some money to let him know if anyone ever came looking for them."

"Did he?" the Assassin asked, unable to contain his smile. "Did he?"

"Yes."

"How are you to notify him?"

"He said he'd call."

"He didn't give you a number?"

"I swear. I'd give it to you right now if I had it."

The Assassin believed her. "Tell me about his lady friend."

The young woman repositioned herself on the bed. "She didn't say too much. I think she's Russian."

"Describe her."

The young woman provided a detailed description. Elena sounded as if she had not yet changed her appearance.

"Is there anything else?"

"I've told you everything I can remember."

"Where were they headed from Palermo?"

"They didn't tell me," she replied emphatically. "I overheard them talking about a ferry."

"Him or her?"

"Her."

"What destinations are available via Palermo?"

The young woman's large brown eyes went to the ceiling. "Uh…Tunis, Naples, Genova, Sardinia…there are others but I don't know them by heart."

"And they didn't say where…you're absolutely certain?"

"I told you…wait…she did say something about sailing overnight and all the following day." The young woman perked up upon remembering this. "That should help you narrow it down. We have a schedule downstairs."

"Excellent." The Assassin's mind changed gears. "But…there's one other thing."

"What?"

"I need his fingerprints…the man's."

"But his room has been cleaned and probably used since then."

"Where else might he have left them?"

"He used the computer but it's also been used since." She shrugged. "I don't know what to tell you."

The Assassin briefly pondered having Gerard examine the Internet activity from the hotel computer but decided against it. "Did the man, Gage, drive your car?"

"No, he sat in the back."

After five more minutes of unsuccessful questioning, the Assassin tossed the pillow back on the bed, continuing to cover her with the Beretta. "So, I will find Gage's fake name on the guest register downstairs?"

"Yes."

"And he sat in the backseat?"

"Yes."

"Has anyone ridden in the car since then?"

"No. Just me."

"And the ferry schedule?"

"Downstairs, next to the train schedules. They're on the wall near the computer."

The Assassin walked to the window, turning his back to her as he looked out. The small parking lot was empty other than his Audi.

"You're going to kill me," she whispered, her crying starting again.

The Assassin was still shaken by what he'd done to the young man in Belpasso. And he quite liked this rebellious young woman. If the situation were different, he'd love to spirit her away from here and throw a little money at her appearance. With a suitable hairstyle, a kiss of the sun on her skin, tasteful clothing and better jewelry, she could transform into a stout little knockout. While she was scared of him raping her now, he knew in his heart of hearts, after lavishing her with the attention she craved, he'd have her begging for it within 48 hours.

He shook his head of the ribald, unprofitable thoughts. After deliberating for a good fifteen seconds, he turned to her. "I won't hurt you, provided you do exactly as I say."

She was about to speak but he silenced her with his hand. "Young lady, if you breathe one word about me to anyone, including your parents, I will come back and I *will* kill you. That's my promise to you." He smiled, almost apologetically. "I've evaded the highest levels of law enforcement for a good portion of your life, so don't flatter yourself into thinking that your phone call will be *the one* that puts me behind bars. Do you understand me?"

She nodded eagerly, her fear evident.

"I'm deadly serious, my dear. Don't confide this in a close friend or a lover, either. Hold it deep inside you, as our little secret, and you shall live your full life minus my retribution." He crossed the room, sitting next to her and almost touching the pistol to her left eye. "So believe me when I give you my word that I will come for you if you do anything—*anything*—other than resume your life."

"I swear I'll do as you say."

He lowered the pistol.

"But when he calls?"

"That's an excellent question." The Assassin tapped the barrel of the pistol against his mouth as he pondered this. "If Gage does call, just tell him the hotel has been quiet and no one has come nosing around to your knowledge. Don't say too much…too many words will unnerve a skilled operator. Just be nonchalant."

"I'll do just as you said."

The Assassin nodded. He believed her.

"What do I do now?"

"You walk downstairs with me. If anyone is here—your parents, a guest—you act as if I'm a man who wanted to see a guest room, nothing more. If no one is here, we'll view the ferry schedule, then we'll get that email address and I will attempt to lift some fingerprints from your car. Good enough?"

"Yes."

"Do you want to know why I'm after Gage?"

She shook her head. "No, and I don't care."

That statement gave the Assassin the reassurance he needed that she wouldn't mention his presence to anyone. "That's my girl."

"Thank you," she breathed.

He cocked his head. "Why are you thanking me?"

"I can't exactly describe what I'm feeling. But I do know this: you're the most serious fucking man I've ever met."

"Just remember that when you're tempted to tell someone." The Assassin patted her cheek. "Come now, let's go down."

From his bag in the Audi, he retrieved the small plastic case that contained several powders, a brush and lifting tape. Though he found several latent prints in the young lady's backseat; the prettiest three came from the underside of the passenger door handle.

Twenty minutes later, the Assassin was on his way to Palermo. In his possession, along with the fingerprints, was a ferry schedule. If what the young woman said was true, about sailing all night and all day, then Elena Volkov and her protector had sailed north to Genoa. No other destination had such a long journey. Once the Assassin confirmed that to be the case, he, too, would head to Genoa.

But not by ferry.

Before that, he hoped to find an identity to go with these fingerprints.

***

Elena wanted a cigarette but decided against it. She needed to appear as approachable as possible, and even something as small as a cigarette might be the difference between this telecom executive agreeing or disagreeing with her proposal. Instead, she sat on the side of the fountain, crossing her legs in a ladylike pose as mostly businesspeople lingered in the sparse shade of the stifling hot plaza.

Elena watched as a man exited the building and headed directly for her. This had to be him. He was wearing a light gray suit minus the jacket. His clothing was modern with a decided European slim tailoring. His air seemed somewhat casual—even his narrow tie was slightly loosened. When he reached her, Elena smiled.

"Herr Konrad Schröder?"

"Yes," he answered in English, glancing around as if someone might be listening.

"I promise I'm alone," she said.

He sat next to her, keeping a reasonable distance and looking straight ahead. "Please explain what you want."

She handed him a folded piece of paper containing every phone number that had called the American killer's mobile phone. "I'd like you to look up each of those numbers. I want to know where they emanate from and who is billed for the number."

"That's illegal," Schröder replied immediately.

"I thought it might be. I already went to the police and they didn't help me."

"Like I said…"

"But I mean no harm, Herr Schröder."

"Whether you do or don't, it's still illegal. I could lose my job."

Elena dipped her head. She remained silent.

"What's this about?" Schröder eventually asked, his voice softening just a bit.

"My husband is leaving me," Elena lied, looking away for a moment. "He's decided he should spend his life with a much younger woman. His girlfriend called him from each of those numbers."

"I'm sorry, but I can't get involved in something like that."

Elena held a tissue under her nose. "I know it's not your business, but do you know what it's like to be replaced by a younger person? To know that you won't be cared for? My husband never even let me get a job…he hardly wanted me to leave the house. Do you know how hard it is here for a Russian who's never worked?" She purposefully didn't reveal her Ukrainian heritage—most people can't tell the difference between the accents. "And now he's leaving me and if I don't prove that he's having an affair I'll have to leave Switzerland. I can't make it on my own. I have to prove his infidelity." She tucked the tissue away. "Herr Schröder, I'm sorry to ask you to break the law. I will never reveal who helped me with this and I'm willing to pay you handsomely for this one favor."

"I thought you didn't have any money."

She produced the wad of bills from her purse, concealing it as she handed it to him. "This is his money…my husband's." She smiled. "My lawyer said I cannot take his money to keep, but I'm free to use it for normal expenses until we're divorced. I consider this a normal expense…when married to a cheating husband."

Schröder concealed the wad of money between them, thumbing the stack of bills. He looked at her. "Something about this seems slightly off."

"There aren't any catches and I'll never utter a word about who helped me. I just need to know the details about those five phone numbers—nothing more."

He faced her. "Are you trying to trap me for any sort of law enforcement or for my company?"

She locked eyes with him. "No, I am not. You can record me saying that if it makes you feel better."

"No." He swallowed before glancing around again. "Can you wait right here?"

"Of course."

He handed the money back. "I'm just going to have a look at the numbers—then I'll decide. It'll probably take me fifteen, twenty minutes. You'll wait here?"

"Yes."

Elena watched as Herr Konrad Schröder, Klarheit senior manager, hurried back into the intimidating chrome and glass structure. She smoked a cigarette, ambling back to the street and catching Gage's eye as he awaited her in the rental car.

Her smile told him everything he needed to know.

***

Several hours later, after Gage had purchased a few needed items from a large bookstore, he and Elena sat at a quiet waterside café on the eastern shore of the sparkling Zürichsee. The sun was now low in the western sky, beaming in at such a severe angle over the water that Gage and Elena sat beside one another, the sun at their backs as they awaited their food.

Once their drinks had arrived, Gage spread the laminated, pre-folded map out before them on the picnic table. Due to the breeze, he weighted down the corners of the map with silverware and the salt and pepper shakers. Then he uncapped the dry erase marker and made a series of three dots on the addresses where the phone calls to the American killer had emanated. The first three numbers belonged to the Park Hyatt Zürich, the fourth to the Alden Luxury Suite Hotel and the fifth number the Sheraton Zürich Neues Schloss Hotel.

Gage capped the marker and pointed to the three dots. "These hotels are all within four blocks of each other."

Elena took the marker and connected the dots with a scalene triangle.

"Interesting that he used hotel phones," Gage remarked.

"Do you think he was a guest?"

"Possibly, but something tells me he called from hotels as a measure of anonymity. They probably have hundreds of lines in each one."

"Anonymity…I know this word…it means so no one would know him?"

"Correct. He purposefully didn't use his own phone in case the American, or someone else, might come looking for him. That's why he used phones from hotels—places where thousands of guests come and go."

"I understand, and I agree."

Gage sipped his water as he poked the triangle. "Why here?" he mumbled.

"Excuse me?"

"Why did he call from those three hotels, especially since they're so close together?"

"Is there a significance with their closeness?"

"You know, Elena, people will often seek the path of least resistance. It's human nature."

"What does that mean?"

"It means, people are oftentimes lazy. And in the center of a bustling city like Zürich, I bet our mystery man walked to those three hotels. Especially with it being summertime. That's why he went to three places so close together. He was on foot."

"Makes sense."

"So, I'd wager he either lives or works nearby."

"I've got an idea." Elena checked the American's phone. "Look at the times on the calls," she said, holding the display so Gage could see it. "The calls were all during business hours."

"Then the hotels are probably near where he works."

The waiter arrived with their food, the intense smells immediately taking Gage back to his years in Germany. Elena had ordered a simple salmon salad. Gage, however, was hungry and splurged for a meal he knew wasn't extremely healthy, but was certainly one of his all time favorites: a large doner kebab platter, piled high with thinly-sliced lamb, shredded lettuce, tomatoes, tzatziki sauce and an order of salty pommes frites.

Yum.

They both ate for a moment before saying anything else. It was Elena who broke the silence.

"Why don't we go over there?"

"Where?"

"That area where the three hotels are," she said, pointing to her triangle on the map. "Maybe we'll learn something."

His mouth full, Gage nodded his assent.

A half-hour later, they walked around the block of the northernmost of the three hotels, the Park Hyatt, studying the nearby buildings. The area itself was quite nice. The older buildings were stately while the newer ones sported classic, yet imposing architecture. The prevalent stone and marble exteriors were softened by the swaying linden trees and an overabundance of colorful flowers in planters and surrounding landscaping. Within seconds, they'd seen branches of large banks like J.P. Morgan and Goldman Sachs. Other boutique banks were scattered about, and between them, high-end jewelers, clothiers, fine restaurants and the occasional tony residence—just the type of places a person would expect to find in the money district.

Despite being understated, it was an area that radiated prosperity.

They walked to the southwest, continuing to eyeball the businesses and not really knowing what they were looking for. In less than two blocks, they found the Sheraton, circling the hotel before walking west on Gotthardstrasse, toward the Alden.

They hadn't walked a hundred meters before Elena's fingernails clawed Gage's forearm. He stopped with her, his eyes following her pointing finger.

Across the street, situated at the corner of Gotthard and Genferstrasses, was a three-story bank that looked more like a wealthy person's residence. It was old and dignified and made of brick and stone. The glass of the gothic-style windows sparkled like mirrors. The home and perfectly manicured yard were surrounded by heavy black fencing supported by decorative brick columns.

And on the brick column at the heavy gate was a gleaming brass plaque. At the top of the plaque was engraved "*Ansteigen Privatbank von Moskau.*" Below the German version of the bank's name was the Cyrillic translation, displayed as "*подниматься частный банк от Москвы.*"

Both Gage and Elena were momentarily silent. They looked at one another.

"But it's a Russian bank," Gage said.

"I know."

"Nastya is Ukrainian, right?"

"She speaks Russian fluently, Gage. And Georgy *is* Russian."

"Is this their bank?"

"It very well could be."

"Before we get too excited, let's look around a bit more," Gage suggested.

They continued on, searching the surrounding blocks for a full hour. They walked until the sun was down and found nothing else remotely interesting.

"What do you think?" Gage asked.

"I think the man who arranged my botched assassinations works at the Ascend Private Bank of Moscow."

"I wouldn't argue with you."

Elena's breathing picked up and her neck grew splotchy.

"You okay?"

"I'm fine."

"You look anxious."

"It's excitement, Gage," she said with a trembling smile. "Believe it or not, this is exhilarating to me."

Gage laughed.

With a kick in their steps, Gage and Elena headed back to the east in search of a smaller, local hotel. There, they would craft a plan.

If they knew what awaited them tomorrow, they wouldn't be so excited.

Chapter Nine

DUE TO the altitude of the airplane the Assassin rode in, he could still see the lemon tip of the sun in the west long after it had officially "set." Thus, the strong light in the cabin was in stark contrast to the growing sea of darkness below him. Though he'd hardly paid attention, the northwesterly flight had afforded the Assassin fine early evening views of Naples and Rome on the starboard side of the aircraft. Now, dead ahead, the burgeoning lights of Genoa loomed.

After receiving such a handsome fee for this flight, the pilot had offered the Assassin the right seat, "and a chance to take the yoke of the Ferrari of the skies." The airplane was a Socata TBM-850, a ridiculously fast single-engine turboprop. It was quite obvious the pilot was proud of his airplane and he seemed more than a little miffed when his distracted passenger declined his benevolent offer. Instead, the Assassin quietly positioned himself in one of the rear seats—without a headset.

Any other time, the Assassin might have been impressed by 330 knots of cruise speed in a single-engine prop aircraft. But on this evening, he was far more interested in what lay ahead. Foremost on his mind were the fingerprints he'd lifted, scanned and emailed to Gerard at Interpol. Would Gerard be able to learn this Gage man's true identity, and would that information be awaiting the Assassin upon his arrival in Genoa? Second, and perhaps more pressing, was the answer to why Gage and Elena had fled to Genoa? Why there? Was Genoa simply the best location as a jumping-off-point to continental Europe, or did her protector have a destination specifically in mind?

Put simply: Were they blindly on the run, or did they have a purpose in where they were headed?

The airplane's forward speed slowed dramatically while the attitude changed to one of descent. As the sound of the turboprop decreased, the pilot spoke fluent English over his shoulder. "I'll have you on the ground in ten minutes. That'll put us from Palermo to Genova in *only* eighty-eight minutes! The only other airplane in Palermo that could have done that for you would have been a Volotea 717. But then you'd have had to go through security and the whole bit. That would have blown your time parameters all to hell. You got the best pilot, the best airplane and the fastest service on all of Sicily." He turned all the way around, his face beaming. "So, friend, what did you think?"

Struggling not to display his exasperation, the Assassin nodded. "Fabulous. My compliments on the swift flight."

"I appreciate it," the Italian replied, but he didn't stop there. He continued to talk as he descended, extolling the minutiae of his 3 million-euro flying sports car.

While the pilot babbled on, the Assassin powered on his mobile phone, watching the blank signal meter as he awaited the first cellular signals to reach his phone. Just as the aircraft went "feet dry" the meter jumped to two bars. Within seconds, his phone informed him of two voicemails.

Once the airplane's three tires kissed the asphalt, the Assassin listened to the first message. It was from Gerard, relaying the data on the man called Gage:

"It's me. The prints you sent provided a solid hit from the level-one citizenry database of the United States. Your man's name is Gage Nils Hartline, age forty-five, American from New York State. He's ex-military and, other than that, there's precious little to go on. No employment info and nothing medically related, either. But there's something curious about his records...I can see the tabs where he's had open files with the Germans, the French, the Spanish and also two more recent files from the Peruvians. His passport has been stamped in all those places, plus the Caymans, Canada and Mexico, along with others. But the files, which typically involve investigations or criminal activity, have been removed. I'll do some digging but usually when files were there and are now blank it means the investigation or charges were dropped and the host country didn't want the records out there for international digestion. Other than that—"

The voicemail ended abruptly. As the pilot awaited clearance to cross an active runway at Cristoforo Colombo Airport, the Assassin touched the screen to hear the second voicemail.

"Sorry, guess my message was too long. Hartline's file says he's two meters tall and around a hundred kilos. Hair is listed as brown, eyes are blue. I checked the Internet but there's nothing there. Not one hit. I then did an electronic sweep. I found one picture of him in his military records but it's old. Let me know if you want it. And Hartline's last credit card purchase was in Charlotte, North Carolina—that's in the U.S.—last Saturday. His passport hasn't been run in some time. He's obviously here under an alias. That's all I have so far. I've put out feelers on those blank files and will call back if I get something. Listen, I appreciate the fee for this. Call me if you need anything else because I will gladly—"

This time it was the Assassin who cut the voicemail off early.

Dammit! All I got from an exorbitant fee was a full name and an outdated picture. And of course the sonofabitch is in Europe on a false I.D. Probably more than one. He'll be harder to find than a hymen in a whorehouse.

"We'll be parked in just a minute," the pilot said.

"How far is the port from here?" the Assassin barked.

"Port? Well, it depends which one you're interested in. There are actually a few ports in Genova," he said pedantically. "The larger of the ports is used for—"

"The one with the ferry terminal, dammit!" the Assassin roared.

Surprised at the sudden venom from his passenger, the pilot swallowed as he pointed east. "It's not far. Only a kilometer or two."

The Assassin reached into his bag and came out with the fare. He added an additional 200 euro. When the pilot parked at the small private aviation terminal and switched off the engine, the Assassin handed him the money.

"I apologize for my outburst. I'm under a great deal of stress about a business transaction that's shaky at the moment." He pointed to the neat stack of bills. "I've added in a nice tip for you. You're a fine pilot and you've a beautiful aircraft."

The Italian seemed mollified by the compliments.

The Assassin exited without another word.

Behind the desk in the terminal, an older lady in a blue uniform consulted a clipboard and nodded at the Assassin. She asked him a question in Italian that seemed to be in reference to his arriving on the private airplane from Palermo. The Assassin nodded his agreement and pointed through the glass doors to the Socata, where the pilot was chocking the wheels. The pilot looked over and waved. Upon seeing that, the older lady eyed the I-registration on the tail and matched it to her clipboard.

"Where did you arrive from?" she asked in broken English.

"Palermo."

After a perfunctory smile, she told the Assassin to have a nice evening.

"Would you happen to know the best way to the ferry port?" the Assassin asked, using his Midwestern American English.

"Ah…Treno Città," she replied, gesturing to the blue overhead sign. The Assassin saw the arrow to the train station along with the distance of 300 meters. He bowed his thanks and in twelve minutes found himself standing on a nearly empty, two-car city train heading east. The port was only a stop away.

***

The first full day of port surveillance had nearly run its course—and what a boring, fool's errand it had been. How in the hell were they supposed to spot a "suspicious man looking for a man and woman?" Despite the ambiguity of their mission, Antonio and Christopher, both loyal foot soldiers, followed Giuseppe's orders to the letter. A six-man rotation had been set up. Select workers at the port were in on it, too, and they were to inform the surveillance shift of anyone who happened to fit the bill.

This was the second shift, due to end at midnight. Despite their fatigue, Antonio and Christopher had made plans to have a drink afterward. It was summertime, after all. Perhaps they'd happen into some ladies who weren't quite ready to go home yet.

Antonio lifted his radio. "We just pissed away a full day of our lives."

"The boss says stand here and look for a man…so we stand here and look for a man. What choice do we have?" Christopher replied.

"I really hope this gets called off by tomorrow. I've got collections to make. You know he won't be understanding if I hand him a thin envelope."

"Yeah, but he said this was a favor for a friend."

"I know. But sometimes I get tired of hearing…hey…who's that guy?"

"Who's who?"

"Coming around the quay from the stairs, smoking a cigarette."

Antonio turned. "Yeah, I got him."

"What's he doing?"

"Seems to be looking around."

"He's about to move out of my line of sight."

"No worries. He's headed my way. I'll check him out."

***

The main port of Genoa was typical of many Mediterranean ports, protected from the ocean's volatility by manmade jetties that created a picturesque horseshoe shape. Several large ferries were docked in the port's terminal, one of them buzzing with what appeared to be last-minute onboarding activity. The Assassin slowly walked around the upper perimeter of the port, smoking one of his handmade cigarettes as he watched the bustle. He climbed a set of stairs to an adjacent pier, getting a good view of the ferry terminal. There was a man up ahead, adjacent to the head of an unused gangway at an empty slip. He was standing in a darkened area between two lights. Smoking his cigarette, the Assassin continued on.

When he neared the gangway, he was able to get a better look at the man. He was leaning against the gangway rail, quietly murmuring into what appeared to be a handheld radio. The indirect light from the adjacent ferry revealed the man to have a thin face with a narrow, manicured goatee. As the Assassin passed by, the man slid the radio into his pocket and said something. The Assassin pretended not to hear him and continued on.

"*Sei sordo?*" the man asked.

The Assassin stopped and turned, taking a drag of his hand-rolled cigarette as he eyed the man with innocent curiosity. He shrugged and said, "I'm sorry but I don't speak Italian."

The man wore casual, loose-fitting clothing that draped from his lean frame. He switched to rough English. "What are you doing up here?"

"My wife is leaving on that ferry," the Assassin lied, pointing to the busy ferry.

"Oh, she is, is she? What's her name?" the man asked, producing the small hand-held radio from his pocket.

The Assassin tapped the ash from his cigarette, doing his best to disarm the situation with a calm demeanor. "I'm sorry, sir, but do you work with the ferry line?"

"I'll ask the questions, *segaiolo*. Give me your wife's name, now."

"What for?"

"Because I said so," the man warned, stepping closer as his right hand went to his side. It was the move of a man preparing to draw a pistol from his back.

The Assassin dropped the cigarette and crushed it out with his loafer. "Okay...okay...take it easy. Her name's Jennifer and I've got the receipt for her fare right here." He dug into his right pocket—

"Careful!" the man warned.

The Assassin slowly removed two slips of paper and some coins, which he fumbled to the elevated pier. "Sorry," he said innocently. "You're making me really nervous. Her receipt's right there."

Without waiting for the man's approval, the Assassin knelt to pick up the items and in one swift movement he spirited the Beretta 92 Inox from his back, aiming it at the man. It was an impressive maneuver, done in a fraction of a second.

The man was clearly caught off guard.

"Move both hands in front of you," the Assassin ordered, using the tone of a person not to be trifled with.

The man obeyed, still holding his radio, which he motioned to the Assassin's weapon. "Do you have any idea who you're pointing that pistol at?"

Ignoring the bluster, the Assassin spoke flatly. "If you so much as flinch, I'm shooting. Hand me your radio."

The man complied.

"How many others are working the port?"

"I don't know what you're talking about."

"You were talking to someone on this radio. If it were someone who wasn't nearby, you'd use a cell phone."

The man shrugged. "I'm the only person here."

The Assassin let out a slumping breath, as if he was disappointed in his new acquaintance. With a quick glance around, the Assassin tried to determine if anyone was watching. In the brief glance, he saw no one—and this elevated area by this dormant pier was dark and secluded. The closest people were the busy dockworkers and they were two hundred meters away.

"I'll ask you once more. Give me a straight answer, or I will kill you right where you stand. Who else is working the port? And…who are you working for?"

The goateed man offered a thin smile as a show of bravado. "Fuck…you."

"Wrong answer to the wrong man." The Assassin pulled the trigger, halting himself after only one shot as the goateed man thudded backward.

One bullet was certainly enough.

The Assassin's purchase of subsonic ammunition had been an excellent choice. To anyone standing within earshot, the gunshot sounded more like a backfire from a lawn mower. With all the noise from the departing ferry, the sound was unremarkable. The bullet struck the wily man in his left upper chest. Whatever life remained by the time he hit the deck was gone in seconds. He was completely still. The Assassin dragged the fresh corpse behind a compacted accordion gangway, the black blood staining the bleached wood of the deck. After another look around, he walked away at a normal speed.

The Assassin concealed the pistol again in his waistband, covering it with his shirt. He dropped the small radio into his pocket. When he'd descended to the main level of the quay, he walked a hundred meters around the edge of the circular port. There, the Assassin glanced back at the elevated area where the body was. There was no activity. The crew of the departing ferry was bringing in her mooring lines and, other than a few well-wishers lingering behind a long red fence, the activity at the port seemed to be winding down.

He wasn't alone. He was talking to someone on the radio, telling them that I fit the bill.

Continuing on, the Assassin stopped at a small kiosk by the main thoroughfare that led into the port. He ordered a fish sandwich and fries and purchased a beer to drink while he waited for the food. Though he was indeed hungry, he'd parked himself here because it was the perfect vantage point and also an innocuous place for a man to be.

Leaning on a stand-up table, the Assassin concealed the radio behind the ketchup and the vertical napkin dispenser. He rested on his elbows, sipping his beer as he listened for transmissions over the radio. It wasn't until he'd almost finished his food that the radio finally crackled, followed by the quick Italian of the other party. Despite his poor grasp of Italian, the Assassin was able to understand most of the quick queries.

"Antonio." Long pause. "Antonio, you there?" Shorter pause, then a louder query. "Antonio!" This went on several more times, with the final query being followed by a few curse words.

The Assassin sipped his beer and continued to eye the area where he'd left Antonio's leaking body. Minutes later, a short and heavy man hurried past from left to right on the quay. He carried a radio that appeared to be like the one on the Assassin's table.

There he is—Antonio's partner. But is he alone?

The Assassin took measured breaths as he watched the scene play out. Because of the harsh lighting, all he could see was the portly man's silhouette. As the man grew closer to Antonio, the Assassin used two damp napkins to wipe his beer bottle and Antonio's radio. Then he walked forward and casually dropped the items into the water at the head of the nearest berth, satisfied as they sank. The Assassin moved back to the table and waited.

Upon reaching the gangway and Antonio's corpse, the man's hands flew to his head. He stared down for a moment before running back down the ramp to the quay. Running couldn't have been easy for the portly man, but he was doing a pretty good job of it. It wasn't thirty seconds before he lumbered up the main thoroughfare beside which the Assassin stood, deftly concealing himself behind the closed umbrellas at the food kiosk. The portly man wasn't speaking on his radio, nor was he on his mobile phone. His brisk pace suggested he planned to report the news in person.

As the Assassin had noted, the man was quite heavy but he carried the extra weight well. As he passed, it was easy to see that the man was mostly bald and sported a massive black moustache that extended well out onto his broad cheeks. Dressed much like his dead friend, in slacks and a shiny button-down print shirt, the portly man seemed the type to be involved in organized crime. The Assassin knew this was a broad generalization, but such a sweeping guess was often key in accomplishing his missions.

Once the man passed the kiosk, the Assassin went after him. Once in the dark, the Assassin ran softly and quietly, the pace quite easy. After they'd exited the port area, the chubby man turned to the right, cutting through an alleyway into what seemed to be an old part of town. His wheezes were audible from fifty meters away.

The alleyway was long and winding, and the Assassin closed the distance quickly. Forty meters. Thirty. Twenty. Ten.

There was no way for the Assassin to get any closer without giving himself away. Since the alley was deserted as far as the Assassin could see, he put on a burst of speed. This eventually caused the heavy man to turn, his bloodshot eyes bulging as he let out a fearful yell.

The portly man no doubt saw the Beretta come smashing down in a windmill arc.

The two men went down in a heap. In a matter of seconds, the Assassin had gained the upper hand on the panting, overweight man. The Assassin turned him over and wedged the Beretta into his mouth. He clawed at the portly man's scalp with his left hand, speaking Italian and demanding to know why they were watching the port. The heavy man tried to speak.

Prolonging the moment, the Assassin slid the pistol from the heavy man's mouth, the front sight clicking on the man's stained teeth.

"What were you doing at the port?" the Assassin hissed.

Gasping, the man rasped, "We were watching for someone."

"Who?"

"Anyone who might be looking for a man and a woman."

The Assassin moved the pistol between the man's eyes. "Who put you up to it?"

"I can't."

"Who?" the Assassin asked, roughly jabbing the pistol into the man's forehead.

"Please..."

"If you don't tell me, you'll end up like your friend back there...Antonio."

"I can't tell you…"

The Assassin had mounted the man's considerable midsection. Because of the man's large belly, the Assassin wasn't able to fully control the man's two pinned arms as he continued to squirm. There was an almost imperceptible movement of his right arm. The Assassin looked down and to his left to see the portly man palming a very small pocket pistol. He'd probably slid it from his pocket. The man's hand twisted the pistol upward and just as the Assassin lurched forward, the pistol fired, generating a loud report for such a tiny firearm.

Due to the odd angle and the Assassin's flinch forward, the shot missed but it did set things in motion. There was no time now for interrogation. The Assassin easily twisted the small pistol from the heavy man's hand.

Then the Assassin leaned backward while he continued to aim from his corpulent perch. He waited a moment, enjoying the look of horror on the portly man's face.

"Please...I'm sorry," the man cried. "I'll talk...I'll talk if you'll just let me go."

"Too late."

The subsonic 9 millimeter bullet split the portly man's thick moustache in two.

Despite the brief moment of pleasure, the Assassin knew he was now in grave danger. In a confined alley that would do nothing to muffle the sound, there'd just been two gunshots back to back, one subsonic and one full tilt. The Assassin scurried to his feet and continued forward in the alley, hearing a door slam behind him. As he reached the road up ahead, he heard a lady scream. She'd obviously found the portly man whose sinus cavity had been freshly opened.

Shit. Shit. Shit!

Two dead bodies within a kilometer of each other. And surely there were cameras at the port. The police would have a suspect in an hour or two—maybe sooner. The Assassin continued straight ahead, walking into a darkened park. There, he made the decision to stay on foot and to continue on a northern track. If he could avoid detection for several hours, that should put him outside of the immediate danger zone as he determined how he would escape from Genoa.

Who were they? Damn it!

After about a kilometer, the Assassin found a long, dry drainage pipe that ran due north as far as his night eyes could see. There was mud in the bottom, but that was all. The pipe was large, too, allowing the Assassin to jog without stooping. Every so often, the Assassin—jogging blind because he didn't want to risk using his light—tripped and fell over some object that had washed into the drainage ditch. At one point, he disturbed what he thought was a raccoon. The animal sprinted into a connecting pipe in a hail of spits and growls. But the minutes wore on, and the Assassin doggedly jogged, knowing each meter he placed between himself and the dead bodies increased his chances of escape.

As he plowed onward, he turned over the situation in his mind. The fat man said they'd been watching for a man—a man who was looking for a man and woman. *So, obviously, they were looking for me.* But how on earth had this Gage Hartline fellow managed to position two locals on surveillance at the port of Genoa? Or perhaps the oil princess had done it?

Knowing he might never know, the Assassin reconciled himself to recognizing that he was up against a wealthy woman with means—and a capable professional bodyguard. This job was growing more difficult by the minute. It was all that vacuous Georgy Zaytsev's fault for hiring amateur killers. They spooked Elena Volkov and now she was on the run with a pile of money to spend, while protected by an experienced tactician.

If I'd been first, it would've been so damned easy.

Despite his frustration, the Assassin knew that someday he would appreciate this pursuit. While deadly and dangerous, the thrill of the chase could be quite exhilarating.

Tomorrow, when he was well clear of here, the Assassin would need to reevaluate the way he was going about this hunt. He couldn't continue to remain one step behind. Sooner or later, one of Hartline's traps would work, and the Assassin would be no more.

So, it's simple—I must catch them before they set the next trap. Then, the element of surprise will be my own. And they'll be in my trap, where there is no possibility of escape.

After what he estimated was several kilometers of jogging through the central drainage pipe, the Assassin was struck by an inspiration. This was summer, after all. When he'd gone a bit farther, he would find an exit and begin to search for a middle-class residential area.

Chapter Ten

ZÜRICH was cool and rainy the following morning. Last night, after quite a bit of searching, Gage and Elena had found a small hotel and rented the only vacant room—a family suite. It was actually a regular hotel room with a small, "bambino" side room designed for a child. Despite Elena's protests, Gage slept there, having to curl into the fetal position to sleep on the short bed that he estimated at five feet long. He'd slid the pocket doors nearly shut, leaving a small gap so he could hear Elena. As had been the case each day thus far, Gage was up before Elena. Seeing no threat, he locked the room door and went downstairs for food and coffee. After a light breakfast and a cup of black coffee for himself, he poured a cup for Elena. When Gage entered the room, he heard the shower running. He placed the cup beside her bed and went back into the bambino room.

Ten minutes later, Elena knocked on the pocket door. She was in a white robe with her short wet hair in a towel. "Thanks for my coffee," she said, taking a sip.

"Sleep well?" he asked.

"No. Not really. I missed my dogs."

"They're probably getting a Swedish massage right now."

She smiled. "How'd you sleep?"

"Too much on my mind about today."

"Still feel good about our plan?" she asked.

"As good as I can. Kidnapping an executive in the middle of a major city usually gives me a little heartburn."

"And you think that's the only way we'll get him to talk?"

"Remember, I'd rather not go down this path. But, yes, that's the only way I think he'll talk. He has to fear for his life. And since we have proof—even though it's negligible—of what he's done, I don't think he'll be too keen to report us afterward."

"Do you think he'll warn Nastya and Georgy?"

Gage chewed on his bottom lip for a moment. "We have to scare him so badly that he won't."

"I'll leave that part to you." She motioned to the bathroom. "I'm done in the shower."

"Do you need to dry your hair?"

"You're learning. But I'll do it later. And now it's so short that it doesn't take long."

"You hungry? They have breakfast downstairs."

"I'll eat later."

Gage grabbed his bag and made his way into the cramped confines of the bathroom. After brushing his teeth and a quick shave, he eased into the cramped confines of the small shower, loosening the adjustable showerhead and moving it all the way up. He made the water cool and set about shampooing his hair and cleaning his body.

Today would be critical. Nabbing a banker in Zürich's financial district had to be among the craziest things he'd ever pondered. While it might not hold much water with the local authorities, if he got caught, he'd simply tell the truth. What else could he do? The police would learn about the attempts on Elena's life. While her situation might soften the blow somewhat, Gage couldn't imagine a Swiss judge being too lenient with him. Vigilantes are frowned upon in nearly every culture. And the peace-loving Swiss would probably have as little understanding for Gage's current mission as any society on earth.

With closed eyes, Gage faced up into the stream of cool water. Suddenly, the water temperature warmed. He stepped back, clearing his wet eyes as he glanced around. The shower door was cracked open and Gage heard the bathroom door click. He leaned out of the shower, seeing no one.

Gage looked at the single shower handle, finding it over to the right. He'd clearly positioned it almost all the way to the left.

What the hell?

"Elena?" he called out.

"Yes?" she replied, her voice distant.

"You okay?"

"Yes. I'm fine. Why?"

"Just wondering."

There was a brief pause before she said, "I'm starting to get an appetite."

Gage's mind raced. "Okay...be right out."

He shifted the handle all the way to the left—full cold. He wiggled the handle, feeling its easy movement, wondering if he'd accidentally bumped the lever.

That had to be it.

Right?

***

Far to the south of Gage and Elena, the Assassin had spent the night in Genoa, with a good eight kilometers between him and the men he'd killed.

He removed the coffee pot from the Braun drip machine and poured himself a cup. The coffee was good and strong, indicating that the grounds he'd found in the sealed container on the counter were fresh. Wearing Sal Unilla's light robe, the Assassin surveyed the neat Italian home, concluding that the Unillas preferred Ikea and Muji. He went through the stack of open bills on the counter, also deducing that the Unillas were largely debt-free and almost certainly wouldn't be home before their trip itinerary called for.

Last night, after the Assassin had jogged out of the Genoa metro area, he'd exited the drainage pipe and walked west for a short distance. His first acquisition was a leash, which he stole from an attached carport at one of the first homes he'd come across. The leash was hung on a nail beside the carport door, along with a collar. He then carried the leash with him, whistling occasionally and calling out for "Pio-Pio", his *missing* dog. Doing so provided the Assassin with the perfect excuse to scrutinize driveways and front porches.

On his third street, the Assassin found what he was looking for: a stack of newspapers in the slot under the mailbox. After casually surveying the home, he had pronounced it empty and easily picked the two locks on the rear door. There was no evidence of an alarm—an unneeded item in most of Europe. Many of the interior and exterior lights were on, operated by the astronomic timer in the coat closet. Once he'd cleared the home, the Assassin exited the back door and concealed himself behind a small shed bounding the rear fence. After an hour, the police had not come. The Assassin felt confident there was no hidden alarm.

Back inside, the Assassin found the itinerary in the Unillas' small home office. The Unillas had traveled by air to the Croatian coast and weren't due back for three more days. A quick survey of the photographs in the home revealed the Unillas to be childless and probably in their mid-thirties. The wife was considerably more attractive than the husband, making the Assassin briefly wonder what it was the man had going for him. Using his burner phone and a prepaid calling card, the Assassin dialed the Unillas' Croatian resort and asked to speak with Salvatore Unilla. The polite resort worker asked him to wait and a short time later informed him that there was no answer in the Unillas' suite.

"That's fine," the Assassin replied in English. "I can call tomorrow morning if they'll still be there."

"Oh, yes. They're here till Sunday."

"Excellent. I will call tomorrow. Thank you."

After confirming the Unillas weren't coming home soon, the Assassin felt safe enough to take a long, soothing shower. Afterward, he used several of the Unillas' lotions and toiletries, making certain he replaced each of the items in its proper place. Once clean and comfortable, he ate a varied meal of cheeses, crackers and two energy bars, leaving five more in the large box.

Again, his goal was to consume items the resident family wouldn't know were missing. The Assassin then slept on the sofa for eight hours and awoke feeling quite refreshed. The Unillas' Ikea sofa was surprisingly comfortable.

Today, the sun was already high overhead and the birds were singing. The Assassin slid the back door open and felt the positive energy of European summertime as he took a great breath of the sweet-smelling air. After making sure the neighbors couldn't see him, he took his coffee outside, feeling the familiar aching in his balls that had tormented him since the age of 13. He thought back to the young hotelier in Sicily—the last woman he'd had significant contact with. The Assassin pondered her purple hair and piercings—such a rebel—she would have probably been a helluva lay, open to fresh ideas and new sensations. He'd done his best not to be insulted by the rape talk. The Assassin would never rape someone. In fact, since he'd had a bit of time, he might have come on to her had she not killed the mood with her mention of rape. Pity.

He shook the thoughts away. Now that he was on the mainland, there was no time for sex. Ending Elena Volkov's life would give him a license to live as he pleased for the rest of his days. He had a lifetime of leisure in front of him. He could afford to be horny for a few more weeks.

After his coffee, the Assassin would need to heavily alter his appearance while he pondered his next move. He checked his watch—he couldn't leave yet.

As he enjoyed his second cup of the dark coffee, the Assassin switched on the PTV news. He turned on the closed captioning and switched the language to English while he waited for the top-of-the-hour report. There it was, the very first story, involving two murders near the Port of Genoa. While the details were sketchy, the reporter indicated that a source with the police felt the murders were related. According to an official statement from the police, there was no threat to the general public—that made the Assassin smile. The reporter said the authorities believed the killings to be related to organized crime. However, the names of the deceased had not yet been released to the public.

"The police are searching for a man who is approximately two meters tall, with brown hair, blue eyes and a neatly-trimmed beard." An artist's rendering appeared on the screen. It looked quite similar to the Assassin. The reporter continued. "Here is the police rendering of the person of interest. He was last seen around the port wearing a light blue shirt and tan slacks." The camera cut back to the reporter. "Anyone in the viewing area having seen a stranger of this description should please call the number on your screen."

Leaning backward, the Assassin shut his eyes and massaged the bridge of his nose. If the organized crime connection to the deceased were true, he wasn't very concerned. In fact, that would probably send investigators in a completely different direction. More concerning was the description and sketch—not to mention the overarching question of where was Elena Volkov and her protector?

The Assassin walked to the nearest mirror and eyed himself. The beard had to go. He ran his hands through his hair, pushing the hair the opposite way and squinting, imagining. He walked into the Unilla's office, finding a worn Atlas on the bookshelf. The Assassin opened the map to Western Europe and eyed it carefully. Sicily to Genoa was north by northwest. He rested his index finger on his current location.

Why Genoa? Why did they come here? Why not Tunis? Of all the Palermo destinations, Tunis seemed to be the most sensible departure from all of Elena's troubles in Europe. While Tunisia was rather advanced, it would have provided a gateway to the largely anonymous African continent.

The question hounded him: why did they choose Genoa? Why?

After retrieving his bag, the Assassin connected his phone to his computer, connecting to the local wireless network. He first tested the masking system before he dialed a number. There was no answer. The Assassin cursed and redialed the number. This time Georgy Zaytsev answered.

"I told you to keep the phone with you," the Assassin said, listening as his software spoke the translation to Georgy.

"I was pissing," Georgy answered. "What's going on? Were you...successful?"

"How did you hire the American assassin?"

"Where are you? Is it done?"

"I'm close and I don't have time to chat. How did you hire the American assassin?"

"Through a third party."

"What third party?"

"A trusted advisor."

"I need to know who."

"He's a banker."

"A banker. You used a banker?"

"He's not just any banker. He does all sorts of things," Georgy replied.

"Where is this banker?"

"Are you going to hurt him?"

"Don't be ridiculous. Tell me now."

"Zürich."

The Assassin's index finger dropped like an executioner's blade on Switzerland's largest city.

That's it. That's where they're going. Gage Hartline, smart bastard, interrogated the incompetent American killer and learned that a Swiss banker had put out the hit on Elena. And now Gage and Elena were headed to Zürich. Sonofabitch.

"Are you there?" Georgy asked.

"Which bank?"

They spoke for another minute. The Assassin hung up and disconnected his equipment.

A Russian banker in Zürich hired the American. And rather than run away, Elena Volkov was facing her problem—going after the banker. The Assassin admired her guts.

After finishing his coffee and having a handmade cigarette on the back patio, the Assassin pilfered a few items from the rear of the Unillas' closet. He chose clothes he didn't think would be missed and laid them on the bed.

Next, in the bathroom, he took a photo of his face with his iPad. Afterward, he shaved his beard and used peroxide to add a great deal of white-blond to his hair. He used lemon juice from the refrigerator to remove the peroxide smell. The Assassin then showered and donned Sal Unilla's clothing, including a shimmering black button down and off-white slacks that were only a half-size too large. From his own pack, the Assassin retrieved his thick black frame eyeglasses, reminiscent of the glasses that were popular in the 60s and now worn by fashionable artsy types. The glasses were fitted with non-prescription optical lenses.

The Assassin typically parted his hair from the side and swept it backward. He'd found hair gel in Sal Unilla's toiletries and once his hair was dry he used the gel to provide spiky volume to his newly-colored locks. His look complete, the Assassin held the iPad selfie next to his face, eyeing himself in the mirror.

Perfect. He was a new man.

Twenty minutes later, the Assassin concealed his backpack inside a larger black bag he found in the Unillas' attic. The bag had a shoulder strap and would do fine to conceal his own bag until he was clear of Italy. After returning the Unilla home to its original state, the Assassin left the way he'd come, absolutely certain the Unillas would never have a clue he'd even been there.

Without a shred of fear of being questioned, the Assassin walked to the nearest bus stop, paying two euro to ride back to the center of Genoa, only a kilometer from where he'd killed two men ten hours before. A short time later, the Assassin was on a Eurocity train headed north. The journey would take six hours and ten minutes, the only major stop being Milan. The Assassin settled into his first-class seat, watching the Piedmont region of Italy slide by. He checked his watch, content that he would be at Zürich's Hauptbahnhof with more than five hours of daylight remaining. Who knew, perhaps he might catch a break and get to Elena Volkov and her protector before they moved on?

He charged his computer and phone and put on his headset to make a quiet call to a man in Geneva that he'd used many times before. The man was older and discreet and specialized in weaponry. What the man didn't have in selection, he always made up for in concierge-like service. After quietly discussing what the Assassin would buy, with no quibbling over the price, the seller agreed to drive the items to Zürich and have them waiting in inconspicuous packaging. As soon as the Assassin secured a rental car, he'd meet the man and pay him for the weaponry. Once that was agreed upon, the Assassin powered down his devices and made the conscious decision to relax.

He viewed the people in the railcar, seeing no one of note until he turned to his left. Across the aisle, an attractive woman in her forties caught his eye. She was quite petite and appeared to be traveling on business. Judging by her conservative clothing, the Assassin guessed her to be a lawyer or accountant. She smiled before looking away. He continued to eye her.

She finally turned back to him, dipping her chin as she tasted him with her eyes.

And there were still six hours left on this mundane journey, six hours with nothing to do.

Ah, liberty.

***

It was a few minutes after 4 P.M. in Zürich. Gage and Elena were parked near the corner of Gotthard and Genferstrasse. The light rain had grown heavier, obscuring visibility and making Gage worry that they wouldn't be able to identify their man. She had left the car running with the air conditioner on so the windows wouldn't fog over. Three times Elena had pushed in the car's lighter and lifted an unlit cigarette to her mouth. Three times Gage had cleared his throat and shaken his head.

"You're killing me," she mumbled.

"No. Those cigarettes are killing you."

The rain intensified.

"You have your iPad?" he asked.

"Yes."

"Can I see those paintings?"

"No."

"Why not?"

"No."

"And you do them under a…what do you call it…a pen name?"

"Yes. But I'm not showing you."

"You said that. How much do they sell for?"

"Doesn't matter. You're sure he'll exit through the front?" she asked.

"Nice change of subject."

"Answer me."

Gage eyed the color print of the banker. They'd visited a copy shop earlier, printing the photo from the bank's website. There were four senior executives at the boutique Russian bank, and this one was the only Russian expat. According to his biography, he specialized in wealth management specifically for Russians.

"Yeah, he'll exit this way," Gage replied. "No one used the back door at lunch."

"What if he's with someone?"

"Then we follow till he's alone."

While they waited, Gage used one of the new prepaid phones, impressed at how good the browsers had become on cheap devices like this one. He scanned the English language mobile page of La Sicilia, checking to see if there was any news about a dead American found stuffed in a drum of dry sweep. He'd just been moving his finger to the "X" at the corner of the page when one of the headlines on the sidebar caught his attention.

```
Belpasso Teen Dead in Scooter Crash
```

Gage touched the headline and read the brief story. According to the rote report, Paulo Christopher Almano, 18, perished after losing control of his scooter and running off the road near the end of his own street. The medical examiner said he died of blunt force trauma. An autopsy was pending but the results wouldn't be available for several weeks.

Rubbing his eyes in frustration and sadness, Gage briefly struggled over whether or not to show it to Elena. After a moment he handed Elena the phone and told her to brace herself.

She took the phone and, after only a few seconds, gasped as her hand covered her mouth.

"Paulo!" she cried. "No...no...no. That sweet boy."

Gage allowed her to vent for a moment before he said he was sorry.

Elena handed Gage the phone and used a tissue to wipe her tears. Afterward, she gripped the steering wheel with both hands as her sorrow turned to anger. "I hated that scooter. In the brief time I was there, I'd see him zooming up and down the street. He drove too damned fast."

"Elena..."

She turned to him.

"Elena, I doubt Paulo wrecked his scooter."

"What?"

Gage stared at her.

"What're you saying?"

"You know what I'm saying."

"That he was killed? Is that it?" she asked, her voice rising.

"Try to stay calm. I can't be sure, but the timing is far too coincidental in my book."

"Why would someone kill him?"

"They came looking for you and figured out that he knew you."

"But why kill him?"

"Whoever did it made it look like an accident. They don't want us to know they're onto us."

"Are they onto us?" she asked.

"Not that I've seen," he said, slowly scrutinizing the area around the car. "But this demonstrates why we have to remain ultra-vigilant."

"I can't believe he's dead."

"I'm sorry."

Elena stared at the bank again. They were both quiet for a while.

Over the next fifteen minutes, several other people exited the bank, many of them carrying briefcases and umbrellas. None were the banker in question.

"You okay?" Gage asked.

"Yeah," she breathed. "I'm sad but I know I need to focus on what we're doing."

"We're okay, right now," he replied.

Earlier, after a great deal of searching, Gage had stolen license plates from a car parked at a grocery store. It was the exact same car, down to the year and color. He'd tossed the rental plates into the bottom of a dumpster. Hopefully, if the Swiss captured any of what they planned to do on traffic cameras, they'd spend their first day on a wild goose chase.

Gage's first burner phone rang. He stared at it. To his knowledge, only one person had the number. He answered it.

"This is your friend in Genoa." It was Giuseppe, Colonel Hunter's friend, who had sold Gage the weapons and arranged port surveillance.

"Did you get something?" Gage asked.

"Yes. And both of my men are dead because of it."

"What?"

"Dead. Killed last night."

Gage straightened. "And the one they were looking for?"

"Gone. No sign of him. But his description is all over the news."

Gage listened as Giuseppe gave a detailed description of the alleged killer. Then Gage said, "Your people wouldn't have known where we were headed."

"Of course not. Nor do I."

"I'm sorry. I didn't think something like that would happen."

"It's not your fault. But I thought you should know."

Gage rubbed his forehead. "What can I do?"

"When you kill him, make him suffer. Or, better yet, bring him to me."

"Deal. Is there anything else?"

"If I learn more I'll let you know. As you might imagine, we're searching for him, too. Good luck." Giuseppe hung up.

Sonofabitch! What sort of Charles Manson did they hire? First the kid, now two Mafiosos?

"What was that?" Elena asked. "What happened?"

"I'll tell you later." He used a second phone to call the Sicilian hotelier's daughter. The call went to voicemail. "Shit." Despite his better judgment, he left her a message, warning her that someone very dangerous might come snooping around. Gage knew the killer had probably already been there, since he'd found his way to Genoa. Gage jabbed the end button on the burner phone and shifted irritably.

"What's wrong?" Elena asked. "Why did you say you were sorry on that call a minute ago?"

At that moment, the bank door opened and Peter Karlerenko exited, his bald head glistening in the rain. Behind him, a guard waved and said something before closing the door.

"Isn't that him?" Elena asked.

"Yes."

Elena pushed in the clutch and found first gear.

"Not yet," Gage said.

Frowning, the small Russian banker looked to the sky and immediately tucked his eyeglasses into his overcoat. He opened his umbrella and hurried through the front gate. After crossing the street, he walked east on the sidewalk, directly past Gage and Elena.

"You ready?" Gage asked.

"Was that Giuseppe on the phone? What happened?"

"Tell you later. Remember, follow me at a distance. When I take the banker down, pull up and stop right next to us. We'll get in the back."

"Okay."

He looked at Elena. "Are you sure about this? Once we do it, we're on the wrong side of the law."

"We have a very good reason. Yes, I'm sure."

"Elena…we could both go to jail."

"Then let's not get caught."

After a deep breath, Gage exited the car, taking up station behind the petite Russian as he hurried east.

There was no telling how far the man was going, so Gage preferred not to waste time. The banker could be headed to a bus stop, looking for a taxi or hurrying to his own car. Thankfully, the rain provided excellent cover sound for Gage to close the gap. The rain also had cut down on sidewalk traffic. In fact, no one else was nearby.

Gage was ten feet behind the banker now. Glancing backward, he decided to wait a bit longer. Several cars were passing. He held out his hand to Elena, just so she'd know he was waiting. They approached an intersection and the Russian had yet to turn around.

At the intersection, Karlerenko turned right on Tödistrasse. Gage sped up.

There were no cars passing, no pedestrians nearby. This was it. Now or never. Gage closed to within five meters of the slight man.

Up ahead, a car turned right to head Gage's way but had to stop at a traffic signal. It was still 200 meters away and Gage didn't think the driver would get a clear view.

Gage scanned the area, seeing no one else. He lurched into action. After quietly closing the small gap, he gave one good swipe from his right foot. The swipe tripped the Russian, sending him sprawling. A few papers slid from the man's open-top briefcase.

Cursing, the Russian turned to get up and was met by a crushing right to his chin, flattening him. The Volvo scrubbed to a wet stop beside the curb and Gage hoisted the little man into the backseat. Gage went back for the soaked briefcase, tossing it inside along with the papers. Just as Gage was getting in the car, the Russian began to scream.

After pulling the door shut, Gage aimed the American assassin's Sig at the Russian's face and told him to shut the hell up and put his head down between his knees. The frightened Russian complied.

Several minutes later, with his head still down, the banker asked a frantic question in Russian. Before Gage could say a word, Elena responded, also in Russian.

The banker lifted his head, his mouth falling open as he eyed Elena. She turned and stared at him. He'd obviously not seen her in the car until now. Gage had no idea what she had said, but whatever it was, along with her presence, scared the little man far more than the nine-millimeter pistol.

He shrieked.

Elena merged onto the Autobahn and, at Gage's urging, obeyed the speed limit as they headed north out of Zürich.

***

The Assassin had been in Zürich for no more than thirty minutes. Upon exiting his train, he'd rented a car at the Hauptbahnhof and driven directly to the rendezvous with his Genevan gun dealer. That meeting was done with Swiss expediency, allowing the Assassin to drive directly to the Russian bank.

As soon as he reached the 8000 block of Gotthardstrasse, where the Ascend Private Bank of Moscow was located, he saw the flashing blue lights reflecting off the rain-soaked buildings a few blocks to the east. The lights unnerved him. He parked his rental Volkswagen in a metered spot near the bank, noting that this area didn't require a *Parkschein* after four in the afternoon— probably due to all of the cushy banks with their early closing hours. While continuing to eye the lights down the street, he touched the call button at the heavy gate of the bank. The man who responded, probably a guard, spoke German with a strong Alsatian accent. He said the bank would reopen tomorrow at 9:30 A.M. The Assassin thanked him and headed east toward the flashing lights.

There, near the intersection, two police cars sat idle. Standing under blue police umbrellas, a few officers spoke to an older woman in civilian clothes. She was speaking animatedly, pointing in several directions and to the very spot where they stood. She seemed distressed and was quite emphatic about whatever point she was making.

The Assassin took a deep breath, wondering if he should do this.

Yes...yes, I should. There's little risk and the chance of coincidence is too damn high.

He walked up to the nearest police officer and spoke in his most neutral German accent. "Excuse me, officer."

"Stand back, sir," the policeman said, using his arm to edge him backward.

"Is this about Peter?"

The policeman, a youngish man with an under-bite and a harsh, heavily-lined face, cocked his eyebrow and walked from under the umbrellas. "Did you see something here, sir?"

"Well, yeah...maybe...if this is about Peter."

"What'd you see?"

"A while ago, when I was on Genferstrasse, right around the corner, I saw my friend Peter running down the sidewalk, headed this way. Did something happen to him?"

"Peter who?"

"I can't remember his last name," the Assassin shrugged. "He's a Russian banker at the bank around the corner. I just know him as an acquaintance from living here in the neighborhood. We'll sometimes say hello over coffee or a beer if we run into one another."

"Stay right here," the policeman commanded. He walked to the other grouping of umbrellas, returning with a middle-aged man in a rain-mottled overcoat. "This is Detective Renner. Please tell him what you just told me."

The Assassin repeated his words without any embellishment. He had no way of knowing if this involved the Russian banker who'd hired the American assassin.

"Describe your friend," the detective said.

The Assassin recalled the banker's description from his Russian employer. "Short. Glasses. Bald. Maybe mid-forties. Not really a remarkable looking man other than his wardrobe."

After nodding at the policeman, the detective asked, "Was there anyone running after your friend?"

"Of course," the Assassin answered smoothly, "but I don't think he was *after* him, per se. It's raining, so I just thought they were both running to catch the bus, you know, like people do when a summer shower arrives." *Damn, I'm good.*

The detective took a step closer. "Wait. Do you know the man behind him?"

"Yes," the Assassin answered, puzzled, acting as if he'd missed something.

"Who was he?"

"Peter's boyfriend," the Assassin lied. In the event Peter had been snatched by Gage Hartline, the police were the last people the Assassin wanted finding him and Elena.

Now it was the detective who appeared confused. "Boyfriend?"

"Yes."

"Are you certain?"

"Quite. I see them together often. I feel like I missed something. Is Peter okay?"

"His boyfriend?" the detective repeated, clearly puzzled.

"Yes, officer. Peter is gay."

After taking a few steps away, the detective and the policeman conferred in low voices.

While they deliberated, the Assassin could hear the testimony of the frightened female witness. He overheard her saying something about a white Volvo sedan. She said the big man punched the little one and threw him in the backseat. After the smaller man was thrown in, the bigger man jumped in the back with him and the car made a U-turn and headed north.

The detective and the policeman came back to the Assassin. "Your testimony is appreciated, but I have another witness giving me a much different tale."

"What's she saying?"

After only a few seconds of what looked like indecision, the detective said, "She told me that a small bald man in a suit was being pursued by a bigger man down Gotthardstrasse. The small man fell here," he said, pointing, "and the big man hit him, then picked him up and tossed him inside the backseat of a car. They said the small man was yelling in protest from the backseat."

It was all the Assassin could do not to react. As a cover for his emotions, he forced himself to laugh. His laugh was a knowing chuckle, the type a person uses when a situation has been blown out of proportion.

"What's so funny, sir?" the detective asked, hands on his hips.

Leaning close, the Assassin said, "Peter and his boyfriend are into…different activities. I see them out sometimes. They and their *friends* enjoy the…you know…spicier side of things. When I saw him running from his boyfriend, he was clearly laughing."

The detective was pissed. "Are you sure?"

"It's summertime, detective. The weather is hot. Peter just got off from a long day of work." The Assassin turned his palms skyward. "There's a cool summer shower and a whole evening ahead…you can put it all together."

"But what about the car? Being thrown in the backseat while yelling?"

"Probably just carousing with friends. I've seen them do far more extreme things."

"And you're sure the man's name is Peter?"

"Yes, sir. From the Ascend Private Bank of Moscow," the Assassin replied. He thought about this Gage Hartline, about his actions thus far. The man knew what he was doing. Certainly he knew if he were to take down a prominent banker in the middle of Zürich that there would be witnesses. He'd account for that, wouldn't he?

Think, damn it…think! Hartline is smart. Very smart.

"You should call him," the Assassin casually added, taking the calculated risk.

"Call Peter?" the detective asked.

"Sure."

"Do you have his number?"

"No, but it shouldn't be hard to get. Everyone has a handy." The Assassin had to struggle not to hold his breath.

The detective walked to the other officers, telling them what he'd just heard. Then the detective called dispatch on his radio. He requested they call the bank to get Peter's mobile phone number.

The Assassin stood there on the sidewalk, trying to appear pleasant while his mind raced and his pulse redlined. *Please, Hartline, you prick—please do what I think you'll do.*

***

A moment before, the Russian banker's cell phone had rung five times. When it stopped ringing, Gage had the banker reach into his jacket and get the phone. Knowing they could be tracked by the signal, Gage had powered the phone down and considered destroying it since the battery couldn't be removed. As they continued north, away from the city, Gage pondered the kidnapping. A takedown of a prominent banker in the middle of the city was almost certainly an invitation to a manhunt. There had to be witnesses. He turned and pressed the pistol painfully into the Russian's side.

"Do you want to make it out of this alive?"

"You know I do," the Russian cried.

"I'm going to turn your phone back on. When the cops call you, or your bank, or anyone checking on you—you'll speak to them in German and tell them you're fine, you got that?"

"Y-y-yes."

"If you pull anything cute I will shoot you here and now and dump you on the side of the road, understand?"

"Do you promise to let me go?"

"If you comply with me…yes."

"I don't believe you."

"I don't give a shit!" Gage answered, jabbing the handgun against his ribs. "I'm all you've got."

"But what do I say if they ask me about being thrown into the car?"

"Just tell them you fell and hit your shin because of the rain and that's why you were yelling. Don't tell them too much. Just laugh it off."

"I'll do it, I swear. But only if you let me go."

"When we're done chatting."

"You're not who we're after," Elena turned and said. "But you still make me sick."

Gage powered the phone back on.

***

The Assassin watched the scene, his mind running scenarios of what might happen if Gage and Elena were to get picked up for kidnapping. Given her money and resources, she'd probably manage to get released in a day or two. Hartline would take the fall and she'd once again find herself in a vulnerable position.

But the Assassin felt it was far too risky. What if she didn't make bail? What if she remained confined until after the deadline? Or, what if she spilled her guts about the attempts on her life? No, the Assassin felt what he'd done had been best, and he was gambling that Hartline would threaten the banker into pushing the police away.

"He's not answering," the detective said, wagging his phone. "It rang at first and I got voicemail. Now, the phone's picking right up. It must be turned off."

A polizei lieutenant had arrived by this time. Violence in Zürich, especially in this wealthy area, was extremely uncommon and not the type of thing the local government or business leaders would stand for. "Try it once more," he breathed to the detective.

The detective complied. "Ringing," he said loudly. "Yes, hello. This is Detective Hans Renner with the Stadtpolizei Zürich. To whom am I speaking?" He listened for a moment before nodding at the lieutenant.

The detective's elocution was slow and clear. "Might you prove your identity by telling me your occupation, your date of birth, and your current address?" The detective stared at the lieutenant's iPad as he listened to the testimony of the alleged victim.

"Very good. Now, please tell me the middle name of your business partner whose first name is Peter." The detective listened, then smiled and nodded. "Excellent, Herr Karlerenko. We're just down the street from your office due to a report that you might have been attacked."

The detective listened for a moment, his eyebrows arching. "So, you were *not* attacked?" Looked at the lieutenant and shook his head. "We received a report that someone of your description was attacked just east of your bank. Were you running west on Gotthardstrasse approximately thirty minutes ago? You were? Yes, sir...the testimony of a local resident was that you were attacked near the intersection and thrown into the back of a car while yelling."

The detective listened intently. He smiled again before putting a finger to his throat and dragging it across.

The Assassin read that as a signal to shut down the small investigation.

The detective mouthed to his lieutenant, "*Er war es. Ihm gut.*" It meant, "It was him. He's just fine."

After a few more questions for full corroboration, the detective hung up the phone. The Assassin overheard him talking to the lieutenant.

"It was him. He didn't go into the boyfriend angle, I guess for obvious reasons. But he admitted to running west down Gotthardstrasse in the rain. Claims he was yelling because he hit his shin as he was falling into his *friend's* car."

The lieutenant rubbed his chin, motioning to the streetlights. "I could call city traffic control and get the video pulled from this intersection."

"I don't think it's necessary, sir. He sounded incredibly relaxed. The woman is just confused about what she saw. I've seen people horsing around before that I thought were being serious."

Five minutes later, despite the female witness's insistence over what she'd seen, the policemen wrapped up the incident as a misunderstanding. The Assassin was thanked for his testimony and was never even questioned about who he was or where he lived.

It was Zürich, after all. The great majority of the crime here was performed with quiet keystrokes and flourishing signatures from Mont Blanc pens.

The policemen departed the scene and the neighborhood quickly subsided to its customary quiet affluence.

The Assassin walked back to his car, his phone pressed to his ear as he called Gerard at Interpol. He considered asking Gerard to ping Peter Karlerenko's phone but thought better of it. Now that the cops had been called off, Hartline would either power the phone down or dump it. No…the Assassin would go after the car. Gerard didn't answer. *Dammit!* The Assassin hung up and called him two more times in a row. On the third try, Gerard picked up.

"I was in a meeting," he said without concealing his irritation.

"Fuck your meeting. Listen closely…I'm in Zürich. There's a car that's nearby, a late-model white Volvo sedan. It might be headed north and it probably has three passengers—two men, both in the back seat—and a woman. Can you find them?"

Gerard exhaled into the phone. "Do you know how big a deal it is for me to do a traffic camera sweep in Switzerland? Do you have a license plate number?"

"No."

"We'll have to take over their entire system and then I'll have to have a dozen technicians manually comb video. I'll need all sorts of authority to do this. What time period?"

"They've been on the run for less than an hour. I can tell you exactly where the car started from."

"That helps, but it's still a big deal."

Rolling his eyes, the Assassin asked, "How much?"

"I'll have to pay off a number of people."

"I don't have time for your obvious negotiation tactics."

There was a pause. "Thirty-thousand. Maybe fifty."

"You skipped forty."

"Because I may have to bribe the captain."

"I'll pay ten for trying. And the balance if you steer me to them."

"But I can't even make the pay-offs with ten."

The Assassin was silent.

"Twenty. And twenty more when I find them."

"Fine. It's done. Call me when you find the Volvo and talk me in."

"Move the money now."

"I will. And you better produce," the Assassin warned.

"Keep this phone on."

The Assassin entered the Volkswagen and performed a U-turn, heading back to the west before turning north and driving slowly. As the Assassin merged onto A1, the hairs on the back of his neck stood on end as he was struck with the powerful sense that he was getting close to the Ukrainian oil princess.

Chapter Eleven

THE RUSSIAN banker was quiet and relatively calm as Elena searched for someplace remote. They'd driven north out of Zürich, past the Flughafen and eventually across the border into the south of Germany. She drove through the small town of Jestetten, located where the border of Germany acts as a jutting fingerlike promontory into Switzerland. Here, where the Rhine snakes its passage through its eponymous valley, dense forests bounded the river. The gray sky hung ominous and low as heavier showers threatened. For now, no rain fell. Just past Jestetten, Elena steered the Volvo into the thick forest at a pine needle-covered trail. She halted at the large warning sign hanging from a length of chain that blocked the trail.

"Unclip the chain," Gage said from the back seat.

"Are you sure?"

"It's fine," Gage said. "The Germans aren't used to rule breakers, so they'll assume we have authorization to drive in the forest. Just unclip it and drive forward at a slow speed."

Once she'd done as Gage suggested, they motored down a slight decline that went on for about a kilometer. They stopped at the lowest point of the forest path. As soon as the engine was switched off, the sound of trickling water could be heard.

The forest was deep and thick, with little undergrowth due to the thick carpet of pine needles. Precious little sunlight infiltrated the thick canopy of trees. Other than the chirping of birds, the forest was hushed, made even quieter by the dampness of a recent rainfall. Any other time, Gage would have loved to have spent a few hours in this forest, reading and enjoying the peace and quiet.

He exited the back seat, motioning the Russian out with the Sig. Gage spoke German to him, telling him to kneel in front of the car and lace his hands over his head.

When the banker complied, Gage said, "I'm going to ask some questions. Despite what you did earlier, with the cops, I just want you to know if you try to mislead me, this is going to end badly. Understand?"

The shuddering banker nodded.

"And, to test you, I'm going to throw in some random questions I already know the answer to." Gage cocked the hammer. "Lie to me one time and I'm taking out that right knee...for starters." The Russian banker began to cry.

***

Through the use of Swiss and German traffic cameras, Gerard guided the Assassin to within three kilometers of Jestetten. At that point, with Jestetten being in such a rural area, the trail had gone cold due to a lack of traffic cameras. The Assassin was on the side of the road awaiting further instruction when the ringtone pierced the silence of the car. He answered his phone on the first ring.

"You should drop to your knees and thank God for knowing me," Gerard said.

"Why?"

"Because I just saw something better than anything you'll ever find on a traffic camera."

"And that is?"

"I still can't believe it. I'm staring at it right now."

"Dammit...what?"

"Our good friends, the Germans, have an unrelated manhunt going. A womanhunt, actually—some federalist, fem-bot wackjob who sliced off a local politician's ear."

"What the hell does this have to do with anything?"

"They've thrown all assets into her capture and made us privy to a number of satellite images. One of those images was just taken, literally five minutes ago, from 35,000 kilometers above us and broadcast, right here, to our dingy little building. I grabbed it and zoomed in and..."

Gerard explained.

After jamming the Volkswagen in gear, the Assassin fishtailed onto the two-lane road and roared to the north.

***

The interrogation of the Russian banker continued.

"You know who this woman is?" Gage asked as Elena coolly lit a cigarette.

"Of course," the Russian blubbered.

"And you ordered a hit on her, you piece of shit. A *murder.*"

"No."

"Yes," Gage countered.

"I didn't *order* the hit—I was only following orders…passing a message."

Gage eyed Elena and nodded. So, it *was* him. They had the right man.

"Peter Karlerenko, you called the failed American assassin from multiple hotels, thinking you were being slick by using their phones instead of your own. But you were too lazy to walk more than a kilometer away from your office. That's how we found you."

"I didn't know her before," he cried, turning his head to Elena. "Now that I look at her, now that I see she's a real person, what I did makes me sick. But, they'd have killed me if I hadn't done it."

"I don't give a shit about your justifications," Gage said.

"Before…it didn't seem real. Now, it does."

Gage paused a moment. "Well, Elena and I now have a decision to make."

"What decision?"

Gage made his smile thin and cruel. "We can't decide whether to turn you in—we've plenty of evidence, including a confession from the American you hired—or to just kill you here and be done with it."

"You told me you wouldn't kill me!"

"I said I wouldn't kill you…*if* you comply."

"But I helped you with the polizei, and now I'm going to do anything you say."

"Assuming you do that," Gage said, "are you going to report us when we let you go?"

"No!"

"I'd expect you to say that now."

"I swear…please…why would I report you when it implicates me in a murder-for-hire scheme?"

Gage stepped closer, aiming the Sig at the top of the banker's head. "Because you're obviously loyal to your clients, and if you're willing to arrange murders for them…"

"No! Please! Please don't kill me!" The banker removed his hands from his head, gesticulating as he pleaded.

Elena dragged on her cigarette as she watched the scene. Gage walked over and leaned close to her, whispering. "You think he's ready to talk?"

"I think so," she replied, pointing her cigarette to the puddle of liquid on the trail between his feet.

"Ugh. That's a sign of weakness. Saw a guy do that in SERE school and they booted him on the spot."

"I can't help it," Peter blubbered, staring down at his own urine.

"Okay, Peter…here's your test," Gage said, walking back in front of the banker. "I may or may not already know the answer to this question so, if you lie, you're playing true *Russian* roulette with your life."

"I—will—not—lie!"

"Who were you arranging the murders for?"

Hands on his head, the banker dipped his chin to his chest. "I did it for her sister and brother-in-law: Nastya and Georgy Zaytsev."

"Step-sister," Elena corrected as she flicked her cigarette away.

"And they have hundreds of millions invested with you?" Elena asked, crossing her arms.

The Russian banker shook his head. "Not nearly as much as they once did. They spend much more than they make." He took a steadying breath. "They told me, if I were to help them with this, that they would invest over a billion dollars with me."

"And all you had to do was have someone killed," Gage said.

"They told me she'd die anyway, so why shouldn't I get the investment?"

"Yeah, that makes it all better," Gage mused.

"I'm sorry," the banker cried.

"Sorry *now*," Gage replied. "Everyone's sorry when they get caught."

"Okay, enough of this," Elena said. "Let's end it."

"Please don't kill me," the banker whispered.

"You mind?" Elena asked Gage.

"He's all yours."

Elena leaned forward, face-to-face with Peter. "Are you listening?"

"Yes."

"Peter, if you answer this truthfully, you're a free man."

"Ask me anything."

"Where are Nastya and Georgy hiding?"

"This's all you want to know?" Peter asked, face brightening.

"Yes. And provided you tell the truth, and never breathe a word of any of this," Gage said, "then you'll live a long and healthy life."

"Oh...thank you. Thank you. Thank you!"

"Enough talking," Elena said, standing up straight. "Where are they?"

"They're in Odessa."

"Where?"

"On the beach. Georgy rents the same house each year."

Elena looked at Gage and nodded. "I know this house." She turned back to the banker and leaned down again.

"If you say one word about this to—"

Suddenly, in a peculiar sequence of actions, Elena Volkov was off her feet. She'd fallen to her right, onto the side of the pine-needle trail. It looked like she'd been tackled by an invisible person. Peter had been cut off by the jarring physical occurrence and stared wide-eyed at her.

A distant report reached them and already registered with Gage.

"Get over here!" Gage yelled, grabbing Elena and pulling her behind the front wheel of the Volvo. Blood was streaming down her left arm and upper back. She didn't seem to realize what had happened.

Gage had begun to turn back to the banker when he heard a smacking sound that sounded like a thick steak being dropped onto a butcher block. By the time Gage's eyes were all the way around, he saw Peter Karlerenko on his side in the forest roadway, blood and gelatinous brain surrounding his head as he lay lifeless, his eyes wide open.

The second report rang out. This time, Gage got a bead on the shooter's angle.

And he and Elena were down in this depression—like sitting ducks.
Shit!

***

Two hundred meters away, the Assassin lay prone on the carpet of pine needles. He'd been forced to hastily choose this spot after Gerard spotted the Volvo on satellite. While his vantage point was on the high ground, the Assassin realized its positional weakness. He couldn't see Elena or Hartline where they'd hidden behind the car due to the angle of the rise he was perched on. And, dammit, she'd had to make a jerky movement just as he'd applied the necessary pressure to the trigger. A realist, the Assassin certainly didn't think he'd killed her. Based on her movement, and the quick image of blood on her shirt, he felt he'd hit her in the upper chest or shoulder. Though he hoped he'd hit her in the neck, he certainly wasn't counting on it.

So, his hasty choice of firing position had been his first mistake.

The second mistake was not firing again as Hartline dragged her behind the car. There'd been far too much movement for the Assassin to make precise aim, but he certainly could've hit flesh and bone on one of them. But, for whatever reason, the frozen-with-fear banker had been far too tantalizing a target for the Assassin, so he'd simply pivoted ten degrees to the left and ended the blubbering little man's life with a shot through his right ear.

And now Elena and her defender were hiding behind the Volvo. The Assassin hoped they would slink into the car and attempt to drive away. The thin sheet metal and glass of a Volvo would be no match for a close-range .308 with Federal Gold Medal ammunition.

After a moment's deliberation, the Assassin decided against taking out the driver's side tires of the Volvo. Doing so would dissuade what he hoped would happen—them escaping by car. The last thing the Assassin wanted was Hartline to determine the origin of the shots and to creep backward while using the Volvo as cover.

Peering through the scope, the Assassin checked his left and right limits. Yes, sliding backward was the only clear escape for Hartline and Elena. It would lead them down and out of sight. If they went that route, the Assassin's only counter would be to stand up and charge forward.

But that maneuver held great risk for the Assassin—it would expose him. Who knew how Hartline might react?

So, for the moment, he kept a watch through the Volvo's windows, searching for any clue of what might be happening.

***

Gage knew better than to peer over the car. He thought about the angle at which Elena had fallen and he took another look at Peter the banker—he'd fallen at roughly the same angle. Both of those angles were consistent with their inverse, the direction in which Gage had heard the muffled reports. Therefore, he estimated the shots were coming from the Volvo's ten-o'clock position. Elena was now hidden behind the cover of the Volvo's tire.

Gage, on the other hand, was somewhat exposed if the shooter could see beneath the Volvo. Gage peered under the car, seeing a slight rise on the other side of the Volvo, meaning he should be protected at the moment.

Less than five seconds had passed since he'd dragged Elena behind the car. She was nearly flat on the ground, her right hand probing around her left shoulder.

"Stay behind that tire," Gage said.

"I can't believe I got shot," she replied, sounding almost conversational as she said it.

"Let me see that." He pulled her shirt away, finding a diagonal channel wound across the top of Elena's left shoulder. It was bleeding profusely. Whipping open his knife, Gage cut off a strip from the bottom of his own t-shirt. He wadded it long-ways and pressed it onto both ends of the wound. He moved Elena's bra strap over to hold it down.

"You're gonna be okay," he said. "The bullet just grazed you."

"Is it just one shooter?" she asked, surprisingly lucid.

Gage turned her so they were face-to-face. He needed to make sure she didn't go into shock. "Look at me. You okay?"

"I'm pissed I got shot."

"It's just a skin wound. It'll heal." He motioned behind them. "Do you want to get out of here?"

"Of course, I want to get out of here."

"Can you move?"

"Yeah," she answered, testing her left arm.

"You're going to be okay. Stay with me, alright?"

"Gage, it hurts like hell but I'm fine. Just worry about him, not me."
She rubbed her face with her right hand, leaving a smearing of blood. "Tell
me what to do."

It wasn't the first time Gage had seen someone take a gunshot in
stride, but he couldn't help but be impressed. In fact, it almost seemed she
was edgier now—more engaged. It gave him confidence that she could excel
at what he had in mind.

"All right, Elena, listen carefully. You're going to go first and we're
gonna trap that sonofabitch. I want you to start backing away and..."

***

At least ninety seconds had passed—enough time to unnerve the Assassin.
The twosome hadn't even tried to enter the Volvo. He'd have known it by
the excellent view he was afforded with the scope through the front
windshield of the sedan. So, Elena and Hartline were either hiding on the
other side, dealing with her injury—or they'd backed away, using the car as
cover.

Hartline, whoever he was, knew what he was doing. While brazen—
doing things like snatching bankers in Zürich in broad daylight—he'd also
had enough sense to unflinchingly pull Elena to safety, probably before he'd
even heard the supersonic crack of the bullet.

Because of Hartline's good sense, the Assassin was sure they were
backing away with the car between him and them. He removed his phone,
viewing the map of his current location. He was perched at a slight elevation
over the car and forest road. Beyond the road, where they would be slinking
away, the forest continued to drop down to what looked like a creek. The
Assassin switched his map to satellite. There were too many trees for good
detail but he could see the creek in spots. It branched off just to the north.
That would give them multiple avenues of—

What the hell was that?

The Assassin's head jerked up above the scope as he stared at the
Volvo. Someone had just gotten in the car. He clearly saw the overhead light
go on. So, they were either in the car now or had opened the door for some
reason. He couldn't see any heads through the windows but certainly they'd
be smart enough to duck down.

It was all the Assassin could do to fight the urge to start shooting.
Because, while he knew he could turn the car into a veritable tomb, Hartline
would know the same. The Assassin thought about letting loose, anyway.
The .308 rounds might penetrate both sides of the car. Might. But sending a
blanket of lead downrange would completely reveal the Assassin's current
position. What if Hartline had a rifle?

Dammit…how to play this one? Did someone get in the car? Were they crouched down? The Assassin could think of only one way to find out.

Voi vittu!

Leaving everything other than the rifle, the Assassin began to low-crawl forward.

***

Gage had slid behind the rear tire of the Volvo. He eyed the spot where Elena had been, seeing the dots of dark blood. As he prepared the items he'd purchased from Giuseppe in Genoa, he turned his head. She was thirty meters away, inching backward very slowly, feet first. Gage motioned with his hand, altering her direction. She complied, adjusting her angle of retreat. In another minute, she would drop out of sight as the ridge steepened down to the creek.

From there, hopefully she'd do just as she'd been told.

With his items at the ready, Gage gnawed on his lip while he thought about how to initiate contact. Whoever this sonofabitch was, he had a high-powered rifle trained on the car. Gage lifted the telescoping mirror—it was no bigger than the small mirror a dentist uses in a person's mouth—and peered through the windows of the Volvo. He had to take a deep breath and tell himself to relax. Viewing a broad expanse of forest on a tiny mirror, while looking through two car windows, was a tedious task.

Using a method he'd perfected years before, he first did a quick sweep to make sure the shooter wasn't charging the car. Gage felt sure he'd hear him if he did, hence the pistol in Gage's right hand. When the quick scan showed no one, he started at the horizon and worked slowly left to right. There were, of course, hundreds of trees.

Gage was about halfway through the slow scan when he saw him. A section of pine needles seemed to be moving. Though Gage couldn't see many details about the man, he could see the dull shine of grease paint on his face.

While it was difficult to determine distance with the tiny mirror, Gage estimated the man was about halfway between the ridge—where the horizon appeared—and the Volvo. That meant he was approximately 100 meters away.

Still too far.

Gage eyed the man, estimating that he was crawling forward at maybe 10 meters per minute. It wouldn't be long before he was far enough down the hill to get a shot underneath the car. Repositioning himself behind the tire, Gage made sure his two feet and ankles didn't give himself away once the shooter was able to see below the Volvo.

Licking his lips, Gage briefly eyed his small arsenal. He slowly slid the four items in front of him, hopefully putting them out of the shooter's incipient view. Gage wished he'd purchased more of the items he planned to lead with.

But he didn't. He'd just have to deal with what he had.

Palming one of the items, Gage attuned his ears to the area around him. As he awaited his moment, he watched as Elena began to disappear over the lower ridge, beginning the steepest portion of her descent to the creek.

Gage gave her the OK sign. He could tell by her face that she was in great pain, but she returned his signal before urgently gesturing beyond the car.

She was referencing the shooter.

Gage nodded. He knew.

It was nearly time.

***

Something was amiss. The Assassin was now about 30 meters from the Volvo. If he flattened himself completely on the pine needle forest floor, he was able to see a sliver of light beneath the car. He could see the lighter colored forest path and the beginning of the pine needles on the far side of the Volvo. But what he couldn't see were people. And that was a problem. That would indicate one of two things to the Assassin, though he knew other permutations certainly existed.

Either they'd gotten into the car or they'd backed away. He'd definitely seen the car's overhead light turn on and off. But if they'd gotten into the car, why hadn't they stayed low and tried to drive away? It would only make sense. But they hadn't done that, so the Assassin assumed they weren't in the car.

If they'd backed away, why did they wait all that time to go into the car for something? Was there an item in there they needed? Did they have to grab it before they hauled ass? Looking beyond the Volvo, the Assassin could see where, after perhaps fifty meters, the ground dropped away and out of sight, presumably to the creek he'd seen on the map and satellite. If Elena and Hartline had gotten something from the car and slowly backed away, they'd probably be close to that ridge by now, if not already there.

The Assassin briefly eyed the splayed body of the Russian banker. Through the scope, he could see a swarm of first-responder flies were already feasting on the wound.

Two more to go...

Nearly every instinct in the Assassin's finely honed psyche told him to charge the car. If they weren't there, he could subsequently rush to the ridge in safety. Because if they were past the ridge, they would be running by now and, if he didn't go soon, the cause would be lost—at least in the near term.

While his instincts told the Assassin to charge the Volvo, a small receptor in his brain rang an alarm. What if Elena had retreated but Hartline, the snake, had remained in wait? That would mean, if he charged, the Assassin would fall right into Hartline's trap.

It would also mean Hartline was willing to die for her. And that bit of chivalry was going to make the Assassin's task extremely difficult.

He peered under the car again. It was conceivable that one, or both of them, could be hiding behind the tires.

When he'd gone five more meters, it all came clear to the Assassin.

And it was made clear by tangible obfuscation—a literal smokescreen.

First came the blur, then the thud of the canister. Hartline had known to throw the grenade slightly upwind, although the air was barely moving. Within seconds, gray smoke enveloped the area between the Assassin and the car.

He's behind the car—playing the chivalrous bastard. I'm not letting this smoke stop me.

Bolting to his feet, throwing a bit of caution to the wind, the Assassin charged.

***

With more items hanging from his pants and belt, Gage peered through the windows as the heavy smoke wafted in front of the Volvo—providing him with an odor he hadn't smelled in some time. The wind was light but it had shifted slightly, turning toward him. In his hands was an assault rifle Gage had never before fired—in fact, he'd never even seen one before—a Polish Karabinek Tantal in 5.45 caliber. He nestled the folding stock into his right shoulder as he waited for the shooter to burst through the smoke.

As the smoke grenade continued to spew, the shooter didn't appear.

By this point, Gage grew a bit anxious. He checked behind him, making sure the shooter didn't take a circuitous route under the cover of the smoke. When twenty seconds had passed, and still no sign of the shooter, Gage retreated to the ridge. When he arrived at the drop-off, he turned back toward the Volvo and saw the muzzle flash from an area of thinned smoke. Gage immediately felt the slicing of skin on his upper shoulder as he fell to the ground.

He glanced left, seeing his own blood. *Damn!*

Still in control of his faculties, Gage slid forward to a tree and peered down the steep earthen drop to the creek. He spotted Elena. She'd bunched pine needles around her in an effort to not be seen by the shooter but signaled Gage with her hand.

Knowing his rear end and legs might be exposed, Gage reached around the tree with the Tantal and let loose several bursts in the direction of the shooter. Using the cover of the tree, Gage then held a closed fist to Elena—their signal to stop.

Though his mind was occupied with many things—including the gunshot wound to the area where his shoulder met his neck—he found himself briefly transfixed on his employer. She seemed to be smiling. It was an expectant smile, the type he usually associated with adrenaline junkies. He shook his closed fist until she acknowledged with a closed fist of her own.

Reaching down to his side, Gage grabbed his last smoke grenade and pulled the pin. He waited a moment before popping to his knees and hurling it toward the Volvo. As soon as the gray smoke began boiling, Gage cut loose with the Tantal again. In between bursts, he pointed to Elena then pointed to the creek, then made a running motion to the south—away from the shooter and back toward the town of Jestetten.

As she was coming to her feet, Gage repositioned himself, shooting slowly and in earnest in the direction of the shooter.

Though Gage could see little due to the smoke, he knew he'd provided his employer cover to escape.

***

Having realized what Hartline was doing, the Assassin reasoned that Elena Volkov was escaping via the creek. So, when Hartline popped smoke again, the Assassin rushed around the north side of the Volvo and down the steep hill to the creek. Although he'd made a bit of noise, Hartline had been steadily providing cover fire and might not realize the Assassin had changed positions under the cover of the smoke.

As he dropped into the creek bed and saw no sign of Elena Volkov, he knew what had happened. Despite the wind pushing the smoke to the north, the woman had gone south, toward the town. And now her protector, armed with smoke grenades and a rifle, had provided the avenue of escape.

So, as the man called Gage Hartline pranged away with sporadic gunfire, the Assassin leaned back against the bank of the creek, completely protected and obscured by a large Durmast oak. Due to bends in the steeply banked creek, the Assassin wasn't afforded much of a view to the south. He couldn't see anything.

So, he waited. But he might get a clean shot at Hartline, yet.

***

Above the shooter, about 40 meters away, Gage waited, too. He was aiming over a fallen tree, using the trunk as a shooting platform. He'd replaced the

164

magazine on the Tantal, finding the weapon quite nice and easy to shoot. But now he couldn't see the shooter and had no idea which direction he'd gone. Could he have retreated away under cover of the smoke? Or had he dropped down to the creek to the north, using Gage's own smoke as cover?

Regardless, Gage had a defensible position and was unwilling to relent. Sooner or later the man would reveal himself.

***

Leaning back against the uncomfortable roots of the towering tree, the Assassin closed his eyes and willed himself to have patience. Something told him that Hartline was up above, awaiting movement. At some point, the wounded Hartline would give up and move on. He'd have to—because the oil princess was clearly wounded, too. Unfortunately for the Assassin, he had to accept that this encounter might not end with her death. There was still time to complete his mission so, for the moment, his current objective was to live and fight another day.

But, assuming Elena Volkov was still alive after being shot, she and Hartline now knew that a man was close on their tail. This would create an even higher degree of difficulty for the Assassin.

First and foremost, he needed to get the hell out of here so he could continue the chase.

The Assassin began to feel a scraping pain down around his feet. He looked at both of his athletic shoes, seeing the problem. Around his submerged ankles—they'd been scratched by briars earlier—several crayfish had begun to make a meal of his flesh.

Of all days to wear ankle socks.

Gritting his teeth, the Assassin decided to bear out the nuisance. He shook both ankles slightly, dislodging the pests for but a moment. They moved back in with ease, continuing to rip away at his growing wounds.

Fifty million bucks. Just keep thinking about the prize.

The crustaceans' feasting continued…

***

Despite his gut feeling that the Assassin was down in the creek, biding his time, Gage's worry about Elena began to swell. How badly was she bleeding? Despite her earlier lucidity, was she now in shock? Had she managed to get back to Jestetten? By waiting here, was Gage missing crucial seconds that might lead to her death?

He cinched the rifle closer, taking a careful appraisal of the area he believed the Assassin to be in. The Assassin could have moved to the creek using the cover of the smoke. And with all the shooting Gage had been doing, he wouldn't have heard him. Gage scanned the creek. He saw nothing other than what a person might expect to find in a summertime forest.

Nothing, dammit!

Time was up—Gage had to go. He had to take the Volvo and find Elena. Then he had to get help for her wound.

Without looking, Gage appraised his own wound, experienced enough to know—solely by feel—that it was beginning to clot. The bleeding wasn't bad enough to alter Gage's actions.

But Elena's was.

Suddenly, an idea occurred to Gage. In Genoa, at Giuseppe's, Gage had purchased the rifle he currently held, a shotgun, multiple boxes of ammunition, extra magazines, the two smoke grenades and two other items.

Using his left hand, Gage found one of the two other items he'd placed at the ready earlier. He continued to maintain his aim throughout with his right hand. Still no movement...

He chanced a quick look upward, making sure there were no branches that would interfere with the trajectory. The arc looked clear.

Don't overshoot. 40 meters is nothing to sneeze at, but with 7 or 8 meters of elevation, the ballistics change.

One final look—he still could see no evidence that the Assassin was even down there.

Regardless, this would tell the tale.

Gage leaned the Tantal against the log and pulled the pin on the grenade. He came to his knees, making a flat throw and gritting his teeth as the grenade arced to earth.

Go! Go! Go!

The grenade struck the ground on this side of the creek. The throw had been short. But with a nice initial bounce and a generous roll, the unexploded grenade disappeared over the bank.

Then...

A white geyser burst upward, mushrooming out as it climbed. Before the droplets had come back to earth, Gage had slung his pack and was aiming the Tantal at the creek.

As the serenity of the forest returned, Gage debated on whether or not to descend the hill. He knew he was rather close to the small town of Jestetten. He seriously doubted they had a police force, but with all the gunshots, the smoke, and now an explosion, he had no doubt that the nearest polizei were on their way.

Gage made his decision.

Fifteen seconds later, he'd done a half doughnut in the manual Volvo and raced up the trail, headed back toward the main road. He scanned for Elena the entire way.

***

The Assassin didn't reveal himself for two full minutes. If the grenade did one good thing, it relieved him of the crayfish that had ripped at his flesh.

That was the only good the grenade did.

When it had first splashed into the water behind him, the Assassin thought it was another smoke grenade. But there'd been a difference in shape. The smoke grenades looked like a gray canister of shaving cream. This object was more rounded. It had fallen into the creek about 10 meters from where he crouched. Succumbing to years of training, the Assassin dove the other way, also opening his mouth while covering his ears. He did each of these things less than a second before the grenade detonated.

Afterward, he had remained hidden, despite the agonizing pain of his wounds. He'd grasped his rifle from the water, aiming, waiting for Hartline to come down and peer over the bank.

Oh, how the Assassin was going to relish this man's death.

But Hartline didn't show for two full minutes. Knowing he was taking a huge risk, the Assassin had finally breached the tactical situation and peered over the roots of the tree, doing so very slowly.

The Volvo was gone. Because of the extreme ringing in his ears, the Assassin hadn't even heard it.

Still not trusting Hartline, the Assassin had been very careful as he exited the creek. Once he reached the forest trail, he saw the half doughnut of dark earth where Hartline had made a U-turn and sped away.

This was a critical moment. Unless they'd been meticulous about their rally point, it was entirely possible that Hartline hadn't yet found Elena. The Assassin felt she'd escaped in the creek to the south. Hartline was a smart operator, but there were no guarantees that he'd find her quickly. And who knew how badly she was injured? The Assassin might not get another chance like this one.

He reached around to his lower back, wiping his tattered shirt. When he brought his hand back around, it was covered in blood.

Tilting his head back to the heavens, the Assassin slowly came to his decision. He walked to the dead Russian banker, removing his watch and emptying his pockets. The banker had a nearly full pack of Gauloises cigarettes. The Assassin kept these, knowing the taste would pale in comparison to his hand-rolled delights.

But still, a smoke was a smoke and heaven knew he needed one at the moment.

As sirens approached from the southeast, the Assassin trudged west through the forest to where his rental car was parked about a kilometer away, off a perpendicular trail to the one Hartline had departed on. Once there, the Assassin drove slowly away, using his wet shirt to wipe his face.

Once he'd driven a few kilometers, he slid his back left and right against the seat, feeling the slickness of the blood. Without knowing for sure, it felt as if his back was riddled with shrapnel wounds.

He was going to have to do something about this, and soon.

Chapter Twelve

WHEN GAGE had reached the main road, he'd turned left and sped to the bottom of the hill. There, at the road's low point, the creek ran directly into the small town of Jestetten. Gage eased the car off to the right side of the road, peering downstream. He could see where the creek fed into a much larger river at the center of town. The town itself appeared to be exactly what the world thought a small, German valley town would look like. Neat, tidy, narrow streets with lots of exposed wood and a charming bell tower. Any other time, Gage would have loved to spend a few days here. Right now, however, he was fearful for the woman he was trying to protect.

Where was she and, after the blood loss, was she still conscious?

He lurched from the car and crossed the road, dropping down through the high grass toward the concrete culvert that guided the creek into the town. He estimated that he was about one kilometer from where the battle with the other man—the Assassin—had taken place. As Gage neared the creek, he looked over the opposite bank, seeing a number of residents behind their homes. They were staring off into the forest in the direction where the gunfight had taken place. No one took notice of him.

Gage heard the sirens in the distance.

Knowing there wasn't much time, he eyed the length of the creek that headed back into the forest. He didn't see Elena so he continued his descent down to the culvert. As soon as he rounded the concrete abutment he saw her. She was huddled against the radius of the culvert, her head buried in her arms. Gage rushed into the head-high pipe, saying her name. She lifted her head, her face brightening.

"I thought you were dead," she said.

"We've got to haul ass," he said, holding out his hand. "Unless you want to stay and tell the police the truth."

She stood and shook her head. "No. We keep going."

"I want you to be sure. There's a dead banker in that forest. If we run, the police may think we killed him."

"I want to leave." She hissed when she saw Gage's shoulder. "You're bleeding."

"I'm fine." He lifted a finger between them for emphasis. "Know this—if we run, we're criminals. Before, we were simply on the run. Now, if we run, we're going to be wanted for a host of things." He pointed the finger back toward the forest. "Sooner or later, someone in Zürich is going to determine that it was us who snatched that dead banker."

"How?"

"They will," he said with finality. "We can talk about it later. If you want to keep going, we need to leave right now."

"I do."

"Then follow me." The sirens seemed to be farther away than before. Gage assumed the gunshots and explosions were hard to pinpoint, especially when they'd probably been reported by numerous people. Maybe the police were coming into the forest from the other side.

At the end of the culvert, he turned to her. "The car is up on the other side of the road. When we get up there, duck down and wait until I say go. If anyone sees our blood, the game is up."

Beside the road, he stooped down in the high grass. There was a car approaching from the left. Gage motioned her to stay still. He turned, seeing that smile on her face again.

She's enjoying this.

After the older Mercedes had passed, he and Elena crossed the road to the Volvo and headed off to the east, away from the sound of the sirens. Gage turned on the car's air conditioning and, after making sure Elena was okay, he settled in and told her they needed to drive for a while before they stopped. He noticed her shoulder didn't seem to be bleeding very much and the pressure bandage had held nicely under the bra strap.

Elena went into her bag and handed him a scarf. Gage wadded it and pressed it onto the shoulder wound. When he'd viewed it in the mirror, he realized just how lucky he'd been. It wasn't too dissimilar from Elena's shoulder wound. Had the bullet struck him one inch lower, it would have hit bone and Gage wouldn't be driving a car right now.

Several minutes had passed when Elena turned to him. "I know I'm playing this like a game…but it's not a game. And if you want to go and tell the police what happened, I'll understand."

"What do *you* want to do?"

"I want to find Georgy and Nastya. I want to confront them."

Gage had remained on the two-lane, eastbound road. He downshifted as he entered the western edge of the town of Flurlingen. "You want to go to Odessa?"

"Yes."

"Do you know where in Odessa?"

"I know the home he rents."

"You think he'll rent the same one?"

"Yes. Georgy's too stupid to change his habits."

"Does he rent it at the same time each year?"

"No. They stay in dozens of places. Cancun. Miami. Thailand. But, when he's in Odessa, he stays in the same place."

They passed through the small town. Gage accelerated when he saw the town sign with a diagonal slash—meaning, he was now out of the town limits. "When we stop, we can try to come up with some sort of plan to get out of here."

"How can the polizei track us?"

"It'll be more than just the polizei." Gage dug out his Chapstick and applied it to his lips. "Let me think about things a little more. I've got an idea about what we might do."

Several kilometers after the town, he turned north.

"Where are we going?" she asked.

"A place where I have some friends. Well, sort of."

"How far?"

"I don't want to use a GPS right now, so I'd guess about a hundred and fifty kilometers."

"That's a long way."

He pointed to the blue and white autobahn symbol up ahead. "We can be there in an hour."

Once on Bundesautobahn 81, the Volvo easily managed 150 kilometers per hour. As Gage cruised in the right lane, he held the scarf firmly against his wound, making sure Elena applied pressure to her wound, also. They discussed the underpinnings of his plan.

***

Far to the south of Gage and Elena, the Assassin had driven to the Swiss city of Winterthur—the sixth-largest city in Switzerland. His back was throbbing, radiating pain straight through to his gut. He was still in his rental car, the windows rolled down as he studied the faces of people as they exited the building. *She's a no. She's a no. He's definitely a no.* Though the Assassin knew it was not helping his condition, he'd smoked two of the Russian's Gauloises cigarettes. He chose to save his remaining handmades for when he was feeling a tad bit better. There was just something about the soothing effects of a cigarette after a fresh injury...

Based on the amount of blood that had trickled down his back, the Assassin felt many of his shrapnel wounds were small enough that they'd already clotted over. The worst of the pain came from the wounds near his middle and upper spine. He was hopeful he'd soon be able to view his injuries in a mirror. For now, he simply smoked, swilled water and watched the employees as they left work.

It was nearly an hour before he saw his mark.

She exited the rear of Kantonsspital Winterthur, the largest hospital in the city. The woman wore scrubs and had the look of a nurse. Judging by her gait, she was exhausted, beat down—probably coming off of a 12-hour shift that lasted 14 hours. She waited for a bus to pass before trudging across the road and entering the large lot where the Assassin waited. He watched as she clicked her key fob, the lights blipping on a Volkswagen Golf. The Assassin eyed the car, not noticing any protruding baby seats in the silhouette of the interior. The Golf was a few years old and seemed to be in fair condition, despite several battle scars on the plastic bumper.

At first appraisal, she seemed the ideal target.

The Assassin eased his car behind hers just as she reached her door. He didn't want to scare the woman so he politely greeted her in what would pass as native German. She didn't seem at all scared as she turned and eyed him openly with her door open.

"Do I know you?"

"No, but can you help me?" he asked.

She tossed her purse into the car. The Assassin guessed she was in her late thirties and multiracial, especially due to the thick dark hair that was held upward by the bright empress hair wrap. She had light almond skin, full features and was slightly overweight. Although the nurse seemed exhausted and certainly wasn't at her best, the Assassin found her attractive and unique-looking. Her large light green eyes were her most striking feature.

Though he was completely guessing at her socio-economic circumstances, the Assassin had deliberately waited for someone like this woman. As she'd walked to her car, he'd envisioned the adult period of the woman's life…

In her twenties, she'd had the world by the balls. Pretty, and different from most of the locals—and perhaps even hailing from some other country—she'd finished her nursing degree and was ready to launch herself into the Swiss middle class where she could truly make a difference. But once she'd begun working, things had slowly unraveled. She'd dated a series of losers, ending with a long-term affair with Switzerland's biggest asshole, probably a pampered surgeon. That black hole of a man had sucked away four years of her life, leaving her high-and-dry and approaching middle age with ten kilos of extra weight. And, about the weight, she could shed it if it wasn't for the long 12-hour shifts and her residual fatigue on her days off. Each exercise phase she began fizzled for one reason or another and now the years plowed steadily on as the dreaded age of 40 loomed like a dark storm in the distance.

She was absolutely perfect.

So, the Assassin was confident that, despite his current disheveled appearance, she was intrigued with him. She had to be…

"Do you work here?" she asked him, her tone skeptical.

"No."

"Then security is going to run you off," she replied. "This lot's for employees only."

"Lady, I need your help. I've been injured."

"Emergency room is around front."

He smiled wanly. "I know. My injury is...well..." he let out a regretful breath, "it's private. And I think you're a nurse, right?"

"I'm a nurse practitioner."

"Even better."

She seemed curious. "Why are you talking to *me*?"

"I was watching employees as they came out. When I saw you, I thought you looked like a nice person...and pretty."

The nurse frowned at his flirtation but there was a hidden twinkle in her jade green eyes. "What kind of injury are we talking about?"

"Will you help me?"

"What...kind...of...injury?"

"One that could cause me to lose my job."

"What job?" she asked. "What are you talking about?"

The Assassin lifted a wad of euros. "Look, I have a wad of cash. If you'll help me, I'll pay you and I'll never tell a soul."

This time her frown was genuine. "Are you in some sort of trouble?"

"No," he said, making sure he sounded casual and unworried. "I'm pretty far from home and...well...I did something stupid that's going to require some medical help. I just don't want to go to the E.R. because if my health insurance notifies my employer about this, I'll be in deep shit." He smiled and shrugged at the same time. "That's the reason I'm out here. I'm happy to pay you more than I'd pay a doctor...I just can't lose my job."

Despite his current condition, the Assassin was curious to find out how close he was in his hypothesis of this woman's past and present. And he knew he *would* find out because he could tell she was about to say yes.

She glanced around. "I'm not sure I could even help you...I don't have a whole lot of stuff in my medical bag."

"That's okay. I can tell you what you'll need if you could run back inside and get it."

The nurse practitioner deflated. "I can't get you drugs."

"No, I don't want drugs." He motioned a thumb over his shoulder. "It's my back...it's cut up all over and I can't get to it with my own two hands."

"How did you cut your back all over?"

"Long story. Please..."

"Was it a knife?"

"No!" he yelled, smiling disarmingly. "There were no laws broken or anything like that. When I show you, you'll understand."

173

She gnawed on her lip and glanced back at the hospital building. "Tell me what you think you need."

He did and, once she realized his requests were innocuous, she agreed. Once the deal was struck, he waited as she walked back inside. This would be the critical moment. Would she see a friend and confide in her—and subsequently be talked out of helping—thereby destroying more than a critical hour of his precious time? Or would she hurriedly gather the items, intoxicated by the prospect of making some serious cash along with the bonus prospects that an attractive stranger offered.

The Assassin knew the situation was in hand when she reappeared, walking with a purpose through the employee exit. Though she was attempting to appear serious, he could sense her excitement when she reached her car.

"You okay to drive?" she asked.

"Sure," he replied.

"Are you sure you're not some psychopath?"

The Assassin showed his palms. "I'm just a regular dude."

"Let's just go to my house. It's ten minutes away."

"If you'll give me your address, I just have to make one quick stop before I'll be there." He read her face and gave her a reassuring look. "Don't worry, I'm a nice guy."

The nurse gave him the address and he watched as she drove away. A few minutes later, the Assassin drove to her street and parked in a grocery store parking lot a few blocks away. After pulling a sweatshirt over his bloody shirt, he walked in great pain to her duplex. During the walk, he prepared himself for the agony of the coming extractions.

As well as the pleasure he predicted would soon follow.

***

Gage and Elena were still on the autobahn, headed north. As had been the case with so many other injuries Gage had received, his shoulder was now throbbing. Typically, the initial pain wasn't very bad. Soon after came a stinging and burning feeling. Then, the throbbing—the current stage. After the throbbing came the radiating pain, which Gage knew would make it difficult to use his left arm. It appeared the bullet he'd taken had only damaged flesh. Elena's appeared worse but, to her credit, she hardly complained. Women almost always did better with severe pain than men. To pass the kilometers, he slowly relayed his plan to get them needed medical attention. When she agreed, Gage instructed her to use a specific mobile phone from his bag.

"Just power it on, then press and hold the number one. If he answers, tell him you're with me and put it on speaker."

"But you emailed him before."

"I know. I was taking less risks, then. But now, we're in a critical state so I've got to risk putting info out over the airwaves."

She did as instructed with the phone. Hunter answered and she put him on speaker.

"Sir, can you hear me?" Gage asked.

"Barely. Lots of scrub noise."

"Yeah, we're driving and you're on speaker. I don't think we're compromised, sir, but in the event we are, I'm going to be somewhat indirect."

"Roger."

"Sir, you know the group of friends of ours who are over this way? 'The *Best*?' And, inside 'the best...the *first*?' " Gage asked, referencing "The Best" which is the 10th Special Forces Group's motto and "the first" which was in reference to 10th Group's First Battalion. The First Battalion was based north of Gage and Elena at the Stuttgart Region's Panzer Kaserne.

Gage had received significant help there a few years ago from his fellow Green Beret, Kenny Mars, after Monika Brink's murder during the business with the Hitler diaries. But Kenny had recently retired and was now working as a high-paid civilian contractor in Kabul. Unfortunately, Gage couldn't think of anyone he knew currently serving in 1st Battalion of the 10th Special Forces Group.

That's what happens when you get old.

"Yeah, I know who you're talking about," Hunter said. "Why?"

"We'll be in the neighborhood soon and both of us are in need of some needle and thread. You think you could plug us up with a delta?" he asked, referencing an 18-Delta—a Special Forces Medic.

"Is it bad?"

"No, but not good either. We both need sewing."

"Damn, son," Hunter grumbled. "Wish you could've avoided contact all together."

"That makes two of us."

"About the delta...I can try. Not sure my name holds much water anymore. Let me shake a few trees. What's your timeframe?"

"We should be there in about—" Gage stopped talking midsentence. Both of his hands constricted tightly on the steering wheel as his face went rigid.

"What is it?" Elena asked.

"You there?" Hunter asked.

"One second," Elena said to Hunter. "Your friend looks like he just saw a ghost."

Gage's face was alive with energy as he still continued to stare straight ahead. His knuckles were white on the steering wheel.

"Hey," Elena said, touching his right arm. "Are you okay?"

"What the hell, over?" Hunter asked, clearly talking to Gage.

Snapping out of it, Gage blinked several times. "I'm good, sir. Something just occurred to me. Something big. Will you please check on the delta and we'll call you back in exactly one hour?"

"I'll see what I can manage. Don't be surprised if you have to do this one on your own."

"Roger that, sir. Six-zero-mikes...talk to you then," Gage said, clicking his Timex.

Gage had slowed considerably as traffic whizzed past in the left lane.

"What happened to you back there?" she asked.

He licked his lips, still gathering his thoughts. "Something occurred to me...a new approach."

"Okay...what is it?"

"First, pull the battery off that old phone of mine."

When she did, Gage scratched his stubble and looked at her injury. "How's your shoulder?"

"It hurts like hell but I'm trying to be quiet about it."

"No...I believe it's much worse than that."

She looked at it. "Well, I think it stopped bleeding thanks to the bandage under my bra strap."

"No," he replied. "It's bad. Very bad. Possibly fatal."

Elena screwed up her face. "I'm confused."

"So was I. But not anymore."

"Can you please explain what you're talking about?"

"Before I tell you, I want you to lean your seat all the way back and close your eyes."

"Why?"

"Please."

She complied. Hardly able to contain his excitement, Gage did explain—after insisting she lie perfectly still. Though he didn't know how to distribute the "big news," he felt Elena might be able to fill in the missing pieces.

***

The Assassin had dreaded the explanation. How exactly does one explain away shrapnel from a grenade? Maybe the nurse would know what the flecks of metal were—maybe she wouldn't. But the Assassin didn't want to chance it. He decided to be truthful with her, up to a point.

Her home was small and comfortable, if a tad messy. She'd made him wait at the front door for several minutes after he'd rang the bell. She was no doubt still straightening up the small duplex. Once inside, he eased the sweatshirt over his head.

"Look at all the blood!" she said, eyeing his shirt. "It's everywhere."

"I'm fine. I think most of it's clotted by now."

The pain around his spine was quite debilitating. Sitting for so long had made it much worse. It had gotten a little better as he walked, although it had taken all he had to walk normally.

She tugged on his collar. "Your shirt has clotted to the wounds," she said. She gently pulled his shirttail out and peered underneath. "You've got gouges everywhere on your back. What the hell happened?"

"Can you go ahead and start working on them? I can tell you while you work—maybe it'll distract me."

"Fine. Leave your shirt on and come with me," she ordered, now in full medical mode.

As the Assassin trudged through the living area and down a small hallway, he saw no evidence of children or a husband. The living area consisted of a sectional sofa, a chair and a large flat-screen on an entertainment center. He noticed several empty beer bottles and, on the counter that separated the living area from the kitchen, a nearly empty red wine bottle.

The blinds covering her sliding back door were open. Her back yard was a small, enclosed postage stamp of a space with scraggly grass. A privacy fence in disrepair extended around the small yard. In the middle of the yard was a cheap chaise lounge and, beside it, a small table covered in beer bottles.

The nurse was standing at a hallway door, watching him. "Sorry about the mess. My girlfriends come over here and trash the place. With all the hours I work, it's hard to keep up."

"You should see my place," he lied.

She'd been waiting at the guest bathroom. Beside the toilet was a stand-up shower. She turned it on, making the water very warm.

"The water should break up those clots. Just let your back soak for a few minutes. I'm going back in there to set up a few things. Stay in the shower and let it soak. I'll be back."

Once she'd left, the Assassin used his feet to remove his shoes. He winced as he pulled off his wet socks, followed by his pants and his underwear. The blood had mingled with his sweat and creek water, turning all of his clothes a shade of pink. He stepped into the hot stream of water, fighting not to hiss as the hot water went to work on his injuries. True to her prediction, the shirt slid right off. He dropped it to the bottom of the shower. With his back still facing the showerhead, the Assassin was aware of each individual stream of water licking at his shrapnel wounds.

Despite the pain, he decided to fully clean himself. He was filthy. There was no shampoo, not that it mattered with his peroxide-bleached hair.

He used the brand new bar of green soap that sat perched on the small wire basket. The Assassin washed his face and scalp, taking deep breaths as the stinging soap coursed over his back wounds. He took his time, rubbing the soap over his entire body that had been covered in dirt, sweat, blood and grime.

"You okay in there?" she yelled.

"Fine. I got the shirt off," he answered. "Want me to come out?"

"Can you do it on your own?"

"Yeah. Be right out."

He toweled off and mottled her white towel with his blood. He wrapped the second towel around his waist and emerged, finding her waiting in the hallway, hands on her hips. She seemed momentarily at a loss for words, finding him only wearing the towel around his waist.

"I was dirty," he explained. "Hope you don't mind I took a full shower."

Despite his exhaustion, the Assassin knew he possessed a fine body, browned by the sun and sculpted through hours of gym and ocean fitness. He also knew the thoughts that probably warred in this lonely woman's mind. In fact, he encouraged them, saying, "And I just wanted to make sure I was clean for you."

Finally managing to avert her eyes from his torso, she motioned to the living area. "I layered some sheets on the sofa. Lay there for me, on your stomach."

He did as she requested, closing his eyes as she pulled on surgical gloves. He prepared his story.

"What exactly happened?" she asked, her operating room authority returning. "You must have forty wounds on your back."

"It'll seem really silly to you. And because something similar to this happened once before, it'll piss my boss off to the point of firing me—if he finds out."

"What are you talking about?"

"I collect militaria. Uniforms, guns, knives…that kind of thing."

"And?"

"I'm also interested in weapons and ordnance. Believe it or not, selling these old items, this militaria, especially from the Second World War, is *big* business." The Assassin generated this tale from an encounter he'd once had on a commercial airplane. The exuberant man he'd sat next to was a well-known militaria collector and had traveled all the way to France from the U.S. to make a deal for a single pilot's uniform. Because of this, the Assassin knew his cover story was solid.

The nurse was preparing her tools. He could hear her ripping packages open and placing items on a towel on the coffee table. "Go on."

"So, I was out in the forest, near the German border, because I knew numerous units had been marshaled there starting in forty-one, waiting for the Germans to invade with their dreaded Operation Tannenbaum. Using a metal detector, I found some old equipment. One buried item happened to be a grenade." The Assassin was facing away from the nurse. He smiled as he lied because it sounded so damned good. "Anyway, the top of the grenade, where the pin is, had corroded and when I pulled the grenade out of the dirt the whole top of the grenade fell apart. It stunned me for a second. When I realized it might blow up, I turned and ran and I guess I was about five meters away when it went off."

She didn't speak for a moment. Finally she said, "Are you insane? Who picks up a grenade that's seventy years old?"

"I know," he chuckled ruefully. "Like I said, something like this happened before and I missed a week of work. My boss still hasn't gotten over it. And that's why I came to you. If my insurance reports this, I'm toast."

"Unless we hit a snag, I think we can get you patched up," she said.

Her first order of business was giving him an IV of Lactated Ringers on a slow drip. She hung the bag from a heavy floor lamp. The Assassin declined her offer of pain pills.

"It's only Tylox," she said. "It's nothing heavy."

"I hate pain medicine."

"You're gonna hate the pain worse. Do you know badly this is going to hurt when I start digging?"

"I'll live." He could tell she was impressed with his bravado. The Assassin gritted his teeth as she set about picking out the jagged shards of metal.

"This is like pulling out barbed fish hooks," she breathed, dropping the second piece of metal into a small porcelain cup. "Each one has jagged edges that makes it hard to pull out."

"Just clamp and pull," he said. "Don't worry about tearing more skin."

"Okay," she sang in a tone that told him she thought he was insane. She grasped the next piece and yanked it out, causing him to flinch. "How was that?"

"Perfect," he answered.

As the nurse worked, she closed his wounds with a combination of stitches and butterfly bandages. The entire process took 90 sweat-inducing minutes.

When finished, the nurse changed the sheets on the couch. After guzzling a tall glass of ice water, the Assassin thanked her and slept as soundly as he'd ever slept before.

***

Nearly five hours had passed since the incident in the forest. Gage and Elena were now in a nature park a few kilometers outside of the southern Germany city of Böblingen. They'd parked and walked and were currently waiting in a hidden glade several hundred meters from the Volvo. Being near Böblingen was surreal for Gage, as several haunting memories of Monika's death floated to the surface of his mind. It had all happened because of those damned diaries. While he remembered Monika during nearly every waking hour, and even occasionally thought about that horrible night she died, his memories today were things he'd not once thought about since the tragedy. One of them was the awful despair Gage had felt upon hearing the policeman's words that there'd been a shooting in that dingy old hotel. At that moment, Gage had felt the way he imagined a person feels when slipping and falling from a deadly cliff. When the person knows they're going to die but they have several seconds to ponder it.

It was one of the two worst moments of Gage's life.

Move your mind elsewhere…

Doing his best to remain in the present, he found himself asking Elena mundane questions as they sat there on a fallen tree, awaiting their rendezvous with the Special Forces medical sergeant.

Holding a fresh gauze from the Volvo's first aid kit on her wound, Elena turned to him. "Why are you asking me these things?"

"Just curious and killing time."

"We've had hours together—days together—and you never asked me any of these types of questions before. Are you nervous?"

He nodded and shrugged, though the movement made him wince.

She narrowed her eyes. "Look, if you don't trust these people, then why are we here? I can go on with my shoulder the way it is. Just drive to a pharmacy and—"

"That's not why I'm acting this way," he said, cutting her off.

"Okay. Then why?"

Standing from the log, Gage rubbed his face. "This city…meeting a soldier from the First of the Tenth…it brings back some memories. Awful memories."

"War memories?"

"Actually, no. I served alongside many people who were stationed here, but the thing that's bothering me doesn't involve the military. In fact, it wasn't all that long ago." Gage realized his voice was distant, as if he were down in a well. He cleared his throat, knowing her question was coming—he answered preemptively. "My girlfriend was murdered in Frankfurt and this is where I came afterward."

Elena was quiet. She sipped from her bottle of water before she whispered a condolence. Then she said, "I didn't know about this."

"I know. Hopefully, it doesn't shake your confidence in me. After what happened today, I wouldn't blame you if it did."

"How could you have predicted today?"

"Considering the money that's at stake, I should've known someone would eventually find us."

There was a long period of silence before Elena said, "Well…since we're being honest, I can't help but feel sorry for that banker."

"Don't," Gage commanded. "I know that sounds cold, but anyone who gets involved in the business of ordering hits on an innocent woman doesn't deserve sympathy." He looked at her. "Okay? That man knew, as soon as he made that first call to whoever tried to kill you in Prague, that he'd crossed the line."

She nodded.

"I'm serious."

"I know you are." A sly grin formed on her face. "To hell with that little Russian-Swiss bastard."

He chuckled. "Much better."

"But Paulo," she said.

"Yeah. The kid didn't deserve to die."

"And right before you left the car in Zürich…who did you talk to?"

"The man from Genoa. He'd stationed a few of his men at the port."

"And?"

"And they were killed. The man that just attacked us killed them."

"Are you sure?"

He looked at her. "Had to be."

"Who'd you call after that?"

"The girl who drove us to the train station. I warned her."

"How could someone just leave a trail of bodies and get away with it?"

"We're lucky to be alive, Elena. That guy today, he's not like the others that have been after you."

She didn't respond.

As the time dragged on, Gage said, "When we were in the middle of all that today, I saw something."

"What?"

"You were…smiling. It looked like you were enjoying what was happening."

"I was smiling?"

"Yes. But 'enjoying' is the wrong word. You just seemed invigorated by what was going on."

"One of my painter friends once told me that I'm happiest when all around me has gone crazy."

"Were you scared?"

"No, I don't think so. I was shocked by getting shot and by what happened to the banker. But I don't think I was ever scared."

"Makes sense, for a certain kind of person."

"I guess."

"You sure you want to keep going?"

"Of course. If you think your plan will work?" she asked.

"It might, but we shouldn't underestimate this assassin they've hired. He killed Paulo. He took out two mobsters. And he found us once—he can do it again."

"Do you think you hit him with the grenade?"

"Doubt it. I'm not that lucky."

After a moment, Elena squeezed his hand. "I'm sorry about your girlfriend. I don't want to know what happened, but I want you to know that I understand the pain of losing a loved one."

Gage nodded his thanks.

"And Gage?"

"Yes?"

"You know how you told me not to feel sorry for the banker?"

He nodded.

"Your girlfriend surely loved you," Elena said, touching his arm. "She wouldn't want you to be sad."

Gage nodded his thanks and looked away. Neither person talked for a while.

The nature park was quiet save for the occasional passers-by out on the trail, chatting in their distinctive Swabian accent. The crickets began to chime in with each measure of growing darkness. A pleasant evening breeze pushed thick warm air through the glade, making Gage crave a long period of uninterrupted sleep.

He was suddenly keenly self-aware. Just minutes before, he'd been haunted by visions of Monika and her grisly murder. But the simple act of opening up to Elena had relieved him of nearly all of his current angst. Now he was tired but actually felt quite good.

Why? What did those escaping words do for him? Or was it Elena's kind words? And her touch?

"Should we talk about something else?" she asked.

"You sleepy?"

"Yes," she admitted. "Now that it's almost dark, my eyelids feel so heavy. I could stretch out in that grass out there and be asleep in seconds."

"We'll get a room later," he said, sitting back down. "I'll stay up tonight while you sleep."

Her head whipped around. "Why? Could he really know where we are this quickly?"

"The man from today?"

"Yes, of course."

"I don't know, Elena. I really don't. And it may not just be him. It could be *they*."

"What do you mean?"

"I mean, that man might not be the only person after us."

He recognized her Ukrainian curse word.

"How would he, or they, have found us?" she asked.

"That car," Gage replied, pointing. "It's the only thing I can think of, which is why I had you lay back in the seat. He tracked us right to that town and into those woods."

"Does the car have a GPS inside?"

"Yes, but the GPS is passive. It receives but doesn't send. Since it's a rental, I thought it could have a tracking device, too, installed by the rental company. But Colonel Hunter checked with someone who would know and told me it doesn't. I trust him. He wouldn't have given me such a definitive answer if he didn't know."

"So how could the man have followed us? Did you see him behind us?"

"He wasn't behind us. The only thing I can come up with is traffic cameras."

"How could someone follow us to a specific spot with traffic cameras?"

"Whoever he is, he'd need access to traffic cameras, both in Switzerland and Germany. And I know for a fact that, here in Germany, the highway cameras are run by the state."

"Is this Bavaria?"

"No, but we're close. We're actually in Baden-Württemberg."

"How could someone access those cameras?"

"Germany and Switzerland are among the most wired countries in the world. You run a red light here, you get an expensive ticket a few days later with your picture on it. They have multiple cameras in each intersection." He gestured to the way they'd come. "And the autobahn we were on…it has traffic control cameras everywhere."

"That doesn't explain how the man had access."

Gage shrugged. "Hackers, maybe. A bent cop. Maybe some civilian employee that had been paid off…"

"It's scary that someone could follow us all the way."

"That's the world we live in," Gage breathed. "Makes me jealous for the way my parents lived." He looked at her. "Just think about it…years ago, if my dad had to take a long drive, he'd get in the car, turn on the radio, and just cruise. No cellphones, no cameras, just him and his thoughts, or maybe the radio."

"But what about the car…shouldn't we get rid of it?"

"We will. For now, we're going to need it to draw their attention back our way."

"How do you know they won't shoot us right here where we sit?"

"Because I took a route into town that wouldn't be covered by cameras."

"That's why you cut through those forest roads?"

"Exactly," he replied. "For now, we just need to get patched up. After that, we'll get some shuteye and set things in motion, okay?"

Elena leaned toward him. Gage didn't move. Her face hovered inches from his as her green eyes flicked back and forth. Gage was aware of the rise and fall of her chest. Just as he was wetting his lips, headlights shattered the dusky reverie, followed by the sound of an engine. Gage peered through the bushes at a car that had roared up behind theirs. The lights went out and two men stepped out, one of them carrying a sizeable black tube.

"Don't move," Gage whispered. He continued to watch the men, hardly able to see details with the waning dusk. The driver looked all around before tapping the back of his head, making his moves very obvious. Then he made a come-to-me motion with his right hand.

That was the signal and Gage could think of no way that it had been intercepted.

"Stay here," he whispered, easing well to his right to mask where she was. He emerged and talked to the men before coming back to Elena and telling her to come out.

"My friend's going to patch us up while the other one changes the car's color."

"He's going to paint it?" she asked.

"Something like that."

Elena went first and, when the 18-Delta was finished, she had a total of nine stitches on both sides of her left shoulder. By this time, the other soldier had applied black vinyl to the hood, the roof and the driver's side of the car. While Gage was worked on, the foursome chatted about how to proceed with Gage's plan. It was decided that Gage and Elena would hole up on the military post tonight. They'd be safe there and could rest in peace. Then, tomorrow around lunchtime, when they were well rested, the "show" could begin.

Chapter Thirteen

WHEN THE Assassin finally awoke, he could see the gray light of early morning through the drawn blinds. Several times during the night he'd stirred, reminding himself where he was and willing himself back to sleep. But he'd now slept long enough and stifled a groan as he sat up. His wounds still throbbed painfully under the latticework of fresh stitches. The nurse had tried to count his wounds, telling him that he had "about" 38 lacerations on his back, 16 of which had required at least one stitch, the rest covered by small bandages. The worst wound was the painful one to the left of his spine. He'd viewed it in the mirror, a vertical gash that she'd closed with five stitches. As she'd dug out the jagged shrapnel on the long wound, she said the depth was better than 5 centimeters.

"If it had gone deeper, it might have hit your pancreas or stomach. One centimeter to the right and you'd have had your spine severed," she'd said academically, dropping the spiky, blood-soaked metal shard into a ceramic bowl. "Good thing you've got all these muscles to protect you."

He recalled the way she'd brushed his shoulder with her gloved hand when she'd commented on his muscles. He'd appreciated the comment then, but now—especially after a night of rejuvenating sleep—it turned him on.

Fortunately for the Assassin, he'd suffered no serious injuries. In fact, he was rather pleased that he felt as good as he did. After visiting the nurse's guest bathroom, he swallowed the ibuprofen she'd left out for him, following it with several tall glasses of water. Then he made himself at home, preparing a large pot of coffee and wolfing down two cups of yogurt along with a browning banana. When the coffee was ready, the Assassin poured a mug of the strong black brew and walked out into the nurse's small backyard—it was 5:12 A.M. and fully light despite the sun that had not quite shown itself.

He eased down into one of the cheap garden chairs, wincing at the pressure on his stitches. After he'd settled in, he smoked one of his handmade cigarettes, holding off on checking his phone. He wanted the ibuprofen and caffeine to kick in before he did anything requiring something other than a basic amount of concentration.

Following the cigarette, he poured a second mug of coffee and retrieved his mobile phone, sliding the battery onto the back and powering the phone on.

Closing his eyes, the Assassin said a prayer to the heavens that he was still anonymous after yesterday's fracas. He waited for the phone to sync with the network, eyes still closed as he heard three chirps—three messages. He held down the number one, listening to three messages from Gerard, his Interpol contact...

Message one: *"The local polizei searched the forest where your gunfight took place. They found the dead Russian banker along with significant expended brass in several locations. There was no mention of anyone else's blood found anywhere. I did find the Volvo again. It came north out of Jestetten and made a few turns as if headed towards Stuttgart. On the clearer videos I can see the man driving and the woman in the passenger seat."*

"Damn it!" the Assassin hissed, angered that Elena had made it out of there.

Message two: *"Are you okay? Still haven't heard from you. I don't mean to sound greedy, but you haven't paid the balance of what you owe me—and you said you would—and I'm hoping something hasn't happened to you. Anyway, the Volvo turned off the autobahn just before Stuttgart and headed west. I'm trying to pick them up but the non-autobahn cameras are in a different menu. It could take some time but I'll track them down. And on the last few video images I found, the woman in the passenger seat was laying all the way back with the seat fully reclined. On each of the videos, taken many kilometers apart, her hand positions were exactly the same. I dunno, maybe she was just sleeping. But the Volvo's speed slowed considerably after she reclined in the seat."*

The Assassin's heart rate redlined. Could Elena Volkov be dead? Could the bullet she took in the Jestetten forest have killed her? The last message was the shortest of the three...

Message three: *"The Volvo had to have stopped or turned off between Steinenbronn and Schönaich. There are cameras in both towns and the Volvo departed Steinenbronn but never reached Schönaich. I'm sure of it. There are no roads that your man could have taken between the two towns, unless he cut through fields and I don't know why he would do that. Oh, in the last video, the woman was still reclined all the way back in the exact same position. Call me."*

Sitting back down, the Assassin controlled his breathing as he phoned Gerard. The Interpol official answered almost immediately.

"Tell me," the Assassin demanded.

"Thank God you're okay. Did you listen to your messages?"

"Yes. Give me the update."

"My money?"

"As soon as the bank opens. Talk."

"As far as the Volvo, nothing new since that last one. Your man departed Steinenbronn around sunset and never made it to Schönaich."

"How far apart are the two towns?"

"Five or six kilometers."

"So, presumably, he stopped somewhere between, correct?"

"Yes."

"How many residences are on that stretch of road?"

"Not many. It's fields and farmland."

"No businesses?"

"No." Gerard paused for a moment. "Listen, I don't know your objective but I think it's important you know that, when I personally ran the videos through our digital enhancer, it seems the woman who was stretched out had blood on her shirt around her left upper chest…near her heart."

"I knew I hit her."

"You did. And the driver of the Volvo was on a cell phone in the last video."

"Can you pull that cell number?"

"With some effort, yes. Look, I've got traces on his credit cards and passport under a completely different investigation, but if I call for a triangulation on that phone call based on the date and time and his position, it'll send up a shitload of red flags. I can guarantee I'll be shut down as they investigate what I'm doing. Right now, I'm working within approved parameters for my paygrade…this is all I can do."

"Dammit to hell."

"Can't you get over to that stretch of road and find them?" Gerard asked.

"Yeah…it's just going to take some time. I've got to lay on new transportation and make sure I'm clean."

"Well, no one's onto anyone from the Jestetten shootout other than the body that's cold in the morgue. The locals are looking at the same traffic cameras I am, and the Volvo and your rental Volkswagen are on the list along with 122 other cars. But if I make too much noise, someone will put it together that it was the white Volvo that was involved in that shootout."

"No witnesses have come forward?"

"None that saw anything. That spot you were in was very remote. The locals heard the shots and explosion."

"Don't call attention to the Volvo. I don't want those two apprehended by anyone other than me."

"I wouldn't worry about it. For now, the locals are chasing their tails and most of the investigation is revolving around Switzerland."

"What about those satellite photos? That's how you found the Volvo."

"Two separate investigations by different police forces. Hopefully no one thinks to look."

"And I assume you're watching all the cameras around those two towns where you last saw the Volvo?"

"Yes. There was a similar Volvo last night that passed through Schönaich but it was the wrong color, wrong plates and the driver had black hair."

"Anyone in the passenger seat?"

"Nope. And I checked—there are more than 26,000 Volvos of that type and year in Baden-Württemberg. Wasn't the same car."

"Alright. I'll keep this phone right beside me."

"My money?"

"Keep working, Gerard. I'll send the balance when the bank opens." The Assassin hung up and finished his coffee as the sun began to peek through the slats in the nurse's wooden fence. When he went back inside, he checked the coffeemaker, eyeing the timer—it could be programmed to turn on at any time and date. He checked the back, finding a panel for the battery backup, presumably so the clock and timer wouldn't scramble if the power blinked. The nurse's kitchen "stir drawer" had the AA battery he needed. Once he inserted the battery, the Assassin eyed the hot plate as the idea formulated in his mind.

Down the hallway, the bedroom door at the end of the hall creaked. He could barely see the nurse between the darkness of the hallway and the scant centimeters she allowed the door to open.

"How are you feeling?" she asked, her voice scratchy.

"All things considered, I feel pretty good. How'd you sleep?"

"So-so."

"Want some coffee?"

"Maybe later." She opened the door just a bit more, revealing herself to be wearing a long t-shirt. Her almond legs shifted nervously.

"When do you have to go back to work?"

"I'm off for two days," she replied, biting her bottom lip and pulling the door open a bit wider.

"That's good news." The Assassin walked to the hallway, allowing his eyes to licentiously move up and down her body. "If you don't mind, I'd like to take a shower."

"Sure. Everything's already in there from your shower yesterday."

"No."

"No?"

"That's not what I meant."

Her face clouded. "What did you mean?"

He paused dramatically. "I want to shower in *your* bathroom, *with* you."

She blinked several times. "Are you serious?"

"Very."

"I can't believe you just said that."

"But you're glad I did, aren't you?" He stepped closer. "Aren't you? You drive me crazy, and you have from the moment I first saw you. Forgive me for saying it, but I want you so badly."

The nurse was clearly nervous. But over a matter of seconds, her nervousness built into elation, as she couldn't help but smile. And her smile told the Assassin all he needed to know.

***

At that same moment, Gage Hartline was 131 kilometers to the north. He was outside, walking around Panzer Kaserne, in Böblingen. He'd been to this Kaserne—a German word for "barracks"—more times than he could remember, but it was his last visit that was still burned into his brain. The visit after Monika Brink's murder.

Deep breath, Gage. Deep breath and drink in this weather. And remember how talking about it last night relieved you of your sorrow. Just accept things and try to relax.

The weather on this Friday was exactly what German summers are advertised to be. There's an old saying about Germany's weather: the sun "goes in" in September and "comes back out" in June. But for three months, Germany's weather is nearly as nice as anyplace on earth. As the sun was just coming up over the trees, Gage guessed the temperature to be in the mid-sixties—slightly cooler than the previous mornings. The sky was a deep blue and cloudless, with a breeze stirring the tops of the tall pines.

He shook his head, unable to stop thinking about Monika Brink. Gage stared skyward, imagining what that sweet woman would say to him right now.

First, she'd tell him to let her go—and she'd reiterate that what happened wasn't his fault. She'd thank him for the time they had together and she'd demand he move on with his life. And, to be fair, Gage had certainly done that. But being back here awakened feelings he'd long since boxed up and put away.

Suddenly, Monika's voice came to him as if she were standing behind him, whispering in his ear. "The lady sleeping on that cot in there is a kind soul and she needs you. Don't think about me—think about her. See this through so she can finish her life in peace."

"I'm still sorry, Monika."

"No need to be. What happened was out of your control."

"I avenged you."

"That wasn't necessary, either…but I'm glad you did."

Squeezing his eyes shut, Gage was nearly overcome with the memories of his girlfriend.

He growled audibly, shaking his head as violently as he could. "Focus on today," he grunted to himself. "Do what she said…go look after Elena."

Gage walked back to the old warehouse building where he and Elena had slept. He looked through the window, seeing Elena safely nestled under her blankets on the familiar green Army cot. She was still soundly sleeping.

He wished he could take a run but decided against it. The medic had told him to avoid heavy physical activity for a few weeks. Instead, Gage walked up the short street between several other empty warehouses, following his nose to the closest mess hall. He could smell the cooking bacon and it made him instantly hungry. Though the day's physical training—known simply as "P.T."—had already ended, several sweaty soldiers could be seen in their shorts and t-shirts. Others were already in uniform. All of them had a kick in their step and it made Gage think back to his days as a young soldier, when Friday was easily the second best day of the week.

The two soldiers working head-count eyed Gage curiously, probably unused to seeing disheveled, lightly-bearded 40-somethings in old t-shirts and blue jeans. Plus, the bulky bandage on his shoulder was visible around his neck and it made him more conspicuous.

"Mornin' fellas, any way you guys could rustle up a couple of to-go breakfasts with a few tall cups of coffee?"

"Do you happen to have your meal card, uh, sir?" the older of the two soldiers said, struggling over how to address Gage.

"It used to be 'sergeant,'" Gage said with a smile. "I'm retired. I'm here, on post, as a guest. Came out for a walk this morning and left my government I.D. back at quarters."

"I'll check with the mess sergeant," the older one said, walking away.

"I've got cash if I need to pay."

While he waited, Gage moved into the lobby area of the dining facility, viewing the pictures of the chain of command. He didn't know anyone listed. As he eyed a full bird colonel, the post commander, Gage trumpeted his cheeks—*he's younger than I am. I remember back when the post commander seemed like an old man. But now…*

Life was like those coin funnels Gage sometimes saw at stores, next to the gumball machines. You drop a quarter in the top and it starts circling the funnel slowly. That's youth. Then, as it gets lower, it begins to move more quickly. Circling. Descending. Circling. Descending. That's where Gage was now—in the middle, with each revolution quite a bit faster than the one before. Then, at the bottom, the quarter becomes a whirling blur—old age—before it disappears into the abyss—forgotten.

Life dissipates like a vapor and sooner or later, no one even remembers your name. No one knows you existed. Others take over and time moves on.

"What the hell is with your mood today, you morbid bastard?" Gage whispered to himself.

His eyes slid to the right as he read about several upcoming MWR-sponsored trips to Berchtesgaden, Paris and Lloret de Mar.

I was in Lloret not too long ago, he mused, remembering how he'd acquired those Star pistols from his Russian friends.

As the head count called out to him, Gage's eyes were focused on the familiar credit card symbols on the bottom of the MWR poster: Visa, MasterCard, American Express and Discover.

"Uh…sir…I mean, sergeant?"

Credit cards. Freaking credit cards! That's it.

"Sergeant? If you will?"

Gage poked the MasterCard symbol and turned around, finding the polite young private first class holding a sack with two covered plates. In his other hand was a drink carrier with two large Styrofoam coffees covered by lids.

"The mess sergeant put cheese omelets, bacon, sausage and toast in each one. He also said there's cream and sugar over by the drinks if you want it."

"That's perfect," Gage said. "How much?"

"Nothing, sergeant. He took one look out here at you and said you look like you could use a free breakfast."

Gage chuckled, glancing down at himself and nodding his agreement. "Thanks to you both," he replied, nodding at the two soldiers. "And thank the mess sergeant for me." He gave a final glance back at the credit card symbols before quick-stepping back to the warehouse that had doubled as their hotel room last night.

Thanks to that MWR poster, Gage had just altered today's plan.

***

Before their shower, the Assassin had vigorously brushed his teeth and gargled the purple mouthwash from beside the nurse's sink. He then wore a towel into the bedroom made dark by the blackout curtains—a necessity for a nurse—and waited while she brushed her teeth. When the faucet turned off, the nurse spoke to him though he couldn't see her.

"I'm sort of nervous," she said.

"Don't be."

"I don't even know you."

He could tell by her tone that she simply desired reassurance. He calmed her by saying, "You know me better than most people do. You know I did something stupid yesterday and, good nurse you are, you helped me with it."

"Okay. But I…" She paused.

"What is it?"

"I feel like you've not told me…everything."

"Of course, I haven't. There's much to learn about you, too."

"No. I'm talking about your accident."

He clucked his tongue. "I wish there was something more exciting to tell you. I'm embarrassed at my own stupidity."

"Do you truly mean that? There was nothing more?"

"Other than me diving into a creek for cover? No…nothing more."

The Assassin could hear footsteps before the shower was turned on. The nurse walked into the bedroom, her head demurely down. "Sorry I doubted you."

"I don't blame you a bit," he replied. "What I did was stupid and it should breed some curiosity—and that's part of the reason I didn't want to go to the emergency room." He stepped to her, lifting her chin with his finger. "And though what I did yesterday was moronic, perhaps now I can redeem myself."

"I'm not normally like this," she whispered. "You know…carrying on with a man I hardly know."

"I believe you." He kissed her, his right hand gripping the back of her neck as his left hand moved south and went gently, but immediately, to work, making her gasp and tremble.

The shower was long and warm and sensual. Both of them used their hands freely, getting to know the other. Their time in bed lingered until mid-morning, as they explored each other's body, doing all manner of things in a creative and pleasurable way. He found her to be a profound and skillful lover, especially once she dropped her inhibition. She had a penchant for being in control, which was good for him and the plethora of injuries on his back. As they finished their third bout, she was astride him, facing away, holding his shin with her left hand while her right hand worked.

She then pulled her feet up beside his hips—a squatting position—her movements pronounced as she yelled out in an uninhibited shriek. Fortunately for the Assassin, her lack of self-consciousness provided him with a spike of inflammation, bringing him off right after her. She collapsed backward, lying beside him, both of her hands massaging her midsection.

"I'm gonna be so sore this week," she groaned while laughing.

"That's quite all right," he said with a smile. "You'll think about me each time it hurts."

Her mirth faded. "Speaking of that, will I see you again?"

"I don't know."

She couldn't help but frown. "What's that mean?"

"I don't live near here but I can make arrangements to come back."

"Do you live far?"

"That's not the challenge."

"What is?" She jerked upward. "Shit...you told me you're not married."

"And I'm not."

"Well, what is it?" she asked, flopping back down.

"I'd just need to know that you're comfortable with the type of relationship I'll suggest."

She stirred. "You just want me for sex, right? Believe me, I work with several girls who have relationships like that and...well...I won't say I'm completely closed off to the idea. I realize I'm getting to the age where life is too complicated to try to date and have relationships, and all that. But..."

"What?"

Her eyes joining his, she said, "I really like you. There's something about you that makes me feel...alive...and a bit like a wild animal." She burst out laughing. "I need a cigarette."

"I like you, too," he said, flicking a certain spot with his hand and making her lurch and gasp.

"So what about us?" she asked.

"I'm too hungry to concentrate."

"Then how about a big breakfast?"

"That'd be wonderful. Let's get some nourishment, then we'll talk about our future."

As she worked in the kitchen, the Assassin spent a bit of time in her bathroom, eyeing his wounds in the mirror before studying his face. Today, before he left, he would shave his peroxide blond locks with a razor and use some sort of cosmetic item from her numerous tubes and containers to darken his scalp, making it not appear freshly shorn. He tugged on his light stubble. When it grew out a bit more, perhaps he would dye it black.

The Assassin walked down the hall and eyed his new friend as she cooked eggs. She was wearing a different t-shirt with only thong panties underneath. Despite their marathon lovemaking session, he twitched with arousal.

"If you don't put on more clothes, I'm liable to bend you over right there."

Her green eyes twinkled. "After we eat, I could possibly do it one more time, if we're careful."

"It's a date," he replied, walking out back. He smoked one of his handmade cigarettes, feeling quite majestic. But within moments, his mind went to work on what Gerard had said about Elena Volkov.

She'd been lying flat in the passenger seat, her chest crimson with blood, unmoving. Was she dead? And, if so, would her protector let it be known? An uncharacteristic spate of panic washed over the Assassin as he pondered the complications that could arise from this situation. What if her protector, Hartline, hid the fact that she was dead? The deal wouldn't go through and the Assassin wouldn't get his money. Even though suspicion of her death would eventually come out, the mission would be a colossal failure if she weren't *proven* dead in time for the deal to go through.

While the Assassin had certainly made enough money with the advance to adequately support himself the rest of his days, he didn't want an adequate life. He desired a sumptuous existence, and $50 million was the number that he'd set his mind on. With that sort of principle, by using tax-free municipal bonds, he could earn at least 5% for the balance of his life. $2.5 million dollars a year, untaxed, was enough to live like a king. Conversely, with only $10 million, he'd probably only manage 4%. And while $400 grand per year was nothing to sneeze at, it would only provide comfort, and not the luxury he so desired.

If Elena Volkov was dead, the Assassin needed to prove it. If she wasn't dead, he had to do everything in his power to kill her. And soon.

"Want to eat outside?" the nurse called out.

He motioned her to him as he took a deep drag on the cigarette, watching her carrying the two plates across the living room floor. He viewed her with fondness, again feeling his arousal as he eyed her long almond legs and her pleasantly wide hips. Despite her slight amount of extra weight, her waist was trim and her breasts were the perfect ski slope variety that cheerily bounced during love-making.

What a fine lady—and a helluva screw. He couldn't wait to be inside her again, to listen to the sounds she made, to feel her nails rake across his chest.

The Assassin closed his eyes…

Killing her was going to be just awful.

***

Last night, the white Volvo had been covered by sheets of adhesive black vinyl, making it appear as if the car were painted black. The two men from 1st Battalion, 10th Special Forces had also brought different license plates to complete the transformation. One of them had even driven the car to Panzer Kaserne. If someone had been tracking the Volvo with traffic cameras, they'd have never known it was Gage's rental Volvo. Now, however, the car had been returned to its original state—save for the badly concealed body in the cargo area of the wagon.

Poor Elena Volkov—killed as a result of a gunshot wound and now stinking up the cabin of the Swiss automobile.

Actually, very little of that was true. Elena was alive and well and, after a long shower, she smelled quite nice. The dead body ruse was solely for the cameras. The 18-Delta, Dominguez, who'd patched Gage and Elena up, had reconnoitered the gas station early today. He'd instructed Gage exactly where to park, giving him the maximum amount of "exposure" to both city street cameras. In order to keep things as genuine as possible, Elena had agreed to be bundled in a blanket and stored in the back of the Volvo. Gage combatted her overheating by running the air conditioning at its highest setting.

He exited the car and peered inside at the wrapped body, then glanced all around the way a person might to see if anyone was watching. He went inside for a bit before returning with several waters and a bag of gas station food. After tossing the food onto the passenger seat, Gage closed his eyes and tilted his face to the heavens, taking a series of deep breaths. He was trying to convey a mournful posture—though he was no Leonardo Dicaprio, he made the regret look genuine.

Gage drove slowly away, headed toward the quiet wooded areas south of Böblingen. It was there the Volvo, along with the body in the back, would disappear.

***

It was rare for the Assassin to be wishy-washy, but that was his current state and he was well aware of it. The nurse had just finished pleasuring him, shaking her head each time he'd tried to stop her. It was almost as if she worshipped him, kneeling before him, caressing his skin as her mouth so skillfully worked. He finally arched his head backward and released, unable to hold back any longer. She stood, smiling and proud. He reached for her nakedness but she pulled back, telling him that she'd had enough for one day.

"You've got to let me recover," she said. "Especially if you want to have some fun tomorrow." Then she went into the bathroom and brushed her teeth again.

As the water ran, the Assassin retrieved his pistol and made certain there was a round seated in the chamber. He sat back down, stuffing the pistol down between the bedroom reading chair's armrest and cushion. When the nurse returned, she'd pulled her light robe on, the one that barely hid anything below her waist. She was smiling and had that glowy look she'd worn all day. Poor woman—she was head-over-heels in love. Who knew how long it had been since she'd been able to demonstrate the affection that had welled up inside her? And while he could see no future with this nurse, the Assassin wondered if there was some way to keep her alive.

Rather than wrack his brain, he had her kneel again where she'd just been.

"Don't tell me you're ready again," she smiled.

"Not quite."

She shrugged. "I'll do it if you want."

"I know you would," the Assassin replied, positioning her just in front of him. "But instead, I'm going to tell you something and I want you to sit and listen without talking, okay?"

Her hand shot to her forehead. "You're married. Dammit, I knew it," she hissed. "This just happened to my friend Nicole. He stayed all weekend and lied about his situation until it was time for him to—"

"I'm not married. Please...listen."

Seeming somewhat relieved, she nodded and settled back into her kneeling position.

"Yesterday, I only told you part of the truth. I was injured by a grenade." He licked his lips. "But the grenade was thrown by another man." The Assassin allowed that to sink in for a moment. "The man I'm chasing."

"Excuse me?"

"I'm certain you heard me," he said, his tone no longer warm. "I've been hired by a group of well-meaning people to find this man, and the woman he's with, and to bring them in. Unfortunately, we had a bit of a showdown in a remote forest and that's how I got injured. That's why I couldn't go to an E.R. and also why I needed a safe place to stay as the heat died down."

She was emotionless but a bit of the color drained from her face. "Is this a lie just to turn me off?"

He frowned. "Please, stop with the paranoia. I'm telling you the truth because I quite like you. If I didn't like you, I wouldn't have told you anything."

"Who are you?"

"My identity is not up for discussion." He gnawed on his bottom lip before saying what he'd dreaded saying. "You're a smart woman, so I ask you this: How can I be absolutely sure you won't ever contact the authorities about me?"

The nurse was clearly puzzled. "Contact the authorities?"

"Yes. When I leave here, what is to stop you from reporting me?"

"Why would I?"

"I don't know. But, however small, it's a risk I cannot take."

The nurse didn't seem to grasp the crux of the situation. She seemed more put off that he was talking about leaving. With a shrug, she said, "I wouldn't contact anybody. Don't flatter yourself."

He didn't want to have to lay all his cards on the table, but now it was clear that doing so was the only option to make her understand. "I can't take any risks. You may act flippant now, but you might change your mind later, and I can't have that. Unless I can be absolutely sure you'll stay quiet, I'll have to *kill* you."

The transformation took a good ten seconds. It started with her mouth, which slowly opened. Her eyes widened and her nostrils flared. Along with that came her breathing, which quickened. The Assassin imagined her pulse spiked, too, but he couldn't tell that visually.

"I can't believe you just said that."

"I'm sure it's a shock," he replied. "But I'm quite serious. It's something I will do if I have to."

She tried to stand but he stopped her.

"No, no, dear. We're talking, here. I'm doing all I can to give you a chance. I suggest you think carefully and give me the reassurance I'm asking for, but only if it's something you can find inside yourself."

She began to bawl.

Willing himself to be patient with all the tears, the Assassin moved her to the bed and allowed her to cry and grieve and moan. After putting up with this for several minutes—which spoke volumes about how much he liked her—he snapped his fingers and told her that her grieving time was over.

As he pulled on his pants, he said, "Tell me now or I've no choice but to end this."

"I don't know what you want me to say," she cried. "I won't tell anyone who you are. Isn't that enough?"

"Not even close."

"Well, what else is there? I'd never go to the cops and tell them that some stranger I *fucked* all morning had been injured by another man who threw a grenade. Why would I do that?"

"Now, see…that's a good point," he replied. "Shame is an excellent motivator."

"Well, I am ashamed. And now I feel like a complete slut."

The Assassin spoke monotone, as he often did when a killing was near. "I'll not stand here and dole out compliments, but you're no slut. The spark between us was genuine. However, I still need a better reason to keep you alive."

She appeared to be struggling with something. Her mouth opened to speak but no words came out.

"What is it?"

"Nothing," she replied unconvincingly.

"As of now, you've not given me enough," he replied. "And I won't wait around much longer. You've made me happy today and I wish I had more time I could spend with you. That's the truth. And I'll come back, if you'll have me, but first we have to come to some sort of agreement. While it sounds callous, if we don't come to an agreement, I will end your life. It'll be quick and painless, but I'll have no other choice."

"You'll get caught if you do that."

"No. I've thought it through. You don't have to go back to work for three days. I checked your phone—you don't make many calls. Perhaps I'm being too optimistic, but I don't think anyone will come looking for you if you go quiet for a day."

"What happens in a day?"

"This duplex burns to the ground."

"How's that quick and painless?"

"You'll die today. The house will burn tomorrow, at rush hour, when traffic is at its peak. That will create difficulty for the fire department, ensuring that any lingering evidence is destroyed."

"How do you manage to decide when the duplex burns?"

"It's not hard."

"I'm familiar with autopsies," she challenged. "They'll know I didn't die in the fire."

The Assassin rolled his eyes, feeling like he were mentally sparring with a sixth-grader. "I said nothing about leaving your body here, did I?"

"I don't want to die," she said, crying again.

"Then give me a better reason to keep you alive."

"If I do...do you promise to let me live?"

"Dear, I don't want to kill you. That's why I've invested a significant amount of time in discussing this. You should be flattered. If you give me a good enough reason, then you and I have a future."

"Promise?"

"I don't make promises. Speak."

She covered her face with both hands, talking through them. "My mother. She lives here."

"Your mother lives here?"

"Not in my place. She lives across town. I'll give you her address as collateral to prove that I would never tell on you. And even though it'll take some time for me to...to come around on all this...I'd gladly welcome you back here again to demonstrate to you that I don't want to hurt you." The nurse took a few deep breaths and lowered her hands. "I'd like to understand what you do because I don't rush to judge other people. You're intense, but I can tell you've got goodness inside you."

Eyes narrowed, the Assassin sucked on his teeth as he pondered her offer. It was actually pretty good, assuming she was telling the truth. He'd need to verify the nurse's mother's presence but, at first appraisal, the nurse's offer might save her life.

However, he didn't believe—not for a mere second—that she wanted him to come back. That was bullshit, although he couldn't blame her for saying it. She was simply lying to survive.

"Well?" she asked.

"I like it."

Relief washed over the nurse. "So, you won't kill me?"

"I never wanted to kill you. Dear, you make me feel like—" His phone rang.

The Assassin grabbed his pistol and instructed her to be quiet. He answered the phone.

"Can you talk?" Gerard from Interpol asked.

"For a moment."

"Listen closely. Gage Hartline just used his personal debit card at an Aral gas station in Böblingen, Germany. I immediately did a street cross-reference and pulled the corresponding video from the traffic camera right outside the station. He's still driving the Volvo and I clearly saw a wrapped bundle in the back. The bundle was long and narrow—consistent with a dead body. The back seat is down to make room."

Holy shit! The Assassin licked his lips as he tried to remain passive. "Anything else?"

"When Hartline came back outside with the items he'd bought, he looked like a man in grief. He stared at the body and then looked like he was about to cry."

"But where've they been? How did he get there without being seen?"

"I don't know, but clearly, the woman he was with didn't make it."

"Call you right back," the Assassin replied. He hung up the phone and eyed the nurse.

"Everything okay?" she asked.

"Maybe," he replied, uncharacteristically gnawing on his fingernail. "Honestly, I'm a bit confused by what I just heard."

"Anything I can help with?"

"I wish."

"What was the call?"

"The man and woman who I'm looking for have been found."

She brightened. "That's good, right?"

"It is," he said, nodding. "Thank you for all you did for me. That was some of the best sex of my entire life and, believe me, that's saying something." He lifted the pistol.

"What are you doing?"

"My timeline just got blown to bits. I'm truly sorry." The Assassin fired, striking her in the center of her forehead.

He watched her fall to the side. He quickly moved one of their sex towels under her leaking head, before too much of her blood and cerebrospinal fluid dribbled onto the carpet. The Assassin shut the nurse's eyes and cursed himself. Then, he remembered Gage Hartline and his damned grenade.

This was all his fault. If it weren't for Hartline, this lonely woman would still be alive.

Wasting little time, the Assassin called Gerard back. As they spoke, the Assassin deliberately moved around the duplex, spreading dry towels and paper and furniture to key locations, increasing the duplex's flammability. After ending the call, the Assassin wrapped the dead nurse in several dark blankets and crammed her into the backseat of her Volkswagen. He was thankful for the privacy of her single-car garage. He then gathered up the bloody towel along with a number of other items used yesterday in his medical procedure, stuffing them in a black plastic bag and also placing them in her car.

Finally, after another shower, the Assassin unplugged the hard-wired fire alarms and removed their battery back-ups. In the kitchen, he worked on the coffee maker's heating element. Using a single piece of toilet paper, he tested the device with the timer, waiting patiently as the seconds ticked down. When the coffee maker kicked on, the toilet paper ignited.

Satisfied, the Assassin set the coffee maker for 6:45 A.M. the following morning. Then he built a tower of light flammables above it. He placed open bowls of rubbing alcohol and cooking sherry in the chintzy cabinet above the coffee maker. Once the burning pressboard cabinet gave way, the two liquids would tumble out, acting as accelerants. Then, the whole place would go up.

Using a battery operated trimmer he found in the nurse's bathroom, the Assassin sheared off his peroxide blond hair. He then shaved the stubble, leaving him completely bald. The Assassin used her makeup to darken his scalp, also adding a light amount to his face to create a uniform appearance. He added his own black, wraparound sunglasses and twin magnet-backed earrings that were made to look like the stud variety. Viewing himself in the mirror, he looked like a different person.

Feeling sufficiently concealed, the Assassin used glass cleaner on her front and back doors. He also cleaned the ashtray out back and brought the garden chair he'd used inside. Then he backed the nurse's car from her garage and drove away.

As far as he could tell, no one took notice of his departure.

Chapter Fourteen

GAGE HAD followed the precise directions of his new Green Beret friends. They'd made certain the local military police and post commander knew what they were doing—using the guise of "specialized training"—and since they were spec-ops, who would be surprised? So, at the south end of Panzer Kaserne, in a heavily wooded area, the Volvo was driven up what amounted to a rabbit-trail, right up to the Kaserne's barbed-wire-topped chain link fence. A section of the fence was disconnected and unrolled, and the Volvo brought back on post far from the watchful eyes of any traffic or security camera. The car was then covered and towed back to the same warehouse where Gage and Elena had spent the night. Once the Volvo was brought inside, it was scoured for tracking bugs and thoroughly cleaned.

Although they'd deflected the police when they'd kidnapped Peter Karlerenko, Gage knew the investigation would be in full swing now that the banker been found shot to death in a German forest. So, certainly the car rental company had heard from the Swiss police about the kidnapping and murder. Because of that, Gage used one of the 10th Group's modified security telephones. The phone was I.P. based, and a predetermined location could be chosen for the phone to seem to originate. Gage chose eastern Austria. He called, telling the customer service person that he'd like to extend his rental until July 7th. Yes, they could use the same credit card, he replied. Once they had his false name, the representative's tone changed.

"Sir, there's a note on your account that you're to call the Statdpolizei Zürich immediately."

"The polizei? Do you know why?"

"No, sir. But the note says it's urgent. In fact, would you please hold on while I transfer you to one of our managers?"

"No. But I'll call the Zürich polizei," Gage replied. He hung up the phone and ceased worrying about the Volvo. He couldn't help but smile as he thought about the hunt turning to the far side of Austria. Unless the investigators knew his true identity—and he didn't see how they could—then they'd have no way of knowing that the real Gage Hartline used his debit card this morning.

But the Assassin, and whoever was helping him, knew Gage's true identity. And hopefully they'd taken today's bait.

It was now time to transition to the more difficult phase of his plan. He walked outside the warehouse, finding Elena sitting on a split log bench that was nestled behind two spruce pines. She was leaning back in the warm sunshine with her eyes closed.

"Glad you're out of those blankets?" he asked.

"I'm just glad to be with you."

Embarrassed, Gage cleared his throat. "So, listen… the battalion commander'll be here soon to chat. I can do this alone if you're not up to it."

"Do you know him?"

"I don't."

"Then let's both meet him," she answered.

Twenty minutes later, an olive drab Volkswagen van arrived, driven by an E-6 Green Beret in his ACUs. Though the man was probably not yet 30, Gage could tell by looking at him that he'd been around. His nametag read McCoy. He nodded at Gage before he walked around and opened the door for the battalion commander, a lieutenant colonel named Davis.

Lieutenant Colonel Davis, probably about Gage's age, had black hair and a tan, weathered complexion. He was an average size man, handsome and the type of person who acts immediately casual—like he's known you for years. He griped about his driver opening the door for him, saying it made him feel like an old woman.

"Ever since I made battalion commander everyone acts like I can't even twist a door knob."

Davis stopped in front of Gage, eyeing him head to toe. "So, you're the retiree who's caused all the hubbub?" Extended his hand. "I'm Barry Davis, *Hard-line*…how the hell are ya?"

"Fine, sir. Thank you for coming and thanks for helping get us off the road last night."

"And this lovely lass, here, must be your Ukrainian damsel in distress." Davis bowed slightly then grinned as Elena grasped his hand, giving it a firm shake.

"Damn, Hard-line…she shakes harder'n you."

"She's a tough one, sir."

"How're those wounds?"

"Both superficial, sir," Gage replied.

Davis looked at Elena.

"I'm fine," she answered.

"All right, let's get inside in case this prick who's after you has managed to divert satellites to do a flyover."

"Could that happen?" Elena whispered as they walked into the warehouse.

"He's just joking," Gage replied, not realizing that their outing in Jestetten had come courtesy of a satellite flyover.

"Do me a favor, McCoy," Davis said to his driver, "find us a few chairs then go outside and get lost in the bushes."

The staff sergeant arranged three folding chairs near the Volvo. He retrieved three bottles of water from his bag, placing one on each chair. "I'll be outside, sir, lost in the bushes."

The threesome sat down and Davis slapped his knees. "Let's get goin', Hard-line…I got the skinny from ol' Colonel Hunter and I'm eager to hear the rest of this tale."

"Did you know Colonel Hunter?"

"Knew *of* him, back in the day. And I know you and me probably even bumped shoulders at some point, seeing's how we were comin' up at the same time. Speaking of time, now that we've bought some, why don't you give me a thumbnail about yourself and then catch me up on what's going on with you and your friend."

Uncharacteristically, Gage spoke for fifteen minutes. Davis was a good listener, but he occasionally interrupted when he wanted to clarify a point that had been made. Toward the end of Gage's recollection, Elena helped with some of the details regarding her situation.

"So, as of today, you may or may not be thought of as dead?" Davis asked.

"That's correct," Elena replied.

"If your sister and brother-in-law think you're dead, what happens?"

"They'll need a death certificate in order to allow the sale to go through."

"Mama always wanted me to go to med school and become a heart surgeon," Davis said, grinning at Elena. "But I took the easy route and raised my hand for Uncle Sam. And even though I'm not a surgeon, I know enough to know that a person needs a body to get a death certificate, right?"

"That's correct, sir," Gage replied.

Lieutenant Colonel Davis moved both hands to his hair, combing backward as he furrowed his brow in thought. "So, by going underground, you two've placed immense pressure on whoever wants her dead."

"Exactly," Gage replied. "As distasteful as it is, put yourself in their shoes. You need her dead to cash in. But to prove she's dead, you need a death certificate for the courts. You know for a fact she was wounded in a gunfight. Then, you might have seen video of her with a bloodstain soon after the gunfight. And maybe even video of her laying flat in the car and not moving." Gage pointed his finger toward town. "Then, the next day, you might have seen a video of what looks like a bundled body in the back of this Volvo."

"Somebody would have to have some unheard-of pull to have access to traffic cameras here in Germany." Davis shifted in his chair, crossing his leg and tapping his boot with his hand. "Hell, I bet if I was on a joint domestic mission with the Kommando Spezialkräfte, I couldn't even get access."

"Tell him the kind of money that's at stake," Gage said to Elena.

She did. Straight-faced, Davis asked if he could borrow ten million dollars.

Elena turned to Gage. "Is he serious?"

"I am if you are," Davis answered, giving everyone a chuckle.

"Forgive my pathetic jokes," Davis continued. "So, let's assume they've paid off the highest levels of government, law enforcement, whatever. And that gunfight you got in...where was it?"

"Right outside a small town on the Swiss border called Jestetten."

"Gunfight outside of Jestetten. Whoever's watching the cameras knows where to look. They pick you up running north while you're on the phone with Hunter, right?"

"Yes, sir."

"You have the idea to make her look dead. You tell her to lean her seat back and not move."

"Correct, even down to her hand positions," Gage added.

"Good. Then, you dump the cameras when you're near here and my fellas bring you in."

"Yes."

"So, they don't know you're at Panzer Kaserne. They could be scouring cameras all over Germany. So, how the hell do they know about the bundled body from a little while ago?"

"There's an Aral gas station down in town, a few klicks from post, sir."

"I know it."

"I parked there, in view of two cameras."

"Okay."

"And then I went inside and used my debit card."

"Gage Hartline's debit card?"

"Yes."

Davis uncrossed his legs and leaned forward. "You're banking that they know who you really are."

Gage told him about Elena's young friend, Paulo, in Sicily, and how he'd died as a result of the scooter accident.

"And he knew your name?" Davis asked.

"Yes, sir. He did."

Elena began to sniffle. "It's my fault," she said. "I made the mistake of telling him Gage's name."

"We think the man we had the gunfight with first went to Sicily and cased her house. The young man we're speaking of was her friend, the landlord's son. He was always looking in on her. I think the asshole who shot us interrogated him and killed him in such a way that it looked like an accident. From there, he may have tracked us to a nearby hotel—we don't know about that, yet—then he knows we took a ferry to Genoa because he murdered two men at the port."

"What?"

"Sure as shit," Gage replied, quickly falling back into the barracks-vernacular. "But those guys had no idea we were headed to Zürich, so he had to track us there by some other means."

"So, you get to Zürich and kidnap a Russian banker..."

"Kidnap is a strong word," Gage said. "That little shit had put contracts on her life."

Davis nodded. "And then..."

"We left Zürich and stopped in the forest near Jestetten to question the banker. He died, we survived a sniper and then hurried here."

"Who the hell is this assassin, anyway? Any ideas?"

"I don't know, but he's good," Gage said.

"And bad," Elena added.

"You know anything about him?"

Both Gage and Elena shook their heads. Gage relayed a bit more about the American assassin—about how sloppy he'd been. "When that failed, I can only assume that they decided to pony up for a true pro."

Lieutenant Colonel Davis scratched his chin. "Hard-line, in the line of work you've taken up, would a kill job like this pay very much up front?"

"I can't really say, but my best guess would be a down-payment with the bulk of the money coming after a successful kill."

"So, he's hungry," Davis remarked.

"That's one way to put it."

The trio was quiet for a moment. Davis spoke first. "So, this means your pursuer...assuming he knows about her injury and then saw your little performance at the Aral station...this means he's going to want to prove she's dead."

"Correct," Gage answered.

"How can he prove it?"

"As you said, he'll need my body," Elena answered.

"But what if there's no body?" Davis asked.

"Then the Assassin has a problem," Gage answered.

"And so do Nastya and Georgy," Elena added.

After asking for a moment to himself, Gage stood and walked away. He passed the cots where he and Elena had slept. He walked to the other side of the pre-war warehouse, looking out the wavy glass panes at the busier area of the Kaserne. Above the trees, Gage saw a medium-size Lufthansa jet that was descending, on approach to Stuttgart. He tracked the aircraft—probably an A319—until it disappeared behind the trees. Gage walked back to Elena and Davis.

"Maybe they saw us at the gas station…maybe not."

"And?" she asked.

"So, if she really was dead…if I failed to keep her alive…what would I do then?"

"You'd get rid of her body," Davis said. "Or hide it, at the minimum."

"Correct. But how?"

Davis answered. "You'd still fulfill her wishes and make sure 'Nasty' and her dipshit husband couldn't get a death certificate."

"Right," Gage said. "After that, what would I do? What do most people do at the end of a day's work?"

"They go home," Elena said.

Gage pointed at her and smiled. "Precisely. They—go—home."

"What're you saying?" Davis asked.

"I need to not-so-secretly bury her body. Then I need to not-so-secretly book a trip home." He motioned to Elena. "Her corpse is the bait, and we wait for the wolf."

They discussed the plan at length.

Once they'd decided on how to go about things, Gage asked Lieutenant Colonel Davis if he could ask him a big favor.

"Sure, what is it?"

"Where's the nearest small-arms range?"

"There's a twenty-five meter range here, on post," Davis answered.

"Any way you could scare up a few pistols and let us pop a few rounds?"

"Of all the crap I've done, that one's the easiest. You wore this beret," Davis said, touching his. "The one thing Uncle Sam is generous to us with is weaponry."

Gage and Elena spent nearly two hours at the range. Once she got over the kick, Elena took to shooting with ease. By the time they were finished, he had her painting the black with a Colt 1911 and an M9 Beretta.

She wore a smile the entire time.

Afterward, since she was feeling so good, Gage asked to see her paintings.

"Not today," she replied perfunctorily.

A bit later, after leaving a rather obvious trail, Gage buried "her" out in the woods. He even had a quick funeral ceremony.

Just in case.

***

It had been an extremely busy day. When he first departed her duplex, the Assassin had driven the nurse's body several kilometers away. He stuck to rural roads and avoided intersections to prevent being tracked in the way

Gerard had tracked Elena and her American protector. Besides, in his experience, many traffic cameras dump memory after a day and re-loop. So, by the time any investigation into the nurse's disappearance began—when her duplex burned down tomorrow—most of the recordings would be long gone.

Three kilometers to the south of her duplex, he drove into the woods and hid her well-wrapped body under a pile of pine needles. Afterward, the Assassin drove her car back to her duplex, parking it inside the garage and confirming that everything was in place. He'd worn rubber gloves in her car, but he rolled down the windows to doubly confirm that the fire might destroy any hairs or fibers he'd left behind. Then he walked from the duplex back to his rental car. From there, he drove back to her body and, finding it undisturbed, he loaded it into the trunk of his rental. Then he drove north into Germany, a distance of only 50 kilometers.

Soon after crossing the border, the Assassin found what he was looking for—a big box hardware store called OBI located on the outskirts of the city of Singen. Not too dissimilar from a Home Depot, right down to the excessive usage of the color orange, the Assassin didn't take long to find the items he needed. After purchasing bolt-cutters, several padlocks, lead counterweights, chain and a long section of blue tarpaulin, he drove around for ten minutes before finding the next item in his deadly scavenger hunt—a secluded car parked behind a warehouse. Using his Leatherman tool, he swiped the plates from the car and used them to replace the Swiss plates on his rental. Finally, he headed to the massive Bodensee, known internationally as Lake Constance.

Weary of all these extra steps, the Assassin promised himself that, if there were any more encounters with Elena Volkov or Gage Hartline, it would be quick and final.

But what if she's already dead? What if she'd taken a bullet, lost too much blood and expired in the car?

Doesn't matter unless there's a body.

Still…what if?

Cruising beside the sparkling waters of the massive lower lake, he forced the speculations from his mind. He'd focus on all the "what ifs" once this bit of unpleasantness was done.

So, as the afternoon sun blazed, the Assassin searched for his ideal spot near the waterside town of Sipplingen. After a full hour of looking, he finally found a lakeside rental cottage that appeared unoccupied and wasn't too close to adjacent cottages. The Assassin backed his rental car into the driveway and stepped out. He glanced down into the small boathouse, seeing a small jon boat with an outboard engine. It looked to be around 4 meters in length and had three bench seats. The boat was chained and padlocked.

He walked around back, listening as the water lapped at the white dock ten feet below the level of the house. He knocked loudly two times. No answer. The Assassin peered through an adjacent window, seeing a welcome basket on the kitchen table along with a note. He could see the logo of the rental company on the note.

Whoever was renting the cottage hadn't yet arrived. And summer is the high season. Would they be coming today, or not until Saturday? He glanced at his watch, guessing check-in to be at 3 P.M. It was currently 1:45.

There was no time to delay. The Assassin had to get to Böblingen before sundown.

He cut the padlock and freed the boat. Before heading out, he slung the chain and padlock into the water. Then, using a small can of fuel he found tucked in the side of the boathouse, he topped off the tank. After starting the engine on the third pull, the Assassin shut it off—it worked and that was all he needed to know. He walked up to the road, making sure the boathouse wasn't visible at road level. It wasn't—it was perfectly secluded.

Back down behind the car, he spread the lengths of chain perpendicular to the car. Then he placed the blue tarp on top of the chain and dragged the nurse's body from the rear of the rental, still wrapped in blankets. He wrapped the blue tarp tightly around her body, then the chain. Before fastening the chain, he lugged each of the heavy 25-kilo construction counterweights from the car, fastening all four to the bundle and padlocking everything with bone-crushing tightness.

The nurse now weighed more than 150 kilos. It would be all he could do not to capsize the jon boat as he dumped her body in the deep lake. The Assassin hoisted the heavy body into the boat, placing it down below the gunwales. After retrieving his pistol, he put the bolt-cutters in the trunk and locked the rental car. Then, the sweaty Assassin pushed the bow of the small boat into the water, stepping in and waiting till he was clear of the boathouse before starting the small engine and puttering due south in the intense sun.

There was a good deal of boat traffic on the lake today. The Assassin's temper crept up because each time he found a quiet section of deep water, a boat full of people or some dickhead on a jet ski would come roaring into his area. He wasn't worried if someone saw the splash of his dumping the nurse's body—from a distance. But if they were too close, they'd see the chains and certainly get suspicious. Therefore, he vowed that he'd require a kilometer of separation before he released the body.

After nearly an hour of trolling, the Assassin pointed the bow back toward the cottage. The north shore of the lake was dotted with homes and hotels, and it felt like every one of their occupants were out here on the water, all of them making it a special point to keep their craft close to the Assassin's jon boat. Then, after a maddening stretch of heavy water traffic, the nearest boat—a pontoon carrying two older couples—slid out of range to his southeast.

Finally, the Assassin found his moment.

He whipped his head in all directions, pronouncing the pontoon as the closest craft at nearly a kilometer away. No other boats were nearby and he was far enough from shore.

Time to sink her.

The Assassin hoisted the weighted body, grunting with the strain of moving it while standing in an already shaky boat. His back seared with pain as the stitches threatened popping from the strain. Just as he managed to get the nurse longways across the bow, a series of small wake waves hit his boat, nearly capsizing him. The Assassin checked again to make sure no boats were near—they weren't. He sat on the foremost bench seat and used his feet to shove the bundle forward, holding tightly when she finally rolled over into the water with a loud splash. The boat nearly tipped bow-down under all the weight. Once the nurse was gone, the boat lurched upward with the loss of her mass and the heavy weights. Then, there was just the sound of bubbles. The Assassin scrambled forward, watching as the bundle filled with water before quickly descending out of sight.

After another glance around, the Assassin let out a contented breath as he checked his back for blood. He found none and took the moment to light a well-deserved cigarette—one of his Gauloises from the dead Russian banker. He yanked the warm engine to life and cruised across the choppy waters of the Bodensee, back to the cottage where his rental car was parked.

The Assassin approached indirectly, zig-zagging as he looked for cars or activity. He saw nothing. He tucked the pistol down into his waistband and puttered into the small boathouse before stepping out and dragging the boat up onto the covered portion of shore. The next renter might be surprised at the absence of lock and chain, but since nothing had been stolen, the Assassin didn't think any special precautions were needed. He stepped from the boat, looking around the boathouse to make sure he'd left nothing that might make the next person suspicious.

"Is that your car in the driveway?" a voice yelled.

The Assassin's heart stopped—briefly.

The question had come from a man and the accent was Eastphalian, similar to what a person would expect to hear around Düsseldorf. After briefly closing his eyes, the Assassin shoved the pistol all the way down into his crotch. He turned, acting as if he were startled—it wasn't much of a stretch.

"Goodness," he said with a smile, touching his chest. "You gave me quite a start."

The man was probably in his mid-60s. He was thin and well-dressed in bright summer clothes. His white hair was pushed backward and the tan of his face, arms and legs gave him the air of a wealthy retiree who enjoyed the outdoors as much as possible.

While the man offered a polite smile, he cocked his head quizzically at the Assassin's presence. "Doesn't that boat go with this property?" he asked, thumbing his hand to the cottage.

"Yes, indeed," the Assassin replied sheepishly. "I suppose you're this week's renter."

The man nodded. "I am. Just got the key from the office in town and came straight over."

"I rented it all this past week," the Assassin explained. "I turned in the cottage keys earlier today. I just wanted to go out for one final bout of...fishing. I truly didn't mean to infringe on your time. Guess since it's so pretty I stayed out too long."

"They biting?" the man asked, his tone convivial.

The Assassin relaxed a tad. "Not today, but yesterday I got a whole cooler full of arctic char."

"I'm looking forward to throwing a hook in the water myself."

"Well, if you're here for a week, you'll have some luck, especially early in the day."

"Good to know," the man replied.

Running the scenarios through his mind, the Assassin believed he could probably leave now with no harm done. It's not as if the man had seen anything untoward—just a man wanting to extend his vacation by a few hours. The Assassin clapped his hands once. "Let me get out of your hair. I do apologize that I wasn't out of here before you arrived. It's just been such a fine week I guess I didn't want to let it go."

The man didn't move, just stood there smiling politely.

Taking his cue, the Assassin began to head up to his car. "Well, have a nice week. Sorry for the intrusion."

"No trouble at all," the man said. He began walking but he glanced back at the boat.

"You here with your wife?" the Assassin asked as they ascended to the gravel drive.

"Nope," the man said, still looking back at the boat. "All alone. I may go see some friends that live in Ravensburg." He half-smiled, half-frowned as he screwed up his face. "Did you say you were fishing?"

The Assassin already knew his mistake. *Damn it!* Without missing a beat, he gestured to the southeast. "Yep. My friend, Klaus, has a place down the shore. I used his gear." Smiled. "Didn't want to fly here with all that stuff."

"I don't blame you. Where did you fly from?"

"Berlin. Been there twelve years now."

"Fun city," the man said as they reached the rental car.

"It can be." The Assassin glanced down, seeing the drag marks leading from the car down to the boathouse. The man seemed to take no notice. He was eyeing the lake and taking great breaths.

It was past time to go.

"This is a rental?" the man asked, thumping the sheet metal of the Assassin's car.

"How'd you know?"

"You just said you're from Berlin, but these plates are local."

"Right."

"You know, I travel quite a bit, and almost all German rental cars have the HH license plate, for Hansestadt Hamburg." Narrowed his eyes. "Strange that yours has a local KN."

This nosy old bastard! Shrugging, and fighting to maintain his composure, the Assassin said, "Just what they gave me at the airport."

"Which airport did you use?"

The Assassin genuinely hated this man. "Stuttgart."

"Really? Why? Friedrichshafen is just down the road and has direct flights to Berlin."

Removing the polite tone from his voice, the Assassin said, "I had business in Stuttgart."

"Ah," the man replied. Then he frowned and allowed his tone to change, also. He made no attempt to disguise his suspicion. "Seems odd that they'd give you a Konstanz tag all the way up in Stuttgart."

"I'll make sure I ask them why when I return the car." The Assassin extended his hand. "Once again, I'm sorry I disturbed the first few minutes of your holiday."

"I hope you have a pleasant trip," the man replied, taking the Assassin's hand and giving it a firm pump.

Once he had a good grip, the Assassin yanked the man to him and twisted, pulling the thin arm up behind the man and feeling his shoulder resist for a moment before it popped—a clean dislocation. The man yelled out but the Assassin cut it short by clamping his left arm under the man's neck. The Assassin shoved him forward, the two of them thudding to the gravel behind the cover of the cottage.

The man spasmed under the Assassin, making gurgling noises as the Assassin held firm, adjusting the chokehold for maximum constriction.

I hope you die slow, you meddlesome old prick.

In the midst of his dying, the man vomited. The last thing the Assassin wanted was to be doused in puke, so he clamped down even harder. Hardly any of it escaped the man's mouth and before long his exaggerated movements fell to mere twitches.

Eventually, the man's twitches ceased but the Assassin held fast, halting sufficient blood to the brain for a protracted period of time. When he was sure the man had perished, the Assassin rolled to his back, wincing at the pain and gasping for air. He felt like he'd ripped all his stitches apart and his lungs were on the verge of exploding. He lay there for quite some time, catching his wind as a few stray clouds scudded through the azure sky.

Sonofabitch! He'd been just minutes from being able to proceed without any loose ends—but this busybody had to show up. Though he was in a hurry to leave, the Assassin forced himself to slow down and think. What had been nothing more than a jon boat with a missing lock was now a crime scene—or, at the very least, the location of a man who would soon be reported as missing. The Assassin could wipe down the boat and leave the scene as it was. If he took the man's wallet, the cops might just write this off as a robbery gone wrong. But would there be one critical loose end that might somehow point the detectives to the deep? Could someone come forward, maybe someone from the shore that the Assassin hadn't seen, remembering a man heading out in the cottage's jon boat with a large blue bundle?

After hiding the man in the jon boat, the Assassin walked up to the cottage, using his shirt to open the unlocked back door. Inside, he found the man's luggage by the door and rental paperwork on the kitchen counter beside seven bags of groceries. The Assassin opened the front door, seeing a BMW 545 with "D" license plates. He'd been correct about the man being from Düsseldorf but, unfortunately, he was in no mood to find satisfaction over his knowledge of German accents.

He couldn't burn this house, like he'd done with the nurse. They were too close and someone might put the modus operandi together. So, now he had to stay until nightfall, at which time he'd dump the man's body in similar fashion to the nurse's. The Assassin found rubber gloves in the kitchen. He donned them and washed them thoroughly with dish soap. Then he stowed the man's groceries and unpacked the suitcases.

His final order of business involved a bottle of whiskey that had been in the man's groceries. The Assassin opened the bottle and carried it to the boathouse, dumping all of it in the water. He pressed the bottle to the dead man's lips and even canted the man's head to allow a small amount of vomit-tinged saliva to dribble in and mingle with the splash of whiskey that remained in the bottle. The Assassin made sure the old man left plenty of fingerprints on the bottle before dropping it on the covered dock next to the boat.

Just as the Assassin was finishing up, his cellphone rang. It was Gerard.

"Your man disappeared for a bit before popping back up on a few traffic cameras not too far from where he was this morning."

"And?" the Assassin asked.

"He drove into the woods on a fire trail. He was in there maybe twenty minutes and, when he came back out…"

"The body was gone from the back of his car."

"Precisely. The back was empty."

"Are you still on him?"

"No. I've lost contact but I'm looking."

The Assassin committed the details about the possible gravesite to memory and hung up. After changing his shirt, the Assassin locked the boathouse and cottage and drove all the way back to Singen, where he made identical hardware purchases as earlier.

Later, after an "alcohol-related mishap," the dead vacationer would join the nurse in the deep of Lake Constance.

Chapter Fifteen

IT WAS early evening in south central Germany, though the sun was still high above the western horizon with summer solstice having been less than a week ago. Gage and Elena were in the rear of Lieutenant Colonel Davis's Army Volkswagen van. The windows had been curtained shut, allowing them to snooze over the long drive. The commander's aide, Staff Sergeant McCoy, drove the van—he was quiet except for the few times Gage spoke to him. Every now and then, McCoy checked with the commander by phone and told Gage nothing had happened out at "the grave site." As they neared Frankfurt, Gage and Elena discussed exactly what would happen tomorrow.

"Are you sure you don't mind footing the bill for this?" Gage asked.

"Are you kidding?"

"It's a lot of money—a stunning amount, in my opinion."

"For this special occasion, I don't mind."

Elena was on the rear bench seat. Gage was in the seat just in front of her. He was turned sideways, his back against the curtained window.

"Do you think he'll go to the spot?" she asked.

"The *gravesite*? No," Gage replied with a firm shake of his head. "Not unless he's far more stupid than we think."

"Because he knows it could be a trap?"

"Yep. And there's no reason for him to go. He can anonymously report 'the body' to the cops and, if I'd actually buried a body there, the cops would find the body, check the DNA and if it was you—voila—the assassin would get paid for a job well-done."

Elena seemed puzzled. "So, even though you don't think he'll go, it was worth your friends going out there anyway?"

"Colonel Davis insisted."

"What'll happen to the assassin if he does go out there?"

"McCoy, you listening?" Gage asked.

"Tryin' not to, but this van's mighty small."

"Don't worry about it. Tell Elena what will happen to our nemesis if he shows up at that grave site."

"Depends on whether or not the polizei is out there."

"If they're not."

"He'll be up against twelve of the world's finest soldiers. They'll take him down with extreme prejudice while making sure he stays alive. Then he'll get a free ride back to a little facility we keep for such occasions. At that point, after some cajolin', he'll tell us what we want to know."

"Cajolin'?" Elena asked.

"Encouragement," Gage replied with a wink.

"And that will make him talk?" she persisted.

"He'll talk," Gage replied.

Elena seemed suddenly nervous.

"Does it bother you to hear that?" Gage asked her, puzzled.

"No, not at all," she answered. "If I'm anxious it's because I wish it would come true. I want hard proof about Nastya and Georgy."

"What do you want to do then?" Gage asked. He'd asked this question several times before.

"I don't know," she answered, firmly shaking her head. "And I'm unwilling to tease myself by thinking about it since it seems so far from reality."

"Regardless, I don't think he'll show at the mock grave site. But don't worry. This plan is going to flush out all the rats sooner rather than later."

"You don't know that," she said.

"No. I don't know it for sure, but I think it's a good plan."

Despite her consternation, she smiled.

Forty minutes later, the Army TMP van was allowed through an electric gate on the service side of the towering Frankfurt Marriott. McCoy eased the van through and followed the ramp downward. In the basement garage, the hotel manager met them, placing their bags on a cart and apologizing that they would have to ride the freight elevator.

"Give us a moment, please," McCoy said to the polite German.

"Certainly." The manager walked to the freight elevator and held it open.

"Hartline," McCoy said, handing Gage a cell phone. "Press and hold any number other than zero on this phone and it will call me. I'll be here in the hotel all night and then I'll meet you in the morning. You're gonna take the subway to the airport, correct?"

"Yes. The S-bahn."

"Colonel Davis told me to tell you that the room and room service are all on Uncle Sam. Said there's a special arrangement here with that manager—he's a friend of ours."

"Thank you," Gage said, shaking Staff Sergeant McCoy's hand.

"If that phone rings, it's either me or the colonel."

"Will he call me direct if something happens?"

"Probably."

"Roger."

"Colonel also said to keep your head down till you're wheels-up."

"We won't leave our rooms," Gage replied.

"Y'all go on up. I'm gonna secure the van and I'll head up afterward."

Gage thanked him again before he and Elena entered the freight elevator with the manager, riding it to the 37th floor. The manager gave them two passcard envelopes, replete with room service breakfast coupons and WiFi codes. Their rooms were side-by-side at the end of the hallway. When they reached the rooms, Gage gave the manager 20 euro and thanked him.

"No need to tip me," the man said.

"Then give it to one of your workers who can use it."

The manager dipped his head. "I will be here until eleven. Call if you need anything at all." He gave Gage a card with his cell number. The two men shook hands before the manager walked away.

"How's your shoulder?" Gage asked.

"Feels okay. The bandage catches on my shirt sometimes, but other than that it just feels sore and achy. How about yours?"

"It's fine."

"Really?"

"No, but there's not much I can do about it."

"Hungry?"

"Very," Gage answered.

"Want to have dinner in your room?" she asked.

"That'll work. I need a shower first."

"One hour?"

"Perfect."

"Can we check on my dogs?"

"I'll see what we can do. See you in an hour."

Gage's room was quite nice, decorated in black and cream with accents of burgundy. In the center of the room was a very un-German king-size bed across from a massive flat-screen TV. Between the bed and the large window, there was a work desk and a recliner. It was the same 4-star hotel room a businessperson might find in Hong Kong, Los Angeles, Moscow or Sydney. Though all business certainly wasn't Gage's style, he'd be a liar if he said he wasn't excited about a good night of sleep on the massive bed.

Get nice and clean and then load the stomach up with good food, heavy on protein. Drink copious amounts of water right now—so you're not pissing all night—and then hit the rack before 11. With a 10:45 A.M. flight, that should amount to a good eight hours. When was the last time you had eight hours…eight good hours?

He couldn't come up with the answer.

In the black marble-dominated bathroom, Gage turned on the shower, making the water cool. He showered for fifteen minutes straight. When he exited, he eyed his wound—it looked good—so he added a fresh bandage. Then he donned the last of his clean clothes, a black t-shirt and a tattered pair of cargo shorts.

"Real nice outfit," he muttered. He'd just been ready to wash his clothes in the sink before he rang the manager.

"Any way someone could wash a load of clothes for me tonight?"

"If I have them back to you in ninety minutes, will that be sufficient?"

"That's great. My friend, too?"

"Of course." The manager gave Gage some simple instructions. Gage called Elena's room and she agreed to prepare some laundry for cleaning. After placing his items in the small laundry bag and hanging them outside his door, Gage rested on the bed, his eyes open as he stared at the ceiling.

Though everything about this night felt quite right, something about the overall situation felt quite wrong.

And he had no idea what was unnerving him.

A bit later, after Gage had wolfed his food, he pushed his plate to the center of the rolling cart. Hand on his stomach, he leaned backward, taking large breaths.

"I'd say you were hungry," Elena said, cocking her eye at his clean plate. For the first time since he'd met her, she'd not dried her recently-shortened hair. It was hanging straight and damp, still occasionally dripping onto her t-shirt. She'd worn old jeans and a simple pair of flip-flops. Despite the simplicity of her outfit, Gage was taken by her natural beauty. She looked even better with no makeup.

"Want to talk about tomorrow?" he asked.

"Can we not?"

"Sure."

"I just want a night off." She sipped her wine. "Know what I mean?"

"Believe me, I get it. You done eating?"

"Yes. I'm quite full."

Gage kept the pitcher of water and the bottle of wine before rolling the food tray out into the hall. When he returned, Elena had a cigarette in hand.

"Where can I smoke this?"

"Do you have to smoke?"

"Yes," she laughed. "I told you—if you can get me through this situation, I'll quit. But, for now, I want a cigarette. Maybe two."

After a moment of thought, he slid on his old tennis shoes and told her to follow him. He led her up the enclosed stairwell across from his room. They climbed ten flights of stairs to find a steel door at the top. In German, English and French, a sign at eye level forbade any unauthorized personnel from opening the door. The word "alarm" was used several times.

Gage eyed the simple magnetic reed switch on the upper portion of the door. The builder hadn't even gone to the trouble of embedding the switch. He removed his knife and lifted its compass to the switch.

"What are you doing?" she asked.

"Checking polarity. But I think I've got a better idea." First, he unscrewed the wire clip several feet to the right of the door. This would buy him the slack he needed. Then he ripped a length of duct tape from the insulation on a nearby wall. The tape was still relatively sticky. He pressed a bit of it against the door where he could reach it. Then, he used his knife to carefully unscrew the two sheet metal screws on the magnet end of the switch.

"Hold this in place," Gage said. "Don't let it move." As Elena did as she was instructed, he unscrewed the two screws from the frame side of the door. Then, holding the switch together, he used the duct tape to keep the magnet in place. With the slack in the wire, Gage carefully laid the reed switch on the support beam to the right.

"Wow," Elena said. "That's impressive."

"Actually, it's not," Gage replied. "All I did was keep the circuit in place. If they'd have installed that the correct way, we couldn't have gotten out on the roof without them knowing. And we still might not. Ready?" he asked.

She squeezed her eyes shut.

"Three-two-one." Gage pushed the door open. The only sound was the breeze and the distant din of the nighttime city far below.

"You'd make a good burglar," Elena teased. He shrugged.

The Frankfurt Marriott's building was called the Westend Gate. Though neither of them knew it, the building had been the tallest in all of Germany until 1978. The height of the building served them well as they walked to the southeast corner, able to see the bulk of the inner city, the snaking rail lines of the Hauptbahnhof, and the Main River. To the west, an orange and pink horizon still added a bit of a glow to the buildings of Germany's banking center.

There was a stiff yet warm breeze at the corner of the building. Gage took the ornamental lighter from Elena's hand. "Let me help."

"Wait," she said, pushing the cigarette back into its pack. She drew close to Gage, looking up at him. "After Dmitry died, I didn't think there was a man on this earth who could make me look his way."

Easing backward, Gage said, "Elena, you might be confusing mutual trust with actual attraction."

"Don't tell me what I'm feeling." She grasped the back of his neck and pulled him toward her.

He resisted, but only for a moment. The power of their attraction wasn't unlike the two magnets that held that reed switch together. In one instant, not only did he see her lovely face coming toward his, he felt the press of her breasts along with the pull of her hips as their bodies came into full contact.

Just as her mouth closed on his, the Special Forces cell phone rang. The noise was loud and irritating and unwelcome. But it stopped them as Gage stepped backward and held the phone to his ear. He looked at Elena and mouthed "McCoy."

Gage gave McCoy his room number. "No, we're not there—we're on the roof. Be right down. What? She was having a cigarette. Don't worry. No one's up here."

"What is it?" Elena asked as Gage hung up and started for the door.

He stopped and turned, motioning her to hurry. "There's a man poking around in the woods at the gravesite. Come on."

As Gage turned and ran toward the door, Elena gripped the safety rail at the edge of the building. She squeezed her eyes shut and dipped her head.

"Elena, come on!"

While descending, he glanced back at her. "You okay?"

"Fine."

"You're bummed that you didn't get that cigarette."

"No, Gage. That's not why I'm bummed."

His mind dizzied by the prospects of catching the Assassin, Gage completely missed what she was trying to tell him.

***

While a strip of light might have existed on the western horizon, the forest south of Böblingen was oil black. Lieutenant Colonel Barry Davis had personally led two alpha teams here to deal with the man who'd shot up former Green Beret Gage Hartline and his friend, Elena Volkov. Though Davis thought the Assassin, whoever he was, would be foolish to come out here and see for himself, the colonel had been around long enough to know that sometimes even the brightest people do stupid things. So, it wasn't a complete surprise when Davis heard one of his men announce that a car had pulled in off the main road and stopped at the locked swinging gate of the fire road.

"Talk me through," Davis replied. His men were concealed in a perimeter around the obvious gravesite and, because of a ridge, he couldn't see the gate.

"Got a male getting out of his car. The car is a late model sedan. The male seems average height and size. No other details until he gets closer. Okay, now he's climbing the gate and using a flashlight. He's walking up the path, swinging the light in arcs. It's obvious he doesn't expect any trouble."

"Is this guy that stupid?" Davis asked. "How far?"

"He's a hundred meters from first contact."

Davis was farther up the hill, well past the shallow grave of four potato sacks bundled together. While he felt confident that his men could take this man without much incident, he knew he'd be breaking all sorts of international laws by doing so. Although the Germans were accommodating and welcoming hosts, Davis doubted that they would smile upon an American military takedown of a citizen on their soil—especially without clearing it with them first.

This could set off an international incident. There'll be congressional hearings. Pressure for us to leave Germany. The Germans will say we are out of control—a war machine that's grown beyond itself. To cover his own butt, the Secretary of State will barbecue my ass for weeks, and then all I'll have left is my book tours and an afternoon slot on Fox News.

All valid points—and, regardless of his political leanings, Lieutenant Colonel Davis hated news channels. So, he counseled himself the same way he'd been counseling himself since the age of 12, with the very same phrase: *Don't get caught.*

"You think this is our guy?" one of the team leaders asked.

"He's in a suit jacket and it looks like he's harnessed," replied the team member who was down the hill.

"Green light first opportunity," Davis said. "Non-lethal unless he retaliates."

"Roger."

As the man came over the crest, Davis peered through his night vision monocular, the device nearly blinded by the garish sweep of the man's flashlight. Seconds later, there was a burst of light followed by a thundering report. Then there was quiet—followed by moaning that grew to yelling. The yelling was quickly muffled.

Bound and gagged, the man with the flashlight was carried into the back of a large green truck with German business markings on the side and doors. While the truck advertised a bakery owned by the Fahlberg family, it carried 13 American Green Berets and one man howling and complaining through a gag.

The man had taken a non-lethal, 12-gauge rubber shotgun slug squarely between his shoulder blades. It had knocked him forward onto the path, splitting his chin before he was pounced on from multiple directions.

The bakery truck arrived at the "business" 14 minutes later. The interrogation began immediately.

***

A short time earlier, the Assassin had approached the gravesite from the west, low-crawling to the crest of the hill. Below him, the hill fell away to the freshly-tilled earth and, eventually, the swinging gate at the fire road. He'd deftly concealed himself with items from the forest floor and waited as the day's light evaporated. Shortly before dusk, using a night vision monocular similar to Lieutenant Colonel Davis's, he spied on the fire road that led in from the main road.

Eventually, after the forest was fully dark, shadows slid into place, moving silently and without rapid motion. Rather than sweep his monocular, the Assassin focused on one shadow in particular. It was a man and he was wearing nighttime fatigues. He was armed with several weapons and his adroit movements indicated years of training and a high degree of self-discipline. Once the man was in place, the Assassin slowly inched the monocular around, eventually able to spot numerous other men waiting patiently, waiting to pounce.

Mildly crestfallen, the Assassin had been almost sure this was a trap. Even if the oil princess were dead, this Hartline bastard wasn't completely stupid. He wasn't going to dump his client in a shallow grave and leave. No, much like a hollow point bullet, he was going to cause some collateral damage on his way out.

Once the men, whoever they were, had settled into place, the Assassin carefully covered his silenced burner phone and pressed send on the already-prepared text. Then he waited.

Twenty-two minutes later, he watched as the private detective's car halted at the gate. Then he witnessed the man climb the gate before walking dumbly with a swinging flashlight.

Here I am! Come and get me!

While all of this played out in a manner that was unsurprising to the Assassin, he was floored by the shotgun blast. The report was unmistakable, followed by all the black shadows swarming onto the private detective's downed body. The audacity of these people...

Straining through the budget NV monocular, the Assassin swore he saw one of the shapes using zip-ties on the downed man's wrists and ankles. But the shooter had only been a few meters behind the private eye, and the Assassin had seen him hurled forward by the powerful blast.

Meaning, they'd shot him with a rubber slug or a beanbag. The man's yelling confirmed the round's non-lethality.

While that softened the blow just a bit, the Assassin knew the policies and procedures of Germany's formidable police agencies. And though they could be aggressive at times, they wouldn't have taken down a non-threatening citizen in that manner unless he'd been carrying a weapon in his hand.

But the Assassin had seen the private eye clearly—all he'd been carrying was the flashlight.

A minute after the takedown, a medium-size straight truck quietly backed to the scene. The truck didn't have a telltale safety beeper that engaged while reversed—nor did the backup lights illuminate. Within seconds, the private eye was hoisted into the truck, followed by all the black shapes as they silently climbed into the truck's rear before it purred away.

Though there were letters on the side of the truck, they didn't contrast well and the Assassin was unable to read them. Not that it mattered—the truck was camouflaged as a work truck but was obviously modified for stealth.

He remained in place for fifteen minutes, just in case. During that time, he carefully extracted the battery from the burner phone. A short while later, as he drove over a bridge, he flung the phone and battery into the Berstlach Stream.

So, one question was answered tonight, but two remained: First, and most important, was Elena Volkov dead or alive? Second, and perhaps most puzzling, who the hell was this Gage Hartline? What the Assassin just witnessed amounted to a spec-ops-style takedown. How could Hartline have laid something like that on so quickly?

***

209 kilometers to the north, in Gage Hartline's Frankfurt Marriott hotel room, Staff Sergeant McCoy relayed the takedown to Gage and Elena. Elena squealed with delight but Gage shook his head.

"What is it?" she asked, crestfallen after she saw his grim expression.

"It's not him."

"Roger, we're standing by," McCoy said to whoever was on the other end of the line. He turned to Gage and Elena.

"Whoever they took down had come in about as un-tactically as a person could. He had a flashlight and came loping down the forest lane as if he were out on an evening stroll."

"He sent a patsy," Gage said. "Dammit!"

"Yeah," McCoy breathed. "It looks that way."

"What are you two talking about?" Elena asked.

"Mister Hartline is thinking that your assassin indeed learned about the fake grave site. Then he sent this other man in to have a look. He did it to flush *us* out."

"Do we know that for certain?" Elena asked.

"Not yet. We'll know soon."

The threesome sat that there for what seemed an eternity. Gage turned on the television, finding a friendly soccer match—Mexico versus Costa Rica. He turned the volume low and tried to lose himself in the struggle. It was almost 30 minutes before the phone rang again. McCoy didn't listen for very long. His face was sour as he nodded and spoke only a few words. When he hung up the phone he shook his head at Gage and Elena.

"He's a private detective from Ulm. Whoever hired him did everything by text and paid him by dead drop. Told him exactly where the gravesite was and paid him two thousand euro to go investigate. Didn't tell him what was allegedly buried there, though. So, the private detective wasn't breaking any laws and was happy to make two grand for checking on a spot in a forest. Damn near got him killed."

Gage rested his head in his hands and spoke without looking up. "Will he know who took him down?"

"No chance. They blindfolded him and no one spoke in his presence, other than the interrogator—one of our German language specialists. He speaks like a native."

"What's the private eye supposed to tell the assassin?"

"They wrote the text for him. The text said there was a woman's body wrapped in plastic and blankets in a shallow grave. But Colonel Davis had someone at CID check the phone number the assassin used. It was offline and not transmitting at the time of the text. They're keeping it on constant ping and will let us know if it goes active again."

"Damn," Gage breathed.

"What about the private eye?" Elena asked.

McCoy shrugged. "They'll blindfold him and drop him somewhere remote. He'll be told not to breathe a word of any of this, or else, and he'll also get an extra five-hundred euro in his pocket for his trouble. Tomorrow, he'll wake up confused and sore as hell between his shoulder blades. And when he gets the urge to call the cops, he'll remember what happened and think better of it."

Despite his frustration, Gage couldn't help but chuckle.

"Do you think the real assassin was out there?" Elena asked.

"What do you mean?" McCoy asked.

"I mean, could he have been near the gravesite watching to see if he'd been set up?"

Arching his eyebrows, Gage said, "She makes a good point. And that'd explain his phone being off by the time the text was sent."

"Too late now," McCoy answered. "If he was there, he's gone."

Gage shrugged. "Well, if he wasn't there, he'll have to turn on his phone at some point to get the private eye's message."

"So, now what?" Elena asked.

"Now, we proceed as planned," Gage said. "Tomorrow, I 'fly' back to the United States. We have to assume the assassin doesn't know you're alive, so you remain hidden."

"Then, we take a little trip," Elena added.

"Exactly."

McCoy relayed Gage's decision to Lieutenant Colonel Davis. A bit later, when Staff Sergeant McCoy departed, Elena averted her eyes and said she'd better get to sleep.

Not believing the words escaping his mouth, Gage stopped her at his door. "That, uh, security door up on the roof is still disconnected, in case you, uh, still want that cigarette."

Her eyes were focused on the door handle as she mulled it over. After a moment she said, "No, I'm fine, thank you. I'll be ready in the morning as we planned. Good night." With that, Elena was gone like a flash. Gage heard her door open and close in the room next to his. He walked to the phone and made a room-to-room call.

When she answered, he said, "You okay?"

"I'm fine, thank you. Just need some rest."

"You sure?"

"Yes…I'm just a bit embarrassed."

"Don't be."

"Thanks."

"Lock your door and if you need me tonight, you call me. But we're safe here, so you rest well, okay?"

"Goodnight, Gage."

Despite his angst, Gage knew he needed sleep. He brushed his teeth and washed his face and nestled into the comfortable king size bed. As sleep confounded him, his mind was awash in the cunning of his opponent and what might have been up on that high roof above the Frankfurt skyline.

Then it hit Gage—he realized why Elena had seemed regretful as they'd come down the stairs. She was upset that they'd been interrupted, and now—so was he.

When Gage finally slept, he dreamed of Elena Volkov, his Ukrainian oil princess.

***

Late that night, after driving to the forest south of Böblingen and back, the Assassin wore his rubber gloves and pressed the German vacationer's lifeless hands all over the jon boat. Then, after a quiet ride to the big water of the lake, the Assassin dumped the old German in the depths of the Bodensee. He slowly guided the boat back to the boathouse. However, without docking the boat, he killed the engine before switching the power back on but not cranking the engine. He stood on the small dock and shoved the boat away, watching it slowly drift out toward the center of the lake.

Minutes later, the Assassin relaxed on the deck of the cottage, staring at the shimmering waters that lay out before him. He dragged deeply on his final cigarette of the day, attempting to zone out the pain radiating from his back and upper buttocks. When he was halfway through the cigarette, his Interpol contact phoned. The Assassin stared at the vibrating phone, finding himself inexplicably angry with Gerard. The Assassin shut his eyes, taking a steadying breath before answering.

"You okay?" Gerard asked.

"Peachy," the Assassin replied in English. His tone belied the one-word description of his current state.

"Something just came across my alert screen."

"And that would be…?"

"Hartline booked a plane ticket home."

"Under what name?"

"George Nathan Howell, the same man who flew into Cantania, Sicily a week ago. The departure closes out his European visit on his passport."

The Assassin refused to get excited. "Are you telling me he booked the fare with his *Hartline* debit card?"

"No. He used the debit card for Howell. It's attached to a bank account at a regional U.S. bank called Southern First. I was able to pull the account. It's rarely used other than a few systematic deposits and automatic drafts."

It was late and the Assassin was tired—he was having difficulty concentrating. "So, he used his debit card to trick me into coming to the grave site. But does he know that I know his Howell I.D.?"

"That I don't know."

Why not pay cash at the airport? Why book in advance with a credit card? If Hartline were to walk up to the counter, sure, he'd take a haircut on the price, but he'd give zero time for anyone to react. By doing it this way, he's setting himself up.

It doesn't seem like him, this meticulous meddling bastard who's fouled up my mission.

"You there?"

"I'm thinking," the Assassin muttered.

Another trap? Doubtful. Hartline would know that few people would be stupid enough to try something untoward at Frankfurt International Airport.

"Tell me his middle name again?" the Assassin asked.

"Nathan."

"And Hartline's?"

"Nils."

"George Nathan Howell and Gage Nils Hartline…both G.N.H. He's either careless or arrogant," the Assassin breathed. He drew deeply on the Gauloises cigarette. He'd decided to deny himself of his premium hand-rolled cigarettes until he brought this situation under control.

"Agreed about his arrogance," Gerard replied. "The ticket is on Delta to Atlanta, and he's got a regional flight connecting to Fayetteville, North Carolina about two hours after he lands."

"Do you, in any way, see this as another trap?"

"What could you do at the airport?" Gerard reasoned.

"Exactly. What could I do?"

"Do you think she's dead?"

"I don't know," the Assassin answered truthfully. "Do you?"

"She sure looked dead on those traffic cameras. How would he know to fake that?"

"Because, thus far, he's been as crafty as a fox. When I tracked him to that forest with a rifle in my hands, he realized how good I am. He's been matching me play for play.."

Gerard was quiet for a moment. "You might be overthinking things. Think about it. She dies and he tries a last gasp effort to get even with you at that mock gravesite. When you didn't show, he said to hell with it. But he's almost certainly hidden her body in such a way that you won't be able to prove she's dead."

"Yeah, maybe," the Assassin replied, unconvinced. "Different subject...the straight truck that departed the forest with the soldiers and the private eye...did you find it?"

"Yeah, but I'm not sure it'll be much help. I finally found one grainy shot of it on a traffic light camera. It's lettered like a *Backerei* truck. Ran the plates and they're in Germany's system, but there's no information attached to the registration in the database."

"What the hell does that mean?"

"I don't know. Never seen something like that before, but it's very un-German to have an incomplete vehicle registration."

The Assassin pulled deeply on the harsh cigarette before dropping the butt into his water bottle, hearing the quick hiss. "Another question...the U.S. once had a special operations unit in Bad Tölz, down near Garmisch—Army Special Forces. Are they still there?"

"Hang on." Keystrokes.

Reclining backward, the Assassin viewed the sky full of stars above the Bodensee expanse. The waning moon was just a sliver, allowing for better stargazing. A mild breeze pressed in from across the water, whispering over the two aqueous graves. Although the Assassin was unwilling to use the inside of the cottage for fear of leaving a stray hair or some other telltale sign of his presence, he wished the nurse were still with him. There'd now been sufficient hours since his last climax that he would welcome her kneeling between his legs. He genuinely missed her adoring company.

Dammit, how did this one go so wrong?

"Found it," Gerard said. "Those Green Berets aren't in Bad Tölz anymore...but they're still in Germany. Wanna guess where?"

"Just tell me. I'm too tired for games."

"Böblingen, just south of Stuttgart."

Closing his eyes, the Assassin shook his head and snorted his disgust. That was mere kilometers from the fake gravesite. Too convenient. Too mother-fucking convenient. So, how the hell did Gage Nils Hartline rate the assistance of the frigging United States Special Forces?

"You think that was them at the gravesite?" Gerard asked.

"It was a dozen highly-trained soldiers," the Assassin mumbled. Few groups of men moved so adroitly, so expertly, and with such stealth. And the fact that Hartline was American, originating from...*wait!*

The Assassin sat up. "Where did you say Hartline's flight is scheduled to terminate?"

"The one he just booked?"

"Yes."

"Fayetteville, North Carolina."

"And where did he originally fly from?"

"Hang on...got it right here...uhhh...Charlotte, North Carolina."

"Sonofabitch!"

"What?"

"Charlotte *and* Fayetteville. Fayetteville is where Fort Bragg is located and Charlotte's not too far away. Fort Bragg is the *home* of the United States Special Forces. I knew those pricks were more than just guns for hire."

"Do you think your lady is being protected by them and not just him?"

"No, or they wouldn't be acting clandestine about it. He's alone, but he's supported by them."

Gerard spoke in a reasonable tone. "Be that as it may, think about it. Why would he fly back to Fayetteville if she weren't really dead? Maybe his friends are hiding her body and the gravesite trick was just to smoke you out? Why else would he have tipped his hand by booking a ticket to the home of the Special Forces?"

"Indeed, why?"

There was a bout of silence between the two men.

"I know you're busy," Gerard said. "Is there anything else can I help you with tonight?"

"You can help me tomorrow by telling me whether or not Hartline gets on that plane."

"Of course. I can check any flight's manifest from right here."

"You're sure. Even if he tries to fake it?"

"He can't fake his ticket being scanned. I can absolutely get you that information."

"Good. Call me back then."

"Do you mind if I go home until an hour before his flight? I've pretty much been living in this chair."

"Just make sure you call me when they start boarding."

After he hung up, the Assassin reclined the chair as far as it would go before pulling the store-bought blanket up over him. While it wasn't an ideal place to sleep, it would do the trick for one night. Tomorrow in the early morning, he'd hose off the deck and lock the cottage. It would probably be days before the police connected the missing vacationer, the drifting jon boat and the empty bottle of liquor.

As he drifted off to sleep, Hartline's curious actions, and his background, confounded the Assassin.

Chapter Sixteen

ON THE following rainy summer morning, Gage Hartline stepped off the S-8 into the train station beneath Frankfurt International Airport's Terminal 1. With a studiedly sad expression, he flung the fake pack over his back and made his way upstairs to ticketing and check-in. There, after queuing with dozens of vacationers headed home, or heading to their vacation, he finally was able to check in. From there, Hartline ate a quick breakfast at the upstairs food court before making his way through two layers of security, carrying a ticket for George Nathan Howell. Because Howell had no status in Delta's Skymiles program, he boarded last, with Zone 5.

Just behind him in the boarding line, a small German family struggled with their strollers and head pillows. Gage allowed them to board the jetway first. He took a melancholy look around the now empty gate before shuffling into the moveable corridor, disappearing from sight. He dragged his feet, making certain the family had boarded the aircraft before he reached the airplane.

Once there, as the cooperating first officer of the 767 stood in the door of the aircraft, Gage hurriedly donned the blue and yellow reflective uniform of Frankfurt International's ramp workers. Wearing a hat low over his head, he hoisted two suitcases and opened the door leading to the ramp. After carrying the suitcases down the metal jetway stairs, he carried the suitcases to the aft of the airplane and handed them to a "rampie." Then he rode on a food truck back into the lower level of Terminal 2. There, the captain of the 767 stood with Staff Sergeant McCoy. As Gage stripped off the ramp-worker safety garb, the captain spoke to McCoy.

"The Germans would probably throw me in prison if they knew what we just did."

"You were the easy part," McCoy said. "We also had to bribe five ramp workers and their manager."

"Anything to help Uncle Sam."

McCoy grew serious. "Captain, you're certain our friend here will appear on the manifest?"

"Yes. His will be the only empty seat on the flight, but it won't be reported that way. We're going to report to the Delta computer that the flight is full and everyone who checked in boarded."

"Thank you, sir."

The captain, a rather statuesque looking man who was probably nearing 60, eyed Gage. "Is there any point in me asking what this is all about?"

Gage had just finished tying his shoes. He straightened and said, "Sure. There's a situation here…a man who's trying to harm a very nice lady. We're trying to help her. We want the man to think I'm heading home."

The captain narrowed his eyes. "You trying to lure him out?"

"Yes, sir."

"Good," the captain said, nodding. "I hope you bust his ass. I don't cotton to men who harm women."

Gage shook the captain's hand. "Neither do I, sir. Thanks for your help."

Twenty-nine minutes later, the 767-400ER lumbered into the rainy sky, loaded with fuel, luggage, 3 dogs, a coffin, numerous packages, the Delta crew and 246 passengers. Actually, there were only 245 passengers, but according to all records, the airplane was completely full.

It would land in steamy, summertime Atlanta in approximately 9.5 hours.

***

Though the Assassin had already spoken to Gerard once this morning, he called again following a sumptuous breakfast at a lakeside café.

"Hartline definitely departed for Atlanta," Gerard said. "The plane was completely full."

"How do we know it wasn't someone else using the Howell ticket and passport?"

"That one was easy. Frankfurt's airport is on the open security grid and it's about as wired as anyplace I've ever seen—I'm assuming due to terrorism. I personally watched the security monitor at the checkpoint. It was Hartline. Then, I found the monitor at the Atlanta gate. He handed his ticket to the agent and boarded the airplane. He's gone."

"And no reports of a woman's body matching Volkov's?"

"Nothing. By the way, Hartline looked pretty desolate."

"Good, but that doesn't help me. I need the princess's body."

"Working on it."

"How about Winterthur?"

"There's a big fire at a duplex. That's all I know. Three alarm. No bodies so far."

A relief. "Suspicious?"

"Not yet."

"All right. Keep your phone on." The Assassin hung up and put ten euro under his coffee cup. An unlit cigarette dangling from his mouth, he walked outside, feeling disheveled and in need of a shower.

He'd been somewhat worried that the nurse's neighbor might sense the fire and get the fire department there before the flames had destroyed all evidence of the Assassin's presence. But if the place burned completely to the ground, he didn't think they'd find evidence of foul play.

Her disappearance was likely to be a confounding case. On to the next problem...

The Assassin kept thinking about the rest of the money Georgy Zaytsev owed him. Right now, the Assassin had the ten million plus the money he'd had left before taking this job. If he quit now and carried on with his current lifestyle, the cash would last him five or six years. There wasn't enough principle to live off the interest. That was the first problem.

He also worried about the future. What if he got some debilitating disease, like cancer? Though the Assassin had all the confidence in the world in himself, he couldn't guarantee he'd be healthy forever. What then? What if the disease stayed with him for years? Would he have to scrimp and save and live like a pauper as he withered away?

Negative.

The Assassin wanted the forty million—needed it. With the full payday, added to what he currently had, he was confident he could live the remainder of his days without ever working again. A life of comfort; a life of status; a life of debauched nights with strange, yet beautiful, women.

He indulged his base desire, thinking about tall, lithe women—arrogant and haughty and secretly wanting to be taken down a peg. Short, voluptuous ladies, with hidden tattoos and tits like watermelons. Nineteen-year-olds who were still discovering themselves and open to adventure, just waiting for him, a "father figure," to teach them about life's hidden pleasures. And he thought about all the women who fell somewhere in-between.

In other words: a life worth living.

As he lit one of the few remaining Gauloises cigarettes, a minivan parked outside the café. Two children un-assed the vehicle like elite soldiers charging into battle. They ran up and down the sidewalk by the café, yelling and clacking plastic light sabers. Then came the father, a mousy little man who looked tired and probably ready to get back to his normal routine of escaping to work each day. Last was the mother, mid-30s, slightly plump but with everything in the right place. She glanced at the Assassin as she shut the van door.

The Assassin removed the cigarette from his mouth and openly winked at her. He licked his upper lip, allowing only the tip of his tongue to show. The woman's eyes widened at his boldness and, probably due to her surprise, she tripped over the concrete parking stop, falling to her hands and knees. Her husband and children were already inside.

"Are you okay?" the Assassin asked, lifting her.

Laughing, she said she was, speaking rough German. Her accent sounded Polish. She brushed off her hands and knees.

"You're so beautiful," the Assassin said, touching her under her chin. "I know you're with your family, but I just can't help myself."

The woman seemed to be a combination of startled and mesmerized, staring up at him dumbly.

Then her husband could be heard. He was standing at the café door, having walked back outside. Though the Assassin couldn't understand him, he was probably asking her if everything was okay.

"She just had a little fall," the Assassin replied in German. "And you, sir, are a damned lucky man."

The mousy husband didn't move but he immediately broke eye contact with the Assassin. He made a nervous gesture to his wife to come inside.

"Danke," the wife whispered to the Assassin, hurrying into the café. The husband could be seen urgently questioning her as they walked to their table.

Quite brazenly, the Assassin puffed his cigarette and walked to the front window of the café, seeing the foursome being seated at the plate glass window with an excellent view of the Bodensee. It took her a minute, but the women finally looked over her shoulder and saw the Assassin. She quickly looked away before turning back after a moment, biting her bottom lip as the corner of her mouth turned up.

Damn, she'd be fun.

It was too bad the Assassin had to leave. A woman like that would be so easy to corrupt, and her pathetic little husband would even keep the kids busy during her 24-hour dalliance. He'd ignore the fact that the strange man was in a hotel room with his wife, teaching her advanced sexual techniques that would allow her to always orgasm explosively during sex. The cuckolded husband would gladly take her back tomorrow, wanting to believe her ridiculous line of bullshit that she'd just needed some time to herself.

Unfortunately, none of that was going to happen. It was time for the Assassin to go.

And just that little interlude with the bored mother displayed why the Assassin needed the full payday. Once he was paid in full, he'd be free to find such distractions, cultivating each one to their ultimate glory before moving on to the next.

Fuck living comfortably. The Assassin wanted it all.

Flicking the cigarette under the Polish family's van, the Assassin entered his rental car and drove to a secluded area. There, he retrieved his third phone, sliding the battery onto the back and turning it on. There were several voicemails which he ignored. He paired the phone with his computer, sitting there as all the systems initialized and he connected with a wireless network. When the system and translation device was online, the Assassin took a deep breath and phoned Georgy.

The Russian picked up on the second ring, breathless.

The Assassin made no preamble. He spoke directly and succinctly, saying, "Elena Volkov is dead. And you now have twenty-four hours to get me my forty million."

As the Assassin listened to the expected response, he lit one of his handmade cigarettes, inhaling deeply on the premium product as his mind wandered to a breezy beach and a fine ocean villa. He pictured that Polish wife underneath him, tears in her eyes due to the intense pleasure he'd provided.

The long and satisfying final chapter of his life awaited.

***

Ten minutes earlier, Georgy Zaytsev had sat down to a lunch with his wife. They hadn't stayed together last night—hadn't slept in the same bed for nearly two years, for that matter. Nastya's overly-muscled, tattooed Albanian standing outside was almost certainly his wife's flavor of the week. Nastya was wearing an impossibly tight dress; some sort of one-piece tube thing that was no doubt designed for skinny girls 25 years her junior. It looked like a getup worn in an 80s hair band video. Her huge, silicone-loaded breasts strained the fabric of the dress, making her husband wonder if the patrons at the fine Odessan establishment might get a free show if but a single thread gave way. Nastya lit a cigarette, an American menthol, before she'd said a word. Several diners turned and frowned.

"You can't smoke in here," Georgy said.

"Fuck them." Nastya stared at the menu then looked around. "Do we have a server or what?"

Georgy turned and waved over the young server. She arrived, her pad at the ready as she nervously glanced at the cigarette in the ashtray. Georgy crushed it out, his action hidden by the menu in front of his wife's face. He mouthed an apology to the cute young waitress, guessing her to be no more than 20.

She had an impoverished look about her, though he couldn't put his finger on what gave that away. Maybe it was a hollowness in the eye sockets and below the cheekbones—signs of insufficient calories and a poor diet. Regardless, it made the poor young thing all the more alluring to him. He loved that type of girl—young and not too intelligent. Flash a little cash, pamper them, and they'd do damn near anything he suggested.

"Vodka martini...Putinka, with extra olives, and it better be right," Nastya demanded. "Just go ahead and bring me two. And I'll also have the American burger, very rare with extra bacon and heavy on the onions. Fries, with extra salt and a large ketchup on the side." She shut the menu and went for her cigarette before loudly cursing her husband.

Ignoring Nastya's rebuke, Georgy smiled at the young waitress. "*Buzhenyna* and *holubtsi*, please. And I'll just have a beer." He made sure his left leg touched hers. She flinched at first contact before smiling at him.

With his left eye—the eye Nastya couldn't see—he winked. When the young waitress walked away, she glanced back two times.

"So, did you bring me here to watch you flirt with some teenage heroin addict?" Nastya asked, her tone bored. "Or, perhaps you called me with some good news."

"No. I haven't heard anything actually."

"You dumb bastard. You dragged me all the way down here to hear nothing? I could've been doing something worthwhile."

"What, like getting your withered old clam split open by that anabolic *durak* out there? You think he's really attracted to you? He loves the money, honey—he doesn't love *you*." Georgy snorted. "You're about as fresh as a mushy black banana."

The bell had rung. The verbal clash was on.

Unfortunately, Georgy's insults seemed to have no effect on his wife. She smirked. "Your obvious jealousy flatters me. It shows how badly you wish you could have me." She cocked her head. "You do realize the reason you have so many one night stands, don't you?"

He didn't respond. Just stared.

Nastya tapped out another menthol, allowing the moment to draw out. "None of your little sluts have any desire to come back for a second night because of your pathetic little, Viagra-loaded penis. If I were you, I'd be so embarrassed I'd never show that tiny thing to another soul."

Her words cut him deep as she knew they would. Nastya was a mean and vicious woman who could, and would, burn anyone down once she'd determined their insecurity. Georgy should have known better than to engage her but, with all that'd gone on, he wasn't thinking clearly.

"Are you done?" he asked, aware of his perspiration.

"I'm done with you and your little dick. Have been for a long time."

Georgy took a needed sip of water. "I wanted to tell you that I think we should ask Suntex for another month to get the sale in order. Maybe we give them some sort of discount and tell them we need the extra month due to a medical situation with one of the shareholders."

She rolled her eyes. "They're not going to give us any more time, you dumb shit. Haven't you read the offer?"

"We don't know if we don't ask."

The server arrived with their drinks: two cloudy martinis for her and a tall Lvivske for him. The server stood in exactly the same place and made sure her leg touched Georgy's. This time, he was too distracted to notice.

"Your food will be out in a few minutes," the girl said. She lingered for a moment, waiting for him to look up.

"Fine," Nastya said, turning hateful eyes upward. "So, leave." The server hurried away.

The wife glared at her husband and poked the table for emphasis. "You've been tasked with one thing, and one thing only. And thus far, you've failed just like you've failed at everything else you've ever tried."

He opened his mouth to retort but Nastya cut him off.

"Our lawyers have asked for extensions numerous times. I don't even know how many. They were all denied. I never told you because I wanted you focused on getting rid of *her*. And now, here we are, down to the damned wire and you've got no news at all from this prick who probably stole the entire ten mill—"

Georgy's shrill cellphone ringer cut her off. Both of them started at the phone.

"All zeroes," Georgy said reverently. "It's him."

"Then, answer it."

He did, listening for just a moment before every feature of his being brightened. He was like a light bulb connected to a rheostat that had just been turned all the way up. Both rows of his surgically implanted teeth shown in his widest of smiles. The whites of his eyes could be seen above and below his irises. And even his deeply tanned neck and upper chest, quite visible due to his shirt only being buttoned halfway up, splotched a deep red.

He was the picture of jubilation, the fortunate man who'd just won the largest Powerball lottery in history.

"Would you mind holding on just one moment?" Georgy asked. He touched the mute button and looked at his wife, his lips whitening as he pressed them together, trying to contain his grin.

Nastya, obviously sensing his euphoria, opened her hands. "What? What? What?"

"Do you want to hear the most beautiful words I've ever uttered?"

She clenched her eyes shut. "Please...say it."

"First, who do you love?"

Nastya slumped. "Don't do this."

"*Who*—do—you—love?"

"I'll blow you in the bathroom if you tell me what I hope you'll tell me. You know I love you."

"Apologize."

"What?"

"For what you said."

"Georgy...I don't believe this...I'm sorry. Your prick is beautiful, okay?"

"That's better," Georgy replied, taking a satisfied breath. "Listen closely...that disease who Dmitry married...Elena Volkov...the oil princess..."

"Yes?"

"Wait for it...wait for it...she's...*dead!*"

Nastya shrieked with joy. Her screech was so loud it caused her Albanian bodybuilder to come running inside. The husband and wife stood from the table, dancing and yelling despite the shock of the other diners. Nastya guzzled both of her martinis and grasped her surprised boyfriend's face, pressing it into her cleavage as she continued to hoot and holler.

Feeling oh so good, even with his wife's public display of affection with another man, Georgy took a large quaff of his beer and used the napkin to wipe tears from his eyes. The server had come running back, politely asking them to keep the noise down. Georgy peeled off several bills from the wad in his pocket before laughing and pressing the entire roll into her thin hand. He blew her a kiss before taking his beer and muted phone outside to the patio.

There, he unmuted his phone, apologizing for the delay but explaining that it was a time of celebration. Still speaking through the voice modulation device, the man on the other end of the line uncharacteristically agreed.

"So," Georgy whispered, lightheaded, "how did the bitch die?"

"Gunshot."

"Excellent. I hope she suffered."

"She did, actually. I'd have rather it been cleaner but it was a long shot while she was running away. She died about an hour later, probably from blood loss."

"Good!" Georgy shut his eyes, tilting his face back toward the heavens, breathlessly mumbling to himself more than the Assassin. "Oh...this solves everything. Everything is better now. Life can go on."

"I'm pleased for you," the electronic voice said. "And now, per our agreement, I want my money."

"That will be no problem, believe me. I've already got it sitting in a clean account ready to be transferred." He sipped his beer, wanting more. "Same process as before?"

"No. I have new instructions."

"Hang on," Georgy said. He motioned the server out, asking her for a pen and paper. She gave him her order pad and pen. Mouthing his words, he told her he'd find her later before sending her away with a licentious pat on the ass.

"Okay, I'm back," Georgy said into the phone. "Before I take down the instructions, where is her body located? I need to let the lawyers know so they can do whatever they have to do to get the death certificate. At this late date, every minute counts."

"I don't know where her corpse is," the mechanical voice replied. "Nor is that my concern. She's dead and I saw video evidence of her death."

Frowning, Georgy paused for a moment. "Okay, well, I'm sure she's at a morgue near where you saw her die. It shouldn't be that hard for us to figure out. Where were you?"

"Near Stuttgart, Germany. Just south of there."

"Germany? Interesting. Well, I'll get the team of lawyers on it right away," Georgy said, trying not to let this revelation trouble him. It was probably just a small speed bump—something that would cause a delay of a half-day. There was still time—barely.

Georgy cleared his throat. "Once we confirm that she's dead and get the death certificate, then you and I can straighten out this money situation."

A brief, spooky pause.

"There's nothing to straighten out. She *is* dead and I want my money within twenty-four hours of this call. That was the agreement."

"But…" Georgy rubbed his hand backward on his shiny scalp as the situation came clear to him. "While she might be dead, her death does us no good until we get a death certificate."

"I don't care. You made a deal with me to kill her. I upheld my end of the deal. Rather than me become unpleasant—and I've reached that point, just so you know—you should agree to send the money and I will exit your lives. Then you can set about doing whatever else you need to do. My portion of this is done."

"But we can't complete our business deal without her death certificate."

Silence.

"Are you there?" Georgy asked.

"There is no place you can hide. No corner of this earth that will provide you enough shelter. That's why I take such a large retainer upfront. If someone ever tries to stiff me, I will gladly spend that retainer doing what it takes to kill them. And that will keep all my future clients in line. Do you understand? If you go one minute past the deadline, I promise you a gruesome death."

"It's not fair," Georgy pleaded. "You knew what we needed."

"You hired me to kill her, nothing more. You now have twenty-four hours to pay me. Tomorrow, at zero-nine-four-two, Greenwich Mean Time, I will come after you. Just so you know, I may already be nearby. Every minute you live past the deadline will be a minute of jeopardy. I will kill you. And I will kill that slut wife of yours. And I will kill the remainder of the Volkovs, the Zaytsevs, and anyone close to them. And there's nothing on this earth that will stop me." The mechanical voice paused. "Or, you can easily prevent this by wiring the money."

"I can't believe you would act as if you didn't understa…hello? Hello?"

The line was dead.

Standing and pacing the patio, Georgy took deep, chest-expanding breaths. *Stay calm. Stay calm and think. Think!*

Rather than panic—yet—he called his personal attorney and explained some of the situation—leaving out the portion about hiring an assassin to kill his sister-in-law. He told the attorney to speak with the rest of the deal attorneys and associated parties and to begin canvassing the municipalities in and around Stuttgart, Germany for Elena Volkov's corpse, or someone matching her vital statistics, in case she'd been admitted to a morgue under an alias.

"Do you know the cause of death?" his Moscow-based attorney asked.

"Gunshot."

"Gunshot?"

"Yeah, gunshot! Now, get to fucking work. I've paid you millions and now it's time for you to pay off. No one sleeps till she's found or you're all fired. You have twelve hours to produce her body or I vow to put the weight of the Volkov name behind crushing you and your shit law firm."

"But I need to know—"

"Find her!" Georgy hung up the phone. Acting tough to the lawyer was the easy part and it did make him feel a mite better, but only for a moment. Now Georgy had to face the firing line that was Nastya—and her Albanian bodybuilder, assuming the big lug could comprehend any of this.

How could I be so happy minutes ago…and so crushed minutes later?

Trudging back inside, Georgy steeled himself for the verbal bludgeoning he knew was coming.

***

When the Assassin hung up the phone and disconnected his computer, he felt quite liberated. He knew better than to try to envision the frantic discussion between Georgy and Nastya Zaytsev. Despite all their bravado, they had to be terrified. They'd pay the money—they'd definitely pay.

His liberation didn't last long as a cold jag of regret traveled up the Assassin's spine. What if the oil princess wasn't dead? What if, after the deadline passed, she surfaced?

The Assassin's sterling reputation would be ruined. Decimated. Though no one in his field communicated with his or her competitors, the Assassin would be a laughing stock. Of course, the money was his main concern. But he also loved being the best in the world.

Regardless, you'll still have the money—fifty million U.S. dollars. So why would you give a shit about your reputation? You'll never have to work again. No one will know where you are, or who you are.

The Assassin shut his eyes and focused his thoughts. He hadn't been the same since taking the shrapnel in that blasted creek. Before that, even—it had all started after he'd murdered the young man in Sicily. Since that moment, this job had been as dirty as any he'd ever worked. He'd had to kill tertiary citizens, dispose of bodies, burn buildings, cover tracks…

There'd been little time for methodical, deliberate thought.

The Zaytsevs, trashy as they were, would want their money back if the oil princess were to somehow still be alive. If the Assassin didn't refund the money, they'd likely send someone after him. And, despite his skill, the Assassin wasn't unrealistic. If the Zaytsevs were to enlist a team of skilled operatives and promise them half of the recovered money, the Assassin would find himself one of the world's most-wanted men. He'd never be able to live on his beach in peace. He'd be the hunted.

But, on the other hand, what if Elena Volkov was dead? If so, then the move he'd just made was correct. It wasn't his fault that the American, Hartline, concealed her corpse as a final Hail Mary for his client's wishes. If the Assassin had killed her, he deserved his money, plain and simple. There'd never been a show-clause involving her cadaver.

He vigorously rubbed his face. Something about the situation was askew. And it had been askew for quite some time. The Assassin wasn't accustomed to being a step behind, but he felt at least that far back during this entire pursuit, except for those tantalizing moments when he'd caught up to the duo in that forest.

Why did that bitch have to jerk forward just as I pulled the trigger?

And what about Hartline, the prick? Maybe he was the key. Rather than seek the oil princess, perhaps the Assassin should have spent a bit more time on her protector. He was the reason she lived as long as she did. The Assassin checked his watch, assuming that the flight to Atlanta was about ten hours in duration. That meant the flight would land around 8 P.M. the Assassin's time. Flipping open his burner phone, he called Gerard. When he answered, the Assassin jumped right into his request.

"When that Delta flight lands in Atlanta, I want you to tell me if Hartline gets off the plane."

"Whoa…listen, I know you're uncovering every stone, but I'm telling you—Hartline boarded. I watched him go through security, watched him get his boarding pass scanned, and I saw the final manifest of the plane that took off. It was full and he was aboard. What you're asking for is unnecessary."

"I don't give a damn, it's what I want. How much?"

"Seriously?"

"Am I one to joke?"

"Hang on…might take a few minutes…was just getting ready to leave," Gerard mumbled. The Assassin could hear keystrokes for several minutes. Then he heard the murmur of a phone conversation as Gerard spoke his native French. After a moment, he was back on the phone.

"Atlanta has cameras but not at every gate. No way to confirm remotely. I'd have to find somebody to go down there and actually count heads while watching people exit the plane."

"How much?"

"Shit, man…I don't have an open American investigation to act as an umbrella for this. North America is not my area."

"How much?"

"Theoretically, I'd have to nibble around with someone in Atlanta, probably a local cop, and promise him some dough for doing this on the side. And, by doing that, I'm taking an incredible professional risk."

"Bullshit," the Assassin snapped, knowing that Gerard was simply angling for more money. "If your bosses found out that you paid some beat cop to watch a flight, they wouldn't have a clue what it's connected with. Don't act like this is a risk to your job."

"Correct, but then they might scrutinize the remainder of my investigation and ask what it's tied to."

"So tie what you're doing to something legitimate."

"I know how to work the system," Gerard replied.

"So, tell me…how much?"

There was a pause. "Ten grand for me to have someone go to the airport and confirm that Hartline exits the flight."

"Euro?"

"Yes."

"That's way too much but, since I'm in a hurry, I'll pay. Text me when it's set up and call me as soon—the very second—that Delta flight has de-planed."

"I can't promise that I can find someone to do this."

"Stop lying. You'll pay no more than five hundred dollars and pocket the rest of my euros. Get to it."

Gerard cleared his throat. "Pay me now."

"What?"

"In case something happens to you, I'd like to get paid now. You owe me more than just this request."

"Pull this one off, and I will call the bank and wire the full amount."

"That's perfect. But what about—"

Ignoring him, the Assassin hung up the phone. Gerard would continue to perform. He wanted his money and he knew what would happen if he halted.

Suddenly, the Assassin felt the cold shiver again. Something told him that Hartline had pulled every string in the book and faked his boarding.

If so, what was he up to? What was his angle? Maybe he did it to throw the Assassin from his trail? But, if Elena Volkov were truly dead, why would he go to such trouble? As long as her body was hidden, the final portion of his job was accomplished.

But if she were still alive, he did it to protect her. And he was with her right now.

The Assassin made a concrete declaration: If Gerard proved that Hartline wasn't on Delta flight 15, then Elena Volkov was alive and well.

The Assassin had to make peace with the fact that he wouldn't know about the Delta flight for a bit. And he'd already made his power play with Georgy over the forty million. So, without much else to do on this day, he figured he'd at least put himself into better position.

Hartline's last known position was Frankfurt International Airport. The Assassin drove to a petrol station where he filled up his tank. He purchased water, power bars, almonds and two bananas. He also purchased a new pack of Gauloises—his smoking of the most recent handmade had been premature, dammit.

Resigned to extending the three-hour drive into four, the Assassin drove at a moderate speed with the windows down. He silenced the radio and welcomed the noise of the road and the rushing wind. Though he was frustrated, he liked the fact that he was thinking more clearly—and think he did. He created scenario after scenario, dissecting each one for his best possible tactics.

And his instinct, the visceral intuition from his very core, told him this wasn't over just yet.

Chapter Seventeen

GAGE HARTLINE had, indeed, made his flight. It was quite pleasant, and despite his penchant for simple living, he'd have been lying if he said he couldn't get used to it. But he hadn't been upgraded to the land of lie-flat seats and five-course meals, no. Instead, he'd caught another flight altogether. He'd met Elena at the private terminal of Frankfurt International, on the airport's south end. Now the twosome were the only passengers on a Hawker private jet. Gage was in one of the plush leather seats, his legs stretched out before him as he stared at the raven-haired beauty across from him. Despite the fact that it would cost her thousands of extra euro, Gage and Elena had first flown to Zürich—even though it wasn't their final destination. Because, in the unlikely event the Assassin learned that Gage hadn't flown on Delta flight 15, they didn't want a charter flight to Odessa to be seen on the list of departures from Frankfurt International.

The flight to Switzerland was swift and they now stared at the rain-covered tarmac of Zürich Kloten Airport. In fact, it was raining so hard at the moment, it sounded as if dozens of hands were beating on the skin of the aircraft. Gage and Elena were at the rear of the cabin while the German pilot, also in the cabin and facing them, spoke to his dispatch on a mobile phone. He muted the phone and lifted his head to Gage and Elena, speaking English with very little accent—typical for a pilot who flies internationally.

"We're fine to fly on to Odessa from here once we gas up. I don't typically get involved in this type of thing, so please know I'm simply relaying the message. To fly from Zürich to Odessa International, they tell me it'll cost an additional nineteen thousand euro. If you want us to wait for you and fly you somewhere else—and that can't be more than forty-eight hours—then the company will give you a twenty-percent discount on the flight there, as well as the return flight to Frankfurt or any suitable European airport."

"Why's that?" Elena asked.

"Because, otherwise, we'll be flying back empty unless they can find someone looking to head back to Germany. It'd be cheaper for us to wait for you, but only for a day or two."

Elena looked at Gage. He shook his head. "That may not give us enough time...if...well, you know."

She nodded her understanding and turned to the pilot. "No, thank you. You shouldn't wait for us."

"Understood. Are you okay with the trip to Odessa costing nineteen thousand euro? Are they clear to run your card? They have to before we depart," he said with a shrug, as if apologizing. It was clear the pilot didn't enjoy this part of his job—and since Elena changed the destination as soon as they landed, situations like this were probably a rare occurrence.

"Yes," she answered. "Except I didn't pay for this flight by credit card. I did it by bank transfer from a company that's owned by my attorney. I will call and have them send the money right now." She lifted the burner phone before suddenly halting. "Oh, will the fee be any different if I bring along two small, well-behaved dogs?"

"No, ma'am," the pilot replied. "You're taking possession of two dogs here in Zürich?"

"Yes," she said with a smile. "They've been staying here at a resort."

"A resort?" The pilot's struggle to remain passive was obvious. He looked at his watch. "I'd say we'll need about an hour to gas up, file a flight plan and grab a quick bite. If you want to step off the plane, there's a little café in the terminal there." He glanced outside. "Looks like the storm has let up some, too. Take these." He handed them large, golf-style umbrellas. Elena took one but Gage politely declined.

Elena's first order of business was calling the swanky dog kennel. They offered to drive her two dogs over immediately. At the café in the upscale private aviation terminal, Gage and Elena both ordered sandwiches and waters and took a seat by the window. The summer storm had all but stopped and there was a strip of blue on the horizon. The two pilots, a man and woman, walked inside as a fuel truck parked next to the handsome Hawker 850XP.

"Well…have you decided?" Gage asked before taking a large bite of his sandwich.

"I think so."

"And?"

"Which do you think I should do?" she asked.

He shrugged as he chewed his food. "Both have merit. I could make a case for either."

"Which would *you* do?"

Gage snorted. "I'd drop the hammer and then smoke that killer out of the woodwork."

"I don't mean, which would Gage Hartline do?" she said with a smile. "I mean, if you were me, in my situation, which would you do?"

He didn't hesitate. "I'd stay hidden."

"I thought that's what you would say."

"But that's not the choice you're going to make."

"No," she answered. "It's not. Unless you can talk me out of it."

"I kinda figured you were leaning that way," he said. "Hence this private, cloaked flight to Odessa."

She took a bite of her sandwich and chewed for moment. "You didn't know that for sure." Mischief danced across her face. "Maybe I just wanted to get you to the Black Sea for a few days."

"Sounds nice."

"It's perfect," she replied. "And I honestly can't wait to share it with you."

Gage was somewhat embarrassed. He averted his eyes to his food and said, "Elena, if we do this, we can't make any mistakes."

"I'm not doing the public announcement," she said with a firm shake of her head. "That's not me...not who I am."

"People are trying to kill you," he countered, looking up again. "Forget about who you are for a moment."

"I will not," she snapped. "I'd rather die than have to resort to a stunt. I will handle this with dignity, no matter what happens."

He nodded. They were silent for a bit.

"You're angry with me," she said.

"No."

"No?"

"I just don't want something to happen to you. I want you to come out of this alive. I'm doing my best, but there's a limit to my abilities, and yours. And I'm just afraid that we're walking into a pit of vipers."

"I know you're trying to keep me safe," she replied. "I appreciate it. But I want this to end and I want them to feel a little of the heat I've been living with."

"I'm guessing they're already feeling a little heat."

"Okay, a lot of heat."

"Understood." He sipped his water. "So, since we've got some time, tell me all you can about Nastya and Georgy. And tell me how you think they'll react to the news of your alleged death, and the news that's coming."

That conversation lasted over lunch, through a tearful reunion with two pups, and didn't resolve itself until they were 39,000 feet over Romania, a mere 40 minutes outside of Odessa International Airport.

***

It was nearly 9 P.M. in Frankfurt but daylight wasn't close to yielding its powerful summertime presence to dusk. Recognizing he needed rest to promote healing, the Assassin had sprung for a luxury hotel room overlooking the Main River, just south of the teeming Konstablerwache. While he craved a sexual encounter, he abstained, ordering a sensible dinner in his room. The drapes were pulled wide open, affording him a view of the iconic Main River, Frankfurt am Main Süd and, to the southeast, the broad concrete plain that was Europe's third busiest airport.

As the Assassin chewed his last piece of heavily-seasoned chicken, his phone rang. It was Gerard. The Assassin had been waiting for this call because Delta flight 15 had landed almost an hour ago.

"Yeah?"

When Gerard delayed for a few seconds, the Assassin knew what had happened.

"Hey...listen...I'm sorry but..."

"Hartline wasn't on the flight," the Assassin said flatly, knowingly, bitterly.

"Unfortunately, you're correct. Listen, I did all I could to verify that he was flying. He went through security. He gave his boarding pass. He walked down the jetway. He was listed on Delta's manifest. Faking all that is incredibly difficult."

"Yet, somehow, he did."

"It appears so."

"Appears?"

"Sorry...he did fake it."

The Assassin shut his eyes and took a deep breath. Now wasn't the time for anger. Gerard was correct—he had done everything in his power.

"I understand," the Assassin answered. "So, he obviously still has people helping him. He either boarded another aircraft or he departed the airport by some other means. I need you to find him."

"That's going to be damn near impossible unless he used his other I.D. that we already have. And he's not that stupid."

The Assassin paused as his mind calculated the value of this proposition. "If you can find him by zero-eight tomorrow, I will pay you one hundred thousand euro, on the spot."

Silence.

The Assassin didn't speak either.

Finally, sounding out of breath, Gerard asked a question. "When you say on the spot?"

"I'll pick up the phone and wire the money *before* you tell me where he is."

"That's worth trying."

"That's why I'm making the offer."

"But you said you'd also pay me today what you owe me thus far."

"*If* Hartline exited that Atlanta flight."

"I...uh...I thought you said you'd pay me if I could get the job done."

"And clearly you have not. Tell you what, I'll pay you the full balance of what I owe you plus a hundred grand to find him. Are you in or out? I don't have much time."

Gerard breathed loudly into the phone. "Can I involve one other person? I trust her."

"That's up to you. You have to live with the consequences."

"You mean, on my end?"

"All consequences. If you draw negative attention to me...well...need I say more?"

"No. And just to be clear, are you referring to tomorrow, zero-eight-hundred Frankfurt time?"

"Yes."

"I'm on it," his contact said. "I'll be in touch."

The Assassin hung up. He finished the mixed vegetables and coarse mashed potatoes his chicken had come with before he drank the remainder of his *Mineralwasser*. Then he opened his balcony to smoke the last cigarette of the day. He stood outside, completely nude, smoking and staring broodingly at Frankfurt International. Aircraft landed and took off, purple against the fading sky, their lights blinking in the frenzied dance that was controlled from that central tower.

He smoked half of the cigarette before flicking it away, watching it tumble and move with the wind currents before striking a roof below with a flash of sparks. The Assassin gripped the rail, gritting his teeth as his entire body shivered with rage.

Elena Volkov, the Ukrainian oil princess, was still alive. And that meddling bastard, Hartline, was with her. Wherever they were, they were taunting the Assassin. Laughing at him.

***

Four hours later, a black Mercedes limousine snaked north on Odessa's beachside road, Zdorovya Track. Though it was Sunday morning, to the revelers, it was still Saturday night. The time was 2 A.M., the hour when the biggest stars and public figures showed themselves at the Black Sea resort's most-exclusive clubs. And for this summer's jet-set, no club was more exclusive than Itaka, an establishment that had spared no expense on décor, lighting, sound and location. Itaka fronted the beach and was designed after the Greek ruins of Athens. Marble columns towered fifteen meters above the dance floor. On the north end of the club, the Parthenon stood sentinel over the 30-meter-long fluorescent purple bar. The bartenders wore togas and the female staff didn't wear much of anything. With pulse-pounding music and a line of bouncers deciding who got in and, in most cases, who didn't—Itaka was Odessa's most exclusive venue to drink, dance and be seen.

While the club was packed with beautiful and wealthy people, tonight had been a slow night for celebrities. Two paparazzi lurked in the shadows 10 meters from the bouncers. As they did every night, the bouncers and the local paparazzi put on a little skit. First, the bouncers made a big show of running the photographers off around midnight. That was all bullshit. The club owners—a group of cocaine-snorting, stripper-loving Muscovites— needed the paparazzi as bad as the paparazzi needed them. Perhaps worse. If the paparazzi were to go to another club, then that club might quickly become the place to be. So, the act had played a few hours ago and now, if a celebrity were to show up, the paparazzi would ambush them from the shadows. They'd successfully get twenty or thirty seconds worth of pictures and video before the bouncers "noticed" their intrusion. At that time, the bouncers would scowl and yell and lightly shove them back to their shadowy hiding area.

It was a good system for everyone, especially the underpaid bouncers. Depending on the quality of celebrity who showed up on a given night, the paparazzi would tip each bouncer between 500 and 1,000 Ukrainian Hryvnia—at the current exchange rate, between $15 and $30. One time, when an extremely popular Australian starlet had "accidentally" flashed her goods while getting out of a limo, the bouncers were each overjoyed to receive 3,000 Hryvnia each. And on top of that, they'd all gotten a front-row view of her laser-treated mons pubis. What a night that had been. And the pictures, of course, sent the already-popular starlet to the A-list.

The process worked well for everyone.

So, as the two paparazzi nudged each other upon seeing the limo, they dropped their cigarettes to the ground and ceased flirting with each other. One paparazzo readied his video camera while the other prepped his camera and lights. The head bouncer, known as a cooler, even turned his head to make sure his friends were ready for the arriving limo.

"Probably another damned carload of British lads who pooled their steroid money to arrive in style one night in their pathetic lives," the videographer muttered.

"That's not a bad guess," the photog replied. "But it *is* a Mercedes. I'm going to go with two or three sixty year-old wealthy Saudis who wish they were oil barons, here to tell every young slut that they *are* oil barons."

"I could see that."

The two men were in position now, chuckling over their guesses as the bouncers held back the sidewalk traffic who'd also spotted the limo. Both paparazzi were proven wrong as soon as the driver opened the rear door of the Mercedes. Two long, tan, shiny legs emerged, led by the telltale Christian Louboutin high heel shoes with the stark red soles. When the remainder of the woman was visible, the crowd gasped and the paparazzi feverishly worked to make sure their shots were of the finest quality.

It couldn't be—could it? Was it really her? What about her was different? The hair! Yes, the hair—plus she was a tad leaner. Leaner and more radiant. And stunning.

This was the collective thought.

Because it really was her—the rags-to-riches royalty of the Ukrainian people—one of their own—the oil princess, Elena Volkov, a woman who had virtually fallen off the map since her husband's death.

"Elena! Please! Over here!" the photog paparazzo yelled, overcome as genuine tears filled his eyes.

She was fully out of the car now, flashing a dazzling smile at both paparazzi before turning to the rapidly assembling crowd and blowing them kisses.

"Your hair is so short and so blonde!" an adoring woman yelled. Elena's smile grew wider as she acknowledged the woman by touching her freshly coiffed and colored hair.

She'd colored it earlier, learning that going from black to blonde is a painstaking process.

"Elena, where've you been?" the videographer yelled.

"Just traveling," she replied.

"What happened to your shoulder?" the videographer asked, referencing the fresh bandage.

"I'm a bit clumsy," she replied, turning back to the crowd and blowing more kisses, doing her best to acknowledge each person.

One of the bouncers offered his hand and ushered her up the three stairs that led into the exclusive club. Elena turned back to the cameras and crowd, waving one last time before disappearing like a wraith into the purplish light and fog machine smoke.

The crowd, the paparazzi, and even the bouncers, were dumbstruck over what they'd just seen. Elena Volkov's appearance would be the boon of the summer season. After tipping the bouncers handsomely, the two paparazzi raced away on their scooters, anxious to start the bidding. They knew that multiple celebrity-covering fan websites would pay top dollar for the photos and video of the reappearance of the Ukrainian oil princess. If someone wanted an exclusive, they were damn well going to pay for it.

Though the news was Tweeted almost instantly, the first decent images didn't hit the wire until the following morning, just before 10 A.M. The reason for the delay was the intense haggling over the cost of the pictures and footage. The most credible rumor had the videographer selling his video for 60,000 U.S. dollars.

Once the pictures and video appeared on multiple websites, the accompanying stories didn't offer much substance other than the backstory of Elena Volkov's tumultuous life since her husband's death. Not even the most enterprising of reporters knew about the murder attempts. Months back, there had been sketchy stories that she'd been struck by a car in Prague. Soon after, word leaked out that she'd only suffered minor injuries and the story was quickly forgotten. But now, the reclusive celebrity was back and partying at the Black Sea's finest club. Most reports claimed Elena Volkov spent the balance of her evening in a private, ultra-exclusive Itaka suite with other celebrity friends.

None of the stories reported the truth—because their authors didn't know what happened once she went inside—it had all been fabricated by the club's general manager. He was as surprised as anyone about her presence, and couldn't find anyone other than the bouncers who'd even seen her. Not wanting to seem ignorant of her presence, the general manager made up the part about her spending time in the private suite. What else was he to do?

The truth was much more boring. After walking the red carpet, Elena Volkov strolled through the dark and frenetic club, sticking to the lightly crowded perimeter in an effort to prevent a panic attack. She walked straight to one of the restroom hallways and slipped out the side door into an alley. There, her male escort—Gage Hartline—awaited her in a rather plain rental car.

Regardless, her reemergence caused quite a stir and was a windfall to Itaka. The line of hired cars on the following evening was nearly unmanageable. The general manager and owners—their nostrils flaked like sugar glaze on fresh doughnuts—couldn't have been more thrilled.

And for Elena Volkov—mission accomplished. The following morning, she reached out to several of the players that had been involved in her crucial reappearance. Their help might be needed again.

Chapter Eighteen

THOUGH he physically felt much better, the Assassin awoke the next morning extremely frustrated. He ordered a large breakfast and, despite his hunger, left at least half of the food on the tray. He hardly even touched the coffee—and it was quite good. The day outside was gloomy, with rain threatening. The low, ominous skies added negativity to his mood. Hoping a cold shower might snap him from his current state, he took one, cleaning himself thoroughly. When he exited the shower it was 7:43 A.M.—his phone rang. It was Gerard from Interpol and, by the tone of his voice, the Assassin could tell he was excited.

"Did you find them?" the Assassin asked.

"Yes."

"Are you absolutely certain?"

"I'm certain."

"There's a difference," the Assassin said.

"Wire my money."

"Tell me first."

"That wasn't our deal."

"Just tell me. I won't stiff you."

"That's not fair."

"Nor is life. Tell me."

Apparently, Gerard and the woman he'd brought in had worked throughout the night, chasing every possible lead they could think of. First, they checked other commercial flights. Then, they checked the numerous short and long-distance trains that had departed the train station under the belly of the busy airport. Finally, the female had decided to run the flight plans of the private aircraft that had departed the airport within several hours of Gage's alleged flight to Atlanta.

"So, when she came up zeroes," Gerard said, "bloodhound she is, she checked subsequent flight plans."

"I'm not following," the Assassin replied.

"She found a medium-size business jet that departed Frankfurt International forty minutes after Hartline's flight was to have departed."

"And?"

"It flew to Zürich, a very popular destination for business jets departing Frankfurt. The jet is owned by Frankfurt-based MJAC Aviation.

Oddly enough, they've had a rash of non-safety-related issues, mostly involving pilot scandals."

"What does that have to do with anything?"

"Probably nothing, sorry. Anyway, the flight in question was chartered by a limited liability company based in Ukraine. Upon landing in Zürich, the pilot immediately filed a new flight plan. Want to guess the destination?"

"No guessing games."

"It was going to Odessa, Ukraine. It departed Zürich only an hour after landing."

"Who were the passengers?"

"I've been unable to get that from MJAC."

"So, a flight went from Zürich to Odessa. That doesn't prove a damn thing."

"Agreed. So, we got in touch with dispatch at the private aviation terminal in Odessa. There were no cameras for us to check. We spoke to a person in security who saw the passengers." Gerard paused dramatically. "A man, mid-forties, with heavy stubble. He was well-built. With him was a woman with short dark hair, late thirties or early forties. Attractive."

"Still not good enough."

"The woman's summer clothing revealed a large white bandage taped over her left upper shoulder. She also had two small dogs. Oh, the man had a bandage on his shoulder and lower neck."

The Assassin was silent, aware of his deep breaths.

"And, if you're still not convinced, I found the taxi driver who took them to their hotel. And I, of course, have the name of the hotel. So, please, wire my money."

"Good work. You'll get your money when I confirm it's them."

"That was not the deal," Gerard protested, a tremble in his voice. "When I see the money in the account, I'll call you back with the hotel."

Gritting his teeth, the Assassin agreed. He hung up, phoned his bank and provided terse instructions. Yes, he was willing to pay the extra and exorbitant fee to expedite what probably amounted to the Belgian asshole banker on the other end of the line having to tell someone in the office to "wire the money now."

When the Belgian sweetly relayed that the wire had gone through, the Assassin placed his phone on the table and got dressed. Seven minutes later, the phone rang and Gerard gave him the name of the hotel.

"I must inform you that I cannot be available to you any more over the next three days," Gerard said.

"Why?"

"I need to leave here. I've been dogging this investigation too long without a good excuse. People are getting suspicious."

Rather than reply, the Assassin simply hung up the phone. If Gerard had duped him—which was certainly a possibility—then he'd die for it. Otherwise, the Assassin currently had no more use for him. Besides, if Elena were at the hotel, this whole thing would be over in less than 12 hours.

Using the Internet feature on one of his phones, the Assassin searched for private aviation at the Frankfurt airport. Though he was tempted to use scandal-ridden MJAC Aviation in order to glean a tip or two about their passengers from yesterday, he decided to approach Odessa as anonymously as possible. No point in tipping Elena Volkov and her protector off to his presence.

The first aviation company wouldn't have a free airplane until tonight. Too late. The second company he called had a very expensive Gulfstream V at the ready. It was far more aircraft than the Assassin needed, but it was gassed up and waiting with two fresh pilots.

"Can we be wheels-up in thirty minutes?" the Assassin asked the polite woman.

"If you're here and pay us, we can."

"I'll be there, and I'll have my bank wire the amount right now."

Five minutes later, he was in the cab, heading southeast as he spoke to the Singapore-based Belgian banker. Once again, he endured the haircut for the fast transfer and overpaid for the flight.

No matter. Elena Volkov would soon be dead and the Assassin would be swimming in money, pondering his retirement. After they'd crossed over the Main and driven across the busy German plain to the airport, the Assassin began thinking about the excuse he'd feed Georgy.

Surely Elena Volkov had traveled back to Odessa to prove she wasn't dead—to rub everyone's face in it. And such brassiness would result in her own death. But the Assassin needed a very good reason for telling Georgy that she was already dead.

Somehow, over the luxurious two-hour flight, the Assassin was positive he could come up with something.

***

A distant thudding awoke Georgy from his alcohol-induced slumber. His vision was blurry and the light was bright enough that he cursed himself for forgetting to pull the drapes. The little waitress grunted and hooked her leg over his midsection as she mumbled something about needing more sleep. Despite his hangover, he couldn't help but begin to touch her, making her coo with delight.

"Not now," she muttered after a moment. "Need sleep."

"We can sleep later."

More thudding, followed by, "Wake up, you stupid fat bastard!" It was yelled by a grating and familiar voice outside the door of the villa.

"Who is that?" the waitress asked, sitting up.

Georgy rubbed his eyes, his stomach already churning with acid. Only one person on earth spoke that way to him. It was *her*.

He stood, rather unsteadily, and after gathering himself he walked to the front door of the villa. He didn't bother with his robe. After all the booze and sleep, he needed to urinate. The urge, and the touch of the waitress, had provided him with a partial erection.

Let her see it.

Georgy opened the door.

Unfortunately, Nastya's Armenian bodybuilder had been the one banging on the door. The Armenian looked down and curled his lip, saying something in his native language as he jumped backward, almost as if Georgy was holding a poisonous snake.

Then, with his beady brown eyes still on Georgy's midsection, the Armenian sniggered.

A very small poisonous snake.

Muscle-bound prick.

Rather than demonstrate shame, Georgy didn't flinch. He cut his eyes to his wife and asked her what the hell she wanted.

She wore even fewer clothes than usual. Today, her outfit consisted of cut-off jeans that hardly concealed more than a thong would. Most of her fleshy midriff was bare, revealing a spangled belly-button ring. Nastya's massive boobs were barely covered by some sort of lace cover-up over her floss-thin bikini top. Instead of her typical, caustic response, she surprised Georgy by speaking calmly and in a pleasant tone, saying, "I have one question for you."

"Yeah?"

"Did you send the money to the Assassin?"

"Not yet. But it's ready to go. All I have to do is call but I still have time before the deadline. Did the lawyers find Elena's body?"

"No."

"We still have to send the money," Georgy said with a shrug. "I don't know what else to do unless we all want bullets in our heads."

"The legal team has worked nonstop. They've called every hospital and morgue in Germany."

"Then where the hell is her body?"

"I called off your search an hour ago," Nastya said, her mouth building into a malevolent smile.

"Why?" Georgy roared.

"Searching for her body in Germany is pointless."

"What the hell are you talking about?"

"She's been found."

Georgy's eyes widened. "Are you kidding? That's great!"

"Is it?"

"Will you please stop playing games?" Georgy asked.

"Show him," Nastya commanded her bodybuilder.

The Armenian swiped at an iPad a few times before lifting it to Georgy's eye level.

The iPad displayed a well-known gossip website. Translated, the headline read: *Ukrainian Oil Princess Makes Grand Reappearance at Posh Odessa Nightclub.* Below the bold headline was a picture of Elena Volkov. She had shorter, blonder hair and was walking the red carpet at what looked like one of the exclusive dance clubs by the shore, not all that far from his villa.

"That's fake," Georgy said.

"This was last night, you dumb bastard," his wife snapped.

"Do you realize the type of money at stake, here?" Georgy asked, looking at both of them. "That picture could be a year old."

"There's video, too," Nastya replied. "It's not fake. Dozens of people saw her *last night.* Look at her shoulder."

Georgy took the iPad and increased the size of the photo.

"Your inept assassin shot her, alright. Looks like he scratched her."

"Real good job," the Armenian growled.

Suddenly embarrassed by his nakedness, Georgy said he'd be right back. He walked to the nearest bathroom, grabbed a towel and returned. "Are you certain this isn't another deception?"

"It's not a deception!" Nastya yelled. "You need to realize that you've already pissed away a significant portion of this family's remaining money. And now Elena is here in Odessa rubbing your ugly face in it while your psychotic assassin is out there threatening our lives."

Georgy felt faint. He grasped the doorframe.

"And you were about to send him forty million more!" she yelled. "What did I ever see in you?"

"I had no way of knowing she wasn't dead," Georgy rasped as the world spun.

"Oh...and one other thing," Nastya said. "While Elena's been running and hiding all this time, her presence here—the sheer audacity of it—makes me think she might be plotting some sort of revenge."

"What revenge?"

"I don't know...maybe she has proof that we tried to kill her? Ever think about that?" Nastya asked, her tone patronizing, as if Georgy were too slow to keep up.

Before he could answer, the brain-jarring ringtone from his dedicated mobile phone could be heard. Holding the towel around his waist, Georgy turned and ran for the bedroom. Nastya and her bodybuilder followed.

As Georgy reached his phone, Nastya saw the waitress and immediately began spewing filthy insults at her husband. The waitress buried herself in the sheets and the bodybuilder slyly tried to sneak a view of the young woman.

But Georgy didn't notice a thing. His phone displayed all zeroes. He held the phone with reverence.

"It's him," he whispered.

"Probably calling you to laugh at you," Nastya said. "And tell him he can't shoot for shit."

Ignoring her, Georgy answered the phone. "Hello?"

The computer-generated voice replied after a brief delay. "The ruse worked."

"Ruse? Your ruse to steal our money?"

"I didn't steal your money and you haven't wired it yet."

"You told me she was dead! Then, today, I wake to find that she's here in Odessa. Last night she showed up at a club and walked the red carpet as if nothing was even wrong."

There was a momentary pause before the voice said, "Listen carefully. Elena had you compromised the entire time. She had to believe that everyone thought she was dead, including me. Now that there's such little time before the deal deadline, she doesn't think you have the time, or guts, to lay on another hit. Most of all, I think she's simply rubbing your nose in it."

"Why are you calling me?"

"Because I'm here in Odessa, and I'm going to kill her once and for all."

"I thought we were compromised. And, if so, why would you tell me this?"

"You're not compromised anymore. She thinks you paid me. She's humiliating you because she thinks it's all over."

"How do you know that?" Georgy asked.

"I know. Don't worry about your advance money—it was well-spent and I'm not a thief."

"What are you going to do?"

"As I said, I'm going to kill her. You and your family need to behave normally during the next twenty-four hours—which, is to say, you need to act angry as hell. Don't hesitate to throw around the fact that you're out fifty million dollars. But if you see her, I need you to alert me."

"How?"

"We'll get to that."

"What if she tries to get us arrested?"

"She won't."

"How can you be so sure?"

"That red carpet stunt tells it all. Her sole objective is to embarrass you. Get a pen and paper." The Assassin provided a phone number to call if anyone spotted Elena.

"You do realize there's only twelve hours remaining," Georgy said. "We need a full day to get the death certificate."

"Elena Volkov will be dead tonight."

The line went silent.

As Nastya and her bodybuilder waited expectantly, and as the young waitress poked her head out from under the covers, Georgy stood frozen after all he'd heard. He was awash in bewilderment as well as relief. Before he could say anything, he collapsed onto the bed, staring at the mirrored ceiling as he gasped for breath.

"I think we're going to be okay," he managed.

"What did he say?" Nastya asked.

It took a full minute of steady breathing before he was able to relay the entire story.

***

Less than a kilometer away, the Assassin completed the relay system with his phone and computer. If the Russian called the burner phone, it would trigger the Assassin's toggled computer to send a text message to his other phone. The computer and toggled phone were now plugged in and sitting on the chintzy desk in a cheap hotel room on the western edge of the city. The Assassin had reserved the room for three days.

It was time to acquire some weaponry. He'd used a reputable website that had yet to fail him. Still, with the information being out on the Internet, the Assassin was always more careful. He called the dealer, satisfied at the precautions the woman on the other end of the line insisted upon. When he departed his hotel room, he hung the "do not disturb" tag from the doorknob before walking downstairs to his rental car, another Audi, this one an A6 sedan. The Assassin peered eastward, at the rows of high-rise hotels. Elena Volkov and Gage Hartline were in one of those buildings, the two of them believing they'd outsmarted everyone.

They'd soon be proven wrong.

***

Though he had a number of things wrong, the Assassin was indeed correct about Gage and Elena being in one of the high-rise hotels near the shore of the Black Sea. They'd booked a room on the 17th floor. Later, however, Gage had moved them to a room on the 9th floor, using his clean Garrett Healey identification.

After moving rooms, Gage had departed alone several hours earlier. Like the Assassin, he'd gone to buy weapons and implements. But his first mission had been trying to spot the Assassin arriving at the airport. Gage had just returned, nodding triumphantly as soon as he walked through the door.

"Got him," he said, wagging her phone.

"Let me see."

Elena opened her photos and slowly swiped through the four shots of the man seen exiting the Gulfstream aircraft.

"According to Flightaware, his charter flew straight here from Frankfurt International," Gage said, uncapping a bottle of water. "Sonofabitch must have been right on my tail and then somehow figured out I wasn't on that Delta flight to Atlanta."

"How?"

"Hard to say, but it shows how far-reaching his resources are. Thankfully, we anticipated this. I still think he's got some well-positioned law enforcement type who's helping him."

"Who?"

"Not sure we'll ever know."

Gage leaned down, eyeing the photos as she went back and forth through them. The Assassin was a decent-size man—probably six feet and around 200 pounds. Maybe a bit taller. His head was newly shaven, with only a few days' worth of growth. He'd probably shaven it after the incident in the Jestetten forest—and his scalp was markedly lighter than his tan skin. His clothes were casual but well-fitting. Earlier, Gage had thought the Assassin walked with an air of athletic confidence. Overall, he was a rather handsome man who could have easily doubled as a former footballer or just a businessman.

In the photos, the Assassin wore gold aviator sunglasses, preventing any views of his eyes. From where Gage had been concealed in an adjacent parking lot, he saw the Assassin remove his glasses in the terminal, but was only able to see the back of the man's head.

After leaving the terminal, the Assassin, one hand loaded with rental paperwork, walked to a black Audi A6, cranked the car and sped away. Gage had snapped a few shots of the Audi but the license plate was unreadable. The traffic had been heavy and two policemen had been parked at a nearby intersection, preventing Gage from running the red light and following the Assassin.

It was no matter. They now knew the Assassin was in Odessa. They knew what he looked like. And they knew what he drove.

Advantage: Elena and Gage.

When she'd viewed each photo several times, she looked up at Gage. "Tonight?"

"Yes, for two reasons. One, the deadline is coming up, and if they accomplished their mission it would still give them plenty of time to get a death certificate."

"You can say the words, Gage."

"I don't like saying it."

"Thank you. Second reason?"

"Every minute we delay allows the man in those pictures to prepare. The less prepared he is, the better off we are."

"Okay," she replied, chewing on one of her fingernails.

"You all right?"

"I am. Just ready to get on with it."

He rubbed his eyes. "I know you are. I'm ready for it to all be over with, for your sake." He checked his Timex. "I'm meeting the attorney in two hours."

"Is he bringing the security man?"

"Yes. From what I was told, the guy sounds solid."

"See? I'll be fine."

"What if there's more than one assassin, Elena? What if the situation is more than this security guy can handle?"

"They don't have another assassin."

"You don't know that."

"I just want to do it the way we discussed. This is personal for me. Regardless, I want you to stop worrying." She crossed her arms. "It's you I'm concerned with."

"Don't be. I'm not stopping for anything."

"What if *he* stops you?"

"I'll be okay, Elena."

She closed her eyes, her nostrils flaring as she pulled in a breath. "You can't understand how satisfying it's going to be to confront them."

"Just be direct and get the signatures and don't waste time."

"You think they'll sign?"

"If they're as greedy as you say, I don't see how they'll have a choice."

A smile formed on Elena's face. "I'd really like to slap Nastya."

After giving Elena a moment to indulge herself, Gage said, "Mind if I call the concierge?"

"You think he can find one?"

"Sure, if he's resourceful and has cash on hand. I'd think if he visits a few stores he'll find a manager willing to part with one."

"Have enough money?" she asked.

"Yeah. Still have plenty."

"Okay. I'm going outside." Elena dropped to her knees and crawled over the threshold of the sliding door. Both dogs followed. Per Gage's orders, she had to recline fully on the sun lounge if she went onto the balcony. This concealed her behind the concrete wall and prevented anyone from seeing her—and most important, taking a shot at her. He watched as she lay on her back and lit a cigarette, smoking with her eyes shut and her left arm draped over her eyes and forehead.

After speaking to the concierge on the phone, he arrived within two minutes. Gage spoke English to him in the sitting room, showing the man a wad of money and presenting him with what would probably be the most curious challenge of his career. As with any good concierge, the man didn't question the bizarre request. In fact, as soon as the words were out of Gage's mouth, he narrowed his eyes as if he were already pondering where he might "acquire" one of the items.

"I don't know what one costs," Gage said, pressing the wad of money into the concierge's hand. "But that should be more than enough."

The concierge thumbed through the bills. "I agree."

"Make sure you put it in the car," Gage reiterated, handing the concierge the key fob to the rental Renault Latitude.

"Got it."

"You sure you understand?" Gage asked.

"Indeed, sir," the concierge replied.

"And you know where the car is parked?"

"I'll get the space number from the valet stand."

"If anyone asks you about me or my friend…"

"I will act ignorant and, when they're gone, I will call you immediately."

"Perfect," Gage replied. "Make sure it's just as I described. And it can't be cheap, either. It needs to be of good quality."

"I understand."

"Just so you know, there will be a sizeable tip for you when you return."

The man nodded politely before departing.

Gage walked to the balcony and slid the door open, standing off to the side so he wasn't visible. Elena was done with her cigarette and was still reclined in the late afternoon sun. Her eyes were shut and she appeared a bit more placid than before.

"You awake?"

"Oh, yes."

"Maybe you should come in and take a nap. Might do you good."

She sat up and quickly ducked inside, remaining in her crouch. Once the dogs were inside, she pulled the door shut as well as the drapes. Other than the bright light around the edge of the heavy fabric, the room was quite dark. The dogs nestled next to one another in the corner. They were exhausted from the kenneling and the trip.

Gage remained still, eyeing her in the darkness.

Elena put a peppermint in her mouth, keeping it in her cheek as she talked. "When this is all over, I'd like to paint you."

"What color?"

She snorted. "I'm serious. You wear so many emotions on your face. And at the very same time, you somehow manage to appear emotionless. I haven't quite figured it out yet. I think maybe it's your eyes that tell the tale."

Gage was flattered. "That's...well...thought-provoking to hear."

"It'll be a challenge to capture on canvas."

"Elena, I know you haven't painted since Dmitry died. Please don't feel like you have to paint me."

"Why do you say that?" she asked, sounding if she'd taken mild offense. "I wouldn't force myself to paint. Believe me, my desire is genuine."

"Does that mean I can finally see your paintings?"

She produced her iPad and opened a separate photo album. Gage took his time, going through each of the portraits. He knew nothing about art but, like most people, he knew quality when he saw it. Gage guessed she worked in oil. The portraits she painted were classic, similar to what one would see of a president or the head of a major corporation. But it was the minute touches, things like the veins on hands or a slight crease in an earlobe that demonstrated her skill and attention to detail.

"These are amazing."

"Thank you."

"I mean it. The way you paint every little detail..."

"I appreciate your kind words. Now, let's talk about something else," she said, clearly uncomfortable with the praise as she took the tablet from him.

Gage crossed his arms. "Tonight, you need to make absolutely certain you wait until I message you before going in. We can't risk their assassin being close enough to make it back in time."

"I know."

Gage illuminated his Timex. "I've got about an hour and fifty minutes—"

"Before you go talk to the attorney and security man. Nervous?"

"Hell, yes," he answered.

"I'm nervous, too. But I've enjoyed this adventure, Gage."

"I can't tell you how surprised I was to see you grinning with excitement in Jestetten, after you'd been shot."

"I didn't want to die, but there was something exhilarating about being in the midst of such danger. You know that feeling," she said, her tone indicating that it wasn't a question.

Gage frowned, pondering her statement. "Yeah, Elena...I guess I do. But unlike you, I forget I'm having fun once I get hurt. Then, I don't like it so much."

They both laughed. Then Elena said, "I'm not quite ready for my adventure to end."

"We can find something a little less risky for you when this is over. Maybe we'll go skydiving."

"I'm not talking about the life-or-death part of this adventure." She took a step toward him. "I'm talking about my time with you."

Gage couldn't find the words to respond. Here she was again, inches from him. He took deep breaths, very aware of his pulse in several areas of his body.

"I never thought I'd have feelings for another man." Her words came quickly and thudded into Gage with great force. She removed the peppermint and dropped it in the trashcan, moving even closer afterward.

"Elena, please don't do something you'll regret."

"I won't regret it, Gage. I've thought about it for days. I want to be close to you."

"Still…you might feel different once you get a little time to yourself."

Elena came to him, wrapping her arms around his neck.

"Elena," he whispered. "Make sure this is what you want."

"I'm absolutely and completely certain."

They stood there kissing for some time.

"Take my clothes off," she whispered. He complied.

"Now, take your clothes off," she said, sliding back onto the bed. He complied.

Her next words were the prettiest words he'd heard in quite some time—almost as lovely as the paintings he'd just viewed. "Make love to me, Gage. And it's okay if it's quick, because we've got an hour and forty-five minutes to get it right. And I want us to get it right."

They got it right.

Chapter Nineteen

GEORGY glanced at the caller ID. He didn't recognize the phone number so he didn't answer it. A minute later, the phone rang again. He didn't answer—no one had the number of this phone, so it had to be a mistake. It rang a third time. He finally answered, spitting his words as he informed the idiot on the other line that they'd dialed a wrong number.

"Hello, Georgy, you son of a bitch…this is your sister-in-law, Elena."

Georgy's flash of anger evaporated, leaving him with a slack jaw as he dumbly tried to formulate a response. He was unsuccessful.

"Yes, Georgy, I'm still quite alive, despite your persistent efforts."

"I don't, uh, know what you mean."

Her laugh was sharp and quick. Then, in a calm voice, she continued to speak Russian as she said, "I want to meet."

"Meet?"

"Yes. But I will tell you now; we're *not* selling the company. Get that out of your limited mind. I'm only willing to punish myself with your disgusting presence because I'm going to restructure the ownership of UkeOil, especially given how you and your bitch of a wife have behaved."

"I still don't know what you're talking about."

Ignoring his denial, she asked, "Do you remember Dmitry's dacha?"

"Yes."

"I want you and Nastya to meet me and my attorney there, tonight, *alone.*"

"Why?"

"I'm going to offer you two some money to give up your shares and go away. It's a—*lot*—of money. But if you don't take it, I'll proceed with lawsuits and you'll both eventually end up losing your ownership. Given your spending habits and your abhorrence for work—you'll be broke in months, not years. And once I prove you tried to kill me, you might find yourself in prison. I bet the other prisoners will love you two."

"This is crazy. We've done nothing wrong. I don't even know what you're talking about."

"Fine, then let's forget the meeting. The Suntex offer deadline will pass, I'll still be alive, and I'll sue the ever-loving shit out of both of you. So, you lose everything. Concurrent to that, I'll go meet with the feds and tell them everything. It's not just my word, Georgy. I have proof and a *confession* from the American who tried to kill me in Italy. Goodbye."

"Wait! Please don't hang up." Georgy struggled to think quickly enough. "When do you want to meet?"

"Ninety minutes. My attorney is already there. He has the paperwork ready to be signed."

"I can't get ready and then drive all the way up there that quickly."

"I've made it fast to prevent you from trying to kill me...again."

"I need a few more hours."

"Ninety minutes, Georgy. I'm leaving in ten minutes. You tell that bitch, Nastya, that the two of you better come alone. Don't even think about getting cute. I have a security man with me who knows exactly what he's doing."

"But I—"

The line went dead.

Georgy massaged his temples and tried to concentrate. Elena obviously had no idea the Assassin was in Odessa. Despite his presence, was there time?

Take the money and run or make one last effort at killing the bitch? She did say she was offering a lot of money.

But there was a big difference between a "lot of money" and billions.

Georgy thought about the remote dacha and the long, black stretches of Ukrainian road between here and there.

Fuck her.

He frantically dialed the Assassin's number.

This might just work out after all.

***

Elena hung up the phone and stared at Gage. Neither person said anything for a moment. Finally she asked, "How did I do?"

"It sounded good to me," Gage said. He took the phone from her hand, dropped it to the floor and smashed it to bits.

Elena watched as he separated the wafer-thin battery and dropped the items in the trashcan. "Do you really think they'll send the Assassin to the dacha?" she asked.

He sat down on the bed and clamped his hand on her thigh, squeezing it affectionately. "Are you absolutely certain that the company charter makes no provision for foul play or murder?"

"I'm certain. My lawyers have combed through the charter a dozen times."

"And the courts wouldn't block the sale if you're murdered?"

"Our company is Ukrainian, Gage. And after all those lean years under communism, the economy is now booming. It didn't get that way by accident. It's like the wild, wild west. Anything goes."

"You don't think the American oil company will balk at buying UkeOil if you wind up dead right before the deal date?"

She narrowed her eyes. "They'll buy the company and then handle any negative blowback with their New York City P.R. firm. Oh…I'm sure they'll promise an investigation. They'll feign outrage whenever foul play is suggested. It'll be all the usual crap." Elena laughed. "They don't care about me and, in the privacy of their boardroom, they'll be glad I'm dead."

"Then, yes, I absolutely think they will send their assassin to the dacha."

"I wish I could see the look on his face when he realizes he's been duped."

Gage cocked his head. "You're enjoying this, aren't you?"

"I'm enjoying the strategy of it all. And I'm especially looking forward to confronting Nastya and her idiot husband. But my biggest worry is with you." She pointed north. "Whatever you do, Gage, don't stop."

"I'll be fine."

"Tell me about the security man."

Gage nodded. "His name is Nazar. I quizzed him from some odd angles. He knows his stuff and, most importantly, your attorney vouched for him."

"What's he look like?"

"Big guy. Black hair with a low forehead. Bushy black eyebrows and a heavy jaw. His nose is crooked, too."

"Sounds lovely."

"Well, he's not trying to win a beauty pageant." Gage touched the other burner phone. "Go ahead and let them know that we're on."

After she'd made the call, Gage reinforced their plan. "Remember, when you get out of the car, make sure you crouch down and stay hidden until he's passed. Then you high-tail it to the next street over and get in your attorney's car."

"Right."

"What kind of car?"

"A silver BMW 550. I'll do it just like you say."

"Good girl. And when you get to the beach house, if you see anything that unnerves you, regardless of what either of your escorts say, just back off. It's not worth it."

"You got it."

"You sure you feel good about this?"

Rather than respond, she kissed him.

***

While Georgy finalized details with the Assassin, Nastya extracted herself from her boyfriend and made her way to the rear of the villa. There, from the quiet media room, she phoned a former lover, a man deeply embedded in Odessan organized crime. He answered on the second ring, forgoing pleasantries and immediately asking Nastya something ribald.

His suggestion made her smile—and remember. But there was business at hand.

"Maybe later, lover," she cooed. "For now, I need a favor. Are you in Odessa?" When he said he was, she explained what she required, what she would pay, and gave the man the address of the oceanfront villa.

"When you get here, just come around to the back, to the far side of the swimming pool," Nastya said. "There's a small cabana out there. It's unlocked. Just pull back the curtains and watch from inside. I already checked—you can clearly see the entertaining salon from the cabana window."

"So you want me to just stand guard?"

"Yes. It's probably unnecessary, but I want you there just in case. If you see anything out of the ordinary, please protect me."

"What about your husband?"

"Protect *me*."

"Understood."

"When can you be here?"

"Hour…hour-and-a-half. Am I doing this *only* for money?"

"If you'll help me with this," Nastya promised, "then you can do anything you want to me."

It certainly wasn't the first time Nastya had uttered those exact words.

***

Twenty-two minutes after the phone call with her brother-in-law, Elena Volkov and Gage Hartline exited the elevator in their hotel lobby. Gage knew the next few minutes would be extremely dangerous. He was banking on the Assassin's desire not to get caught. Otherwise, if the Assassin were reckless or desperate, he might try to knock her off right here in the lobby or out front as they waited for the concierge to arrive with their car. Though he needed to be prepared for anything, Gage didn't think the Assassin would have the gall to take a crack at her in such a public place.

Trying to appear as casual as possible, Gage exited the elevator first and scanned the people. There weren't many. He motioned Elena forward, satisfied as she walked directly into the gift shop, just as they'd planned. Gage then made his way to the double sliding glass doors of the main entrance, peering outside and to the left. There it was, 100 meters away, a black Audi A6 parked on the street. Gage had spotted it from upstairs and could now see the silhouette of a man in the driver's seat.

After spotting the Audi from the window by the elevators, a piece of Gage had wanted to use the service elevator to exit the hotel. Maybe he could sneak up behind the Audi and put a bullet in the driver's head. But that notion presented several problems. First, he wasn't positive it was the Assassin. Second, Gage had eyed the angles of approach and couldn't find one that wouldn't leave him exposed for the Assassin to easily spot with his mirrors.

No, it was best to stick with the plan.

After signaling Elena, she joined him and they stopped between the double front doors as the concierge—acting as a valet—ran down into the garage with a yellow valet ticket in his hand. Gage moved Elena to a hotel television monitor, pointing at it as the twosome feigned interest in the timeshare video. He did this because the monitor was in a protected area near the front desk. The area would lower her vulnerability from a sniper's bullet.

While there, Elena pressed something into Gage's hand. He looked down—it was her cigarettes and lighter—Dmitry's lighter. It was ornamental, made of silver and adorned with red stones.

"I told you I'd quit," she said.

"You promised to quit when it's all over."

"Won't it be?"

"I hope so."

"Then, I've quit for you."

"But this lighter was Dmitry's."

"Please keep it," she said. "He'd like that."

"Thank you."

He pecked her on the lips before tossing the cigarettes into a trashcan and stuffing the lighter into his pocket. Only about a minute passed before the "valet" zipped into the portico in the white Renault Latitude. Though they both walked quickly from the hotel to their car, Gage and Elena tried to appear casual as they stepped from the hotel into the warm salty wind of the Odessan evening.

Elena was in the car first, her seat an extremely tight fit since there was already an "occupant" reclined there. The third occupant was out of view and partially extended onto the center console and into the backseat. With the seat fully reclined, Elena had to sit up without a backrest.

Gage tipped the "valet" and reminded him to walk Elena's dogs every two hours. Then Gage seated himself in the car. He was very tense.

"Keep your hand on the door handle and, when you get out, you make damn sure you get fully clear of the road and into the shadows."

"Don't worry about me, Gage," she said. "I promise, I'll be fine."

"Get straight to the attorney's car."

"I understand."

Easing the car away, Gage watched for the correct sequence in traffic. He saw the black Audi edge forward, headlights off. *It's him, the bastard.* When a taxi approached, Gage accelerated from the hotel circular drive directly in front of the taxi, putting it between himself and the Audi.

Perfect.

The taxi driver honked and gestured angrily. Gage roared forward and made a fast left turn on Mors'kyi Lane. As soon as he'd made the turn, he used the handbrake to stop the car in the pre-designated area.

"I love you," Elena said unexpectedly. She bolted from the car and lurched into the shadows behind a shuttered kiosk.

Gage sat briefly, stunned.

Then he accelerated naturally and used his right hand to raise the passenger seat and prop up the mannequin where Elena had just been. Once it was upright, Gage looked at the mannequin.

The concierge had done a fine job. Though the mannequin's hair was a bit more full than Elena's, "she" would suffice as a reasonable facsimile provided the Assassin didn't get too close.

Gage eyed the rearview mirror as the black Audi made the turn and sped up the street. There was one car between them. Through the center car's windshields, Gage could see the Assassin, glancing around as if he were just any old Ukrainian driver, not a man bent on killing an innocent woman over money.

But not just any woman—Elena Volkov. And Gage was taken with her. He smirked as he thought about their first meeting, when she snapped at him over his brusqueness.

From then until just now...when she told me she loved me.

Surprised by her revelation, his reciprocal response was quickly shoved aside by worry. Yes, Gage was pulling the killer away from Elena, giving her the time she needed. But he didn't know much about Nastya and Georgy. If they were the type of people to hire an assassin—they'd probably also kill if they had to.

But Elena had insisted on this approach. He'd tried to change her mind but she was adamant. And Gage, a man who'd sought revenge of his own, certainly understood.

Relax. She's got the security man, Nazar, with her. The Assassin is right behind me. Everything will be fine—it's all going to plan.

When the light turned green, Gage accelerated normally, watching as the Assassin followed, believing that his target was seated next to Gage in the Renault.

"Joke's on you, asshole," Gage said, finding third gear and punching the gas. "Joke's on you."

***

Crouched in the shadows, Elena waited until the Audi passed. A tiny piece of her wanted to yank the pistol out and shoot the Assassin in his big head. Wouldn't that be a surprise for everyone? When the two cars were stopped well up the street, she stood, remaining hidden but holding her hand over her mouth. She suddenly had a very bad feeling about this entire plan. It had nothing to do with what she planned to do—her worry was centered on Gage. If something went wrong, he'd be matched in a duel against a professional killer. If Gage died, it would be her fault.

"You can't think that way," she could hear him saying. He'd say it in that calm, almost laconic voice that managed to be reassuring and sexy at the same time. "Just do your part and I'll do mine, okay? And if you promise not to worry about me, I'll do my best not to worry about you."

It was as if he were standing right beside her.

When the two cars accelerated from the traffic signal, eventually turning north toward Dmitry's dacha that was about 70 kilometers away, Elena adjusted the long, lightweight sweater. She walked to a nearby store window, turning to her reflection to see if the Walther PPS that was tucked into her waistband bulged.

Satisfied, Elena walked one block over and carefully peered around the corner. True to his word, her lawyer, Aleks, sat facing the opposite direction in a silver BMW 550. Next to him was the security man, Nazar. She walked to the car and Nazar jumped out and opened the rear door. He politely asked her to lie down on the seat.

"Why?" she asked.

Nazar shrugged apologetically and said, "We can't have someone taking a shot at you."

Once they were all inside, Elena asked for the legal paperwork and a phone.

Aleks handed the documents over the seat. "Why do you want a phone?"

"I'd like to use the flashlight so I can read."

"Sorry," Aleks replied, passing his iPhone to her. "It's in airplane mode, just in case. Are you ready?"

"As I'll ever be," she replied. "I'll read as you drive."

The legal documents seemed to be in perfect order. They'd be at Georgy's villa in less than 15 minutes.

Chapter Twenty

AFTER calling Georgy to inform him that he'd successfully acquired the "subject," the Assassin followed the white Renault out of Odessa to the north. He'd already entered the Petrivka address of the dacha into the rental Audi's dash-mounted GPS and was satisfied as Hartline was following the route to the letter. Given the busy two-lane road they were on, and the fact that Hartline didn't seem inclined to pass any of the slow-moving cars, the Assassin settled in for what would likely be a ninety-minute journey. Since this sticky yet lucrative job was nearly finished, he decided to reward himself with one of his last hand-rolled cigarettes.

He spirited the silver case from the bag that was on the passenger seat. In a reverent manner, he clicked the case open and carefully removed one of the final three handmade Portuguese products from behind the silver elastic band. After taking a great sniff of the length of the 105-millimeter cigarette, he placed it between his lips and set it aflame with the car lighter. Easing his seat back, the Assassin rolled down the windows, allowing the breeze to whip through the car as he enjoyed the cigarette in the manner of a man preparing to set off on a lifelong vacation.

Because, tomorrow, that's exactly what he would do.

The car that had been between him and Hartline veered right on an exit ramp outside of Odessa, allowing the Assassin to close behind the white Renault. He watched Hartline's head, seeing him glance at the rearview mirror, but only for a split-second. Beside Hartline, Elena Volkov's newly blonde hair shone in the light from the Assassin's headlamps. Her head moved as she adjusted herself to the right. Everything seemed quite normal. The Assassin backed off a bit—no sense in spooking them. Besides, the traffic was easing the farther they drove from Odessa. Maybe the ride would only take an hour.

He drove on for some time, finishing the cigarette as he pondered this meeting.

Why way out in the woods, like this? Was Hartline stupid? Or was he planning on exacting a little revenge on Elena's family?

Stop over-thinking.

The Assassin forced himself to relax a bit before the big finish that awaited him in Petrivka. His mind turned to other pleasurable thoughts.

On the private jet from Germany, he'd made his final decision to spend the next three months in three different places. Four, actually, if he were to count the quick trip he'd make to Istanbul. There, one of the finest forgers on earth—a woman who was linked into multiple government databases—would provide him with several pristine identities, replete with bank accounts, credit cards, driver's licenses, the works. Each I.D. cost a whopping hundred thousand euro. Fortunately, she'd parked a sizeable sum of cash in each I.D.'s bank accounts months before. Net, each I.D. would end up costing about half of the entire fee.

A bargain.

After his time in Turkey, he'd first travel to Bermuda, a place he'd lived and knew quite well. Bermuda was a fine British territory but grew a bit too chilly in the winter for the Assassin's tastes. Still, he was prepared to give it another chance due to its exclusivity and refinement. While there, he'd cultivate a new appearance and style. Though few knew what he looked like, there was no point in giving fate a chance. Other than fine living, a new facade would be his primary goal while in Bermuda.

But the Bermudan winter, it may be a touch too much, the Assassin recalled. The Atlantic moderated Bermuda, regulating its temperature. Still, it could be wet and miserable for months on end. He recalled his home, as a boy, when he'd be knee-deep in snow and dreaming of the beaches he'd only seen in pictures and movies. Those dreams crystalized during the ultra-brief summers when the Assassin worked at the small marina down at Julkula. He'd see the women with their summer tans, with their long legs and wandering eyes. They'd come off the boats with their loud and ugly husbands, the ones with the bad teeth and big bellies. When the Assassin was 17, he'd had a brief affair with one of the wives. It had been like first blood to a young lion—from then on, his mission was singular. How many had there been since then?

The thought warmed him.

Despite the cool weather he'd likely encounter, he'd still give Bermuda a shot, for old time's sake if nothing else. From there he planned to head to the lushness of Playa Avellana, Costa Rica. While he'd traipsed all over the Central American country, the Assassin had spent precious little time on its Pacific side. Unlike Bermuda, in Playa Avellana the Assassin could purchase a grand palace for what amounted to a pittance. He'd be able to hire 24-hour security and would have an unending stream of willing women to choose from. But though it was a safe haven for thousands of expats, there was still something about Central America, an atmosphere of instability, which gave the Assassin the slightest bit of pause. Regardless, he planned to give it a fair shake through the winter months.

His final destination, and his favorite so far, was Koro Island, Fiji. The Assassin had visited there once, and since then he'd not been able to shake it from his mind. Primo weather, affordability, pristine beaches and gorgeous women. And despite all the beauty and lavishness of the island, the Assassin was unable to forget something that he'd experienced there for only eight fleeting seconds: it had been an orgasm, brought about by the deft hands of an older Fijian woman. He'd been in his twenties at the time and she'd been at least fifty. She'd used strange and taboo techniques to lead him to the precipice, and the result was more than breathtaking. In fact, the sensation was so overwhelming, he'd momentarily passed out. Afterward, she'd lovingly bathed him and prepared a meal fit for a king.

Needless to say, Koro Island, Fiji, held a special place in the Assassin's heart—and libido.

For now, however, work had to take precedence. The traffic had indeed all but disappeared, and Hartline was leading the way at better than 140 kilometers per hour. A quick glance at the GPS revealed the dacha as only ten minutes away. Time to refocus.

Unless something changed the Assassin's mind, such as the presence of other people, he planned to take Hartline as he exited the car to open the gate. According to Elena's brother-in-law, the road to the dacha was blocked by an old-fashioned iron gate. Hartline would have to stop and get out and use a hidden key to open the giant padlock. The Assassin planned to back off when they neared the dacha. He'd watch from a distance and pick off Hartline once he was out of the car.

After that, killing Elena would be the white meat of the evening's feast.

The Assassin uncovered his new purchases. He had a Sig Sauer SSG 3000 with a Bushnell tactical scope; a nifty MP5A3 that was nearly new; and a sexy Makarov 9x18 pistol in chrome with black grips.

Earlier this afternoon, he'd spent twenty minutes zeroing the rifle in the forest north of Odessa. While his preparations had been hasty, he felt confident in a shot up to 500 meters, even at night. Though he'd not been able to recon the dacha, he seriously doubted he'd need anything close to such range.

The exit for Petrivka was approaching. The Assassin could feel his heart rate increasing. His hands began to perspire. His mouth grew dry. He knew that life boiled down to several key moments, and none for him had been more important than this one.

Forty million dollars. Added to what he already had, he'd soon claim a net worth of right at fifty-one million, U.S. The top fraction of the world's one percent. Yachts. Private jets when needed. Servants. Access to the finest doctors, tables in restaurants and, of course, hand-rolled cigarettes. A life in the lap of luxury. For that sort of money, he'd gladly kill his own—

The Assassin jerked upward in the seat.

He didn't take the exit. Hartline didn't take the damned exit!

The Assassin stayed with the Renault, watching as his own GPS recalculated the route to the dacha. It took the device a moment before it displayed the new course in yellow. There was another turn only three kilometers ahead. The change in route only added one kilometer to the entire trip.

"Okay," the Assassin breathed, trying to calm himself. Hartline was simply taking a different road. No need to be so jumpy. Who knew, maybe Hartline's GPS was leading him this way?

Three kilometers later, Hartline signaled and turned right to take the exit. The Assassin had dropped well behind. He allowed Hartline to get all the way up the exit and to turn right at the stop sign. As soon as the Renault disappeared to the right, the Assassin pressed the accelerator and roared up the exit. As he exited, he switched off the car's fog lamps, which would give the car a different appearance and hopefully help Hartline believe he wasn't being followed. Once the Assassin had turned right at the top of the exit, he spotted the Renault up ahead, driving normally.

The GPS displayed four kilometers remaining to the dacha.

Almost there.

***

After making the turn, Gage accelerated normally and kept his eyes on the rearview mirror. Another car exited after him. As it went under a streetlight, he could see it was painted a dark color. When the car turned, it appeared different than the one that had followed him. This car had two headlights rather than four. Then it hit Gage.

He's turned off his driving lights. Smart prick.

Gage continued on at a normal pace. The Assassin's simple maneuver of changing his car's image provided Gage with the slightest bit of disquiet. He already knew the Assassin was a formidable opponent, but the man's attention to detail was impressive.

He might have a strong attention to detail, but he has no idea he's following a woman made out of plastic, Gage thought, thumping the hollow leg of his synthetic passenger. So far, everything tonight had gone to plan.

But, for whatever reason—Gage had a feeling that would soon change. He hated it when his instinct bubbled up from the pits of his being, warning him of danger much in the manner that wild animals sense predators long before they come into sight.

At this point, the wheels were in motion, and Gage could do nothing other than focus on his part. He slowed down, hoping to draw out the seconds before the Assassin realized he was a patsy.

***

Elena and Aleks waited in the BMW. Five minutes earlier, they'd parked down the mansion-lined street from Georgy Zaytsev's villa. Nazar told them to sit tight while he reconnoitered the property. When he returned, he said there was no visible external security.

The threesome walked to the edge of the property, stopping behind a stand of vegetation that separated the villa from the neighboring mansion on the south side of the property.

Situated a short distance from Odessa, Georgy's rental "villa" was actually a palatial estate, perched just inside the sheltering dunes from the Black Sea. The sprawling home was a single story and rather new, constructed in a modern style that Elena could only describe as tacky. The architect had chosen different materials for separate areas of the exterior. The right side was made of stone, while the center and left side were constructed from varying textures and colors of stucco. Nearly all the windows were large, floor to ceiling, many of them canted inward so they faced partially to the sky.

Unfortunately, like all the homes in the Kyivs'kyi Beach area of Odessa, Georgy's was well-lit with architectural lighting. Elena looked at the neighboring houses, noting their understated diffused lighting that threw pleasant light against the structures. Georgy's rental, however, was cast in garish multi-colored exterior lighting, projecting spotlights against the villa that were more suited for a wild Otrada nightclub than an upscale beachside home in Kyivs'kyi.

It was no wonder that he always rented this estate.

Elena and Aleks listened as Nazar explained his plan. He started by going over their route. As he spoke, Elena eyed the estate.

Parked in the turnout were a large black Mercedes and a late model Range Rover. She'd guess the Mercedes was Nastya's and the Range Rover Georgy's. Just as Nazar had said, she noted no visible guards or cameras.

From where they stood, a light whooshing sound could be heard each time one of the Black Sea's small waves would come in. Any other time, the sound might have relaxed Elena. But on this night, her heart raced over the confrontation that lay ahead.

"I need to update Gage," Elena said. She stepped a few meters down the street and phoned Gage's current burner.

"How's it going?" he asked.

"We're getting ready to go in. Where are you?"

"Good timing. I'm almost at the dacha."

"How long?"

"If I keep driving at this speed, three minutes. Exactly where are you?"

"Right outside the villa."

"Anything out of place?"

"Nothing. We're going around back."

"When Nazar breaches the house, you hide. Got it?"

"I will not."

"What?"

"I'm going in right behind him. I'm sorry, Gage, but I'm not going to cower until he clears the house. I want Nastya and Georgy to shit themselves when they see me come through that door."

"Are you crazy? In just a few minutes, this asshole behind me will realize I'm not going to the dacha. When he does, this entire situation is about to get very real. If something goes wrong, they could kill you. You will *not* go in until he clears the house. Stay back, or abort the whole deal."

"I know you're angry, Gage, but they've tried like hell to kill me. I want payback."

He was quiet for a moment. When he spoke, his voice was more reasonable. "I'm just concerned about the unknown. We think there are just civilians in that house but, until Nazar clears the house, we don't *know* that. If we're wrong, you could die."

"They're not going to kill me, Gage...not without their assassin. They don't have the guts. Thank you for leading him away."

"I've slowed to a crawl. If you guys are gonna breach, go now. Gives them less time to prepare. When this guy tells them that I missed the dacha, things are going to boil over."

"Be careful, Gage."

"Elena, please reconsider about how you go in."

"Thank you for worrying about me," Elena said. "But no. You be careful." She made a kissing sound and hung up the phone, making certain it was set to vibrate. Then, palming the Walther, Elena Volkov stepped back to her escorts. She displayed the pistol and eyed Nazar.

"I'm coming in right behind you."

The two men looked at one another.

"Problem with that?" she asked.

Neither man dared argue.

"Text your friends," the attorney reminded Elena.

"Thanks." She sent the already prepared text to the two men who were parked only a short distance away. In seconds, her phone vibrated with the reply.

"They're ready," Elena said. "Let's go."

Following Nazar, Elena and Aleks slipped behind a large clump of swaying Mauritania grass and slid through the shadows at the edge of the house.

The threesome was headed around to the beach side.

***

The wait was sheer torture. Each minute dragged, the same way time seems to slow when a person tries to hold their breath underwater for a personal record. Tick...tick...tick. Billions of dollars were at stake and all the Zaytsevs could do was sit on their hands and think about how they despised each other, marking each moment with hateful glares and sneers. At one point, Nastya displayed both middle fingers, topped by scarlet red fingernails, to her husband.

Such a lovely marriage.

There were actually four people inside the Russian's villa. The young waitress hadn't even bothered to call her boss today, even though she was supposed to be working right now. She'd landed a whale and didn't intend to leave until she was kicked out, preferably with a wad of *hryvni* in her hand. Her new beau hadn't been interested in sex today, but she did manage to slip into the shower with him earlier, where she made good use of her right hand. He'd only protested for a moment before giving in, having to grip the handrail to prevent from falling over the duration of the "tuggy."

The Armenian bodybuilder seemed to have settled in and didn't seem concerned about much of anything other than the soccer match on television, a friendly between Albania and France. The under-matched Albanians were doing quite well, evidenced by the bodybuilder's constant grunting, flexing and cursing in his native tongue. There were still about forty minutes to go and neither team had scored. A draw would be a tremendous victory for the Albanians.

Finally, Nastya could stand the wait no longer. She walked to the back window, looking beyond the dimly-lit swimming pool. She shook her head before walking back to Georgy. "Call him."

"He said he'd call us."

"He works for us!" she yelled. "Call him right this second."

"Shhh," her bodybuilder admonished from the sectional sofa.

"You shut the hell up!" Nastya snapped, snatching the remote and switching off the television.

"Hey!" the bodybuilder protested, trying to take the remote from her. A quick, flirty game of keep-away ensued.

"I'm not calling him," Georgy said. "Besides, it won't do—"

His words were cut off by a sharp rapping at the back door. The knocking sounded metallic, but there was no knocker at the door by the pool. Someone had struck the door three times with something very hard.

"Who the hell is that?" Georgy said to no one in particular.

Nastya was puzzled. Was it her friend? She narrowed her eyes at the door.

The waitress, wearing a tiny bikini, emerged from the bedroom. "Was that someone knocking?"

"Go back to the bedroom," Georgy commanded. He snapped his fingers at the Armenian bodybuilder. "You, make yourself useful and answer the door."

Arms bowed out as if he were preparing to fight, the bodybuilder strutted to the rear door.

"Check the peephole," Georgy advised.

The bodybuilder did, following his gaze with a shrug. Then he snatched the door open and stared.

"Who is it?" Nastya asked.

He turned, shrugging. "There's nobody here."

But there was someone there. In a swift movement, a large man with bushy black eyebrows lurched through the open doorway and hammered the pistol into the back of the Albanian bodybuilder's undersized head. Though it didn't knock him down, the blow did the trick. The swarthy bodybuilder let out a yelp and cowered forward, both hands flying to the small gash on the crown of his scalp.

"Get over there with them," the swarthy man ordered. "Everyone on the couch!" No one, other than the bodybuilder, moved. The big man fired a shot into the television, creating a hail of dancing sparks and a lacework of ascending blue smoke. "Move!'

Everyone obeyed.

Then...behind the man, strutting through the open rear door, came Elena Volkov.

Elena Volkov, the Ukrainian oil princess.

Georgy was dumbstruck. He gaped at Elena in disbelief.

Nastya, however, seemed distraught and puzzled. She'd made preparations for a situation such as this. She was bewildered over the lack of reaction from her friend. She began typing a text.

As the swarthy man covered the foursome, Elena padded quietly across the tile floor and used her left hand to knock the phone from Nastya's hand.

"Hey!" Nastya protested.

"Shut up, bitch," Elena retorted.

She stood before the quartet, sweeping a pistol back and forth. Her next words were a brief and terse apology to the bodybuilder. He nodded his understanding and, despite his significant musculature, he didn't seem at all inclined to play the hero this evening. When Elena handed him a tissue from a nearby container, he wadded it up, holding it tightly against his head as he leaned back and breathed deeply.

"For the two of you who don't know me, my name is Elena Volkov. I'm the sister-in-law of the Zaytsevs. And for the past months, they've been trying their very best to kill me."

"Preposterous," Nastya spat, continuing to cut her eyes to the open rear door.

"Is it?" Elena asked. "You hired someone to run me over in Prague—and failed. You hired a sniper to shoot me on the yacht in Greece—and failed. Then you hired an American to kill me in Sicily—and failed. And now you've enlisted the assassin who is currently chasing a mannequin near Dmitry's dacha."

"A mannequin?" Georgy managed.

"Indeed," Elena smiled. "Your killer is an hour-and-a-half away, chasing a blonde mannequin from a fashion boutique."

Nastya's curses directed at Georgy were of the nastiest, vilest sort available in the Ukrainian and Russian vocabularies. After the berating, Georgy shot back. Then, talking over each other, the couple engaged in a vicious, verbal fight, as many sordid truths were spilled for the three spectators.

When the fight wound down, when all available insults had been thrown out, the married couple deflated, Georgy first, followed by Nastya. He went silent while she crossed her arms against her bulging décolletage and continued to stare at the open rear door.

After a moment, Georgy said, "What do you intend to gain by holding us hostage?"

"I intend to gain my freedom."

"What do you mean by that?" Nastya hissed.

"Aleks!" Elena yelled.

Upon her beckoning, a man strode through the open rear door. He was not the man Nastya had hoped for. Rather, he seemed like a businessman, wearing suit pants and a white button-down with the sleeves rolled up. In his left hand was a thin black folio.

"The lawyer," Georgy muttered.

"What?" Nastya asked.

"He's a lawyer. He used to work for Dmitry."

"Very good memory, Georgy," Elena said. "This is my attorney, Aleks. Aleks," she said, waving her pistol, "these are my trashy in-laws."

"We've met," Aleks said with disdain. He looked at Elena. "Should I check the front door?"

"Yes, please."

The attorney stepped down the entrance hall, out of sight. The front door could be heard opening and closing. In a moment, Aleks was back. "All clear," he said to Elena. "Everything is in order."

"Good. Let's get started with my idiot brother-in-law, here, and his whore wife."

Normally, Nastya would have fired back at the insult. But she was far too busy using her eyes to search for her protector outside the open rear door.

***

Something was definitely wrong.

Not only did he miss the first exit, but now Hartline had passed the turnoff of the narrow forest road that led to the dacha. The Assassin used his finger to manipulate the map on the GPS—there were no alternate roads.

So, either Hartline had missed the road by accident, or what he was doing was deliberate.

Slow down. Don't overreact. For all you know he doesn't have a GPS and he's simply lost.

The Assassin checked the Audi's clock. They were slightly ahead of schedule. Perhaps Elena and Hartline were going to the nearest town for a bite to eat or something as simple as a few bottles of water. Using the multidirectional controller, the Assassin scrolled forward on the GPS map.

There were no nearby towns. In fact, all that lay ahead for a hundred kilometers were fields and forests.

So, either Hartline was lost, or this was deliberate.

The Assassin thought about Hartline, and what he knew about him from this chase. Hartline wasn't the type to get lost.

Therefore, this was absolutely deliberate.

Before doing anything, the Assassin lifted his phone and called Georgy. Perhaps he might have some sort of insight about what was going on.

***

When the loud ringer of the cellphone erupted, Georgy's hand automatically went to his pocket. Elena tensed, her finger on the trigger of the Walther. Beside her, Nazar aimed his large pistol at Georgy's head.

"I was only reaching for the phone in my pocket," Georgy said, lifting both hands above his head.

"Slowly," Nazar replied.

When Georgy produced the phone, the greenish screen displayed all zeroes.

"Who is it?" Elena asked, snatching the phone away and eyeing the screen.

Georgy was silent.

"Nobody has a number with all zeroes," Elena said. "So you know exactly who it is."

"Who?" Nazar thundered.

"I don't know," Georgy pleaded.

Elena tossed the phone to her left, allowing it to thud dully on the thick white throw rug. In a fluid movement, she turned and put a 9-millimeter round through the center of the phone. The sound inside the house was deafening, causing everyone on the couch to flinch. The young woman in the bikini covered her ears and squeezed her eyes shut.

"I've survived four assassination attempts," Elena said, now alternating the warm pistol's aim between the Zaytsevs. "And after the fourth one, I promised myself that I would respond."

Nastya continued to look to Elena's right.

"Who was on the phone?" Nazar yelled, rapping Georgy in the forehead with the barrel of the pistol.

"Ow! Please don't hurt me," Georgy cried.

"Next time I'm drawing blood," Nazar warned.

"Okay, okay...it was a man we hired," he croaked.

"Hired for what?" Nazar demanded.

"Don't say it," Nastya cautioned.

Nazar moved the pistol closer to Georgy's face. His knuckle visibly whitened as he added pressure to the trigger. "Hired for what?"

Georgy shuddered but he shook his head. He didn't reply.

Elena adjusted the pistol to Nastya. Nastya, despite appearing slightly unnerved, was staring toward the rear of the villa.

Glancing to her right, to the open door, Elena said, "Why do you keep looking over there?"

***

The Assassin stared at his toggled cellphone. Why hadn't Georgy answered? The Assassin called again—same result, only this time the phone didn't even ring. It went straight to a computerized message explaining that the owner of the phone hadn't yet set up his or her voicemail. This caused the Assassin to hurl the phone down, striking the keyboard of the toggled computer. Something was amiss.

Think, dammit, think!

Earlier, at the Odessan hotel, when Hartline and the woman had entered the car, they'd exited the hotel slowly before Hartline had gunned the Renault and whipped into traffic. It had caused the Assassin to lose them momentarily. That had only lasted five seconds or so, after both cars had made a left turn.

Was it possible, during that brief moment, they could have exited the car and someone else was now in it?

No...not possible...there wouldn't have been time.

But *she* could have hopped out. That was definitely possible. But the Assassin didn't think someone else would have had time to get in.

So, if the oil princess had exited the car, and Hartline was tasked with leading the Assassin away, then who was sitting in the passenger seat? Maybe, whoever it was, had already been in the car...been in the car hiding.

You're reaching. Elena Volkov could still be in that car. Your hypothesis has merit, but you have no reason to believe it actually happened. It's merely supposition. For all you know, she's in that Renault right this very second and their missing the turn could somehow be explained away.

As he typically did when applying critical thought, the Assassin countered his own argument:

But Hartline wouldn't get lost. And the meeting spot they chose is remote and dangerous—why would he rubber-stamp such a location in the first place? Answer: he wouldn't—unless he was up to something.

Those two facts, alone, told the Assassin what he needed to know.

You fell for it, you stupid bastard. Hartline sucked your ass right into his little trap and now he's laughing at you. He's looking in the rearview mirror with his beady little eyes and laughing throatily at the sonofabitch who he outfoxed.

Having quickly decided upon his course of action, the Assassin zoomed out on the GPS, eyeing the road ahead on the small device. He saw the road feature he needed approximately four kilometers ahead. The Assassin looked to his left and right. The scant moonlight barely illuminated the faint brush marks of aubergine at the tops of the trees. The Assassin slowly began to back away, increasing the distance between his car and the Renault by about 50 meters over each kilometer. As he did, he checked his Makarov and holstered it on his leg. Then he wedged the MP5 between his seat and the center console, satisfied that it wouldn't be trapped after his next maneuver. The Sig rifle was resting with the stock on the floorboard but the Assassin didn't think he'd need it anymore. He checked the map.

The curve was now 2 kilometers away.

"Laugh at me," the Assassin warned the man in the car ahead. "Laugh at me and see what happens."

***

Gage noticed the headlights of the Audi growing progressively smaller. Certainly by this time the Assassin had noticed he'd missed the turn to the dacha. And for a while, Gage had been content to simply cruise along and wait. He'd thought back through his many years of training, trying to recall training blocks involving the use of decoys. If the decoys were human beings, the last thing he'd want to do is increase the possibility of injury or death. And in this instance, since the decoy was himself, he had added motivation to preserve life. But since the Assassin hadn't visibly reacted, Gage had felt no need to do anything other than lead the man further away from Odessa.

Each minute was a small victory.

But why was the Assassin backing off? And he hadn't backed off by much, either. It was gradual. Maybe he was on the phone? People often slowed as they talked. But this man was a skilled operator, not some gabber taking up the passing lane while chatting.

There was a rather sharp turn up ahead. As soon as Gage had negotiated the turn, he pressed the gas pedal to the floor and decided to stretch out the distance between him and the Assassin. That ought to tell the tale. When the Assassin saw how far ahead Gage was, he'd be forced to increase his own speed.

Gage continued to watch the mirror. No headlights. The Assassin should have been through the curve by now.

Up ahead, a pair of headlights shone in the distance, coming his way. Gage's eyes alternated between the mirror and straight ahead. The headlights belonged to a truck. Still nothing in the rearview mirror. Finally a big lumber truck rumbled past, leaving a trail of flying bark and sawdust that peppered the body and windshield of the Renault.

Continuing to eye the mirror, Gage saw nothing other than blackness and the red taillights of the tractor trailer. Eventually, the red lights turned around the curve and the lumber truck disappeared.

There was nothing around Gage now but the stygian night of the Ukrainian countryside.

He began to consider turning back. When he did, he'd call Elena. But he wasn't sure if she was in a position to answer her phone. They'd discussed this earlier and, if all had gone to plan, she'd cautiously answer the phone while Nazar covered her in-laws.

Once Gage turned back, he would do his best to catch up to the Assassin. This Renault was a stout little car but Gage wasn't certain it had the muscle to run down that Audi A6. Much of a pursuit like that, however, would come down to the two drivers. Over a long drive, aggressively passing cars on the narrow two-lane road that led back to Odessa would probably be the difference in who made it back first.

Assuming Gage had the driving chops, the hunted could become the hunter.

Gage took another look in the rearview mirror as he lifted his foot from the gas pedal. It was time to turn around. When his right foot depressed the brake pedal, his red brake lights illuminated. And for just a split second, Gage saw the iconic four-ring Audi emblem. In that same flitting moment, he heard the menacing growl of the wound-out 2.8 liter FSI quattro engine.

Oh shit.

On that deserted Ukrainian road past the village of Petrivka, the hurtling Audi struck the back of the Renault in an explosion of twisted metal and shattered glass.

At the time of the collision, the Renault had been traveling 108 kilometers per hour. The Audi was hurtling forward at 191 kilometers per hour. In miles per hour, the Audi was traveling 52 miles per hour faster than the Renault.

The results of the impact were catastrophic.

Chapter Twenty-One

NASTYA had indeed been eyeing the open rear door. She turned her eyes back to Elena and spoke through clenched teeth. "Go to hell, bitch."

Elena motioned with her Walther. "Aleks, please go close that door and lock it." The attorney complied, twisting the bolt lock after the door was closed.

"Thank you," she said to Aleks. "Now, go in my bag and get those handcuffs." She didn't avert her eyes as he produced numerous sets of the jangling metal manacles. "Good. Give one set to the girl and put another set on the glass table."

"What the hell is all this?" Nastya asked.

Ignoring her sister-in-law, Elena spoke to the waitress. "Attach one end to your right wrist, and one to the left wrist of muscles, here."

"Who?" the girl asked.

"Him," Elena said, gesturing with her pistol to the Armenian. She watched as the girl did as she was told. "Make them tighter." The girl obeyed, clicking each cuff until it was constricting each wrist.

Elena then pivoted the pistol down and right, uncorking a shot through the thick, beveled glass of the large coffee table. The glass shattered and deposited its contents to the tile floor along with hundreds of shards and pieces.

"Holy shit!" the bodybuilder yelled in his native language, almost yanking the waitress's arm from its socket as he covered his face with his hands.

"You two, sit on the floor and put your free arms through the top, where the glass was," Elena commanded. "Use that second set of cuffs to lock your other wrists together so you're held by the frame of the table."

"We might get cut," the bodybuilder whined.

"Then I'd sit very still." It took a moment to get the mostly uninvolved twosome situated the way she wanted them. The net result was their arms safely entwined in an extremely heavy wrought-iron style decorative piece of furniture. They wouldn't be able to go far, and especially without making a considerable racket.

"Nazar?" Elena asked.

"Looks good to me."

"Good." Elena had the attorney toss the third set of cuffs to Georgy. "Your right wrist to her left. And don't even think of screwing with me, Georgy. I really love the way this pistol fires."

Wide-eyed, Georgy obeyed with zest. Elena made him squeeze the cuffs so tightly that the skin paled on both sides of the steel.

"You know you're going to jail for this," Nastya hissed.

"Let me get this straight...you try to kill me, multiple times, to include shooting me, but that's okay. I hold you at gunpoint without so much as scratching you, but I'm the one going to jail? Okay."

"You can't prove anything," Nastya screamed. She took a calming breath and turned to the rear of the house, her eyes searching the windows. Elena followed Nastya's gaze.

"Why do you keep looking over there?"

"Because looking at you makes me want to vomit."

Moving on, Elena ordered the final set of cuffs to Georgy. "Now, cuff your left hand to the table on the opposite side of your two friends there."

Georgy snapped the cuffs around the wrought iron table, where the beams joined the leg. Then he had to reach far across his wife to cuff himself. "It's uncomfortable," he mumbled.

"Then ask your wife to move."

A fresh argument resulted before Nastya finally adjusted herself to her right. The net result was the foursome tethered to the heavy wrought iron table. The bodybuilder and waitress were most secure, with both arms trapped. Georgy and Nastya, however, were only tethered by his left arm. This was by design. Elena wanted to give Nastya the freedom to move—somewhat.

Sort of like giving a person enough rope to hang themself.

***

The only remaining lights on the country road belonged to the Renault. Its headlights shone into the air at steep angles, steam flitting through both battery-powered beams. The Renault had buckled upon impact, leaving the once-straight chassis of the French vehicle looking like a wide "V" from the side. This was by design, of course, as the car had absorbed tremendous energy when it was smashed from the rear by the slightly heavier Audi. The familiar, pungent smell of gasoline was the first odor to register inside the Assassin's bloody nose. Soon after, the steam escaping from the ruptured radiators reached him. The smell was coolant—much sweeter than gasoline. In fact, enough of the steam hung in the air to brighten the entire wreck as the prism-effect from the twin headlights spread greenish light over a ten-meter radius. This was good for the Assassin. The light would allow him to finish Hartline quickly and finally determine who had been in the passenger seat.

Once his own airbags deflated—which happened almost as quickly as they'd inflated—the Assassin began taking a personal inventory. He was in pain but pronounced himself as serviceable. Once he'd checked that the pistol was still holstered on his thigh, he tugged his MP5 from the mangled center console and checked the action. The weapon was unharmed. His next order of business had involved opening the door of his wrecked Audi. He yanked the door handle and watched as his door nearly fell to the ground. The only thing holding it to the car was a plastic accordion conduit of wires.

Feeling the burns on his face and chest from the airbag, the Assassin licked thick, snot-infused blood from his upper lip. Perhaps his nose was broken. He stood from the wreck and limped ahead, feeling the clicking of a broken bone in his right foot. He ignored the pain and hurried forward with the MP5 at the ready, stepping through several puddles running from the two cars. He'd learned not to underestimate this Hartline prick, and though he liked the chances that Hartline had fared worse in the wreck than himself, he also knew the man might already be prepared to retaliate.

It was because of Hartline's earlier prowess that the Assassin decided not to wait. As soon as he reached what had been the rear quarter panel of the Renault, he unleashed a long burst from the MP5, emptying a third of the clip into the battered cabin of the white car.

When he stepped further forward, thanks to the light from the coolant steam, the Assassin saw the remains of the car's only visible occupant.

She was sitting in the passenger seat. She was still somewhat upright, her torso askew and her head tilted forward due to the car's buckling.

A mannequin. With two fresh bullet holes in her side.

The Assassin advanced, paying no mind to the sharp pain in his foot. He thrust the weapon into the smashed void where the driver's window had once been. As in his Audi, multiple airbags hung deflated. The one from the steering column was marked by a significant amount of blood.

There was no one in the Renault—other than the plastic human facsimile. As the Assassin whirled around, half expecting to take a bullet from Hartline, he bitterly thought about the events as they'd departed Odessa.

Yes, they'd duped him, just as he'd feared. Hartline had sped from the hotel and around the corner. At that point, Elena Volkov had jumped from the car and probably hid behind one of the parked cars on the busy beachside avenue. They'd already had the mannequin in the car, at the ready, and all Hartline had done was prop her up and lead the Assassin far away from Odessa.

Knotting his lips together, the Assassin huffed bloody wet breaths through his nose. He'd been snookered by the American's sleight of hand.

Elena Volkov, wherever she was, was now safe. It was highly unlikely she would perish before the looming deadline. She and her protector, Gage fucking Hartline, had won out. The end result left the Assassin with ten million bucks—not enough—and a significant amount of egg on his face.

Egg on his face that he could never wipe off. The Assassin's sterling reputation had just taken a direct hit.

Most pressing, however, was this steaming and hissing pile of wreckage in the Ukrainian countryside. It was only a matter of time before someone came along and notified the authorities. Fingerprints would be pulled. Blood samples would be taken from the wreckage. The Ukrainians would realize one of the world's most wanted men was nearby and then the hunt would be on.

Dogs. Helicopters. Task forces. News reports. Cops watching every transportation hub. If the Assassin found himself cornered, it would come down to either the bowels of a Ukrainian prison or a self-fired bullet through the head.

Neither of those were acceptable choices. But there was a third choice, and it was quite simple: *Run like hell.*

As he pivoted, he didn't take a bullet from Hartline. In fact, he saw no trace of the man. Where was he? He'd obviously climbed from the wrecked car.

Holding the submachine gun at the ready, the Assassin limped to the shallow ditch at the edge of the road. Hartline wasn't there. The Assassin swept the MP5 over the weedy field, squinting his eyes for any lump or shadow that might be his enemy.

The man was nowhere to be seen.

Gritting his teeth over the pain that was beginning to accumulate in numerous areas of his body, the Assassin dragged himself back to the car. He peered at the threshold of the crumpled driver's door, seeing the scant blood trail that went over the top, where the window had been.

Hartline must have leapt out while the Assassin was regaining his senses.

And now Hartline was out there—somewhere. Either hiding, or waiting for the precise moment to end the Assassin's life.

There was no blood trail below the door. It had been washed away by coolant and gasoline.

What the Assassin didn't see, because it would have required a much closer inspection, were Gage Hartline's two weapons. One, his pistol, was trapped in a mangled section of interior. The other, an antique Skorpion, had been on the floor of the backseat and was now wedged in the deepest portion of the "V".

Hartline had exited the car without a weapon—yet the Assassin didn't know that.

But the Assassin was correct—sooner or later someone would come. He did a full 360, his mind racing over exactly what to do.

***

In Georgy's beach villa, the hostage situation had intensified. Elena had asked numerous follow-up questions, receiving mostly curses in place of rational answers.

"It doesn't really matter," Elena replied to her legal relatives, studying her pistol now that the foursome was securely held in place. "I know exactly what you did, and I can prove it."

"You can't prove anything," Georgy challenged.

"I have witnesses," Elena replied, motioning to the bodybuilder and waitress. "You all but admitted your guilt."

"Them?" Nastya asked, adding a sharp laugh. "A steroid junkie and a malnourished slut? Who's going to believe one word they say? And, besides, we've admitted nothing."

The waitress took the insult without emotion but the Armenian muscleman frowned.

"See what she thinks about you?" Elena asked the Armenian.

"Enough games," Nastya bellowed, jerking her husband's arm and making him protest in pain. "What are you accomplishing with all of this?"

"Why did you want me dead?" Elena countered. "Just tell me and I'll end this."

Nastya and Georgy were silent.

"Why?"

Still nothing.

She'd have to change tack. Elena Volkov shut her eyes for just a moment, ordering her words in her mind. They would have to be spoken just right, just calmly enough to elicit the prescribed response.

"Cover them," she said to Nazar. Then Elena whispered a few things to the attorney. He nodded.

Moving back in front of the foursome, her mind turned to Gage. *Where is he? What is he doing? Has the assassin figured it out yet? And, if so, is the assassin racing back here with Gage on his tail?*

The burner phone hadn't yet buzzed—and Gage promised to call when the situation turned. Elena had to assume all was still well.

***

But it wasn't...

Just like his two weapons, both of Gage's phones were out of reach, lost in the wreckage that moments before was a nearly new Renault Latitude.

Though he'd thought about his weapons and phones mere seconds after the crash, his first and primary impulse had been to get the hell away from the car, so that's what he'd done.

Unfortunately for Gage, as soon as his left leg had touched the ground, he'd realized something was terribly amiss.

It was his femur. Though it may not have been fully broken in two, it gave way when he added his full weight to it. The resulting fall had been less painful than it had been shocking. Usually when a person breaks a bone, they realize it before they attempt to use it again.

But to stand and feel the bisected bone finish breaking inside your thigh; to feel the quadriceps and hamstrings and knee and buttocks all working together, feverishly contracting to compensate for the massive bone structure that had just failed them; to feel yourself falling to the left as the lower portion of the bone bulges out, trying to rip through the muscle and the thick dermis; to claw the pavement in an effort to get away and feel the left leg pivoting in a new location that wasn't a knee or ankle…

The sensation wasn't pleasant.

When Gage had finally tucked himself under the front of the Renault, he'd had to grasp his lower leg and drag it flush with his good leg. Otherwise, it would have given him away as it had remained exposed in an angle that could only be described as grotesque.

Though that exact moment had been extremely tense and only lasted a few seconds, it reminded Gage of a video he'd seen on ESPN some years ago. A major league baseball player was doing his best to beat out a throw to first. He'd stomped on the right side of the bag while running full speed. Due to the elevation of the bag and the way his foot struck, the player's ankle had canted outward and dislocated, leaving the base runner still running, but landing on his right tib/fib where his foot should have been.

His foot was bent all the way inward, and was essentially along for the ride by that point. It wasn't unlike a pirate in a cartoon, thumping along on a wooden peg leg.

The base runner eventually came to a stop and stared down at his damaged ankle in bewilderment. He didn't collapse to the ground until the first base coach and the opposing first baseman attended to him, essentially bringing to his attention exactly what had gone wrong.

And now, as Gage lay under the radiator steam that was slowly dissipating, he understood how that baseball player felt. Things were just coming clear to him.

Elena was back in Odessa, putting the squeeze on her in-laws. The Assassin had fallen for Gage's decoy, followed him out here, and realized his mistake. And he'd just attacked Gage with the largest bullet in the world – a speeding car.

And now Gage lay here gravely wounded. He watched the Assassin's feet as the hired killer paced back and forth, obviously trying to determine what had happened.

By this time, the Assassin certainly knew Elena Volkov hadn't been in the car. He also knew Gage Hartline couldn't have gone very far.

And here Gage was, without a single card left to play. He couldn't shoot. He couldn't call for help. He couldn't stand up and fight.

All he could do was bask in the escaping steam and boiling coolant that burned into the back of his neck.

Upon exiting the Renault and collapsing to the ground, Gage had seen nowhere to go other than the deep blackness directly under the headlights that were now canted upward. He lay there, wedged underneath the wreckage and the radiator that had all but given out of steam. He lay there—impotent.

Gage knew it was only a matter of time.

***

How long was I unconscious? Or was I? I don't remember losing consciousness. But that was a helluva crash, the Assassin reasoned, eyeing the two vehicles that were now melded together by the impact.

And maybe Hartline's dead. Maybe he had just enough juice to jump out and run away. I remember racecar drivers and snow skiers dying from ruptured aortas, blown out due to a sudden jolt. What if that happened to Hartline? He'd have enough blood in the right places to cut and run, but as soon as his body began to fail him, he'd fall where he was and die in seconds.

By this time, the Assassin had walked all the way around both cars. He'd scanned the two ditches as well as the fields on both sides of the road. Hartline was nowhere to be seen.

Maybe he wasn't injured? Maybe I was out longer than I thought? Maybe Hartline jumped out and hauled ass?

In the distance, the glow of distant headlights could be seen. They formed a halo down below at the curve in the road. At that same time, the Assassin heard the low whine of a turbocharged diesel engine. Seconds later, a large truck rounded the bend, the engine quieting once the driver saw the wreckage.

It took the truck half a minute to ascend the gradual slope before it stopped behind the Assassin's Audi with the hissing and popping of pneumatic brakes. The Assassin didn't bother hiding his weapons. He stood there, bloodied, still keeping an eye on the nearby fields.

The trucker emerged, removing his hat and wiping his forehead as he stared at the wreckage in bewilderment. He asked the Assassin a question in cob-rough Ukrainian.

"Do you speak English?" the Assassin asked, continuing to keep his head on a swivel, scanning the area with the MP5 ready to rock and roll.

"A little," the man answered. He was large and heavy with a sparse beard and ruddy face. For whatever reason, he seemed amused by the scene. With a smile on his face, he asked, "Why you hold a gun?"

"I'm a detective," the Assassin replied in his best American Midwestern accent.

"What you do here in Ukraine?"

"I'm hunting a criminal."

"Where other driver is?"

"That's the problem," the Assassin replied. "He ran off." The Assassin cut eyes to the trucker. "Did you call the wreck in?"

"No radio or phone." He looked the Assassin up and down. "You have bleeding all over you."

"Yes. Thank you for your concern. You haven't seen anyone else out here, have you? No one on the road or in the fields?"

"No," the trucker replied, turning a full circle. "Just you. Other man, too, have gun?"

"Yes. And he's very dangerous." Then, with no warning, the Assassin unleashed a short burst from the MP5. The three rounds impacted below, in the center of, and at the top of the heavy truck driver's sternum. He crumpled to the ground, striking the back of his head very hard against the asphalt. As the Assassin continued to shuffle around the car, searching for Hartline, he could hear the faint sounds of the trucker's life quickly slipping away.

The Assassin was at the rear of the two vehicles when he eyed the logging truck, still idling with its headlamps beaming light over the area. A plan came to him. If he were to take the trucker's body with him, he could probably escape by driving the logging truck far away from here, perhaps even back to Odessa.

The police would be all over this wreck, but they wouldn't connect it to a battered old logging rig. Would they?

Think it through.

Hartline is gone. My car is scrap metal. What other choice do I have? I need to get away from here as quickly as possible.

The Assassin grasped the heavy trucker and began to drag him. Thankfully, the 9-millimeter rounds had terminated inside the man, leaving no blood to trickle from his back. Usually, it was reasons like this that the Assassin detested the underpowered MP5. For once, it had worked in his favor.

As he dragged the big man, the tugging caused blood to burble from the chest wounds. The Assassin bunched the man's sweaty shirt around his midsection, trying to contain the spillage and keep it from reaching the roadway.

And a short distance away, through a narrow gap of space under the cars, Gage Hartline watched and waited.

***

Elena stood above the foursome. "You should know, I never agreed to sell UkeOil because Dmitry didn't want it sold. Ever."

"Okay, we get it. You didn't agree," Georgy replied with a shrug. He seemed determined not to get sucked into her ploy.

"But, is there still time?" Elena asked.

"Time for what?" Nastya spat.

"Time to sell UkeOil?"

"What do you mean 'is there still time?'" Nastya persisted. "Why would you give a shit?"

"Let's just say, for the sake of argument, I agree to sell my shares. Could we still manage to get the deal done?"

Georgy and Nastya eyed one another. After a moment, Nastya rolled her eyes. "This is bullshit."

"Tomorrow's the deadline," Georgy said cautiously. "If we're not all in agreement by then, we've been told the deal expires."

Elena pulled up a chair and leaned forward. She still held the pistol but had it pointed off to the side. "I want to propose a deal."

"What deal?" Nastya asked.

"The best deal you'll ever get. That's why I brought Aleks, my attorney."

"Tell us the deal," Georgy said.

"I'll agree to sell my shares if..." Elena let it hang for a moment, "...you two will admit what you've done."

Nastya snorted. "Enough games, bitch."

"I'm serious," Elena replied. She took the sheaf of papers from the attorney. "This is a limited power of attorney. When I sign it, it instructs and empowers Aleks to go to the closing and sell my shares. But it's limited. There's an expiration, a minimum price and it can only be exercised in a sale to Suntex Energy."

"Why would you agree to this?" Georgy asked.

"Because I want closure. Dmitry would want me to have it, too."

Nastya looked like she smelled a rat. Her face was screwed up and she was squinting. "I don't buy it."

"I don't care," Elena replied.

"If you're willing to do that, then what's all this? Why hold us at gunpoint?"

"You've been trying to kill me for months. I wanted you to taste the fear and see what it feels like. How the hell can you live with yourself?"

Nastya smiled without a trace of remorse.

Elena spoke loudly, clearly, officially. "If you will confess to what you've done, I will sign this limited power of attorney, allowing this one specific sale to go through."

Georgy's eyes were wide. He nodded at Nastya.

She, however, still seemed dubious. "Doesn't add up. Why are you hell-bent on a confession?"

"Because I won't be able to live with myself—going against Dmitry's will—until I know for sure it was that or death. Once I know, then I won't be saddled with guilt for selling the company."

"Horseshit," Nastya replied in Ukrainian, drawing the word out.

"It's true," Elena answered, shrugging. "If I sold it for just the money, I'd never be able to forgive myself. But if I do it to save my own life, then I know Dmitry would forgive me."

"I'm not admitting anything," Nastya said. "Not to this cunt."

"We're almost out of money!" Georgy yelled.

"We'll still have our shares," Nastya replied smugly, staring at the floor-to-ceiling plate glass windows at the rear of the home.

"You won't have your shares," Elena countered.

"Why?" Nastya snapped, whipping her head around.

"Because, if you don't admit what you've done, I'm coming after you with all my hundreds of millions. I will employ teams of attorneys who will hire dozens of investigators to prove each of the contracts you hired out on my life. And I swear by everything I hold holy, all my efforts will be aimed at one thing: sending you both to the poor house, followed by prison."

"It doesn't make sense," Nastya yelled, cutting her eyes between Elena and Georgy. "If she truly believes that we did this, why make this deal?"

"Because my attorney also has an airtight agreement you will have to sign. It stipulates that you can never bother me, or even contact me, ever again."

"So, you're willing to do this, to go against Dmitry's wishes, *just* to get rid of us?" Georgy asked.

"Forever," Elena added.

"It doesn't add up," Nastya said.

"Yes, it does," Georgy countered. "She hates us that much and…can you blame her?"

"We can just sit here all night," Elena said. "I'm enjoying watching you two squirm."

"Fuck you," Nastya growled.

Elena moved the pistol inches from Nastya's ear and fired, striking the mirror behind the bar across the room. Nastya spewed curses like a Lefortovo prisoner as the glass fell behind her.

"Stop shooting!" Georgy begged.

"Not until we're done here." Elena produced a pen and signed the limited power of attorney. She held the agreement in front of Nastya, just out of reach. "Simply confess the attempted killings you hired, and this is all yours. Otherwise, I'm calling Dmitry's close friend in the High Council of Justice and I predict you'll be in jail by sunrise."

At that moment, Nastya's phone—on the floor after having been knocked from her hand earlier—chirped with a text. Nastya leaned over and eyed the text in the preview pane. As soon as she read it, she ducked.

Elena lifted the phone and had barely comprehended the words when the plate glass window at the rear of the house shattered with a thunderous boom.

***

Gage watched as the Assassin dragged the large man downhill, presumably toward the idling 18-wheeler parked behind all the wreckage. The truck's headlights revealed plenty for Gage. For starters, the uphill grade was propelling the various vehicle fluids backward, toward the large rig. Though much of the coolant had escaped as steam, a fair amount had dripped onto the ground, along with other slick-looking substances from the engine. But the majority of the liquid was gasoline, having poured from the Renault's gas tank after the impact.

Squinting his eyes, Gage peered beyond his own car, to the wreckage of the Audi. It had taken most of its damage at the front end, meaning its fuel tank was likely intact. Gage thought back to his own fuel tank—it had been nearly full. Gage guessed the tank probably held about 60 liters—approximately 16 gallons.

That should be plenty.

He dug into his pocket, gripping Elena's ornamental lighter, the one that had once belonged to her husband. Using his fingernails, he pinched the wick and pulled it out farther, then tipped the lighter on its side so the lighter fluid would saturate the wick.

Gage spun the flint wheel, watching as the flame burned brightly. He took a steadying breath and flung the lighter under the Renault, watching it strike the car before prematurely tumbling to the fluid below.

***

The Assassin halted his labored dragging. The pain in his broken foot was excruciating, especially when lugging this big Ukrainian bumpkin. But he'd stopped because of a sound. It was a single thump and it sounded like it came from the Renault. He stared, listening for other noises. Nothing. The sound could have come from a piece of the wreckage that had been under tension. Or, perhaps a piece of hot metal had popped from a cooling contraction.

He continued to stare.

Finally, knowing he needed to hurry before someone else came along, the Assassin continued to drag the trucker to his rig.

***

Dammit, what a shitty throw!

Gage quietly pounded the back of his head against the roadway, angered with himself for making such a poor toss. When he'd flung the Zippo-style lighter, he'd tossed it too high and it had struck a hose that was hanging down near the oil pan. This had caused the lighter to drop well in front of the gasoline. It had burned for a moment in the oil and coolant before flickering and going out. And the worst part—it was now out of reach by several feet.

With his left arm extended, Gage wedged himself under the car as far as he could. The front suspension was extremely low—Gage's chest was twice the size of the low clearance. He pushed with his right hand, grunting as he felt the wreckage digging into his left pectoral muscle. Gage's shoulder wound that had been nicely healing ripped completely open. But the pain was nothing compared to the excruciating, lightning pain from his broken femur.

Despite his efforts, his hand was still six inches away from the lighter.

He searched the wreckage above him, tugging on several hoses and pieces of plastic. Just as he was about to give up and consider another ploy, a piece of black plastic came loose in Gage's hand.

It was at least a foot long.

***

The shotgun blast was deafening. The large plate glass window was the first casualty as it shattered onto the tile floor at the rear of the villa. Nazar was thrust forward by the blast, falling onto the bodybuilder and the ruined coffee table that held the foursome. On the right side of Nazar's back were three large holes from the tri-ball buckshot that had ripped into his body. The bodybuilder twisted out from under Nazar, leaving the bloody security man slumped over the top of the shattered coffee table.

The waitress's staccato screams followed.

Elena instinctively lurched backward, dropping down behind the cover of the sofa. This put the foursome between her and whoever the gunman was. Another gunshot followed, sending Aleks spinning to the floor. The attorney yelled in pain and clutched his bloody arm to his body as he slid into an alcove beside the wet bar.

Nazar's silence bothered Elena. She slid forward, risking a glance. He'd slid back down to the floor and was lying on his back in the midst of the foursome. Elena couldn't tell if he was still breathing.

Bewildered by the sudden onslaught, she gripped the Walther defensively while wondering how in hell the Assassin had gotten all the way back here so quickly. Then it occurred to her…

This is someone different. It has to be.

Gage's worst fears were confirmed.

As the adrenaline slowly dissipated, Elena listened to Nastya. She was screaming instructions to the shooter and reaching for Nazar's pistol. Elena could see it through the legs of the end table she was beside. The pistol was out of Nastya's reach but her efforts had begun to drag the heavy frame of the coffee table. Her hand was perilously close to the pistol.

Fear abating, anger increasing, Elena gritted her teeth and vowed to go down fighting. She shut one eye and aimed across the tile floor, shooting Nazar's large pistol and sending it helicoptering away after a flash of sparks. Of course, this coaxed a fresh torrent of curse words from Nastya.

When she'd finished her tirade, Nastya demanded the shooter come inside—to finish things.

Elena stared at her own pistol. She knew, despite her anger and her practice with Gage, that she was no match for a professional wielding a shotgun. To stand up and take the shooter on was to die—that much she knew for certain.

Then how do I do it? What can I use to defeat the shooter?

From across the room, she heard a crunching sound: heavy boots on shattered glass.

The shooter was coming.

***

The rig of the big tractor-trailer was less than ten meters away. Despite the pain of his foot, the Assassin decided to go the extra distance and drag the trucker around to the passenger side. The man was just too damn big to hoist up to the cab, then try and move him over the driver's seat to the passenger side. Thankfully, the gasoline and mingled fluids from the wreck had soaked the road and lubricated the area behind the wreck. This helped the Assassin to drag his load more quickly.

He was moving along at a pretty good pace until the entire world erupted in flames.

***

Seconds before, when Gage had dragged the lighter back within reach by using the piece of black plastic, he'd used his shirt to clean the lighter and make sure the wick would still burn. Once it was lit, Gage allowed the flame to draw up fresh lighter fluid from the reservoir. When the flame was burning brightly, he wedged himself under the suspension and tossed the lighter in a low arc that he knew wouldn't strike the Renault's battered undercarriage.

When the lighter struck the ground, Gage thought the flame had gone out. The lighter hit at the rear of the Renault, right in the perfect spot, surrounded by gasoline. But for just a moment, nothing happened.

Then, when the fumes erupted, the resulting flash of flame scorched Gage's face and singed his short hair.

As Gage scrambled forward, he could hear the Assassin's yells.

***

This wasn't the first time the Assassin had been on fire. Years before, when he'd been in the service, he'd been one of three victims in a careless accident that ignited a petroleum shed. Because of his quick thinking, the Assassin had been the lone survivor that day. He'd felt little remorse as he'd stared at the cretaceous bodies of his two fellow soldiers. Had they acted quickly, they'd have been alive like him. But he hadn't paused for even one second to help them. Once the shed erupted, the Assassin had hurled himself through a wall of flame before rolling on the wet grass. The inferno burned so hot the dead soldiers' skin looked like chalk.

After the blaze was out, the Assassin had only required a few bandages and some special attention from a cute nurse at the clinic.

So, much like the last time, when the fire erupted, the Assassin hadn't waited for anything. As soon as he realized he was standing in the midst of an inferno with flames roaring twice as high as he stood, he'd lurched forward, diving into the weedy ditch on the side of the road. It was there he realized his boots and lower pants legs were on fire. The Assassin rolled in the depths of the ditch before frantically patting the fire out. Then he took stock.

At this early stage, his face, his neck, his arms and his hands felt okay. There was some mild stinging, like when a person with sunburn steps into a warm shower. He knew this would grow worse, far worse. By his estimation, his skin had been exposed to the intense flames for 3 or 4 seconds. He assumed his burns were of the first and second degrees.

The Assassin watched the still-roaring flames, wondering if there was any danger of explosion. The gas that had burned had almost certainly come from the Renault. The Audi was fully engulfed, but the Assassin didn't think the road gasoline would burn for very long. It had dissipated over a sizeable area and it would probably take more than a flash fire to set the Audi aflame.

He viewed the trucker's body, cooking in the center of the heaviest flames. The man's sweaty clothes had melted to his body, revealing fatty skin that was now beginning to bubble. Eyes moving to the front of the wrecked cars, the Assassin noticed that the flames only reached the forward half of the Renault. That was because the grade of the road had propelled the fluid backward.

Next to the trucker was the MP5, out of reach. The Assassin had slung it over his shoulder to drag the trucker. It had fallen to the ground when the Assassin had lurched. As it turned out, strapping the Makarov's holster to his leg had shown prescience.

While the pain on his exposed skin quickly worsened, the Assassin wondered what had caused the explosion. A spark from one of the cars was certainly possible. But why had it taken so long? It seemed reasonable to think that the fuel would have erupted much earlier. The crash had occurred, what, ten minutes ago? So why did the fire take so long to ignite?

The Assassin could think of one reason—Hartline.

Chapter Twenty-Two

WHEN GAGE had witnessed the Assassin sprinting away from the flames, he knew the man would survive. His quick instincts had saved him. The Assassin was nothing if he wasn't persistent. So, gritting his teeth, Gage had slid on his back from under the car, already sweating from the radiant heat of the small inferno. He used his good leg to propel himself around to the side of the blazing car, reaching up with his right hand. Then, in an agonizing sequence, Gage hoisted himself with his arms and his good leg so that he was leaning into the Renault, just forward of the flames.

Mercifully, he found the pistol, and just in time, too. The flames had begun to lick out from under the car, burning his right side. Between the fire and his leg, Gage collapsed backward due to the pain.

This caused his broken femur to once again twist abnormally. The pain was otherworldly. And despite it, Gage still managed to concern himself over his femoral artery. Two sharp ends of bone, both as thick as the handle of a baseball bat, could easily slice through the superhighway of Gage's blood. Because of that, he dealt with the pain as he again carefully straightened his leg, hoping too much damage hadn't already been done.

Now flat on the asphalt, Gage was able to look underneath the cars and get occasional views of the other side between the gaps in the flames. The flames were slowly dying down, but between the fire and the headlights from the truck and the Renault, the area was still quite well lit.

After ten seconds of looking, Gage saw him. Pistol in hand, the Assassin was in the ditch on the other side of the road. He was standing.

Doing his best to ignore the twisting and grinding of his broken femur, Gage propelled himself off the road and down into the ditch on the opposite side of the road from the Assassin. Once there, he battled the urge to pass out. Then, in a highly modified prone shooter's posture, Gage alternated his aim between the front of the Renault and the rear of the Audi as he waited for the Assassin to make his way around.

***

The Assassin didn't know where Gage was, but he suspected he was on the opposite side of the flaming wreckage.

Wherever he is, he's waiting for me to come around the car. And that's when he's going to shoot me.

Not tonight, Hartline. Not tonight.

The Assassin slid back into the ditch opposite Gage. There, after eyeing the truck, he crafted a new and radically different plan. Then, staying below road level, the Assassin began to low-crawl like a snake down the mild grade of the ditch.

***

Nastya spoke native Ukrainian to whoever had just come through the glass. Her words were frantic and maniacal. In short order, she told the person that the man beside her was still breathing, and the lawyer was alive and cowering by the bar. But what Nastya spent most of her time detailing was how urgent it was for the shooter to kill Elena Volkov, the armed woman on the other side of the couch.

In the midst of Nastya's demands, Elena could hear Georgy asking who the shooter was.

"I hired him in case something like this happened," Nastya snapped.

Though she knew she had a number of rounds remaining, Elena had no confidence that she could pop up and hit the shooter. Surely he was holding his shotgun at the ready, and he knew exactly where she was. Perhaps he was a professional killer like the man chasing Gage. Elena had no illusions about the odds of the situation. She searched the front side of the room, trying to spy a reflection or mirror that would give away the shooter's position.

She saw nothing.

"Get on with it," Nastya demanded. "Kill all three. You've got four witnesses who will swear this was done in self-defense. Those three came in and threatened our lives at gunpoint."

"Yeah," Georgy added. "Do it."

"Will the two of you shut up?" the stranger asked. His boot steps came slowly.

In seconds, this would all be over.

Elena had no other choice. What she was about to do was her best defense. She spoke just as the man's pace increased, when he was about to dart into sight and blast Elena's position.

"This is Elena Volkov," she said in a loud voice. "Please don't kill me."

"Hah!" Nastya replied. "Go get her."

"Wait...please. Nastya hasn't told you everything," Elena said, her cheek brushing the back of the couch as she spoke.

The footsteps halted.

"Stop delaying and shoot her ass," Nastya commanded.

"Please listen, sir," Elena pleaded. "I know this situation looks bad, but think about Nastya and Georgy—about their lack of integrity. I was here tonight trying to stop *them* from killing *me*."

"She's lying," Nastya spat, her tone changing to one of concern. "Shoot her this instant!"

"Wait," Elena said. "Before you do anything, I have something to tell you…"

***

Similar to Elena, Gage was also waiting for his enemy to show himself.

He was doing his best to concentrate, trying to set aside his agony as he awaited the Assassin to emerge around one of the two cars. But Gage had been in this ditch now for several minutes and he still saw no signs of his enemy. Now that the flames had all but completely died away, he was able to clearly see underneath the cars. There was no sign of the Assassin where he'd been earlier.

He doesn't know your leg is shattered. He might be prone, waiting for you just as you're waiting for him.

Gage slowly scanned every angle underneath the cars, hoping to get a glimpse of the Assassin. Perhaps if the man didn't see Gage, he could get off a shot or two in the narrow space and end this once and for all.

That hope soon dissolved.

***

Once the Assassin had crawled beyond the powerful beams of the logging truck, he stood, counting on the brightness of the headlights to make everything beyond simply black. His foot was throbbing, having obviously swollen inside his boot. Pushing beyond his numerous injuries, the Assassin gently tugged open the door of the big rig. The cab was utterly filthy, with the floor of the passenger seat littered with food wrappers and picked-clean chicken bones. Ignoring the squalor, he climbed up into the cab and took a spot in the driver's seat.

Then, he indulged himself, staring forward with the benefit of the 2,500 lumens headlamps and two meters of elevation.

There he was…

Gage Hartline was lying prone in the ditch parallel with the driver's door of the Renault. He had his pistol outstretched in a two-handed grip and seemed to be alternating his watch between the front and rear of the two automobiles.

He had no idea what was coming.

Rather than rush it, the Assassin first scrutinized the image of Hartline. Something about his left leg seemed off. It was slightly curved along his left thigh, the curve quite pronounced in the center.

Broken femur. Ouch. You won't be going far.

Chuckling warmly, the Assassin glanced down at the control panel to his right. The large diamond-shaped red button would release the air brakes. And, in the most pleasant surprise of the evening, the Assassin realized the rig was an automatic, not the old 13-speed manuals that took till Christmas to get up to speed.

This way, the Assassin could simply press the gas and be on his merry way—after he'd squashed Hartline into the Ukrainian soil.

***

The very second Gage heard the sharp hiss of the air brakes, he knew what had happened.

The big rig bounced under the diesel engine's torque as the Assassin pressed the accelerator and set the large unit in forward motion.

To say the large rig accelerated slowly was an understatement. But to Gage, the seconds remaining for the rig to reach him went very, very fast.

Knowing he had few options, Gage aimed with his right arm and began squeezing off shots at the driver's windshield. One, slowly. Two, slowly. *Get your aim right.* Three, slowly.

Four-five-six…*shit!…roll away!*

***

The shots the Assassin expected came. He ducked down as he accelerated. Each of the bullets was harmless, whizzing through the glass before terminating in one of the layers of metal or wood behind the Assassin. Just before reaching Hartline, the Assassin sat up, realizing he should have jinked left at the last second. He cursed the American and his expert death roll.

Missed him!

The Assassin looked through the left side knee window, able to see Hartline rolling into the grass with his twisted left leg tagging along for the ride.

Surprised that this lumbering vehicle hadn't gotten stuck, the Assassin kept his aching foot on the pedal as he corrected the large rig back onto the northbound road. He lifted his scorched shirt, wiping sweat and soot from his face. When he looked down at his shirt, he could see numerous pieces of facial skin that looked like pencil shavings.

My burns. That sonofabitch.

Feeling his anger building, the Assassin spoke aloud, talking himself through the situation.

"Just keep going. Forget about Hartline and Elena Volkov. Right now, the victory is life, and it's still yours. Just getting out of this country will be hard enough. And once you do, you'll have more than ten million dollars to lick your wounds with. You can convalesce in style for a decade if you like…just keep that broken foot on the gas and go."

He looked in the driver's side mirror, able to see the still-burning headlights of the Renault.

Ten million bucks…

Not nearly enough to live the dream he had in mind.

All because of that prick Hartline.

The Assassin crested the long hill and began to descend the other side. Up ahead, on the right, was a sprawling gravel lot. In the scant moonlight, the Assassin could see the towering conveyors associated with gravel mines. Underneath the conveyors was a long row of dust-covered dump trucks.

Plenty of room to turn this big rig around.

Don't stop. Get far away. Far, far away…

The gravel lot loomed.

***

"Stop listening to that bitch and kill her," Nastya commanded. "What the hell are you waiting for?"

"Sir? Are you listening? I'll pay you to leave us alone," Elena said. Despite her fear, she spoke the words clearly. Not wanting to give her bitch sister-in-law an opening, Elena followed by saying, "Nastya and Georgy are *flat broke*. That's why they're trying to kill me—for my money. They can't pay you nearly what I can, no matter what promises she's made you. And I will pay you with no strings attached. All you have to do is walk away."

There was a period of thunderous silence.

"Kill her!" Nastya roared, shattering the reverie.

"See…she's scared." Elena countered. "Because what I say is true."

At this point, mayhem erupted. Nastya shrieked her demands. Georgy chimed in. Even the bodybuilder and the girl in the bikini joined the cacophony of people desperate to convince the shooter—whoever he was.

Elena realized that her words had created the perfect diversion. If she was ever going to pop up and fire a shot, now was the time to do it. She turned her eyes to Aleks, her attorney. Despite his battered condition, he gave her a thumbs-up with his good hand.

But Elena knew Aleks well enough to know that his thumbs-up wasn't an encouragement to come out shooting. Aleks was a master negotiator and he obviously approved of Elena's current tack. He motioned her to keep going.

"How much do you want?" Elena asked, making her voice loud. "Name it!"

"You work for me!" Nastya shrieked at the man.

"She's broke. Broke, and going to jail," Elena said, realizing she was smiling. "Now, please, name your price."

The shooter finally spoke enough for her to guess at his background. He was definitely Ukrainian and, judging by his accent, from Kiev. The price he asked for was far less than what she'd envisioned. And, of course, when Nastya instantly screamed she'd pay more, Elena continued to counter by saying Nastya had no more money. Aleks even chimed in, using several fancy legal phrases to further impress the man. Finally, Aleks asked the shooter how Nastya and Georgy would pay him from jail.

"Just go back outside by the pool and wait," Elena said. "You have my word that we will not press charges for the shooting you've done and Aleks will pay you tonight from my account."

"Don't trust her," Nastya spat. "Are you crazy?"

"I know who she is, from the news," the shooter said. "I've always heard good things."

"They're lies!"

"It's you I never trusted, Nastya." Then came one of the most beautiful sounds Elena had ever heard. It was the sound of shotgun shells being mechanically extracted and falling harmlessly onto the floor. Seconds later, the shattered glass could be heard crunching again. The shooter was gone.

And, predictably, Nastya breathed flaming curses and vile threats.

After several steadying breaths, Elena built the courage to stand. She came around the couch, covering the foursome with the Walther. In their midst, Nazar lay there, staring up at her.

"Finish," he rasped. "I'll live."

"Are you sure?"

He nodded and grimace-smiled. "Buckshot to the ribs. Not fatal. Hurt enough that I wish I was dead."

Elena called Aleks from his hiding spot. He'd been hit in his upper arm. Not only was the flesh torn away, but the bone was broken, too.

"You need to lie down," Elena said.

"Just finish and then we'll worry about it."

Elena wrapped Aleks' necktie around his arm as a pressure dressing. Then, at Aleks' insistence, he and Elena tugged Nazar away from the group. After finding a first-aid kit in the kitchen, Aleks used his good arm to tend to Nazar and to himself.

And as he did, Elena went back to work.

***

The evening was quiet. In time, Gage's ears adjusted and he was able to hear the pleasant katydid symphony associated with summer nights. Somewhere down below, in either a creek or a pond, a frog announced his presence with his baritone croak.

These sounds were pleasing to Gage. In fact, he felt almost euphoric—and he was wise enough to know how dangerous such a feeling was. His leg was badly broken. Combined with his other injuries, he knew enough to know he was in a bad place as a brand of shock enveloped him like a cozy blanket. He fought the urge to succumb to its promise of euphoria, knowing that somehow, some way, he was going to have to drag himself to the Renault and pray that one of his phones still worked. Otherwise, he was stuck here until someone came along. And judging by the lack of traffic on this road, by the time someone did come, it might be too late.

He slid the pistol into his waistband and marshaled his bodily troops. *Get it together, soldiers, and let's move this old bag of bones.*

The first significant movement made him scream. Gage wasn't too proud to let loose—it helped bring him back to grim reality.

Fingernails clawing in the loam and weeds, he made it about one meter. A huge victory. He cackled like a madman, tasting a miasma of sweat, blood and coolant dripping from his face into his mouth. He traveled a second meter, shouting maniacal encouragements to himself.

"This ain't shit! Get some! This all you got? Come on, boy...you've had it easy all night...don't be hurtin' on me now!"

He was doing just fine. Then, midway through his third meter, Gage heard the whine of the turbocharger first. Soon after, a rumble and a rushing sound hit him all at once.

He turned, seeing the glow of lights at the top of the hill. The sounds grew.

The turbo with the piercing wail was mated to a diesel. A big one. When the lights crested the hill, Gage knew it was him—his enemy—the Assassin. And somewhere, deep inside the recesses of Gage's mind, a soft voice that he'd never admit existed, spoke soothing words to the rest of his being...

Just let him hit you and end it. Despite all of your bravado, you're tired. You're hurting. You need that dirt nap that everyone—every-damn-body—takes sooner or later.

"You shut the hell up!" Gage yelled.

He wiped his right hand on the side of his good leg, doing his best to clear away the sweat and dirt. Then he removed the pistol, trying to recall how many bullets remained. When he couldn't do the math, he held the pistol one-handed, his left eye shut as he aimed at the driver's window of the rig.

"Get some," he muttered again, this time through clenched teeth. He pulled the trigger.

Shot. *Way too early.*

The big rig plowed on. It was 300 meters away.

Shot. *Nothing. You're wasting ammo.*

150 meters. The turbo singing its staccato tune.

Wait. Wait.

Shot. Shot. Shot. The truck kept coming.

100 meters. 75 meters.

Death swirled all around Gage. He yelled, not from fear and not from rage. It was the yell of life, not unlike the yells sometimes heard from skydivers with failed chutes. A life's final punctuation—a last gasp—an end-run.

You've got maybe a second. Make these rounds count.

Gage's arm traversed like a tank's gun, down and to the left. He squeezed off the remaining bullets at the big rig's front right tire.

Spark. Spark. Hit!

The onrushing logging truck—tractor, trailer, logs—weighed 41 tons. At the time of the blowout, it was traveling 137 kilometers per hour—85 miles per hour. The resulting wreckage, when the tractor swerved to the right and flipped, made the earlier wreck of the two sedans seem paltry and insignificant.

Gage had a front-row seat.

***

In many ways, the Assassin admired Gage Hartline. Everyone needs a capable opponent. Otherwise, what would be the point of life? They say all good stories need conflict—well, wouldn't the same be true for a person's existence? If everything were blue skies and roses, people would kill themselves out of boredom.

So, as the Assassin pressed the accelerator through the filthy floorboard, he couldn't help but watch with fascination and admiration as Hartline lay there, right next to the road, emptying his pistol at the onrushing truck.

In order to give Hartline a fighting chance, the Assassin refused to duck all the way down, watching as the windshield popped three more times. Hartline missed, but the middle shot of the extremely wide grouping was dangerously close and actually cut the Assassin's face with a few shards of hurtling safety glass.

Just before the Assassin had been set to mince Hartline like a slow-moving possum, he watched as the American pivoted his pistol and fired low and to the Assassin's right.

At that speed, with that kinetic energy, there had been no controlling the big rig.

The wheel snapped right as the tire gave way. This caused the massive rim to bite into the asphalt, jerking the rig farther to the right. Just before he was knocked senseless, the Assassin remembered being hurtled toward the roof of the cab as it went over on its side. At the time of impact, the bitter realization hit the Assassin...

Hartline is going to survive this crash. He's a damned cockroach.

***

Six massive logs, each averaging 12,000 pounds, all more than 45 feet in length, broke free of their scant moorings and came at Gage like frenzied rolling pins. Gage had no choice other than to pivot right and into the ditch, flattening himself as all 6 logs went over, spewing dirt, bark and sawdust. It was like being run over by a freight train.

Then, once again, quiet.

I am alive.

Gage propped himself up with his arms. He turned to look at the logging truck, now lying quietly on its side. There was no fire. Gasoline tinkled down to the pavement, though Gage couldn't hear it.

Then, in a moment that defied logic, Gage watched as his enemy climbed vertically through the passenger window of the cab. Once again, Gage flattened himself in the ditch and eyed his pistol. It still had at least one remaining bullet, evidenced by the slide that had not locked to the rear.

Without much caution, the Assassin dangled from the cab before dropping to the asphalt, yelling in pain. He stood and moved with a heavy limp, staggering to the ditch, staggering toward Gage.

The Assassin expressed momentary surprise when Gage lifted up on his left arm and shot the Assassin with his right.

When the bullet hit home, the Assassin went down on his rear end and sat there, bewildered as he stared at Gage. Then, the Assassin fell backward, supine on the Ukrainian roadway.

This time the pistol's slide locked to the rear. Gage had no more bullets.

***

As Aleks worked on Nazar across the room, Elena stood above the manacled foursome. "My offer still stands."

"What?" Georgy asked.

"If you'll confess to all you've done, then I will sign the papers and sell to Suntex."

Eyes narrowed, Nastya said, "This is some sort of—"

"Shut your mouth," Elena said, cutting her off. "If you don't do as I said right now, I'm walking away and Aleks will sue you both for everything and you will lose your ownership. No delays."

"Do it," Georgy urged his wife.

Nastya confessed the attempted killings in one sentence. Based on her tone and her uncaring mien, she might have been confessing something incredibly petty, the way one roommate admits to the other that she was out of food and ate a bowl of the roommate's cereal.

She shrugged as she said, "I wanted you gone so we could sell the company." Nastya nodded afterward. "Satisfied? Now, hand me that signed document and unlock these cuffs."

Elena smiled and shook her head. "Nastya, Nastya, Nastya. I said *confess* what you've done...I didn't say give me a quick and indifferent summary. You do realize this is my life you tried to steal? I was born. My mother nursed me. My father loved me. I went to school. I learned to paint. I had dreams of meeting the love of my life and it came true. Then I lost him. And now, for many months, I've lived in constant fear of being murdered. I was hardly allowed to grieve my husband because of you and your husband. And if you want me to give this company up, the two of you will confess everything—and you'll do it properly."

"Just do it," Georgy pleaded. "So we can get this over with."

"Yeah," the bodybuilder agreed.

"You shut up!" Nastya snapped at her boyfriend. "I'm done with you."

The bodybuilder whispered something to the waitress and they both chuckled.

Elena wagged the sheaf of papers. "Nastya Zaytsev, confess your sins to me and this power of attorney is all yours. I swear on my late Dmitry's good name it's absolutely official and ready to be used."

Nastya closed her eyes and took deep, measured breaths. When she opened her eyes, she began to speak. "Because you have no right to our family company...because you are such a miserable cunt...because I hate every fiber of your being...dimwitted Georgy, here, and I decided that you must die..."

Once Nastya got in a rhythm, she really let it all hang out. Prague. Greece. Sicily. And, of course, the world's finest assassin, who was currently stretched out across a lonesome Ukrainian roadway. Roadkill.

Elena was surprised and impressed that Nastya had gone into such great detail. She'd unapologetically admitted to everything she and Georgy had done, even going so far as to confess that she'd pondered personally killing Elena before the business with the hired assassins had begun.

"I thought about poisoning you," Nastya had said, her eyes locked on Elena's. "But I couldn't do it. And not because I don't have the stomach…it's because poisoning would be too mild. I'd have much rather beaten you to death with a tire iron, you money-stealing witch."

The waitress, the bodybuilder, and even Georgy, stared aghast at Nastya's raw confessional.

"Thank you, Nastya," Elena said, fighting the urge to smile. "Georgy…your turn."

"For what?"

"Confess, in your words…then this is yours," Elena said, tapping the power of attorney with her left hand.

After Nastya snapped at him to get on with it, Georgy began his confessional. It actually seemed somewhat cathartic for him, as his eyes glistened during several portions of the story. He even admitted to secretly lusting after Elena. When he did, he earned a fresh berating from his wife—of course. By the time Georgy finished, he claimed the genesis of the entire plan belonged solely with Nastya.

Elena listened patiently, surprised that she'd gotten all she'd wanted, and more. As she looked toward the front door of the villa, she hoped her plan had worked. All of the gunshots had to have scared them. Hopefully none of the bullets had come their way.

"That's it, bitch. Now are you satisfied?" Nastya asked.

"I am."

"So now you can live with yourself?"

"I can."

"Then give me the papers," Nastya commanded, snapping the fingers of her free hand.

"A deal is a deal," Elena replied, handing them to her.

"Will you let us go now?" Georgy asked.

"In just a moment," Elena replied. She told Aleks to call 112—Ukraine's emergency services telephone number. As he did, Elena spoke to the bodybuilder and the waitress.

"You two might want to duck your heads."

"Why?" the Armenian asked.

"I'm sure they'll do all they can to keep you out of this," Elena answered. "But I'd still duck down."

"What are you talking about?" Nastya demanded. "You got what you want. Uncuff us."

"Sure," Elena answered, uncuffing Georgy's hand that was manacled to the table.

"Now this one," Nastya demanded, lifting her left wrist that was attached to Georgy's right.

"Let's do that one for the cameras," Elena said.

"What?" Nastya asked.

"The cameras."

"What cameras? Are you high?"

"No, but I just thought you might appreciate the chance to claim all you said was done under duress."

As Nastya's mouth opened to retort something profane, Elena cut her off, yelling over her right shoulder.

"Come on in, guys!"

From the hallway leading to the front atrium, two men entered. One man held an expensive digital video recorder. The other man held a parabolic microphone and a still camera.

They were, of course, the two paparazzi from the beachside club, Itaka. Aleks had let them inside at the very beginning of this incident. And now the celebrity-chasers had finally scored the mega-hit they'd always dreamed of.

"Are your friends okay?" the photographer asked.

"They're hurt but they'll make it," Elena answered. "How's the lighting?"

"Good enough," the shorter one replied. "And thanks to all this tile, the sound was perfect. We got everything, clear as a bell."

"Look at her," the taller one whispered reverently, gesturing with his microphone to Nastya. "Make sure you're getting all those expressions. Oh my, that's priceless."

After Nastya had shrieked that she'd been trapped, she provided sound bites of gold—and platinum, and rubies, and diamonds. Then, she'd gone after the two paparazzi with her husband in tow. Her resulting torrent of Ukrainian and Russian curse words, along with her bulging breasts that eventually burst from her strained top, would garner more than ten million hits on YouTube in less than a week. Subtitles were, of course, added and a new Internet meme was born.

"Nastya's Rage and Tatas" was an overnight sensation.

***

At least five minutes had passed since Gage had shot the Assassin. Though he was still alive, it was clear that he would soon be dead. Each time the Assassin breathed, there was an audible burbling in his lungs. He'd been shot squarely in the sternum. The Assassin was still exactly where he'd collapsed. Hardly able to move, himself, Gage remained at the upper edge of the ditch, grinding out the agonizing seconds. He'd adjusted his leg again to make sure he still had blood flow.

"One more," the Assassin rasped in English. "One more."

Gage had no desire to talk to this bastard. Then he watched as the Assassin dug in his pockets.

"Just want a smoke," the Assassin whispered. He grunted with satisfaction when he finally produced a silver case and a lighter.

Gage wanted to warn him about the fuel but he refused to speak to the man.

"It's diesel," the Assassin whispered, as if reading Gage's mind. The Assassin opened the silver case and carefully placed a cigarette into his mouth and lit it, inhaling deeply and coughing a wet, ragged cough afterward.

Gage watched.

The Assassin lay there, smoking and staring at the sky. Several minutes passed.

The last words the Assassin ever spoke were just before he'd finished his cigarette. He could barely speak, blood trickling from his mouth as he did. "These were made for me by a woman in Portugal. I'll miss smoking them." After he'd crushed the bloody nub of the cigarette out on the street, the Assassin breathed for a few minutes before he spasmed to his death, his lungs finally full of blood.

Twenty-one minutes later, a service van approached from the bottom of the hill. Driving the van was an older mechanic who serviced the machinery of the nearby quarry when the quarry was off shift. He found two dead men and one who seemed on the verge of death.

Shortly thereafter, Gage was aboard an older but well-equipped MBB Bo 105 air ambulance helicopter, heading south by southwest to the Regional Clinical Hospital in Odessa, Ukraine. Although he'd been triaged with life-threatening injuries, the attending paramedic and registered nurse agreed that he should survive.

They'd fitted his leg with an air cast and dealt with his numerous cuts and abrasions. The paramedic had treated the large, open shoulder wound with a clotting agent. He'd noted to the nurse that the wound seemed to have partially healed and then been ripped open, evidenced by the scabbing.

Despite the patient's weakened condition and copious amounts of administered morphine, per protocol, he was securely handcuffed to the gurney. Multiple firearms had been found at the curious crime scene—along with several apparent murder victims. For now, this man was the prime suspect.

Unfortunately for everyone involved, the wounded man wouldn't be coherent until 30 hours later.

But before they'd injected him with morphine, the man had spoken to the attending nurse, whispering the name "Elena" again and again. He'd spoken English, inquiring about her.

"I don't know, Elena," the nurse had perfunctorily replied as she worked.

"Elena Volkov," the patient clarified.

Later, when they'd done all they could do, and as the lights of Odessa slid ever closer, the nurse told the paramedic what their patient had said.

"Elena Volkov, the oil princess?" the paramedic had asked.

"That's who he asked about," the nurse insisted.

The paramedic dropped back onto the bench seat and shook his head in wonderment. "Two smashed cars. A logging truck. A charred body. A man with a fresh bullet hole in his chest. And an American, who might be a double-murderer, asking about Elena Volkov, the oil princess." A smile formed on the paramedic's weather-beaten face. "This job never ceases to amaze me. When I retire, I think I shall write a book."

Chapter Twenty-Three

TEN DAYS later, Gage asked to go home. This caused quite a stir with the Ukrainian investigators. Colonel Hunter was there, as was Elena. Through Aleks' recommendation, Elena had added several of Ukraine's finest attorneys to her legal team. Although she and Gage had been extremely cooperative, the attorneys did a fine job of keeping the authorities at bay.

Elena's video of her stepsister's and step-brother-in-law's confessions were inadmissible in legal proceedings and also illegally filmed. Despite that, Elena professed no knowledge of how the video had leaked to the Internet and become a worldwide sensation. Even with the intense investigation into the Zaytsev's activities, Nastya and Georgy were currently weighing a European reality show offer. The producers wanted them to change nothing—absolutely nothing—about their lives, other than to allow cameras in to record every second.

Just as Elena thought, Suntex Energy, upon seeing the "leaked" video, immediately pulled its offer to buy UkeOil. They denied any association with UkeOil and had since stopped commenting on the matter. However, through several anonymous back channels, they'd gotten word to Elena that they would still purchase UkeOil, once the legal problems were sorted out. Elena didn't even respond.

So, eleven days after breaking his femur, Gage—along with the new rod in his thigh—was prepared for discharge. He'd signed numerous hospital papers and promised the doctors he'd consult with an orthopedist upon his arrival in Fayetteville. Gage then had to agree with the Ukrainians that he'd be available for any follow-up questioning and would be willing to come back to Ukraine if necessary. This was also done with several other countries, including Italy, Switzerland and Germany. The United States State Department acted on Gage's behalf, but told him to keep their involvement quiet. Of course, Gage agreed.

Time and time again, Gage asked about the true identity of the Assassin. He was never given any answers. When Hunter had arrived in Odessa, he promised to do some digging and just this morning came back with the answer.

"They don't know who he is," Hunter told Gage. "I talked to the American security officer from the embassy in Kiev. We have a couple of mutual acquaintances. She's a good lady. She gave me the skinny."

"And they can't figure out his identity?"

"Nope. He's a blank."

"How's that possible?"

"I don't know. Supposedly, they've done everything: fingerprints, dental, DNA. All they know are his numerous false identities and the places he lived going back a little over a decade. But before he emerged with those identities, the trail stops cold."

"What else?"

"They know he spoke a host of languages, including English, German, Spanish, Russian, Portuguese and Cantonese."

"I don't know why, but I always felt he was European." Gage said. "Just an instinct I had."

"He'd been in Portugal for a few years. And his DNA showed quite a bit of European heritage. I'm not sure how much faith I put in this witch doctor genome-strand crap, but the lady I talked to said the bulk of the Assassin's genes were," Hunter glanced at his paper again, "Swabian and Walloon."

"Swabian is German. What's Walloon?"

"French descent...Belgium." Hunter adjusted his reading glasses. "He also had Berber, Swazi, Sephardi and Hungarian among trace strands of other ethnicities."

Gage opened his hands. "I know Hungarian."

"Berbers were North Africa. Swazi is Swaziland, in South Africa. And Sephardi are Jews from the Iberian Peninsula."

"So he had everything."

"We probably all do, Gage. But in the end, they don't know shit and they definitely don't know where he was from or who trained him."

"How's that possible? How does he get wiped from every system on earth?"

"They're still digging. The U.S. is helping, as are the Italians, the Swiss, the Germans. So far...zeroes."

"And his body count?"

Hunter gnawed on his lip and shook his head. "After your skirmish at the Swiss border, they think he shacked up with a lonely nurse and romanced her for a day or two before probably killing her. Damn scumbag. And there're a couple of people missing nearby that they can't quite pin on him yet. By the end of this investigation, who knows how many people that faceless prick killed."

"And he killed Giuseppe's men in Genoa."

"Yeah. Giuseppe asked me to keep that quiet."

"Don't the Italians suspect the Assassin?"

"I'm sure they do, but Giuseppe doesn't want cops snooping around so he's keeping mum."

"We may never know who this asshole was," Gage grumbled.

He was correct. They never would know.

In another development, Elena claimed her agoraphobia was markedly better. As Gage had convalesced, she'd performed self-experiments, walking into crowded areas to gauge her reaction. Thus far, she'd not panicked once.

"Maybe we found a cure," Gage quipped. "Anyone suffering with agoraphobia can hire an assassin to almost kill them. Maybe that could be my new business?"

"I think it's because I overloaded myself with fear," she said. "Running due to fear, is one thing. Being afraid for your life and still walking into a deadly situation is another."

"It's definitely a different sensation."

She had offered to fly Gage home by private jet but Gage declined. In the end, he relented enough to allow her to fly him home via business class on United Airlines via Frankfurt. At Elena's insistence, Colonel Hunter would sit up front, too—and she insisted on paying. And, yes, Elena was indeed going with Gage. She currently described it as "a brief visit to the States."

After Gage was wheeled from his room, he stopped off to say goodbye to Nazar. Following two successful surgeries, the security man had been told he'd make a full recovery. Earlier in the day, Gage had received a phone call from Aleks the attorney. He was too busy supervising this case to come down and say goodbye. Other than a bulky cast and eight weeks of healing, he'd be just fine.

Waiting at the hospital's service entrance was a hired van containing a driver with two eager dogs. As Gage was wheeled away from his floor, several of the doctors and nurses stopped by to wish him well. All of them knew something momentous had happened out on that lonely Ukrainian road and, of course, they knew who Elena Volkov, the oil princess, was. But over time, as most people do, they'd come to genuinely like Gage Hartline and simply wanted to wish him well.

Elena eyed the special instructions for the flight. "So, he must get up at least once every ninety minutes?"

"Yes," his surgeon answered. "He should wiggle his toes, move around, tense his calves, his buttocks, et cetera. All aimed at keeping clots from forming. Tell him to take care not to trip and fall with those crutches. Once he's home, I recommend he begin physical therapy as soon as possible."

"And his other injuries?" she asked.

"Healing nicely," the senior nurse answered. "Nothing needs to be done on the flight. When he gets home, just change the dressings as needed. He'll need to tell his doctor that his stitches need to come out in two weeks."

"I'll yank 'em out," Hunter remarked.

Gage thanked everyone and prepared to go. Colonel Hunter rolled him into the hallway.

"There are a few other questions," Elena said, turning to the medical staff. She chose to whisper her queries to the orthopedist, a sober-looking white haired man in his early sixties.

He leaned forward, nodding his understanding. "You're a painter?" he asked.

"Yes."

"Certainly, you may paint him. Just make sure he gets up and moves around occasionally."

Elena glanced at Gage, holding up a finger as if asking for another second. Then she leaned back to the doctor, whispering another question. His eyes went wide once it was out.

The orthopedist answered her in a low voice that no one else could hear. "He can do almost anything he feels like doing but he will be limited, of course." The doctor swallowed. "So...I'd recommend you both be cautious when doing *that*."

Elena smiled and nodded her thanks.

As Hunter pushed Gage down the hallway toward the elevator, he spoke to Elena, asking, "What was that all about?"

"Excuse me?"

"Those questions."

"I'm going to paint a portrait of Gage."

Hunter hitched his head. "Good luck selling that."

Gage's voice was flat. "Yeah, she'd thought about painting you, but she didn't think she was skilled enough to replicate all those wrinkles."

Chuckling, Hunter asked, "What was the second question that got such a big reaction from the doc?"

"I just asked if I could help Gage with his therapy."

"Really?" Hunter asked, backing Gage into the elevator. "Didn't know you were into that kind of thing."

"Oh, yes," she replied, placing her hand on Gage's uninjured shoulder and giving it a squeeze. "I bet I can get more out of him than anyone."

Gage looked up at her and she winked.

As the elevator descended, Hunter eyed them both before turning his eyes to the floor indicator. "I bet you can, Ms. Volkov, I bet you can."

THE END

Acknowledgments

The first draft of this book flew from my fingers. I really thought I was on to something. Then, I gave it to a few of my trusted beta readers. They handed it back to me, several of them pinching their noses. Yikes. So, I rewrote, and rewrote, and rewrote. The book wound up taking six or seven drafts—I cannot recall, nor do I want to count. Hopefully, the end product was enjoyable for you, the reader.

If you made it this far, one of my goals has been attained. I hope this book held your attention. I hope it amused you. I hope you'll want to read more of my stories. That's why I write. I know I'm not Hemingway. I'll never stroke a sentence like Ian Fleming could. My primary goal is entertainment—your entertainment. Thank you for choosing my book.

The Gage Hartline series has been optioned by the visionaries at Solipsist Films. As of this writing, they plan to open the series with TO THE LIONS. Please, if you want to see Gage on the silver screen, don't hesitate to make noise about it on social media. I'm sure studio executives would love to read your casting choices—and I'm dead serious about this. Put your suggestions out there—do not underestimate the power of your voice.

Regarding this book, I owe a big thanks to my beta readers for slogging through a stinky first draft. John Humphries, television magnate and possessor of incredible knowledge of 70s and 80s TV show theme songs: You're a faithful friend and reader and your contributions to my writing cannot be overstated. Thank you. Let's get together and watch some Magnum PI reruns soon. The helicopter diving down to the water during the Mike Post intro still gives me chills.

Charlie Mink, mystery man and purveyor of world-class fake IDs: Your straight-talking style has made each of my books better. I appreciate your willingness to help a man you've never met. I hope we can rectify that soon.

Phillip Day, attorney, real estate mogul, shock comic: You provided the most direction for this novel. I couldn't do everything you suggested but I appreciate the thought you put into every one of my books. You're cheating the world by not writing a book of your own.

Barry Davis, MD—thanks for adding a slice of realism to this book with your medical knowledge. Readers, if you ever need a top heart surgeon, look Barry up. I'm not exaggerating, either. He's world class and, perhaps the best part; he's not a nerd. Thanks for your help, Barry. You can saw me open anytime.

Jake Marcinko: famed skydiver, physicist, putz—thanks so much for lending your IT knowledge to this book. Now you can get back to chasing down jerks who put cameras over ATMs in Roatan, Honduras. (Names, Jake…just give me their names. I'll have Ron take care of the rest.)

My newlywed editor, Elizabeth Brazeal Latanishen, is nothing short of amazing. She's a machine and she turns out high quality work. Thanks for your excellent work and congratulations on your marriage, Eliza. I wish you a lifetime of happiness.

Nat Shane has once again produced an impressive cover. It's certainly not easy to capture the tone of a book with a single image. Nat, you have an impressive range of artistic ability. I appreciate the time you put into your work. Nat's also a new father—a role he was made for.

Finally, I owe a huge thanks to my three proofers: Dina Dryden, Lauren Knight and Sarah Humphries. You three ladies are the masters of detail. Despite all the passes I made through this book, even with the help of my editor, you've managed to help me root out most of the nagging errors. Thank you so very much.

Finally, the Assassin: I left three distinct clues that should tell an eagle-eyed reader where he was from. Hint: I wouldn't get too mired in his DNA. If you figure out the Assassin's home country, please pop me a message. If you don't mind, do not reveal it in a review. Let's see how many readers we can confound.

Speaking of messages, I love to hear from readers. Do not hesitate to pop me an email at chuck@chuckdriskell.com. I'm also on Facebook and I tweet once every blue moon.

God bless.

C.

Photo: Christian Lademann, Giessen, Germany

About the Author
Chuck Driskell is a United States Army veteran who wishes he could write full-time. He lives in South Carolina with his wife and two children. In Her Defense is Chuck's seventh novel.

Made in the USA
Middletown, DE
27 January 2021